Don't miss Teresa Edgerton's retelling of
Arthurian tales . . .
THE GREEN LION TRILOGY:
*CHILD OF SATURN, THE MOON IN HIDING,
THE WORK OF THE SUN*

"One of fantasy fiction's most interesting trilogies."
—*Rave Reviews*

. . . or the romance and intrigue of *GOBLIN MOON* and
THE GNOME'S ENGINE

"For fans of magical fantasy, this is prime stuff!"
—*Locus*

Now return to Teresa Edgerton's world of
The Green Lion, and the untamed Wild Magic of . . .

THE CASTLE OF THE SILVER WHEEL

D0483524

Ace Books by Teresa Edgerton

THE GREEN LION TRILOGY

CHILD OF SATURN
THE MOON IN HIDING
THE WORK OF THE SUN

GOBLIN MOON
THE GNOME'S ENGINE

THE CASTLE OF THE SILVER WHEEL

THE CASTLE of the SILVER WHEEL

TERESA EDGERTON

ACE BOOKS, NEW YORK

This book is an Ace original edition,
and has never been previously published.

THE CASTLE OF THE SILVER WHEEL

An Ace Book / published by arrangement with
the author

PRINTING HISTORY
Ace edition / February 1993

ISBN: 0-441-09275-6

Ace Books are published by The Berkley Publishing Group,
200 Madison Avenue, New York, New York 10016.
The name ''ACE'' and the ''A'' logo are trademarks
belonging to Charter Communications, Inc.

PRINTED IN THE UNITED STATES OF AMERICA

10 9 8 7 6 5 4 3 2 1

A GUIDE TO PRONUNCIATION

For those who take an interest in such things (but otherwise to be ignored) . . .

Generally speaking:

c and *g* are always hard
f is pronounced like *v* in English
ff is just *f*
ll is the Welsh *ll* when it appears at the beginning of a syllable, the English *ll* when it appears at the end
dd is a soft *th*

Vowels are (usually) approximately the same as in Welsh.

With few exceptions, the accent falls on the penultimate syllable.

Specifically:

Tryffin fab Maelgwyn (TRIF-fin vab MEL-gwin)
Gwenlliant (Gwen-HLLEE-ant)
Mochdreff, Mochdreffi (MOCK-dreff, Mock-DREFF-ee)
Tir Gwyngelli, Gwyngellach (Tear Gwin-GELL-ee, Gwin-GELL-ackh)
Ynys Celydonn (INN-us Kel-UH-don)
Mahaffy Guillyn (Mah-HAFF-ee GWILL-inn)
Cado (KAY-doe)
Ceinwen (KINE-wen)
Dahaut (Dah-HOTE)
Garth mac Matholwch (Garth mac Math-O-hhlook)
Meligraunce (MEL-ee-grawnce)
Calchas fab Corfil (KAL-kass vab KOR-vil)
Diaspad (Dee-AH-spad)

Rhianedd, Rhianeddi (Hree-ANN-eth, Hree-ann-ETH-ee)

Caer Ysgithr (Kair Us-GITH-ur)

Camboglanna (Kam-bog-LON-nah)

Cynwas fab Anwas (KIN-wass vab AN-wass)

Brangwengwen (Bran-GWEN-gwen)

Guenhumara (Gwen-hoo-MAR-ah)

Menai fab Maelwas (MEN-ee vab MEL-wass)

Conn, Elffin (exactly the way they look)

Cei (rhymes with "eye")

Faelinn, Traeth, Grainne (FAY-linn, Trayth, GRAHN-yah)

THE CASTLE
of the
SILVER WHEEL

Ynys Celyddonn

N
W — E
S

Cuan

Lech

Oraigh

Murias
Dun Fiorenn
Gorlas
Bargan
Leth Sc

Ynys Moen
Ynys Glastig
Ynys Ysag
Ynys Cadir Carreg
Ynys Monag
Dunn Dessi

Goblyn Hills

Coilldorcha
Tre

Dol Tal Carreg
Uberac Faug

Cambogl

Regann
Caer Cadov
Treledig
Dinas Trachmyr
Teir Mor

Celliwig
Bay of Camboglanna
Drepennin
Pefryn's Grave
Dinas Moren

St. Cybi
Golch
Castell Aderyn
Dinas Moren
Ynys Aderyn

A SCALE OF MILES
25 50 75 100

GORWYNN
MÔN
CAER CELYNNON
DINAS CONN
LLANDALEO
ST. SIANNE
ST. TEILO
PEFYN'S GRAVE
GLANN INGLENANT
CASTELL IORAN
Rhianedd
Ynys Sacha
Ynys Rhennen
DUNN TRAGEN
ARGADUISS
CAER TEINNE
R. TEINNE
DINAS RHIAN
ST. CALL
Ynys Eyrie
LOCH GORM
CAER WYORD
Powell
LLIG
LOCH BEI
DRAGON
MOEL
DINAS DRAGON
ILDATHACH
CASTELL LORRU
Mochrett
ach
YSTRAD YRGOLL
Perfudd
LOCH ARGADN
CAER YSGIDN
R. NENDWY
PENNIGARN
PEFYN'S GRAVE
LLONO
PENNEFYNN
IFARION
Gwyngell
CADIR CERT
R. DEFEYLLA
UNNA
DINAS SPAGEN
Walgan
DYFFYNOG
ST. MADDEN
ABERDAUBEN
CASTELL MAELDUIN
GWERNABY
Ynys Carrea
Ynys Isaf

Ann Myers Maguire

The Lord of Mochdreff was dead: an arrow through the heart and no man knew whose hand had pulled the bow. He had been a stern man, iron-eyed, clutch-fisted, as close and secretive as stone; not even his widowed mother wept when they draped him in scarlet linen and lowered him into the ground. Yet the Mochdreffi felt his loss. They were lordless again, after a single year of cold but meticulous rule, and no heir stood ready to take his place.

Three young kinsmen, each with an equal claim according to the ancient law of Mother Right, three young boys, each with a family of ambitious clansmen ready to spill heart's blood on his account; Lord Morcant had not been minded to single out any one of them as his heir. "A man is a fool, who sews his own shroud," said the Lord of Mochdreff.

Yet Fate spun the linen for his winding sheet even while he spoke—and the thread was exceedingly strong. He took an arrow in the breast as he walked his own battlements at Caer Ysgithr, and the plots were already boiling as he breathed his last. Within the fortnight, the three claimants were two; within a month, an entire clan was massacred in retaliation.

Only the High King in Camboglanna could prevent the violence from spreading, by naming Morcant's heir, by sending an army to set him in Morcant's place. The petty lords and the clan chieftains came together and they composed a letter to the King: "Give us a Lord and spare us further bloodshed."

They gave that letter to the King's young cousin, Tryffin fab Maelgwyn, who was living at that time in defiance of Blood Feud, in the land of Mochdreff. He took the lords' petition, called together his warband, and departed that very same day.

—*From* The Great Book of St. Cybi

1.

Cobwebs and Nettles

The road, which was scarcely more than a path, led uphill through the mist, skirting a thicket of blackberry bramble, then ambling in wide lazy loops up the grassy slope.

Nothing threatening in that, thought Tryffin, as he brought his big roan gelding to a halt and glanced uneasily around him. The only problem was, this range of green hills ought not to exist at all: did not appear on any map that he had studied; had not been anywhere along the road a year ago, when last he passed this way; most certainly had *not* been visible less than an hour since, when the fog first separated him from the bulk of his armed escort as they crossed the boggy lowlands. And even if he had mistaken his road, strayed a mile or two off course—how could an entire range of hills lie hidden in land so bare and flat?

Let alone, no place so green and growing ought to be found in this region of Mochdreff.

Tryffin shrugged a broad shoulder, under his wine-colored cloak. Forward or backward, he had to make a decision, whether he and his squires should retrace their path or continue on up the slope. Though under the present circumstances there was no way of telling whether the road they had followed before was still there behind them.

"Pixy-led or something very like it," said Garth, gone pale under his shock of brown hair. And his brother, Conn, replied very low: "They say the Sidhe in these parts are jealous and spiteful, always looking to do us harm. Curse this heartless land anyway. It has no love for our kind and it never will."

"We'll have none of that," said Tryffin, over his shoulder, more sharply than he intended. "Before God, a man who speaks ill of the very soil he stands on has only himself to blame if he finds the ground crumbling beneath his feet.

"To my mind, we've not been so much led astray as wandered into some adventure," the young knight added quietly, taking up the reins again, urging the big gelding up the hillside. His squires on their lighter mounts trailed behind.

This was not Tryffin's first encounter with the Old Powers—which had ruled Ynys Celydonn in ages past, which had not, even now, entirely relinquished their hold on the wild places of the island kingdom—nor the first time he had been singled out for

2

some otherworldly adventure. Such experiences could be perilous, but a man could also learn something to his benefit, if only the extent of his own courage, his own resources.

"Though I've no idea whatever," he muttered under his breath, "why these adventures should always present themselves when a man is late or traveling in haste . . . or otherwise disinclined to brook delay."

They followed the track uphill, past the blackberry thicket, all hairy leaves and wicked thorns, and around an outcrop of mossy grey stone. The mist grew colder and denser, but the light remained constant, as though the fog itself contained some quality of luminosity. And they could hear something breathing, something much too large to be one of the horses, a vast wheezing and sighing somewhere in the mist behind them.

But once you choose to go on in an adventure of this sort, Tryffin reminded himself, you only increase the danger if you try to look back. Let alone, if he faltered, the boys might panic.

And then, quite suddenly, they were out of the fog and up on the moonlit crest of the hill. While they climbed—could it possibly have taken so long as that?—the sun had died in the west and a raddled three-quarter moon appeared in the east. To either side of the road, the grass glistened with dew in the moonlight.

Now the track took them down and down, until they came to a bowl-shaped hollow between two hills. At the bottom of the hollow, in the exact center of the bowl, was a broad pool of bright water, a natural spring ringed by bushes and great rough stones.

"We'll water the horses, then set up camp here for the night," said Tryffin, dismounting on the slope. The boys followed his example, taking their horses by the bridles and wading through fragrant heather and moon-silvered broom down to the spring.

One moment they were alone in the hollow, the next they were not. Between one heartbeat and the next she appeared: an old woman standing on a rugged shelf of stone on the far side of the pool, a thin, angular old woman with a wild mane of white hair and a rusty black gown; all pointed nose and sharp angles she was, like a creature made out of twigs. At her feet crouched a red fox, scarcely more than a kit, and a rumpled grey owl perched on one crooked black shoulder.

"You'll not wish to drink from this pool or water your horses," said the crone. "A viper came this way, a fortnight since, and discharged his venom into the water."

The boys exchanged a skeptical glance. "Snakes don't do that," said Conn, sounding aggrieved, as though the very notion

3

were an affront to the accumulated wisdom of his sixteen years. "That's just a tale for old wives."

Nevertheless, he kept a tight hold on his chestnut mare, keeping her from the pool.

The woman laughed gratingly. "I take it, young master, you have never met with the kind of serpent who walks on two legs?"

Tryffin frowned; his hands tightened on Roch's bridle. "You tell us that it was a *man* who poisoned this water?"

The bony old creature cackled again; on her shoulder, the owl stretched tall and bated its wings; the little red vixen whimpered at her feet. "The Lord of Penwith, knowing his enemies would pass this way and stop to drink, instructed his warlocks to spell the water. Drink of this pool and you will feel your insides begin to burn, your brains on fire, and your heart aflame."

Garth and Conn made pious gestures, shocked by so callous, so reckless an act—one that might victimize innocent travelers. But Tryffin felt physically ill. To one like himself (who, when he was knighted, had been bound to the realm: earth, water, and stone) the matter was far more serious than that. To poison a spring . . . that was an act of madness, a crime against nature, and a hideous betrayal of that sacred bond which united a Lord to the lands he ruled.

And along with the sickness came a sudden heart-wrenching desire to go home, go all the way back to Tir Gwyngelli, the wild Hill Country where Maelgwyn fab Menai reigned in barbaric splendor, and his Gwyngellach subjects practiced seventy-seven distinct methods of bloody revenge—but none of them involved anything nearly so wicked as this.

"Come with me," said the woman, more gently than before, and the grey owl shrank down again and rubbed its feathered head against her hoary locks. "I can offer you shelter for the night and also sweet water to drink."

"Aye, we'll follow," said Tryffin, squaring his shoulders, assuming once more the placid, almost stolid expression he had used since childhood in order to mask his true emotions. A big, bland, deliberate young man, a man of unshakable tranquility, that was how other people saw him, what they wanted him to be, and for the most part that was what he gave them. In any case, for the sake of the boys, he must not show any weakness now.

She led them to a cottage built of smooth white stones, a little round hut with a reed-thatched roof, a crooked chimney, and bramble and sweetbriar growing around the door and windows. The fox streaked ahead, like a comet through the night, and slipped past the half-open door, but the crone took her visitors around to a rude shelter behind the house.

"You may stable your horses here," she said. Just enough moonlight filtered in through holes in the roof to show that the stable was already provided with fodder for the horses and a big wooden tub half full of clean water. It seemed the old woman had been expecting visitors, and men on horseback at that.

"I think she is one of the Old Ones, a hag or even the Bean-nighe," whispered Garth, as the crone hobbled away.

He and his brother were Gorwynnach, sons of the north, and therefore bred to a horror of all things born of the Wild Magic. Two years living in Mochdreff had broadened their minds but had not altered their instincts.

"No," said Tryffin, taking down the shield he carried strapped to his saddle, placing it in a corner of the stable. "If memory serves me, I've seen this woman before: at Lord Cado's house in Trewynyn. She's Mahaffy Guillyn's old nurse."

The boys exchanged a sidelong glance. "But if she *is* one of Lord Cado's servants," ventured Garth, "then what is she doing *here*?"

"As we don't even know where it is that we are, we have no way of knowing if she belongs here or not," Tryffin replied calmly. "And it happens that Cado Guillyn, in case no one ever told you, is a wizard of some renown."

But he did not think that Lord Cado's kind of magic was at work right now, because he had a certain knack for sensing these things.

The science of wizardry was high and cold and brilliant, all mind and no heart; it made Tryffin's teeth ache like a wind out of the north. But the old Earth magics, they sang in his bones, made the blood run like liquid silver in his veins. The old woman (Ceinwen, he remembered her name was) was undoubtedly a witch; his bones were humming finely now. And Tryffin thought she might be employed, nominally, as a servant in Lord Cado's house, but he had never met the Mochdreffi wise-woman *yet* who was willing to bend the neck and allow herself to be ruled by anything so "puny" as a magic-wielding man. No, whatever peril or benefit the old woman represented, it was all her own and nothing of Lord Cado's.

Still turning the matter over in his mind, Tryffin unsaddled Roch. Then, handing the reins over to Conn, he left the boys to tend to all three horses and went around to the front of the cottage and in at the open door.

He stopped and looked around him. At first, he thought he had got into the mist again, out on the moors with that vast wheezing beast dogging his trail. Then the fog thinned and he saw it was only a cloud of steam rising from an enormous clay pot that hung from a chain over the fire, and the sound he heard was the gentle panting of a silver-grey wolf cub stretched out on the stones by the hearth.

Besides the fire, there were dozens of tallow dips and rushlights casting circles of golden light in the gloom; Tryffin wondered why the old woman should want the place lit up like a church. It was a queer sort of room anyway, larger than he might have guessed from the outside, and parts of it were hard to see, all dim and wavering, as though partially obscured by mist or spiderwebs. What he could see was mostly lined with shelves, shelves crammed with bottles and bundled herbs and bits of crockery and wooden boxes and feathers and bright pebbles . . . and here and there the glitter of a glass ball or a silver mirror, or any one of the other costly trinkets lying like scattered jewels among the more homely paraphernalia of an ordinary village witch and healer. Doves roosted overhead in the rafters. Old Ceinwen sat in a low chair made of woven branches, some of the leaves still on them, sorting through the contents of a large wicker basket she held in her lap. From where Tryffin stood, it appeared to be full of tattered garments of various colors and kinds.

The owl had ascended to the rafters along with the doves; and as the young knight crossed the room, he caught a glimpse of the vixen curled up under a rickety table. As there was no better seat available, he sat down on a little three-legged stool at the old woman's feet, arranging his legs and his sword and scabbard with practiced grace. Not for him the freedom of little men who could fling their tiny limbs about as they would; his every move must be smooth and contained or someone got hurt or something broken.

The crone cocked her head, favored him with a dark, inquiring glance. This close, she smelled a little foxy. "Not too proud to sit so low, son of Maelgwyn?"

"A Prince of Gwyngelli is never too proud to sit at the feet of Wisdom," he replied, in his soft southern lilt.

She nodded approvingly. "Ah, you're a good deal sharper than you look. And someone taught you some pretty manners."

She selected a ragged length of linen—it might have been the remains of a fine cambric shirt like the one Tryffin wore under his mail and leather doublet—set her basket down on the packed-earth floor, and took up a slender golden needle, which she proceeded to thread with a piece of her own coarse white hair. Then she began mending the shirt, sewing up a jagged rent with a row of neat stitches.

Remembering what Garth had said about the Bean-nighe, the fairy washerwoman, Tryffin wondered if there were bloody garments in the basket beside him. Courtesy, however, forbade a closer inspection, and she had already commended his manners.

"Shelter and water you promised. But I've a third boon to ask, if you'll be so kind," he said, stripping off his soft leather gauntlets. Like his doublet, they were crimson leather, and the cuffs were embroidered with gold and silver thread.

"There is a path I will show you tomorrow morning, leading back to your road. And there, perchance, you will find your escort waiting.

"You were not wise to lose them," the witch added, with a frown. "There were many men at Caer Ysgithr, for all they pretended to agree with the rest, who would prefer that the message you carry should never reach your King at all. And you missed one ambush, wandering in the mist, but perhaps you'll not be so fortunate another time. Look to it they don't take you by surprise or outnumber you."

He was only mildly surprised that she knew so much. He had already guessed she was a far more important personage than she appeared at first glance—and maybe young Garth was not so far wrong.

As for the possibility of an ambush . . . He remembered the scene at Caer Ysgithr quite vividly: the petty lords and the clan chieftains signing their petition with great formality. Fully half the sheet of parchment was filled with their flourishing signatures and their great waxy seals. They had passed their petition among them, they had sworn a great swearing of oaths: vowing to abide by the King's decision, pledging their fealty to whichever Lord the King was pleased to bestow on them. But no one had called for an oath that would bind those men against harming the messenger.

That (Tryffin thought wearily) was the Mochdreffi version of honor: to violate the spirit of any agreement, while keeping rigidly to the letter.

And of course he had expected some such treachery from the very beginning. That was why he had armed himself and assembled a formidable escort—only to lose them, in this land of mists and strange magics, before he crossed the border into Perfudd.

"I wonder," he said thoughtfully, "if I was chosen to carry the message, only because the Mochdreffi regard me as expendable."

The witch bit off her piece of thread, tied a knot in the end, and started mending a second hole in the shirt. Tryffin had not thought the length of springy white hair could possibly go so far. In fact, it looked just as long now as it had been when she started.

"I believe you have more friends on the council than you imagine. But also many bitter enemies. You have done well, Prince Tryffin, perhaps too well to a certain way of thinking. You have gained the respect of the petty lords and clan chieftains, a certain grudging affection among the common folk; so naturally there are men who would rather see you dead. But don't think of going back to Tir Gwyngelli (as you did a short while since), for the King will be sending you back to Mochdreff, perhaps sooner than you think."

Tryffin felt a faint stirring of resentment. It was bad enough the uncanny old creature was able to poke around in his thoughts, but she went too far, telling him how to order his life. "And how if I don't choose to return? How if I choose to abandon my post in Mochdreff? Cynwas won't try to stop me if I want to go home. He can't afford to offend my father."

And that was the truth, not bragging at all. The High King would do nothing to antagonize his wealthy and powerful and generous friend. Indeed, it was not so much respect for Cynwas that led Maelgwyn's sons to refer to him by his more archaic title of High King or Emperor. It was more of a gentle reminder, to themselves and to others, that Maelgwyn alone ruled in Gwyngelli, and that his fealty to Cynwas was principally a matter of friendship and form.

"But it's not Cynwas fab Anwas who will compel you," she answered serenely. "You owe the Mochdreffi a debt: one you may repay in blood or in service, just as you see fit."

The accumulated weight of the last two years descended on Tryffin's shoulders. Two years acting as deputy to the Lord Constable of Celydonn, two years studying this land and its strange customs, laboring to bridge the gap which existed between Mochdreffi and Gwyngellach after centuries of feuding. That was his penance for the murder of Calchas fab Corfil.

"But *I* am not to blame for the present wretched state of affairs. Whatever else they may think, no one blames me."

She knotted her hair thread once more and held up the cambric shirt. Tryffin was amazed; the shirt had been little more than a rag a short time since, but now it was just as good as new. He could not even see the places where she had stitched it. "One man blames you," said the old woman. "And the name of that man is Tryffin fab Maelgwyn."

In the rafters overhead, the doves made soft murmuring sounds, the owl hooted twice. Outside, he could hear Garth's and Conn's voices coming around from the stable to the door.

As the boys came into the cottage, the crone left her chair and

8

hobbled around the room, taking down wooden bowls and crockery plates, preparing their supper. Conn and Garth, who were trained to be helpful, obligingly assisted her.

But Tryffin remained where he was, staring moodily at nothing, remembering the deed for which he now did penance.

• • •

Calchas fab Corfil lay sprawled on the cold stone floor, gazing up at the long bloody blade waving just inches away from his face.

"Where can we find the Princess and Cynwas's crown?" said Tryffin's brother Fflergant, very pale but determined. He and his companions had traveled many miles in order to recover the crown and the fabulous sidhe-stone and return them to the Emperor. But they had spent hours searching the Princess Diaspad's fortress of sorcery at Caer Wydr without success . . . until this fortuitous meeting with Diaspad's son.

The Mochdreffi youth made a gurgling sound deep in his throat, but offered no other reply.

Tryffin crossed the room, his face uncharacteristically grim in the flickering torchlight. "You heard the question: Where is your mother and what mischief is she up to?"

Calchas winced as Fflergant nudged him with the tip of the sword, just above the breastbone. "I don't know where she is—no, I swear to you—she doesn't tell me things anymore, she doesn't trust me, ever since—"

Fflergant prodded him again. "Ever since . . . ?"

"Since I tried to bring Gwenlliant with me, when we left Caer Cadwy," said Calchas. "I meant the child no harm; I was trying to save her. She is a taking little thing, and I was fond of her."

The two older boys felt the anger surge through them, remembering how Calchas had attempted to use Gwenlliant for his Black Magic spells, and later . . . No one knew exactly what Calchas had done to her, but she wept afterward and spoke of things no innocent child would know about.

"Oh aye, we remember how you were fond of her," Tryffin said, narrowing his eyes. "And we warned you what would happen if you ever laid hands on her again. But don't worry, we'll give you a chance to die like a man."

Fflergant withdrew his sword and Calchas staggered to his feet. Looking from one furious face to the other, the boy from Mochdreff lost his nerve and began to babble. "You can't kill me, not an unarmed man. I won't pick up my sword . . . and then you will have to spare me. You'd never touch me anyway, not if you

9

knew the truth," he added desperately. "You're Gwyngellach, and kinslaying is the one unpardonable crime."

Fflergant scowled at him and spat: "No kin of ours, you Mochdreffi pig!"

"But I am," Calchas insisted, still trembling. "We're first cousins. My mother and your uncle. You can't pretend you didn't know the two of them were lovers."

Confused, Fflergant looked to his brother for advice. They both knew about Calchas's mother and their Uncle Manogan, but surely that affair had ended years before Calchas was born.

Tryffin's expression was utterly unreadable. "He may know something we don't know." He shrugged. "Ah well, who can say? Take his nasty little dagger and pick up his sword, and then we'll decide about killing him."

Fflergant relieved Calchas of the dagger he carried in his belt, then turned toward the place where the boy from Mochdreff had dropped his two-handed sword. At that same moment, Tryffin turned, as if momentarily distracted. That was all the encouragement that Calchas needed.

He slid a second, smaller dagger out of his sleeve and leapt at Fflergant. Tryffin's sword met him halfway; there was a sickening sound as the blade hit Calchas's midsection, and the boy fell to the floor, cut nearly in half by the force of the blow and his own impetus forward.

"Mother of God!" Fflergant stared numbly at the bloody corpse at his feet. Then he looked up at Tryffin. "You tricked him. We could neither of us kill a man who was unarmed and begging for mercy, so you tricked him into attacking me."

• • •

Tryffin came out of his reverie and looked around him. Conn and Garth had disappeared, but he could hear their voices outside the door again. Apparently, they had taken their supper out to the grassy slope leading up to the door, where they could eat in comparative comfort. The old woman handed him a wooden bowl containing a soup made of nettles flavored with sorrel.

"No one else blames me," he said, just as though their conversation had not been interrupted. "Supposing I had allowed Calchas to live, supposing he had returned to rule Mochdreff in his own right after the death of his mother . . . God knows, he was weak and wicked, the people did not love him. Can you say they would not have killed him before the year was out—as they assassinated Morcant, as they murdered Goronwy?"

He put the bowl down on the floor behind the basket, accepted the hard piece of dark bread, the wooden cup the witch handed him. "No," he said, curling his fingers around the cup. "If I had spared Calchas, if the High King had pardoned his treason, it would be the same now. Calchas fab Corfil would still be dead; his heir, Goronwy, would still be dead; and Morcant, that cold but admirable man, would still be rotting in his grave."

"And you perhaps would be free to go wherever you choose," retorted the crone, resuming her seat in the leafy wicker chair. "But there is an ancient web of love and hate, kinship, murder, and betrayal that binds the men of your house and of Corfil's closer than brothers, for all their bitter enmity. It was to free you all from the tangled skein of history that Calchas came into this world."

Tryffin took a bite of the bread. It was made of cracked grain and dried berries, rough, but not unpleasant to the tongue. "I reckon you did not *know* Calchas. He was not capable of any good thing."

The old woman shrugged. "And so you are alive, while Calchas is dead. These destinies have a way of working themselves out. But after all, you must not consider yourself the victim of Fate. The blood you shared, the wrongs he did you, they were all a part of it. But it was your deed, your slaughter of that poor, weak, wicked boy, that united your destiny and his for all time."

She picked up her basket and began sorting through it again. He regarded her narrowly, as he sat there eating her bread, sipping her water, for her words troubled him. He thought she might be swearing a destiny on him even as he sat there. And a Prince of Tir Gwyngelli was hedged around by geasa and supernatural prohibitions almost from the moment of his birth—he certainly did *not* need to inherit another man's geas as well.

"But enough, for now, of Calchas fab Corfil," said Ceinwen. Under the table, the red fox shifted restlessly, then curled up again with her shiny black nose between her paws.

The witch selected something from her basket: a gauzy yard of cobweb silk shot with silvery thread, the sort of thing a nobly born maiden might wear as a veil, except that the hem was raveled and worn. She replaced the basket on the floor.

"When you leave this place, you will *not* go immediately to the King at Caer Cadwy." She started pulling long bronze pins out of her hoary locks and deftly pinning up the ragged hem of the scarf. "You will go north instead, to Ystrad Yrgoll, in order to stop a wedding."

Tryffin straightened indignantly. "The message I carry is an urgent one."

"The message you carry is an urgent one, but the King is not likely to come to any immediate decision."

He swallowed a last bite of bread, put down his empty cup. "If the Emperor needs time to make up his mind, then I must buy him that time with my haste. Men and women may die while I delay." She had warned him, just a little while since, against those who did not wish the petition to reach the King. Now he was beginning to suspect the old woman might be one of them.

The witch sighed, dropped the silk, pins and all, into her lap. She made a well of her hands, breathed a few words into them. "As you will, then. It is plain that you need convincing. Tell me what you see here."

He leaned forward to look, then started and drew back. How she had managed it he did not know, but her cupped hands were filled with clear water.

"Or is it," the crone asked, with a sly smile, seeing him hesitate, "is it that you are *afraid* to look?"

Tryffin considered for a moment. He had seen pictures in the fire once, on a wise-woman's hearth in Teirwaedd Morfa, and he knew that water might be used the same way, by those who had the power. He was not so much frightened as wary. Yet curiosity always had been and would be among his ruling passions; he bent forward once more and gazed intently into the well of her hands.

At first, he saw only his own reflection . . . *a solemn young man with sun-browned skin, straw-colored hair, and puzzled dark eyes* . . . but that image dissolved to be replaced by another. *A candlelit chapel in a place he did not know, where a saturnine man of perhaps fifty and a young girl in a deep purple gown stood hand in hand before the altar, apparently about to be wed . . . The bride was exceptionally young and exceptionally pretty, and under a gauzy veil her hair was a mantle of palest winter gold falling almost to her knees.*

With a jolt of recognition, Tryffin surged to his feet, reaching instinctively for his sword. "My cousin Gwenlliant," he breathed, his hand clutching the golden hilt. "Holy Mother of God—she's little more than a child! Too young to marry anyone, far too young to marry an aging lecher like Rhun of Yrgoll. As though she's not suffered enough in the past, from the wickedness of men and their desires!"

The witch opened her hands, and the water was gone. "These things have been known to happen: a pure young bride and an evil old husband," she said calmly. "But you—you wish to marry this lady yourself, do you not?"

With an effort, he regained his composure. "I want to marry

12

her, but not until she is a year or two older. I've no desire for a bride of twelve." He sat down on the stool again. "And this wedding, I suppose you mean to tell me, is to happen soon. Why did no one write to me? Why didn't Gwenlliant herself send word? We were always like brother and sister. How could she marry and not tell me?"

The old woman smoothed the skirt of her tattered black gown, then took up her needle and length of silk once more. "Gwenlliant's letter arrived in Trewynyn the same day you left. Though I doubt you would be able to make head or tail of it; it was written in such great haste. Her father came to her at Caer Cadwy—while the King and Queen were away from court and there was no one with the authority to oppose him—announced that he had arranged this marriage with Rhun of Yrgoll, and carried off his daughter that very same day."

Tryffin clenched a big fist. "Cyndrywyn knew I wanted her; he knew I intended to ask for her, when the time was right. Aye, and it would suit his ambitions to marry his daughter to a Prince of the Blood. Ever since her brother disappeared, all Cyndrywyn's hopes have centered on her. Perhaps he thinks this is a fine way of forcing me to marry her before I am ready. He's a strange skittish sort of man, and I suppose he grows impatient. But he risks too much. I have often suspected that Cyndrywyn's fantastical notions bordered on madness; now I am convinced of it."

The old woman regarded him over her sewing. "Then you won't go to Yrgoll? But of course . . . you have your pride. You would not wish this mad and foolish kinsman of yours to believe he can dictate your actions."

"I will go," said Tryffin, grinding his teeth. "Seeing as Cyndrywyn *is* the next thing to a madman, there is no telling for certain what he actually intends, whether he'll force his daughter into this marriage or not."

A vision of Gwenlliant in the arms of Rhun of Yrgoll danced in his brain and it was not a pleasing image. Rhun had already worn out three wives and at least a dozen mistresses with childbearing and brutal ill-treatment, and each new woman was younger than the last.

"And what of your urgent message for the King? What of the men and women who may die while you delay?"

Tryffin gave her a black look under his sandy brows. "As you said: The High King is not likely to make any immediate decision." And then he remembered something that made the cold sweat break out on his skin. "Even if Rhun of Yrgoll were the perfect bridegroom, Cyndrywyn's a fool to take his daughter so far

13

north. She's in mortal danger. My own magical gifts are small, but Gwenlliant's are extraordinary, prodigious. Trees talk to her, stone walls whisper their secrets. Anyone with a trace of the talent can tell: She fairly breathes magic. In the south, we all learn to hide our earth-born gifts as best we can, and everyone obliges by looking the other way. In Mochdreff, as you know, these things are accepted—though perhaps a natural talent like Gwenlliant's, all untrained, would give even the wise-women of Mochdreff something to ponder. But in Perfudd and the north, they take young women like Gwenlliant and they burn them as witches.''

He took a long breath, slowly released it. ''You spoke a while since of the web of history, of predestined loves and hates. I have known for a long time that Gwenlliant was a part of that pattern you mentioned, that she and I share a common destiny—and God help us both if either one should ever deny it!

''I believe you know that, too,'' he added, with another dark glance at the witch. ''Or why should you choose to show me these things, why seek to turn me from my duty?''

''And what,'' said the crone, bending over her sewing, ''if nothing I have shown you, nothing I have said, should chance to be true?''

Tryffin picked up the wooden bowl from the floor, raised it to his lips. The soup it contained was cold and nearly tasteless. ''No,'' he said heavily. ''That was a true seeing. I could feel it in my bones.''

''There are places in this realm,'' said the wizard Glastyn, ''where the powers that ruled this land in ages past still hold sway. There you may meet with speaking stones, sacred wells, floating islands, glass castles, woodland mazes where unwary travelers may wander for days or even years without finding a way out . . . chapels where the severed heads of ancient kings shall be found remarkably well preserved and (rather more remarkably)

2.

The Maze in the Bearded Wood

When it was time to sleep, the witch rolled out three mats made of woven rushes and bade her visitors rest on them.

"And where will you sleep?" Tryffin asked, with a slight frown, for there was no other bed than the ones she was offering, and he was not about to rest easy on a mattress of rushes while the old woman slept on the cold earthen floor.

The witch cackled softly and flapped her arms. "I shall roost in the rafters like an owl, if I grow weary, or perhaps I shall hang from the beams like a bat. You need not trouble yourself on my account, I can nest anywhere." With that, she extinguished the last of the tallow dips and sat down in her chair.

In the flickering light of the dying fire, she might almost have *been* some huge untidy bird, with the white hair standing out from her head like layers of ruffled feathers; her shining dark eyes, as black as pools of ink; and those clawlike hands clutching the arms of her wickerwork chair.

Tryffin shrugged, wrapped himself up in his cloak, and lay down on a woven mat. He had slept in his armor before this. He knew he would be cramped and stiff in the morning, but he was *always* able to sleep.

Tonight was no exception. The next thing he knew it was morning, and a great pot of porridge was boiling on the hearth.

"You look hag-ridden," Conn said to his brother, after breakfast, when the two boys were out in the stable feeding the horses. "How did you sleep last night?"

"I *was* hag-ridden," said Garth. They had brought grain and small dried-up apples with them, and there was still plenty of grass, as well as ample water in the wooden tub. While Roch and the two mares munched and guzzled contentedly, the boys prepared for the day's journey.

"Or anyway, there was a nightmare that came and sat on my chest all night long. It was a great golden beast, rather like a lion, and its weight on my chest was such a pain and a torment I thought it would smother me." Garth lifted the saddle onto Roch's broad back, then bent down to buckle the girth. "If you want to know what I think: I think it was the old woman herself."

Conn grinned at him, unwilling to take this notion seriously. Conn was the younger and more optimistic; Garth was more thoughtful and inclined to be suspicious about reasons and motives—though to do him justice, he was equally suspicious of his own. He had one of those fierce northern consciences that demanded to be examined a dozen times a day. Conn tended to become anxious when he was cold and weary, but on mornings like this, when he was rested and refreshed, when Ceinwen's porridge was still warm in his belly, he was on top of the world.

"If it was the old woman, she's a notable shapechanger. Because I had a dream as well," said Conn. "A lovely young girl with hair like flame. She harped and she sang, and poured me wine in a silver cup—" He stopped, frowning. "Well, I don't quite remember, but I think the dream was unpleasant after that."

Garth might have said more, but just then Tryffin came into the stable. And he and the witch had been so thick and conspiratorial, first last night and again this morning over breakfast, it hardly seemed wise to speak against her. The two boys shrugged and exchanged an eloquent glance.

When the time came for old Ceinwen to keep her promise and take her visitors back to the proper road, she led them around behind the stable and showed them a path that was narrow and steep. "Mind how you go, for the way is treacherous, yet if you follow in my footsteps you will reach the bottom safely."

She carried the little red vixen with her, cradled in her arms like a musky-smelling infant, and the wolf cub trotted along behind her, wagging its tail like a dog. Before long, the ground became so loose and pebbly that Tryffin and the boys had to dismount and lead their horses.

At the foot of the slopes was a wood, a thicket of trees and vines so dense and tangled they appeared impenetrable. The path went in a short way, then disappeared in the leafy gloom.

"You came through the mist—now you must leave by the maze of the Bearded Wood," said the crone. "I cannot go with you, but I will tell you how to go. When the trail branches, turn left and right and left again. You must not attempt to retrace your steps, for if you do there is no saying *where* you might find yourselves. When you come to the stream, cross over. After that, it is right and left and right—as simple as that—and once you come out of the wood, you will see your road directly. No time to thank me or to ask questions, and do not dawdle along your way. You must go swiftly, if you hope to meet with your friends in time.''

She set the fox down on the ground as she spoke, and the wolf cub came around from behind her skirts. And that was the last impression Tryffin and his squires carried with them into the wood: an uncanny old woman in a rusty black gown, with her tame beasts crouched at her feet.

Even after their eyes adjusted, it was dim in the forest—and also very still, except for the occasional creaking of branches overhead. The trees were all willows, poplars, elms, and ancient oaks, strangled with ivy or covered in shabby grey moss, as gnarled and knotted and whiskery as old men. A deep carpet of fallen leaves lay damp and decaying on the forest floor, muffling the hoofbeats of the horses.

Every now and then, some thick twisted root snaked out across the path and had to be stepped over or around. The only light was green and watery, shifting with the leaves as they moved in a breeze too faint to be felt, but there were toadstools and other fungi, pale and phosphorescent against the dark of the trees, and the silver tracks of snails made patterns on the rotting leaves.

The path branched and branched again. Tryffin, who was leading, made certain to turn as the old woman had instructed him, left and right and left. He saw daylight ahead and realized that must be the place where the stream ran through—too broad and deep to allow the arching branches to meet overhead. Already, he longed for a glimpse of sky. When they reached the stream, it presented more of a barrier than he had anticipated; the bank was steep and soft under their feet. Again, they dismounted and led the horses.

They splashed across the brook, wallowed up the steep embankment on the other side, and spent a moment or two searching for the path. Once they found it, it was all very easy: They followed the branching trail, right and left and right, between the ancient trees and came out of the wood on a shallow rocky slope, separated from the road south by nothing more than a thin strip of low, mushy ground.

As they crossed the narrow bit of bogland, Tryffin chanced to glance up at the sky. The sun was low and hazy, when it ought to still be climbing. It seemed that the Bearded Wood, just like the mist, played havoc with time. What had seemed like an easy morning's ride had swallowed up most of the day.

And when he looked back again, back toward the wood, it was not the same place at all: There was nothing there above the slope but a straggling line of leafless grey trees, so thin and sparse that

17

he could see all the way through to the sandy field on the other side.

"Look there," said Garth, as they reached the road. He flung out his arm, gesturing eastward, where a glitter of late-afternoon sunlight on polished metal announced the approach of armed men. Their lost escort came riding down the road, banners flying, green and white, and black and scarlet.

Tryffin awaited the fortuitous arrival of his men calmly. The dark young Captain who commanded his troops was more easily rattled.

"Prince Tryffin," he gasped, at the sight of his master standing at the edge of the dusty road, one hand on Roch's bridle. "We lost you three days since and have been searching for you all this while . . . but I thought you would be halfway to the river Arfondwy by now."

"As to that," said Tryffin, "I have always believed that caution is the better part of haste. For which reason," he added, glancing up at the flags: his own dragon and sunburst, and the green lion of Celydonn, "you had best furl up those banners, at least until we cross into Perfudd. Now that I come to think of it, Meligraunce, we have no need to announce ourselves and our errand wherever we go."

They passed into Perfudd without any incident and slept in a tiny village on the edge of a vast empty heath.

The next afternoon, they turned north and rode for three days through the bracken and the gorse, until they came to a large and busy town by the name of Pwll Gannon. Now and again, the scouts that Tryffin sent out before and behind to scan the country had thought they spotted men riding away in the distance, but nothing ever came of it. By the time they reached Pwll Gannon, Tryffin was convinced that the danger was past, at least so long as they continued heading north.

And if any lord had sent his household troop out to waylay him, they were probably jogging down the road to Camboglanna wondering *why* they never caught up with Tryffin and his men. Turning that idea over in his mind, the young knight thought it might be wise—once he had reached Ystrad Yrgoll and rescued Gwenlliant—to take the long road south, by way of Tregalen and Dol Tal Carreg, and so approach Caer Cadwy from a direction no one expected.

They stopped for the night at a respectable inn: a two-story structure built of the native stone, with a peaked roof made of grey slates and a number of large, comfortable rooms under the eaves.

Tryffin took the largest for himself and his squires, Captain Meligraunce and his Sergeant claimed the next chamber, and the common soldiers took over the public room below.

After a good supper and a long ride, and the weight of his armor gone, Tryffin fell almost instantly asleep, in a wide bed with a feather mattress and a pouch containing the petty lords' petition tucked under his pillow.

He woke suddenly in the dark in the middle of the night, to hear shouting and crashing down in the common room and a rattling of steel in the yard below his window. He rolled out of bed, calling to Garth and Conn, and groped in the dark until he found his scabbard and pulled out the sword.

A clatter of footsteps sounded outside in the corridor. A moment later, the bedchamber door flew open, and Tryffin sprang to his feet, just in time to counter an attack by two armed men who rushed into the room carrying torches and short swords.

Momentarily dazzled by the light, Tryffin gripped his broadsword in both hands and managed to avoid or parry the first few blows. As his eyes adjusted, he aimed a horizontal cut at the nimble little man on his left—a blow that was handily deflected, though it cost the small man his balance and nearly his life—then spun to meet the attack on his right, just in time to avoid a stabbing thrust and to aim a crushing blow at his opponent's sword arm.

There was a momentary shock as the blade cut through leather, muscle, and bone, then the man went down, clutching his wounded arm to his side, though not before tossing his torch into the empty bed and setting the mattress aflame.

By now, the first man had regained his balance. He was a typical Mochdreffi, Tryffin realized, small and dark and agile, much stronger than he looked, with a jagged scar on each cheek and a warrior's keen gaze. As the young knight turned to engage him, the Mochdreffi drew up his short sword and was able to catch the blow on the quillons.

Intent on his own opponent, Tryffin caught only a glimpse of two more assassins entering the room, but a flurry of movement and a clash of steel told him that Garth and Conn had recovered their own weapons and entered the fray.

Overborne by Tryffin's greater weight and force, the man with the scars was pushed back and back toward the wall—another few steps and he would have no place to go. Using his torch like a buckler, he made a desperate thrust at Tryffin's face. But the knight ducked under the burning brand and with a single sweeping movement cut the Mochdreffi down. The man tumbled to the floor, blood pumping furiously from a gash in his side.

The bed was blazing finely now. Tryffin tossed aside his pillow and snatched up the leather pouch, cursing himself for not keeping the petition on him at all times.

But there was not much time to berate himself, for Garth was down on the floor struggling with two men, one of them Tryffin's disarmed opponent. The other still had a sword, so Tryffin dispatched him first, with a deadly efficient blow to the back of his neck. But he was forced to leave the unarmed man to Garth, as a fifth cutthroat, this one flourishing a battle-axe, came charging in through the door.

Tryffin turned, lunged, swung . . . and saw the man fall before his blade even connected, struck down by the stalwart Meligraunce, who had appeared in the door behind the assassin and dispatched him with a two-handed cut. After that, it was only a matter of moments to finish off the two men remaining and rescue Garth and Conn.

But there was still the burning bed, another smoldering fire in one corner of the room, where the second torch had rolled or been kicked. Tryffin and the Captain caught up blankets from the other bed and smothered and stamped the two fires out.

The room stank of blood, sweat, and burning feathers. One of Tryffin's guards came in with a torch, slipped it into a bracket on the wall.

Garth took a few wobbly steps and sat down on his bed. He had a cut on his brow and his knuckles were scraped, he was bruised and horribly shaken, but otherwise whole after his first real battle. But Conn was down on the floor, as white as a ghost, clutching one leg, and his hands were all sticky with blood.

Tryffin took the first piece of cloth that came to his hand, searched around until he found his knife. He tore a hole in the linen and ripped it in half. Then he knelt on the floor by Conn and made a compress to stop the bleeding.

"Not likely to kill you," he said, as lightly as he could. There was no use frightening the lad more than he had been already. "Though I doubt you'll be dancing with the Queen's handmaidens as soon as we reach Caer Cadwy."

Conn managed a weak grin. His face had a sickly cast, and the brown hair was plastered in spikes on his forehead. "I'd have finished the fellow, too—if Meligraunce hadn't decided to inter-fere."

Tryffin sat back on his heels, wiping the sweat from his brow. He considered the bodies scattered across the floor. These were no outlaws, that much was evident, though for certain they had been bold and reckless men, to attack when the numbers were against them, in a house full of so many witnesses. Yet they had been patient men, too, dogging his footsteps, biding their time, then choosing the right moment to strike, when they had lulled him into a false sense of security. These things argued both forethought and determination.

Tryffin shook his head. He thought there must be something more at stake than one of the petty lords or clan chieftains having second thoughts, seeking a way to circumvent his oath. Someone wanted him dead. He had been too efficient, had accomplished too much, during his time in Mochdreff—so the old woman had told him. But she also said he was fated to return.

Yes—and old Ceinwen had gone to some trouble, brewing up her mist, leading him to her door, all so that she could show and tell him those things. Tryffin blew out a long breath. He had a destiny in Mochdreff, that much was certain, and he thought maybe the witch was not the only one who knew it.

"There must be a physician or a healer here in this town," Tryffin told Meligraunce, when the Captain came back to report that three of his guards were dead downstairs, and a fourth man dying.

"Aye, we've sent for him—though I fear he'll come too late for poor Rhufawn," said Meligraunce. Beyond that, there had been injuries ranging from trifling cuts and bruises to wounds that were serious but not likely to be fatal. And the innkeeper, his servants, and the rest of the guests, they were all of them terrified, though none had been harmed.

"But as for the blackguards who attacked in the night, I fear we have killed them all, God save us! And that was a grave miscalculation on my part, Lord, for which you have every right to berate me."

Tryffin ground his teeth. No way of learning, then, who was responsible.

He did not consider himself a cruel man; when forced to kill he preferred to do it as swiftly and cleanly as possible. Yet for all the veneer of civilization he had acquired at Caer Cadwy, there remained that streak of Gwyngellach barbarism. And here were four of his men dead or dying—and young Conn, who might eventually be able to ride and hunt and do all the things he had done before, yet was likely to limp for the rest of his days. Tryffin thought he was *just* angry enough to enjoy the process of interrogation, had there been any prisoners for him to question.

"No fault of yours, Meligraunce. It's not always the easiest

21

thing, taking captives during a surprise attack.'' He set his jaw and squared his shoulders.

"I want to see Rhufawn and the men who were friends of the men who died," he added, rising to his feet. "Though God alone knows what I ought to say to them."

"Aye," said Meligraunce, moving toward the door, "that's like your kind heart—" Then he stopped, and his eyes went wide. "But you, Lord, you haven't a mark anywhere on you, and there you stand in your shirt and your stocking feet!"

Tryffin looked himself over. There he was indeed, in nothing more than his shirt, his brown linen breeches, and his dark woolen hose; yet he alone had survived the battle without so much as a scratch. It hardly seemed possible.

But then he remembered the witch: old Ceinwen sitting in her chair of woven branches, sewing up a bit of ragged linen, with a piece of her own white hair.

She had mended his shirt in advance—and maybe his skin and his bones as well, Tryffin realized with a shudder.

For all that, he doubted the charm would save him a second time. After this, until they reached the safety of castle walls, he would sleep every night in his mail.

• • •

It is through the Marriage of these two, Sun and Moon, brother and sister (which are regarded as one Body, not being formed of one Physical Substance, but by virtue of the Mutual Love which unites them), that many Miraculous things come to pass.

              —From The Magician's Seventh Key

• • •

It was a grey day in Ystrad Yrgoll; the wind howled and the rain fell through the air in sheets. The roads were filthy with mud, but the horses plodded steadily on, for what seemed like years.

And then the storm began to subside. The winds and the rains, which had plagued Tryffin and his men ever since they left the inn, finally gave way, allowing a weak sunlight to pierce the clouds.

Riding in the midst of his troop, weary after this three-day struggle with the elements, Tryffin labored now to master his impatience. Seven days, the crone had warned him, as he sat eating porridge in her little round hut. He had seven days to reach Rhun's castle and save Gwenlliant from an odious marriage, and this was the seventh day.

"They will walk to the chapel when the bells toll the hour of Sext," said the witch. Already, it was well past Tierce, and the

very best he could hope was to arrive in time to disrupt the ceremony.

To a man of his steady and deliberate habits, the idea of bursting into the chapel and making a scene was not appealing. But he would do that and worse besides, if that was what it took to rescue Gwenlliant.

A boggy spot in the middle of the road forced them to make a long detour. After that, there was a bridge down and a swift stream to be forded. By the time they reached the gate of Castell Yrgoll, the clouds had parted, the sun was directly overhead, and Tryffin was far, far beyond considering his dignity.

Two different flags were flying above the gate: Rhun's device, with its knotwork Perfuddi serpents, announcing that the Lord of Yrgoll was in residence; and Cyndrywyn's arms, three ravens *volant,* circling Selgi's iron crown.

"Who comes?" cried one of the guards up on the wall, and Meligraunce shouted back: "In the name of the Lord Constable and of the King, Tryffin fab Maelgwyn bids you open."

The drawbridge came down hastily, but the portcullis stayed in place. Tryffin removed one gauntlet and pulled off the massive gold ring he wore on his right hand. He gave the ring to Garth, who rode up to the grating and passed it through, so that whoever was in charge at the gate might examine the seal: the winged lion of St. March crouching to spring, the badge of the Lord Constable of Celydonn and his deputies.

With a clanking of chains and a grinding of gears, the portcullis rose, allowing Tryffin and his men to ride into the muddy courtyard. There he accepted his ring back from the Sergeant of the Guard, a strapping fellow with a steady eye, rather better than Tryffin had expected to find in Rhun of Yrgoll's service.

Dismounting, the young knight slipped the gold ring back onto his finger, but he did not replace the glove.

"If you'll allow me to escort you to some suitable chamber, Lord, there to await my master's pleasure—" began the Sergeant.

"But it is *my* pleasure to see Rhun *now*." Tryffin tossed back his dark red cloak so the man could see that he came armed and wearing mail. "You will escort me to him at once.

"I am cousin to the bride," he added quietly, "and she has invited me to attend her wedding."

(And God help him if that was a lie—but the old woman said that Gwenlliant had written. It was one of his geasa never to knowingly tell a lie, and the last time he had violated one of those tiresome magical prohibitions a kinsman had died. Just at the

23

moment, he was not particularly adverse to blood on his hands, but he preferred to choose his own victim.)

He followed the Sergeant, splashing across the courtyard, then around a draggled group of stables and cottages, toward a building whose ornate stonework and stained-glass windows proclaimed the castle chapel. The Sergeant hurried on ahead to open one of the massive oak doors, and Tryffin entered the chapel ahead of his guards, with Garth and Meligraunce only a step behind.

The chapel was ablaze with row upon row of fine wax candles in every niche and ledge. Almost certainly Cyndrywyn's doing, for the Rhianeddi were inordinately fond of candles in church. There was a scattering of Rhun's people on the benches to either side of the central aisle.

But Tryffin only had eyes for the group standing by the altar: a gaunt young friar in an ill-fitting black habit; the bridegroom, prematurely aged by years of dissipation; Cyndrywyn fab Dwnn, elegant in black and silver, in the act of giving his daughter away; and Gwenlliant, just as the old woman's magic had pictured her, in a trailing gown as purple as blood and a glittering veil of silk and silver.

A red mist rose before his eyes and a familiar pressure started building inside him.

A whole bank of candles went out in the draft from the door. Everyone turned to look as Tryffin walked down the aisle, his golden spurs jingling in the sudden silence and his gleaming mail hauberk reflecting light from the remaining candles.

Cyndrywyn (who ought to have been quaking in his long-toed shoes, had he known what raged in his kinsman's breast) greeted him with an ill-concealed smirk and a flourishing obeisance. "Prince Tryffin. You have come to attend your cousin's wedding."

With a monumental effort, Tryffin maintained his composure. "I have come to prevent this vile and unwholesome union, as I think you must know."

He heard someone gasp, somewhere in the chapel behind him. There was a general murmur of surprise, and Rhun went scarlet with indignation. "You do me a grave discourtesy," the Lord of Yrgoll exclaimed, "by coming here in this unseemly fashion to disrupt these holy nuptials."

"On the contrary, you should be mightily obliged," Tryffin replied gently. As always, when the savage in blue paint was howling inside of him, he struggled to remain outwardly cool and formal. "Had I arrived a day later, I would be forced to kill you. Whereas now, you may yet escape with your life."

Dropping his gage at Rhun's feet, he stepped past Cyndrywyn, took Gwenlliant's soft little hand in both of his. Now he had it, he was not about to relinquish her, not if the sun fell down flaming from the sky and the earth tilted beneath him. "If you want to marry this lady, you will have to fight for her."

Several more candles flickered and died. Rhun's complexion changed swiftly from red to white. He opened his mouth to speak, but little more than gobbling emerged. When he was finally able to spit out the words, he rounded on Cyndrywyn instead. "You said nothing to me of a previous betrothal."

Cyndrywyn made an airy gesture with his hands. "There is no contract between them, not any I know of, and my daughter is not of age. She is yours—supposing you have the courage to take her."

For just a moment, Rhun favored his intended with a bright lascivious glance. But when his gaze moved on to Tryffin, standing there so broad and determined in his wine-colored cloak and his gleaming mail, then on to the armed men who had entered the chapel in Tryffin's wake, those eyes went dull. And after all, he could always buy himself another bride, as he had bought so many women before, from greedy fathers and complaisant husbands. The price of this one might prove too high.

Standing with the book still open in his hands, the hollow-eyed friar cleared his throat. "Whether or not the lady is of age, any vows, any rings exchanged between them, may present an impediment."

With her hand still clasped tightly in both of Tryffin's, Gwenlliant spoke up for the first time. "But we *have* exchanged rings," she said, holding up her free hand so that the gold bands she wore on her fingers caught the light and sparkled. Sparing him the lie.

Though he was perfectly willing to fight if he must, slice Rhun open and carve out his liver, saving some other innocent girl from his loathsome embraces.

But the Lord of Yrgoll was sadly reluctant to grant him that satisfaction. "If the lady is betrothed to you, she can hardly marry me," said Rhun, turning on his heel and striding toward the door. There was a rustle of movement as his people made to follow him down the aisle. With his departure, the pressure in Tryffin's chest began to ease, his vision returned to normal. It appeared they were all going to be spared an ugly scene.

As for Cyndrywyn, he just went on smiling his slightly demented smile, while the light made a halo around his silvery fair head. "I hope, for my daughter's sake, that you intend to marry her with all due haste."

"Aye," said Tryffin. For the sake of Gwenlliant's good name, he was determined to marry her as quickly and quietly as possible. "I believe I will marry your daughter now."

Releasing her hand, he turned toward his men. "Escort Lord Cyndrywyn from this place—forcibly, if necessary—and then station yourselves in the courtyard, lest Rhun change his mind and attempt anything foolish."

As the others led Cyndrywyn protesting from the chapel, Tryffin nodded to Garth and Meligraunce. "Guard the doors from inside. I'm in no temper to endure any interruptions."

Only when he and Gwenlliant were kneeling before the altar, with their golden heads, bright and pale, side by side, did he think to ask her: "In the name of God, Gwenlliant, I hope you *want* to marry me."

For answer, she lifted her silken veil to receive his kiss. The face underneath was pale, the violet eyes much darker than he remembered, but she looked remarkably serene for a little girl who had narrowly avoided an unthinkable marriage. He wondered if she had known all along that he was coming to claim her.

"I prayed that one of my cousins would save me," she said simply. "I thought it might be Ceilyn or Fflergant—or even the King—but I hoped that it would be you."

Prince Tryffin arrived three weeks later, weary and travel-stained, at the gates of Caer Cadwy. Admitted to Cynwas's private chamber, he presented the petition on bended knee.

"This is not a matter to be decided in haste," said the King, with a sigh. Of all his subjects, of all the tribes and peoples who shared the Isle of Celydonn, the Mochdreffi were the most contentious, the furthest from his affection. It was difficult to love them, for they were not a kindly race.

After many weeks of deliberation, he sent his reply by another messenger. As it was in his power to bestow the degfed *on either of the two candidates, so it was also in his power to withhold the gift. "I am not minded to give you a new Lord so soon," said Cynwas, "only to see him murdered before a year has passed. Therefore, I shall appoint a Governor to rule you instead, to establish order in my dominion of Mochdreff and to make all safe for Morcant's successor when he comes." And he appended a list of five worthy noblemen, officers of his court, for the petty lords and the clan chieftains to choose between them.*

They read the list; they shook their heads and they pulled their beards; not one name was acceptable. After many weeks, he received a reply. "If the King is pleased to send a foreigner to govern us," read their petition, "then give us instead Prince Tryffin, who is not of our blood but has lived among us, who if he loves us not, neither does he despise us."

So the King sent for his cousin and showed him the message. "This is not what I would choose for you. Though I know you are a young man of extraordinary talents, it is a dangerous honor they would have me bestow on you," said Cynwas. "Yet I do not see how I can deny them so reasonable a request: that a man they know should be sent to govern them. Will you be Governor and rule in my name over the people of Mochdreff?"

"I will do as the High King advises," said Prince Tryffin, kneeling again before the King, this time to exchange the oath of fealty.

—*From* The Great Book of St. Cybi

3.

In the Belly of the Wind

The ship was black with moon-colored sails and scarlet pennants, a great broad-beamed galley made of oak, of ancient timbers sucked dry by years of wind and sun.

Like weathered bones, thought Gwenlliant, standing on the deck one afternoon, with the hood of her green wool cloak thrown back, so her pale hair blew in her face and the wind boomed warnings in her ear. *This ship was built of the bones of oaks.*

She shivered. It was not a pleasant thought for a girl who had spoken with oak trees in her time. And surely not appropriate for a bride just short of her thirteenth birthday, sailing to a new life with her handsome young husband.

Gwenlliant shook her head, passed a hand over her brow, as if by doing so she might dispel these morbid fancies.

She heard steps behind her, and turned to see her pages, Cei and Elffin, running across the deck. "Lady, come see. They have sighted land and we are nearly there," said Elffin, the younger, hopping about in his excitement.

Gwenlliant smiled, her spirits lifting. They were bright and active little boys of nine and eleven, these two. Her kinswoman Teleri had sent them as a belated wedding gift, from her house at Regann, with the message that Cei and Elffin had *"served in a wizard's household and so grown accustomed to accept strange things."* Which would apparently serve them well, since they were going to Mochdreff.

Certainly Gwenlliant liked their company better than that of her three handmaidens: Grainne, Faelinn, and Traeth . . . who were probably sitting in their cabin down below, either suffering from sea-sickness or else trying to do needlework by the light of a single lantern. They were kindly practical girls, several years older than Gwenlliant herself, and very clever at dressing their lady's hair and mending her gowns, but they tended to treat her as though she were a doll or a plaything and generally lost interest as soon as they finished dressing her.

She followed her pages up a steep ladder-like stair to the forecastle. There were sailors up in the rigging, shouting orders and climbing the masts (*Like so many spiders*, thought Gwenlliant, *scuttling about in a web made of hemp*), but the three children had the platform all to themselves.

"Look," Cei said breathlessly, pointing a finger.

Gwenlliant gazed out across the bright water, where the wind had stirred the sea into whitecaps. This was not her first sight of the Mochdreffi coast, which had often appeared as a dim grey line just at the edge of vision, but now she could see the jumbled outline of a town, and something taller and darker and grimmer at the center, which she thought must be the castle.

"They say it's all marsh and heath in Mochdreff, and witches and talking pigs and mists and charcoal burners and wicked, wicked heresies," said Cei, mixing the landscape, the climate, the livestock, and the inhabitants promiscuously together.

"Not all marsh and heath," said Gwenlliant. "Tryffin says it is mostly pleasant and fertile in the land by the sea, with farms and walled towns and everything we are accustomed to, and the people grow cabbages and turnips and grains, and raise cattle and horses, and . . . Well, not so very different from Camboglanna. It's inland that you find the mists and the swallowing bogs and all the rest of it, I suppose."

Yet the wind from Mochdreff carried voices that were wilder and colder, harsher yet somehow more poignant, than any wind of the south. *But I don't remember the winds of the north; I was very small when I left. There is something strangely familiar blowing on this wind, but I can't say for certain that it reminds me of home.*

"God love me, I don't think I will rest easy until I've met at least one talking swine," said Elffin.

Gwenlliant laughed. "Well, I hope you may do so. I think I would like to meet a talking swine myself."

Because for all the strange things she had conversed with since she was small: the trees and the stones, the birds in the air, the beasts of the field, and the small burrowing creatures down in the earth—once, even, the bones of her own great-grandfather several generations removed—the pigs she had met were remarkably inarticulate.

As the galley approached the land, her sails were furled, and the oarsmen took over. Progress was slow, and the town actually seemed to recede into the distance for a time, as though the men were losing their contest with the waves. The boys soon lost interest and went below, leaving Gwenlliant alone on the forecastle.

But after a while, the town began to grow large again, and the galley slid past some little fishing boats with parchment-colored sails and docked at the end of a long wooden pier. Two of the oarsmen came up, removed a portion of the rail, and began to lower a wide gangplank down to the pier below.

It was then that she heard Tryffin speak her name and turned to see him climbing the stairs.

He was dressed in somber black from his neck to his feet, relieved only by wide bracelets on either wrist, arm rings of pure Gwyngelli gold, a king's ransom for a king's son. His hair had been bleached by the sun, during this voyage, to a shade nearly as pale as her own. But perhaps that was only in contrast to his tanned skin and the rich, funereal black of his clothes.

Tryffin came and put his arms around her, dropped a brotherly kiss on the top of her head. Then he walked past her and leaned against the rail, where he could watch the activity on the busy docks below. Gwenlliant joined him by the side, slipping a hand into one of his.

One of the oarsmen glanced up at the forecastle, and spotting Gwenlliant standing there with her hair uncovered, made a *sign*—fingers crossed and touched to his forehead—and said something in a dialect she did not understand. But the meaning of those words and that gesture she could guess very well; the men had been signing themselves against evil from the moment she stepped on board.

Suddenly, she was horribly frightened, her hands damp and her knees weak. She was afraid to go into Trewynyn, to ride through its cobblestone streets, where the people could watch secretly from the concealment of their crooked houses, afraid to even glance up at the castle, perched like a gargoyle on an eminence in the center of the town.

"Must we—must we leave the ship today, Cousin?" she asked softly.

"They will send a proper escort down from Caer Ysgithr, but I doubt they will arrive before dark. They need time to make things ready for us." Then, sensing her distress, he added: "You had best tell me what frightens you."

"Some of the men on this ship," she whispered. "They act as though I might wither them with a single glance. Will it happen that way wherever we go?"

She heard him sigh. "Sometimes it will be like that—not always. There will be people who look at you, those with a touch of the gift, and they will see a woman of power, a witch. But you've nothing to fear. Nearly every family in Mochdreff lays claim to a witch or a warlock, usually the clan matriarch. It is a hard unchancy life they lead in this land and any woman who is able to raise most of her children until they are grown is thought to possess some uncanny power. It happens that some few do have genuine gifts, the young and the old alike. But they don't burn witches or hang them here, not for witchcraft only. So long as she abides by law and custom, nobody wants to meddle with a Mochdreffi wise-woman.

"The men," he added, with a shrug, "seem to come by their magical gifts accidentally, after illness or injury brings on a bout of delirium. Of those that survive, many become warlocks. As for wizardry . . . there is little of that in these parts. I've only met but one man who styles himself a wizard, and I can't say he is a man I particularly trust."

Gwenlliant thought about that. For years she had been forced to conceal her gifts—or else lend them a certain left-hand respectability, by studying the "acceptable" discipline of wizardry, pretending it was not the Wild Magic but a wizard's talent she had possessed all along. But how many people had *really* believed that, how many who knew her had *truly* been fooled? Certainly the magic had never been deceived. It wrought as it would and refused to be turned down a different path. And now she had come to a place where people could tell what she was just by looking at her.

But still, she thought, *if nobody wants to meddle with witches, that hardly sounds as though the Mochdreffi love us.*

"Is that why you gave me so many attendants?" she asked. "Why I am never to go anyplace alone after we land? Because people will instantly know me for a born witch?"

He stood up straighter. "Nothing of the sort. That was meant to shield you from *my* enemies. I am certain to have any number now, even if I hadn't before. It would be a fine thing if everyone did look at you and see a powerful witch," he added. "That's the very best protection you could possibly have, far better than any protection I could provide you.

"No one will try to hurt you directly—because what would be the good of it? *I* would still be here, thirsting for blood—but they may find some way, some scandal maybe, and that is why I can't have you going about on your own. Except when you are safe in the tower where we'll live, keep one of your pages with you at all times."

That sounded rather better. Because even if there was something more to be feared, more than he wanted to tell her, Cei and Elffin were just little boys and they carried no weapons but their jeweled daggers. It hardly seemed that the dangers could be very formidable, if Cei and Elffin were supposed to defend her.

"I would never have brought you here," Tryffin said, reaching out to take her hand again, "if I didn't believe you would be well and happy."

He tried to remember when it first came to him, the idea that Gwenlliant would do very well living in Mochdreff. No doubt in the beginning it would seem very strange. The people, too, would need time to warm to her: Gwenlliant with her Rhianeddi eyes and hair. To say nothing of her occasionally astounding precocity, which made some people nervous—though Tryffin himself found it a continuing delight. But in the end, she would realize, the Mochdreffi would realize, that she somehow *belonged,* in this land where the Wild Magic was virtually a palpable presence.

Or was that, he wondered, merely a convenient excuse, one he had invented simply because he could not bear the idea of leaving her behind?

As for Gwenlliant, watching him turn so suddenly silent, thinking she had hurt him by seeming to question his motives for bringing her with him into Mochdreff, she searched for something else they could safely talk about.

"Tell me about the castle, about Caer Ysgithr."

He smiled faintly. "Ah well, I'll not deny it's a weird old place—an uncanny place. I never lived there, you know. I kept a house in the town, but I visited the castle often in the course of my duties. *Mind how you go at Caer Ysgithr,* that's what people used to tell me when I lived in Trewynyn. Though I'm not altogether certain they meant it as a warning, only a way of describing some of the more unusual features. Mostly, it's superstition. The Mochdreffi have been in awe of the place ever since the Princess Diaspad and Calchas lived there."

He might have said more, but just then her handmaidens appeared on the forecastle: Faelinn, Grainne, and Traeth. They stood in a row by the stairs, each with her hands folded demurely in front of her, waiting to be noticed. Gwenlliant sighed. With their broad pleasant faces, their almost identical gowns and cloaks cut from the same drab cloth, they were depressingly similar. If it were not for their voices and the colors of their hair, it would be impossible to tell them apart.

"Lady, your escort will be arriving from the castle very soon," said Faelinn, the redhead.

"And you will want to change into something finer and tidy yourself up," said Traeth, who was dark.

"For you look terribly wild and windblown," chimed in Grainne of the golden hair. It was a habit they had, finishing each other's sentences, as though they had only enough intelligence to hold a single thought among them.

"Yes, I will come," said Gwenlliant, allowing them to shepherd her down below, though she knew very well that it would be Traeth and Faelinn who chose her gown, Grainne who decided how to dress her hair. To argue with them would be no use at all. They would only look offended and ask quite reasonably: What were they there for if not to serve her?

When she came back on deck—properly gowned in satin and velvet, with her pale hair brushed until it shone like silk, then braided in tiny braids at the front, left hanging loose at the back—Tryffin was waiting for her by the gangplank.

He took her hand and kissed it. "By St. Maddieu and St. March, you're the sweetest sight I've ever seen," he said. Which was some reward at least, because Tryffin never said anything that wasn't the truth.

But when she looked down at the docks, down at the multitude gathered there to greet the new Governor and his lady, her heart sank. There were boys with banners, and guards in glittering mail, and dark men, richly clad, on high-stepping horses. Thinking of the Princess Diaspad, Gwenlliant had been half expecting dwarfs and mountebanks and giants—yet this display was sufficiently imposing, even a little intimidating.

When Tryffin led her down the gangplank, a man and a boy in long cloaks swiftly separated from the rest of the crowd.

"Prince Tryffin," said the elder, an angular man with an ascetic, clean-shaven face. He bowed from the waist, very cold and precise, but not very low.

The slender youth at his side went gracefully down on one knee. "Your Grace," said the boy. "The Mochdreffi welcome you." Yet again there was something . . . a note of challenge. And even kneeling, his posture was very far from servile.

He was also, Gwenlliant realized, a trifle breathlessly, the most beautiful young man she had ever seen in her life, with a head of jet-black curls; a pale, flawless complexion; and enormous dark eyes. Or he would have *seemed* the most handsome, she reminded herself loyally, had he not contrasted so poorly with Tryffin's great size and golden beauty.

"Cado Guillyn, Lord of Ochren, and his nephew Mahaffy. The Lady Gwenlliant ni Cyndrywyn," said Tryffin, bringing home the realization that she had landed on foreign soil, had come to a land where clan surnames were used among the oldest and proudest families (which was to say, those of the purest Mochdreffi blood) in place of the patronymic preceded by *fab, ni,* or *mac.*

"And make certain you don't misname any of the Guillyns," Tryffin had warned her, *"for they are* all *of them haughtier than God."*

Now Tryffin made a gesture for the young man to rise. "I've a wish to speak with you, Mahaffy. A desire to better our acquaintance," he said. "I will look for you at Caer Ysgithr."

He drew Gwenlliant on past the man and boy, though not before she had time to see and sense that Mahaffy was just as stunned by this invitation as his uncle was resentful at not being included.

By now, the horsemen had all dismounted. Gwenlliant thought they must be Tryffin's new councilors and officers, they were all so gorgeously dressed and so venerable-looking, with their wise eyes and their beautiful long beards. When they all went down kneeling at once, Gwenlliant was a little taken aback. It was odd to see those old men down on their knees and Tryffin allowing them to kiss his hand—as though he were the King himself.

Though it was really no more than his due, no more than he might have demanded on account of his birth. But Tryffin had never stood on ceremony, not in all the years she had known him.

His rank was as much a part of him as blood and bone; it lent him a kind of arrogant humility.

But he has been a Prince of Gwyngelli all of his life, and the Governor of Mochdreff a few weeks only, thought Gwenlliant. *Perhaps he doesn't yet feel so certain of the one as he does of the other.* It was a new idea, and a decidedly uncomfortable one, that Tryffin, always so strong and confident, might feel unsure of himself.

She tried to be gracious when those men kissed her hand, when they bid her welcome. Then Tryffin motioned his councilors to rise, and there was an immediate stir of movement.

Someone brought Gwenlliant a pretty white mare, and Meligraunce suddenly appeared beside her, dark and respectful and blessedly familiar, to toss her up into the saddle. Once mounted, she took up the reins of scarlet leather and breathed a sigh of relief, now the ordeal of being presented to so many strangers was safely over. Though she still had to endure the long ride through the town.

Tryffin came along on a big red-gold charger, and someone brought ponies for Cei and Elffin, a horse-drawn litter for Traeth and Faelinn and Grainne. Gwenlliant rode up to the mighty gates of Trewynyn, with the stalwart young Captain pacing on one side, Garth and Conn walking on the other, and Meligraunce's men surrounding the entire party. Whether they were there for show or protection, she was glad to have them.

The town was built like a great wheel, with the castle at the center and numerous walls radiating outward, which divided the three concentric rings of Trewynyn into many smaller wards and courts. These in turn were connected by gates and arches, one to the other, so that you could circle the town completely. But to move from one ring to another was not so easy; you had to go a long distance around to find a gate that provided access.

Gwenlliant's first impression as she entered Trewynyn was one of poverty, smoke, and filth. Dwellings in the outer ring were mean and crowded, and there was a pervasive odor of fish and livestock. At first, though she could hear them and smell them all around her, Gwenlliant kept wondering where all the animals were hidden. Aside from an occasional lean and surly-looking pig sitting in a doorway, some scrawny fowl scratching on a rare patch of open ground, the beasts of Trewynyn had disappeared.

But then Gwenlliant chanced to look up, and she smiled in spite of herself. The streets were so narrow, the squalid houses and cottages so ruthlessly crammed and piled together, that the chickens, geese, and goats had all taken to the rooftops, where they scratched and honked and grazed among the thatch just as though they naturally belonged there.

After what seemed like an eternity in the saddle, the Governor's party passed through another fortified gate and into the second ring of Trewynyn. Here the buildings were also crowded, but not so dirty and poor. Gwenlliant saw brick and half-timber freshly white-washed, and roofs newly thatched with reeds or bracken. And there were shops and stalls, and craftsmen hawking their wares from wagons in the market squares, churches and respectable-looking inns . . . But night was falling, the sky was a lurid orange overhead, and shadows gathered in the narrow streets; it became more and more difficult to make out her surroundings.

But something happened as she entered the inner ring of the city, where Mochdreffi nobles lived in great houses built of stone, and the streets were lit by crystal lanterns and burning torches. At first, it was just a vibration in the air, a warm, golden buzzing like a hive of bees, oddly reassuring. When she looked up, the sky was ablaze with lights, like comets and falling stars, only a thousand times more brilliant and all in the most glorious colors.

It was the Earth magic, she realized, only here it was aerial.

The humming sensation came and went, came and went, and so did the comets and the falling stars. The final stage of that ride went by too quickly. One moment the horses were climbing the narrow, twisting road up to the castle, and the next Tryffin was standing in Conn's place and helping Gwenlliant dismount.

"Welcome home, Dear Heart." She thought she heard him whisper it against her hair, but she could not be sure. The moment her feet touched the ground, she felt cold and frightened again. What had happened to her, during that ride through the town? She clung tightly to Tryffin's arm as they walked past a series of iron doors and wooden gates, across paved courtyards, through crumbling stone arches, and into the dark bulk that was the Keep. They went up a flight of stairs, along a twisting corridor, and emerged in a vast room with a fireplace at each end.

There were a great many people gathered around the larger fireplace: more boys and bearded men, and a number of withered but haughty old dames in fantastical silks and great horned headdresses, all bowing and bobbing their heads. Tryffin said some names, and Gwenlliant tried to make the proper responses, but she was growing tired and confused by now, and she was afraid she would not remember any of them in the morning.

"Are the rooms ready for the Lady Gwenlliant?" Tryffin's voice sounded a thousand miles distant. Apparently the response was satisfactory. He took her along a narrow corridor, up and up a long flight of stairs, out onto the battlements, and by what seemed a long and circuitous route, across to a square tower and in through another door.

But before they reached the tower, just for a moment, the golden buzzing surrounded her, and the air was filled with the blazing lights and colors.

It is the magic of Mochdreff reaching out to enfold me, thought Gwenlliant. And she began to believe that she might actually *belong* in this place, that the thing which had terrified her before had only been a presentiment of change.

When she came back to herself, feeling not so cold and abandoned this time, Tryffin was leading her into a broad fair chamber with a vaulted ceiling. Gwenlliant glanced around her with a numb sort of curiosity, realizing that she would live here, perhaps for many years to come.

A fire of sweet applewood smoldered in a cavernous fireplace, perfuming the air with a subtle fragrance. There was a carved bed made of dark wood with green velvet curtains, and a low table beside the fire, set with silver plates and goblets chased in gold, everything ready for two people to dine. A massive chair had been invitingly placed at either end of the table.

As Gwenlliant's attendants followed her into the room, all of them became suddenly very busy. Traeth took the green cloak and bundled it away into a walnut chest. Cei and Elffin lighted more candles. And Faelinn and Grainne plumped up pillows and went poking around in cupboards and cabinets.

A troop of dark-eyed serving men in scarlet livery came into the room, carrying covered dishes and platters heaped with food, and Gwenlliant realized that she was expected to eat before she was allowed to rest. Tryffin took one chair, and she sank wearily into the other.

"Thank you," she whispered, when Garth handed her a cup of deep purple wine. The goblet was colder than ice, and her fingers felt stiff on the stem. When she raised the cup to drink, the wine was heavy and sweet, like drinking perfume—the Mochdreffi vintages were apparently so thin and poor, it was necessary to lace them with honey and orris root.

She was not very hungry and the food was strange; the odd-tasting wine made her drowsy. So she ate what she could and moved the rest around on her silver plate until Tryffin was satisfied.

She felt a dim sort of relief when the meal was finally over, and Conn pulled back her chair.

"Sweetheart, it's an unfortunate thing, but I have to leave you," said Tryffin, materializing at her side. Gwenlliant wondered if she had dozed off for a moment, while still standing. "There are men I ought to meet with, any number of matters awaiting my attention. I've a notion my day is not nearly over."

She tried to smile bravely and thought that she succeeded, because Tryffin raised her hand to his lips, brushed a light kiss across her fingertips, and strode out of the room, taking his squires with him.

It was only after he was gone that she realized: She had never asked him where his own rooms were located—or how, supposing she should have need of him, she could ever hope to find him in this vast, unfamiliar pile?

The man who was Lord of Mochdreff in those days was married to a woman who was a notable witch. They had many sons between them, on whom the Lord bestowed many fortresses and castles as a sign of his favor, but also that they might aid him in keeping the peace.

Now it chanced that Grugyn, who was the youngest son, was also the Lady's favorite, and him she instructed in her magical arts. And when the time came for his father to gift him with lands and a fortress, it was decided instead to build a castle for him, which would be a house of sorceries and weird magics overlooking the sea. And so it was done—and all according to the Lady's wishes, and not to any plan drawn up by the Lord's architects.

When they built the walls at Caer Ysgithr, they used blood to strengthen the mortar, and many spells were chanted and divers strange rituals performed. And the buildings and the courtyards and all within the walls were cunningly arranged to a secret design known only to the witch.

—*From* The Nine Sorrowful Tales
of the Misfortunes of Mochdreff

4.

The Sins of the Fathers

The next morning dawned cold and wet. With nothing to do and nowhere to go, Gwenlliant felt bored and lonely. Her handmaidens and pages had plenty to occupy them: unpacking the chests which had carried her clothes and her other things by sea from Camboglanna, putting her new rooms in order. But when Gwenlliant offered to help, everyone stopped short whatever they were doing and looked just as shocked as if she had proposed something absolutely scandalous.

"Oh no, Lady, that wouldn't be proper," breathed Faelinn, shaking her head.

"Because only think how embarrassing for *all* of us," said Grainne, "if any of the common Mochdreffi servants came in and caught you at it."

Gwenlliant lifted her chin. "Well, anyway," she said to Traeth, "I think I might help you mending that gown. I always mended Sidonwy's things beautifully. She said—"

"As God is my witness, I would die of shame allowing you to do anything of the sort," Traeth said, with her hand on her heart. "It was all very well before you were married to wait on the Queen. But now you are a princess yourself—"

"—you simply cannot be seen mending your own garments," Faelinn concluded.

Even Cei and Elffin looked so appalled, it hardly seemed worth arguing. Gwenlliant was the Lady and must keep order in her household—but she must also be gentle, considerate, and courteous, as Tryffin invariably was, as his mother and sisters undoubtedly were, back in Gwyngelli. She did *not* want to model her behavior after that of her Rhianeddi cousins, who always abused their attendants so shamefully. But how to be kind to these people of hers and still command their respect?

So Gwenlliant spent most of the rest of that morning wandering restlessly from one window to another, watching the rain spatter on the tiny diamond-shaped panes or pacing from one end of her bedchamber to another, with the train of her velvet gown trailing behind her. As usual, the gown had been chosen for her: black velvet with ermine tippets, worn with a jeweled belt. Grainne, Traeth, and Faelinn had all insisted that she look her best, in case any visitors should happen to call. Though who would come out in such dreadful weather?

It was a great relief, in the late morning, when Tryffin finally appeared. But he walked into her bedchamber, sent her women away, and stood by the door, smiling at her with such a warm glow in his brown eyes that Gwenlliant felt suddenly shy and made him a low curtsy, instead of running to meet him.

"May I offer you a cup of wine, Cousin?" This was the first time in many weeks they had been alone together, only one of a handful of times they had been entirely private since they were married, and she thought perhaps he had come for something more than a cup of wine.

"No," he said, that soft southern lilt of his more caressing than ever. "I am just on my way to bed, having spent the whole night consulting with my new councilors and hearing God knows how many petitions . . . as if none of it could wait for another day. But I thought you might wish to know that our rooms are connected by a private stair." He indicated a door at the back of her bedchamber.

Gwenlliant blushed and tried to think what she ought to say. "Perhaps," she ventured, "I should send a servant for some cakes and ale."

He shook his head, not moving from his place by the door. "I've already eaten a substantial breakfast: tripes and sausage, eggs and herring and apple frumenty." Which explained the slightly sated look. He was a man with substantial appetites, she knew—and not only when it came time to sit down at the table. "What you could do, if you've a mind to, is come over here and give me a kiss."

There was no reason for her feet to feel so heavy, her pulse to race so wildly. Yet it seemed to Gwenlliant that she was a long time crossing the room.

When she finally arrived, she lifted her face to receive the usual brotherly kiss on the cheek, but he took her in his arms instead and gave her a long breathless kiss on the mouth. Gwenlliant felt her bones turn to water, a tingling begin in the soles of her feet as his hands slid down to the small of her back, pressing her up against him. He was big and solid and warm. Even indoors, even on a day like this, he smelled of sunshine and heather; his mouth and his hands were gentle. Yet she panicked, suddenly, and tried to push him away.

He held her just long enough to feel the strength in those big hands of his, how helpless she was if he chose to make her so, then he released her. "My apologies. I seem to have difficulty remembering that you are only twelve years old." Then he laughed without sounding like he meant it, captured her hand, and pressed a kiss into her palm. "I confess to God, I'm not usually so clumsy."

But that was a piece of cruelty he had perhaps not intended to cut so deep, reminding her of all the women he had loved before. Yet Gwenlliant took his words sadly to heart. He was not the man to live celibate—and why should he have to, Maelgwyn of Gwyngelli's big golden son? If *she* was too young, too stupid, and too frightened to do her duty, she knew there were plenty of women willing and eager to sleep in his bed.

Meligraunce found him an hour later, in the bedchamber down below, sitting in a big chair drawn up near the fire, frowning at a scrap of parchment he held in his hand.

"Prince Tryffin . . . that is, Your Grace." No one seemed to know precisely what to call him, since vice-regal appointments were seldom made in the island kingdom, and there had never been (so far as anyone knew) a Governor of Mochdreff ever before. "You do not look well, Lord Prince. And I understood that you meant to spend the morning resting."

Tryffin waved Meligraunce toward another chair. "As to that, I find myself too distracted to sleep, having paid a call on the Lady Gwenlliant, earlier today—and been soundly put in my place."

He could not help smiling at the Captain's carefully blank expression. "No need to behave as if you haven't the least idea what I am talking about. You know very well how I spent the first two weeks of my marriage."

Meligraunce removed his cloak—he had been out in the rain and the wool was soaked—draped it across a stool, and took the chair he was offered. He and the Governor were much of a height, though the Captain's build was lean and wiry. He stood high in his master's confidence, partly because he was one of the few men who *could* look Tryffin directly in the eye. He was also intelligent, loyal, and admirably discreet.

"Ah, Lord, that was a difficult time for everyone. Not knowing whether we were safe under Rhun's roof, suspecting there might be men waiting to waylay us the moment we ventured outside. The entire journey south, we were on the lookout for another attack. Who could court a lady, such a very *young* lady, under such deplorable circumstances?"

"Aye," said Tryffin, with a deep sigh. "That is what I thought at the time. But now I am not so certain." Because if he had taken Gwenlliant that first night, in all the excitement of the rescue and

40

the wedding—when she was feeling such relief at finding herself married to *him* instead of to Rhun—it was just possible that she might have responded eagerly.

Instead, he had never even attempted to consummate their marriage until after they reached Caer Cadwy.

"I see," said Meligraunce. "The lady had time to think things over and decided the prospect was far more daunting than she had previously supposed. And you, Lord, being the man that you are, you did not wish to force your attentions, or . . . or suggest to the lady that she had any sort of *duty* that she ought to perform."

Tryffin shook his head. The idea of Gwenlliant submissive and obedient in his bed, as though he were no better a man than Rhun of Yrgoll, appalled him. "There are certain difficulties attending the seduction of a twelve-year-old virgin, one of them being my own outraged sense of decency, and the other—ah God!—the other being that I strongly suspect she has already been subjected . . . not to an actual rape, but to something almost equally vile."

He shook his head. "I ought not to discuss this, I know. These are private things. But you were there at the time, you were one of the Emperor's guards. And I can't believe the rumors did not reach you and the other men at the Main Gate."

Meligraunce hesitated. "We heard something . . . about Calchas fab Corfil wanting her, about the use of Black Magic."

Tryffin clenched his fists, crumbling the scrap of parchment he held between his fingers. "He filled her mind with obscene visions, assaulted her with evil dreams, taught her more of perversion than any good woman ought to know. And yet—oh God, to look at her, to speak to her, who could believe she is not just as innocent now as she was before it happened."

He needed a moment to compose himself before he continued. "I have discussed Gwenlliant with my kinswoman Teleri. Speaking as a physician, rather than a wizard, she says that Gwenlliant may not even *remember* these things, or if she does . . . only dimly. It is one of the ways a broken mind attempts to heal itself, burying such memories as deep as possible. But I am afraid, Meligraunce, I am afraid that something I say or do, some clumsiness—even a moment when I allow passion to overcome good sense—might bring it all back to her." He shuddered inwardly, thinking how close he had come to losing his temper earlier, and how she would have loathed him afterward had he not so narrowly regained his control.

Meligraunce cleared his throat. "If you don't mind my saying so, there are not many men noble enough to forgive a woman these

41

things, to marry a lady who had suffered in that particular way.''

The Governor straightened indignantly. ''Before God. Where I come from, Captain, if a woman is violated, no one blames *her*. Not that it happens often in the Gwyngelli Hills, and not that a man who had done such a deed would boast of it. The penalty is far too messy and protracted. No, if there is any shame attaching to either one of us, it is mine and not Gwenlliant's.''

Meligraunce considered that. ''Because you had failed to protect her?''

''Aye, that's one reason, not the only one,'' said Tryffin. Because the old woman had told him (and he had good reason to believe that she spoke the truth) that by killing Calchas, he had in some way *become* Calchas. And that meant inheriting his sins committed against Gwenlliant, along with the sins of his father and grandfathers.

Was this what repelled Gwenlliant? Her uncanny gifts might well communicate that guilt in some subtle fashion. But if that was so, then Gwenlliant might never *truly* be his wife until Tryffin had fulfilled the mysterious destiny which brought him into Mochdreff.

''I can only hope that as Gwenlliant grows older, as she becomes a woman and begins to feel . . . whatever inclination a woman feels toward a man, none of this will matter anymore.''

He was silent and thoughtful, turning the idea over in his mind, until Meligraunce spoke, breaking into his thoughts. ''The Governor honors me with his confidence. But I think it was not to discuss these highly personal matters that you sent for me.''

Tryffin sighed. ''No more it was. Thank you, Captain, for reminding me.'' He suddenly remembered the piece of parchment he held crushed in his hand. ''I want you to find out who sent his men to murder us in Perfudd. The man with the two scars on his face should be easily identifiable, and if he was a member of any petty lord's household troop or his personal bodyguard, it may be he was right here at Caer Ysgithr when the petition was signed. Find out if anyone knows who he was. Also . . .''

He handed Meligraunce the scrap of parchment. ''. . . here is a list of men that may bear me a grudge on account of my activities as deputy to the Lord Constable—as well as others I distrust for one reason or another. I want you and your men to find out as much as you possibly can about each of these noble lords and chieftains. Be discreet, of course . . . but I already know that I can rely on you for that.''

''Certainly, Your Grace,'' said the Captain, an alert look on his intelligent bony face. "But you know, discreet inquiries always take considerably longer."

Tryffin wandered over by the fire. The grate was piled high with green holly logs, which ought to have burned like wax, but the flames were weak. Even after all these years, he did not understand why fires always burned so poorly in Mochdreff. The native woods aged well—truth to tell, they were practically tinder dry the same day you cut them—but they seemed to lack some essential element necessary for combustion.

While Tryffin brooded, Meligraunce went over the list, sounding out the names one by one. He had learned to read, the Governor had seen to that, but like all skills learned comparatively late in life, this one did not come easily. "I see you have named here the wizard, Cado Guillyn. But surely Lord Cado's grudge is too personal and too trifling . . ." His voice trailed off. "My apologies, I did not mean to insult Lord Cado's niece. No doubt the lady was no small matter to either of you."

Tryffin shook his head. "In fact, I believe Lord Cado was perfectly content that Dahaut should occupy my bed." He turned back toward the fire. "Which may, perhaps, be the very reason I despise him—that Dahaut's affairs never seemed to matter to him at all. Or else . . ."

"Or else, Lord Prince?" the Captain prompted him when he did not continue.

"I'm not quite certain what it is about Lord Cado that makes me distrust him. I have never heard him speak an unfriendly word, and for a man so cold his manner is always remarkably cordial, yet I can't spend more than a few moments in his presence without somehow feeling that he is contemplating some ill turn."

Meligraunce nodded. "He is like a horse or a hound that is too well trained to show his teeth or to snap at you . . . yet you can see plainly enough by the way he stands and he moves that the brute would harm you if he dared."

"Yes," said Tryffin, "that is it. Now that you mention it, there is a kind of a shiver, almost imperceptible, that goes across his skin whenever I approach him—which is reason enough to suppose, no matter how friendly he may otherwise appear, that the man loathes me.

"I feel more easy in the presence of his nephew Mahaffy, who never pretended to like me and used to look murderous whenever he saw me. Now, there is a promising lad," he added. "I wish he would forgive me whatever wrong he holds against me, for I would gladly promote his interests if only he would permit it."

Tryffin laughed, a trifle bitterly. "Ah, Captain, if I had known

I would someday be Governor of Mochdreff, if I knew how all my mistakes and indiscretions would complicate things now, I think I would have led the most exemplary life of any men who ever lived.''

The rain continued to fall the rest of that day and into the next. But the third day dawned clear and bright, and by afternoon the courtyards were dry enough to permit Gwenlliant and her attendants to sally forth and explore their new surroundings.

Stepping through the door, from shadow into light, they nearly collided with Tryffin, who was climbing the steps to the tower, flanked by two of his bearded councilors. Gwenlliant stepped back and sketched a brief curtsy.

Tryffin frowned, not as though he were cross, but as if he were gathering his thoughts. ''And where might you be going?''

Gwenlliant drew herself up defiantly, certain she was about to receive another lecture on proper behavior. ''I wish to learn my way about this place where I am going to live.''

''Aye, and so you should,'' said Tryffin a bit abstractedly. ''Shame on me for not thinking of that before. I should have sent someone—Meligraunce or one of the lads—to show you about.''

He shook his head to expel the last of the cobwebs, then came to a sudden decision. ''I'll do it myself. Lord Caradoc, Lord Dyfan, my apologies. My duty calls me elsewhere.'' And so saying, he took her hand, drawing her between the two gorgeously attired old men and down the remaining steps to the yard, her pages and handmaidens trailing after her.

Gwenlliant allowed herself to be led, not certain whether he had actually altered his plans to suit her or if she had just been used as an excuse. ''Cousin,'' she said, when the Lords Caradoc and Dyfan were out of earshot, ''if you are very busy, you need not—''

''I have hardly been anything *but* busy since I arrived here,'' he said. ''Six months Morcant has been dead, and rather than work together to enforce his laws: One lord issues a writ forbidding the bakers in Trewynyn to make bread on Sundays, and the next makes out a warrant declaring that same practice highly desirable. Then they switch places, and what the first lord warrants—say the right of shoemakers to sell leather pouches—the second condemns. And so it goes from the Seneschal to the Steward, from the Steward to the Marshall, from the Marshall to the Sheriff, with a long string of contradictory edicts and proclamations. And all with no better motive, as God is my witness, than undermining the other man's office and authority.''

He gave her hand a reassuring squeeze, as if to tell her that he carried no grudge after the uncomfortable scene two days earlier. "I had far, far rather take a walk with you than deal with any of that. And since this may be the last time I can shirk my more onerous duties with a clear conscience, let us by all means enjoy ourselves while we still can."

Gwenlliant gave an inward sigh. This was his way of saying that he could not always be dancing attendance on her, as he had done during their voyage. That was true of most marriages—husband and wife leading separate lives, meeting only on formal occasions and in bed—why had she supposed that she and Tryffin would be any different? Certainly he had spent little time with her during the three months they lived at Caer Cadwy. Then he had mostly been closeted with the King, discussing the situation in Mochdreff, or with the Lord Constable, discussing who knew what, or out hunting and hawking with his friends, or practicing broadsword combat with his men. The only difference was that she had her own friends and her own amusements, and had scarcely noticed.

In which case, she thought, stiffening her resolve, *I must just find ways to keep busy here.* It would be a terrible thing, with all his other duties and responsibilities, if Tryffin had to exert himself to keep his bride entertained, as though she were a fretful child. *It is for me to entertain him. I must be bright and disarming, inquisitive, confiding and affectionate, everything he likes me to be.*

And indeed as the afternoon progressed, it was easy to be an agreeable companion. The castle was so odd and so interesting, and it was pleasant to walk from courtyard to courtyard, along the battlements, from room to room, leaning on Tryffin's arm—so long as she did not allow herself to think about the lonely time ahead.

Caer Ysgithr was an ancient stone fortress which had been falling down and building up, falling down and building up, over the course of many centuries. In shape it mirrored the town below (or perhaps it was the other way around), being roughly circular, with a dozen courtyards of various sizes all surrounding the great rambling Keep at the center. Like most old buildings, it talked in its sleep, babbling of battles and surrenders, defiances and conspiracies, coronations and knightings, deathbed curses, the miraculous births of heroes: all the remarkable scenes it had witnessed during its long, complex history.

Gwenlliant had long since learned to listen with only half of her attention, because not all the old stories were good to think about. Besides, it was not as though you could learn anything actually *useful* that way—any building much over two centuries was likely to grow senile, combining the events of a half dozen stories in a rambling narrative that as often as not went absolutely nowhere.

The Keep was just as grand and shadowy by day as it had appeared that first night. Tryffin led Gwenlliant and her attendants down endless corridors, through echoing state chambers, showing them all the principal features of the place. In one room, perched on a dais so high that Gwenlliant had to bend back her head to see the top of it, was an enormous ugly throne. The skull of a boar with great curving tusks still intact was mounted on the back; even dead and stripped of its flesh, the creature had a malevolent look.

"The legendary High Seat, where the Lords of Mochdreff are always invested," said Tryffin. "According to legend, if a candidate should ever be unworthy, the skull will give a mighty shout, shattering the stones that make up the platform.

"It muttered dire warnings, so they say, when Calchas took the High Seat during his mother's regency," he added, with a shrug. "But as the skull steadfastly refused to speak aloud and the dais—as you can plainly see—is still standing, no one dared to challenge his right."

When Tryffin led her back out and into the light of day, it was a relief to breath the air again, and escape from the clamor of the walls.

Outside, the castle was all jagged battlements and winding staircases and dizzily tilted towers and gardens of a sort: the grass sparse, the plants pale and lifeless. The only things that seemed to grow and flourish were a matted woody vine with cunning concealed thorns, and a rich green moss that grew practically everywhere: on flagged walkways and granite walls, on wooden gates and marble statues. These statues were many and various, and they ranged from figures that were brooding and vaguely disturbing to downright frightening: slithering sirens, voracious sea-monsters, and gape-mouthed gargoyles. It was obvious that someone, whether it was the Princess Diaspad or some previous inhabitant, shared the King's grand passion for grotesque statuary.

Near the Keep was a walled garden, an orchard of stunted appletrees. The trees were queer and ugly, with short twisted limbs, desiccated leaves, and withered fruits. Yet those trees spoke to Gwenlliant, rustling their last dry skeleton leaves as she walked by. It was so plaintive a sound that she could not resist stopping and running her fingers over one scaly trunk.

Then she knew something about Mochdreff that she had never known before. "The land is not hard and cruel, it is only ill and grieving. That is why nothing grows as it should, why all the women become witches.''

''Aye, perhaps,'' said Tryffin. He walked over to join her under the tree, placing one of his own square hands on the trunk. ''They say there is a blight spreading through the land; every year, a few more acres lose their fertility. But if that is true, the land of Mochdreff has been ailing for many hundreds of years.

''For myself I think it has something to do with the Wild Magic. You know that when Glastyn tamed the Wild Magic, he bound it under the earth so it might enrich the soil. He sealed it there with his name and the Emperor's name, and the bindings hold: to the north, in Rhianedd, Gorwynnion, and Cuan; to the west, in Draighen, Perfudd, Celliwig, and Camboglanna; to the south, in Gwyngelli and Walgan.

''But for some reason, neither Glastyn's name nor Cynwas's (nor Anwas's before him) has the power to bind in the land of Mochdreff. The spells were weak, they did not hold, so the magic runs loose—loose and sometimes dangerous. That is why the women of Mochdreff become witches. A woman without any hint of power, or a witch in the family strong enough to ward and protect her weaker relations, can only stand by and watch her children die.''

Gwenlliant shook her head. It wasn't like that at all. Remembering what she had seen and felt that first night in Mochdreff, she had an idea the Mochdreffi snatched their magic out of the very air, then bent it to their own purposes . . . when all the time, the earth was begging to be healed. If they put the magic back into the soil where it belonged, their children would grow strong and healthy, and there would be no need at all for their spells or witchcraft.

Later, when Tryffin had shown her as much of the castle as it was possible to visit in a single afternoon, when they were climbing the stairs in the square tower thinking of their supper, Gwenlliant stopped to catch her breath and look out one of the slotted windows. Gazing down at the orchard and the sickly gardens, she spotted a tiny hunched figure moving furtively among the appletrees, as if trying to conceal her movements from any chance observer in the castle up above. There was something familiar about that gaudy little figure, the humped posture, the orange and yellow gown, and Gwenlliant gave a soft exclamation of surprise.

''What is it?'' asked Tryffin, joining her at the arrow slot, looking where she pointed. But by now the orchard was deserted.

"I thought . . . Yes, I am certain I just saw someone that I knew. Brangwengwen the dwarf, who was waiting woman to the Princess Diaspad when she lived at Caer Cadwy. I know that I saw her, though she was moving so quickly."

Tryffin shook his head, gently drawing her away from the narrow embrasure. "I doubt that you did see her. Perhaps it was one of the castle children: a stableboy or a little scullery maid. I tried to search out all of the Princess's servants when I lived in Trewynyn—for particular reasons of my own—but it happened they had all disappeared a long time before."

"Yes, but it *was* an old woman with a hump on her back," volunteered Elffin, from one of the arrow slots below. "I saw her, too."

Tryffin shook his head once more, but now he looked disturbed. Which was to say, his face went more stolid and placid than ever. "If it was Brangwengwen, you are not to approach or greet her, supposing you ever see her again."

"Yes, but—" Gwenlliant started to say. She did not see what harm there could possibly be in talking with a hunchbacked dwarf.

But Tryffin interrupted her. "I mean what I say, Cousin. That woman is evil, as evil and treacherous as the Princess was herself."

Corrig fab Corrig was dead, but no man knew by what means or in what fashion he had died. A delegation came to Menai fab Maelwas at Castell Maelduin where he lived, to see if they could learn what he knew of Corrig's passing.

They said to him: "Lord, your enemy is dead. When he murdered your father by treachery, you took a vow. You said you would hunt him with fierce wild dogs and assail him with evil dreams. You said you would burn the heart out of his body with the fire of your hatred, and likewise boil the flesh from his bones. His head would adorn your doorpost, his entrails would be fed to your hawks and your hounds. These things and many more you threatened, yet now Corrig lies dead without a mark anywhere on him, though on his face may be seen an expression of unspeakable dread. Lord King, will you tell us how this thing has happened?"

But Menai, ever the most gentle and kindly of men, smiled to himself a quiet and secretive smile, and all that he would say to those who asked him was: "Such things are not easily told . . . nor would you be happier for hearing them, if I were inclined to speak."

—From the Oral Tradition of Tir Gwyngelli

5.

Of Duty and Decorum

It was Tryffin's custom to conduct the business of government in a long gallery high in the Keep, which had served in former times as an informal audience chamber for the Lords of Mochdreff. The room was light and airy, with a high ceiling and a row of mullioned windows all along one wall overlooking the town and the sea beyond, altogether more pleasant than the gloomy state chambers down below.

By day, he sat in a massive chair, listening to petitions and attempting to dispense justice, which was a frustrating job at best, since he could rarely rely on the veracity of the petitioners. In the evenings, and often late into the night, he took a seat at the other end of the chamber, before a long oak table that was usually piled high with writs and warrants and edicts and proclamations, which an army of scribes prepared for him down in the Scriptorium. Each of these the Governor had to read carefully before he affixed his seal and signature.

He was engaged in that very task one evening about four weeks after his arrival at Caer Ysgithr—dripping wax on documents and imprinting them with a great silver seal—when Meligraunce slipped quietly into the gallery and stationed himself at one end of the table, waiting to be noticed.

Tryffin sealed the last warrant and glanced up. "Ah, there you are, Captain. I am sorry to call you here so late. But I have decided to make a journey in three days time, and I want you and your twelve best men to accompany me."

"Certainly, Your Grace. Truth to tell, they will be glad of the change. Where will we be heading?"

"To Oeth, and possibly into Peryf . . . to settle a feud between two petty lords and a clan chieftain." Tryffin sighed. "I have a pile of letters here, but I swear it is impossible to determine by comparing them, exactly who is in the wrong. Also, like your men, I find myself longing for a change of scene, after nearly a month of this." He waved a hand, indicating the papers and parchments scattered across the table.

"I am little more than a glorified clerk, and I suspect that Morcant was the same. It amazes me that men were actually willing to do murder in order to sit in his place.

"I wish," he added, with a pang of regret, "that I might take Gwenlliant with me." He thought she was growing bored, now that the novelty of her new surroundings was wearing off. Truth to tell, she was accustomed to a far more brilliant court, with masques and balls and other entertainments, to say nothing of country sports like riding and hawking, which were very poor in these parts. And the last time he found the time to visit her—was that two days ago, or three?—she had looked so pleased to see him, had struggled so hard to conceal her disappointment when he left . . .

Remembering, Tryffin shook his head. He was disappointed, too, had thought being married they would meet more often. Riding to Oeth, they might spend the entire day together, as they had not been able to spend so much as a single day since they arrived in Mochdreff. Yet he knew that Gwenlliant was safer at Caer Ysgithr.

Meligraunce frowned. "Do you anticipate danger along the way . . . or after we arrive?"

Tryffin shook his head again. "Bad roads and possibly bandits, but your men should be able to handle any ordinary outlaws. It is what I *don't* anticipate that daunts me."

He pushed his chair back from the table, rose to his feet, and started across the room. Meligraunce cleared his throat. "Your Grace, there is one thing. I don't doubt you have considered the idea already, but with a journey ahead, I believe you should think again. Your squires *ought* to be tasting your food before you eat, if only as a matter of form."

"Dear God," said the Governor, pausing to look back at him. What Meligraunce suggested was not unusual; it was customary for men of Tryffin's rank to employ sewers, or tasters, to test their food and wine for poisons. Yet it was a custom he had always considered barbarous and cruel. "Are you at all acquainted with my cousin Cadifor fab Duach?"

"I know that the Lord of Rhianedd greatly fears poisoning."

Tryffin laughed mirthlessly. "Fears it? The man is obsessed. He eats comfits laced with arsenic and other poisons in order to maintain an immunity, won't wash in water that's not been previously treated with unicorn's horn, and refuses to eat off any plate, drink from any cup, his squires have not carefully examined. To my certain knowledge, at least two boys have died in his service, tasting dishes which (considering his immunities) Cadifor himself might have eaten in their entirety without suffering so much as a belly ache."

He started across the room again, and Meligraunce hurried to get ahead of him and hold the great oak door open. "If that is so, it appears Lord Cadifor's fears are entirely reasonable."

"Do you think so?" said Tryffin, passing into the torchlit corridor. "But to my way of thinking, he brings it on himself. To hear his name suggests the idea of poisoning and I believe that his enemies consider the thing a continuing challenge. It's a wicked custom, asking children to take poison in a grown man's place."

"That is as may be," said the Captain, matching his stride. "But Garth mac Matholwch and his brother Conn are hardly children. In time of war, they would fight at your side, and consider it an honor to do so.

"I would volunteer to taste your food myself—and indeed I am perfectly willing, if you prefer it—but I think that your squires would take offense. It is their right, as well as their duty."

Tryffin gave him a sidelong glance. He was accustomed to confide in the Captain, just because he valued his opinion, but he sometimes wished that Meligraunce was not so damnably acute. A judgment perhaps for all the unwelcome advice he had been handing out to others ever since he was a boy.

"If I do this thing, the task must certainly fall on Garth and Conn. They would feel slighted otherwise."

"Also," said Meligraunce, "the very presence of a taster is usually enough to discourage assassins from choosing that method. Nor would your squires be in any great danger, taking only a sip or a bite before you eat or drink. Since you do *not* make a habit of eating arsenic-laced sugarplums, there would be no reason for *your* enemies to use such massive doses.

"In truth, Your Grace," Meligraunce concluded earnestly, as they started down a winding stone staircase, "I think you should do this thing, if only to show the people of Mochdreff that you take the responsibilities of your high office seriously."

Tryffin snorted. "Have you any idea just how many distasteful things I have already done for the sake of the Governor's dignity?

You must have, since you were the one who suggested most of them.

"And no need to tell me," he added, as they reached the foot of the stairs, "that it is *your* duty to look after my safety. Let alone, a man in my position had best learn when and when not to take the advice of his officers and councilors. Very well, Captain, it shall be as you say."

Gwenlliant rose in the chill hour before dawn. A long dull day stretched before her, without even the possibility of a visit from Tryffin. While Traeth and Grainne lit candles and kindled the fire, Faelinn laced her into one of the beautiful gowns the Governor had given her.

"I wish—" Gwenlliant began wistfully, then stopped as three pairs of curious eyes turned her way.

"Lady?" said Grainne. But Gwenlliant shook her head. There was no use saying what she wanted, because none of the others would understand.

I wish, she thought, as she donned a silken veil and took up her little illuminated prayer book with the jeweled clasp, *I wish that today need not be exactly like all the days before.*

It was a dreary round: Mass in the drafty castle chapel, with the senile old priest, as often as not, forgetting half the service and gabbling nonsense instead. Then a solitary breakfast of frumenty, eggs, and herring, because none of her attendants were of rank sufficiently exalted to share her meal. Then the morning and afternoon spent in her solar, or sitting room, stitching on a tapestry, or walking sedately in the gardens in company with her handmaidens, or visiting the five sharp-tongued old ladies who lived in the Keep—

"Lady," said Cei, breaking into her thoughts. He and Elffin had appeared in the room. Everyone, pages and handmaidens alike, stood watching her expectantly. "Will you go now?"

"Yes," said Gwenlliant, preserving the pleasant illusion all of them cherished: that she commanded and they obeyed, and not the other way around.

She went out of the room with the boys ahead of her, her maidens trailing silently behind. The square tower (Melusine's Bower, it was called, after some previous inhabitant) boasted three staircases: the private stair between Gwenlliant's bedchamber and Tryffin's quarters, the narrow back stairs which were seldom used, and a broad staircase of polished oak leading down to the two floors below and eventually to the courtyard. To reach either of the latter it was necessary to travel down a long corridor lit by resin-scented torches in ornamental brackets: blank-faced bronze angels with double sets of wings. They looked so stiff and stupid, those angels, that Gwenlliant could never quite make up her mind whether walking the corridor was like ascending into Heaven or descending into Hell.

From the passage to the stairs, from the stairs to another corridor where the torches flared in brackets wrought in the form of vengeful-looking mermaids. Then out through a pair of heavy doors which two sleepy guardsmen held open.

It was still dark as Gwenlliant and her party crossed the courtyards. The air was damp and smelled of the sea, so Cei and Elffin carried candles in crystal lanterns to light the way. Yet early as it was, the castle was beginning to stir into activity around her. As Gwenlliant passed an archway leading to the stables and the outer gates, someone hailed her. She stopped and watched through her misty veil as a tall figure flanked by two torchbearers came striding her way.

"Cousin," said Tryffin, taking her hand and kissing it lightly. Her fingers trembled ever so slightly in his grip. "I meant to visit you before I left. I forgot that you left your rooms so early." He was dressed for travel in crimson leather and silvery mail under a voluminous black cloak. He looked a little weary, as though he had been up most of the night preparing for this journey, but also pleased and excited.

To be leaving Caer Ysgithr where nothing ever happens, to be going out in search of adventure. Something fluttered at the back of her throat, her eyes began to sting, and Gwenlliant was glad for the concealment of her silken veil. Because Tryffin was leaving *her* along with the rest, and she wished he would not make his pleasure quite so evident.

"I've a gift for you, something to keep you occupied while I am gone," he said. And Conn came limping up to present her with three great volumes bound in calfskin.

Tryffin smiled wryly at her look of surprise. "Did you think I would forget that you asked for books?"

Gwenlliant shook her head. No, she had not imagined he would forget, just that he would not take her request seriously. Tryffin was clever—most people said he was like his father, who was widely acknowledged to be the most brilliant man in all of Celydonn—but he generally learned things by asking questions, by watching and listening, and not as a scholar would, by studying books. Like most people she knew, Tryffin believed that book-learning was essentially the province of priests and wizards.

Gwenlliant opened the cover of the book on top; it was a

53

beautifully illuminated bestiary, a collection of odd, exotic animals painted in brilliant colors on creamy vellum. The other volumes appeared to be works on medicine and philosophy.

"Thank you, Cousin," she said softly. This was a princely gift, and not only because the books would be so costly. To find a scholar in possession of such volumes who was willing to sell them, men must have been searching high and low for these books ever since she first asked for them.

Tryffin had gone to some trouble to please her, had known precisely what books she would like, and these things meant far more than the gift itself. Gwenlliant handed the bestiary and the other books over to Elffin and Cei, and lifted her veil to receive Tryffin's kiss.

"You should see me within the week," he said, as his lips brushed her cheek.

It would be a long, lonely week, she thought. But for all that, she must somehow contrive to keep herself amused.

From Trewynyn to Oeth on horseback was a short two days journey. As the Governor's party rode north, Captain Meligraunce kept a careful eye on the surrounding country. Not only was he responsible for Prince Tryffin's safety, but he took a keen interest in the land for its own sake. It would be strange if he felt otherwise, son of the soil that he was, the product of countless generations of Camboglannach farmers and herdsmen.

By his own efforts, the Captain had raised himself to a position of trust in a noble household, yet it was impossible for him to turn his back on all he had been, all that his less ambitious kinsmen still were. And Prince Tryffin, bless his warm and embracing heart, had never expected otherwise. In fact, it was one of the many important principles the two men shared: that the soil was something to be cherished, that the land was sacred and the men who worked it daily deserving of great respect. Sometimes Meligraunce could scarcely believe his good fortune, not only in rising so far and so fast, but in attaching himself to the household of a man he so fervently admired.

This was wild, uneven country, the usual peat bog and pale purple heath alternating with deep gullies and tumbled granite ridges. But not so poor that hardworking farmers could not make a decent living. When he first came to Mochdreff, out of the hospitable south, Meligraunce had been astounded to discover how little people could live on, but he had learned a great deal since. In the fens, there were birds and fishes, and all manner of strange plants that turned out to be perfectly edible. And where the land was dry and bleak . . . well, a man could raise goats and geese, which were good at foraging, and swine—which could live on practically anything. Yet here, where conditions were nowhere near so bad as elsewhere in Mochdreff, the land was sparsely populated.

Probably, Meligraunce thought, as the road took his party into Oeth, because Oeth and Peryf were so near to the vast and mysterious Mochdreffi Woods.

That forest was a menacing dark line marching along the western horizon as far as the eye could see in any direction, and the Captain knew that it went on and on for hundreds of miles more. Strange creatures were said to dwell there—weird survivals from a dim and dangerous past, and even stranger hybrids, the distant offspring of monsters created by the fallen adept Gandwy of Perfudd, in unholy experimentation two centuries before. In the last two years, Meligraunce had heard stories and legends in plenty, terrifying tales of encounters with night-prowling monsters, but he had never but once during all that time heard anyone actually claim a personal encounter.

Not that the Captain doubted their existence. How could he, when the one man who had claimed to have met one—a great scarlet griffon that was at the Princess's fortress of Caer Wydr— happened to be the Governor himself? But Meligraunce thought the number and the ferocity of the beasts must be steadily declining.

He urged his big rawboned black a bit ahead, in order to close the distance between himself and Prince Tryffin. The horse looked awkward and gaunt like so many of the Mochdreffi breed, seemingly incapable of putting on flesh. Yet he was more powerful than he appeared, and Meligraunce had more need of a strong and dependable mount than of anything elegant and showy. In fact, the only vanities he permitted himself, the only signs of his increasing status, were the fine cloak that he wore, the valuable sword he carried, and a quiver full of black-fletched bolts he had specially made for his crossbow. A man ought to have something to set him apart, but it was neither wise nor kind to excite the envy of those in less comfortable circumstances.

As he drew abreast, the Governor greeted him with a smile. "How much further?"

They had neither of them visited this region before, and the maps that were available being somewhat sketchy, Meligraunce had recruited a local herdsman to guide them.

"We should reach Dinas Oerfel long before sunset, if all things continue favorable." It was late afternoon, windy but not too cool.

Ragged bits of cloud passing over the sun cast fleeting shadows upon the earth, but the light was still good and the roads were adequate.

Meligraunce brought his horse in closer. "What do you already know of these men—the Lords of Oeth and Peryf—and of their dispute with clan Llyr?"

Meligraunce had his usual orders: to unobtrusively gain as much information as possible, once they arrived at Dinas Oerfel, as much as he could glean in casual conversation with the garrison, the servants, and anyone else who was willing to talk. He had cultivated a certain air about him (modeled after the Governor, if he only knew it), one of sympathetic and respectful interest coupled with a quiet authority, that generally encouraged other people to tell him much more than they had originally intended.

"I am not acquainted with Teign of Peryf," said Prince Tryffin. "And with the others, only slightly. Dalldaff Llyr is a fussy old man, the sort who is always imagining someone has insulted him. And Gradlon of Oeth: He's proud, as most of these petty lords are, but decent and honorable, so I believe."

"Then you reckon this Dalldaff Llyr to be the source of all the trouble?"

The Governor shook his head. "As to that, I am not so certain. Dalldaff's letters—possibly composed by the son or grandson who served as his scribe—are very well reasoned, not at all what I would expect from the irascible old man. Teign and Gradlon also write convincing, though on some points utterly contradictory, accounts. God help me," he added, with a sigh. "I hope I may settle this quarrel before it leads to bloodshed."

They were nearing the banks of a swiftly flowing stream, not wide but apparently deep; a stout wooden bridge spanned the flood. One of the guards rode on ahead to inspect the bridge, then came back again shaking his head. "Unsound. Two of the beams are cracked. I doubt we could pass over safely."

Meligraunce dropped back to consult with the herdsman, then returned to Tryffin's side. "He says there is a wider place where we might ford, about a mile to the west, near the edge of the Woods. Failing that, we'll have to go five miles east over open country but no roads, to the next bridge."

The Governor considered that. It seemed to trouble him that this bridge should be in poor repair, so near to Gradlon's fortress.

"Open country between here and the next bridge—but what is it like at the bridge itself?"

By this time, their guide had caught up with them, offering the less than reassuring information that there was a little copse of stunted alders within yards of the span.

"Either place offers a fair opportunity for men to lie in ambush. Supposing it *is* a diversion planned by the outlaws," said Meligraunce. "Though even outlaws might be reluctant to enter the Woods. Given the choice, I think they would prefer to lay their trap at the other bridge instead."

"Aye," said the Governor, "I believe you are right. Well then, we had better chance the ford and the forest, rather than the bridge and the alders. Whatever lives in the Mochdreffi Woods, it's not likely to venture out of the trees before dark."

Besides Meligraunce and his crossbow, many of the men carried bows of various kinds, and Tryffin himself kept a crossbow of his own and a quiver full of bolts strapped to his saddle. Now he removed the quiver and slipped the strap over one shoulder. "Order your men to be ready to return fire, if we should be attacked from a distance."

They turned west and set out across a rocky field, heading toward the shadowy line of the forest. The horses were still comparatively fresh after a recent halt, so the Governor encouraged his roan gelding to go a bit faster, and Meligraunce likewise gave his own sturdy mount a light kick in the side, in order to keep up with him.

"Teign and his sons won't be arriving until tomorrow," said Prince Tryffin. "Quite aside from this feud that I hope to settle, I've a particular wish to speak with Lord Teign. *His* grandfather, as you may know, was a witness when *my* great-grandfather, Maelwas the Ingenuous, signed his treaty with Corrig fab Corrig."

"I recall that old tale. The alliance lasted less than a day, because Corrig slew Maelwas out of sheer perversity, causing Menai fab Maelwas to change his politics and side with young King Anwas and the wizard Glastyn instead."

Indeed, Meligraunce had made a special effort to learn everything he could about Prince Tryffin's family history, wishing to know all that he could about the man he admired, the man on whom his own continued advantage so strongly depended. But knowing how little the Governor liked bootlickers and sycophants, he brought out the information casually, as though it were something he had known all of his life.

"So they tell the story in Gwyngelli and Camboglanna. Except in Gwyngelli, we say that Menai was against the alliance all along, and would have thrown in his lot with the wizard and the boy Anwas, except that would have meant siding against his own father. But Corrig's part in the story makes no sense at all. Corrig had every reason to wish for that treaty, it was entirely his own idea—and that being so, slaying Maelwas *for sheer perversity* would be the act of a madman. I would like to hear the Mochdreffi side of that story, what tale Ruan of Peryf passed on to his sons and his grandsons."

Meligraunce raised a shaggy dark eyebrow. "What does it matter? Your grandfather took sufficient revenge for the death of his father, as I have heard."

The Governor smiled faintly. "The wild dogs and the spotted plague. Yes, I've heard that tale and others more elaborate. It's an odd thing: Menai spent the rest of his life dropping blood-curdling hints about the methods he used to murder Corrig, but, in fact, he never admitted the deed straight out. You must know that the Gwyngellach can rarely resist the opportunity to spin an elaborate tale, whether it happens to be true or not. I have an idea of my own that Corrig fab Corrig died a natural death before Menai fab Maelwas ever got to him."

He shrugged. "As to why I might wish to learn the true facts so long after—I think they may be far more important than you might suppose."

They covered the ground quickly and soon arrived at the spot the herdsman had described, on the margin of the wood where the stream grew wide and shallow. The air was scented with pine and the shadow of the trees stretched out to meet them, shadow but no growth. The outermost pines grew in a perfectly straight line, as though defining some otherwise invisible boundary.

There were rushes along the narrow banks, green bulrushes which the guide pushed through, wading across the stream ahead of the horsemen. Meligraunce watched him cross, sitting tense in the saddle. But the dark water came no higher than the middle of the herdsman's chest and the current was slow. He reached the other side easily, scrambled up the shallow embankment, and called back to the others, advising that it was safe to cross.

Two of the guards urged their horses into the murky water, and Meligraunce and Prince Tryffin, flanked by two others, followed after. It was shockingly cold and the black was reluctant, but once in he was a strong swimmer.

When the Captain reached the opposite bank, he circled the black gelding around to see how the others had fared. Garth and Conn had arrived just behind the Governor, and all but four of the guards and two of the packhorses were safely across. As no threat had emerged from out of the trees, Meligraunce began to relax.

And then, with two men and four horses still in the stream, the dark water started to heave and boil. A white wake appeared on the surface as though something large were swimming just below . . . something that was heading straight for the young guardsman at the end of the line.

All three horses suddenly panicked, and the last one started to buck and rear in the shallow water near the bank, flinging his rider back toward the center of the stream. The man disappeared beneath the boiling water, than bobbed up again, coughing and spitting, struggling to gain a solid footing. He gained that footing just as the water rose up in a great spout a dozen feet away, and something huge and clumsy stood up in the center of the stream and shook the water out of its hair.

For just a moment, Meligraunce froze in the saddle, gaping at something the like of which he had never expected to meet in the waking world. In form, the creature was vaguely manlike, but monstrous in size, with arms and legs as thick as tree trunks and a great barrel of a chest. And it was ghastly to look at: skin pale and mottled, head heavy and bulbous with bulging eyes and a wide ugly mouth, and a mass of tattered membranes, which might have been gills, hanging around the neck.

As the reek of the thing reached the embankment, many of the horses panicked and bolted, and even the most disciplined began to stamp and shake their heads, sweating and straining at their bits. Meligraunce came back to himself, pulled in on the reins, and spoke soothing words to the panicky black.

Baring its yellow teeth, the creature out in the stream bent down and swiped at one of the floundering packhorses, smacking her on the flank with a huge clumsy hand. The mare screamed in pain. Then the thing made a grab at the man in the water and just barely missed him, as the panic-stricken youth scrambled desperately toward the embankment.

Meanwhile, the bows were virtually useless, as no one could aim a shot and still control his horse. Giving up the struggle, Prince Tryffin flung himself out of the saddle, taking his crossbow with him. Without his steadying hand, the roan gelding wheeled and fled.

Gritting his teeth (because he was mortally afraid of all those stamping hooves), Meligraunce followed the Governor's example. He landed hard, but quickly recovered. Using both hands, and a foot in the stirrup at one end of the stock, he cocked the bow. He grabbed a bolt and slammed it into place, just as the creature in the stream managed to snatch up the young guardsman and hold him dangling over the water.

His first shot hit the monster in the side of the neck and stuck there. The creature flinched, snarled, but seemed otherwise unaffected, bringing its hands together and beginning to squeeze the terrified guardsman. The youth howled and struggled helplessly in the monster's grip.

Even before Meligraunce could reload his crossbow, two arrows flew past the great bulbous head, and Prince Tryffin's bolt, scarlet-fletched, hit the creature square in the forehead—with no apparent effect. The Captain aimed and squeezed off another shot. This time the sable bolt flew straight and true, landing in one bulging eye, burying itself right up to the feathers.

The monster shuddered, dropped the captive guardsman, and toppled backward into the water with a mighty splash.

Everyone watched to see if the creature came up again. To Tryffin's profound relief, nothing happened—except that the mounted man and the two mares scrambled ashore, and the battered youth came back to the surface, pale and gasping for breath, calling out faintly for help. Some of the men on the bank flung themselves into the water to assist him.

They pulled him out, stripped off his armor and padding, and examined his injuries. Meanwhile the other men calmed the remaining horses, or went out in search of those that had bolted with or without their riders. Garth and Conn had both retained their seats, so Tryffin left it to the pair of them to find Roch, catch him, and bring the roan gelding back again. As fond as he was of the horse, he had men to look after: his *own* men that he had just imperiled with a wrong decision.

And if that poor lad is maimed or dead because I was a fool . . .

Meligraunce, who was kneeling beside the injured guardsman, looked up at Tryffin's approach. "Bruised, but no broken ribs. The monster might have crushed him like an eggshell, if it were not for his mail and his padding."

"Thank God it's no worse, then. That was fine shooting, Captain. This man owes you his life."

Meligraunce shook his head, made a deprecating gesture. "As to that, I believe yours was the better shot. If the creature had not moved precisely when it did, I might have missed entirely."

Tryffin gave him a disgusted look. "If you turn into a courtier, I may have to replace you," he said, only half in jest.

The Captain rose to his feet, grinning sheepishly. "Ah well, if that's how it is. In truth, mine was an excellent shot."

*To any knight who cherishes his honor, deceit is of all things
the most abhorrent. Yet many a fine fellow speaking the truth as he
sees it, convinced to the very depths of his soul that every single
word he utters is as true as the Gospel, has later discovered to his
great dismay that he has been no better than the worst sort of liar:
a man who willfully deceives himself before going on to deceive
others. Therefore, all good knights should be careful when
swearing oaths, that they might not pledge themselves to unworthy
causes, or otherwise find themselves sworn to perform what a
good conscience would, under ordinary circumstances, forbid
them to even contemplate.*

> —From the diary of Anguish of Eyrie,
> Knight of the Order of St. Sianne
> and St. Gall (Rhianedd)

6.

Of Treachery and Deceit

The next day, sitting in the great beamed banquet hall at Dinas
Oerfel, listening to Llyr revile Oeth and Peryf, Oeth and Peryf
revile Llyr, it seemed to Tryffin that truth was a commodity in
short supply.

He had summoned the heads of all three houses (along with
their respective sons and grandson) to attend him, hoping it would
be possible, if they all discussed things reasonably, to uncover the
original cause of their quarrel. But after hours of accusations and
threats, insults, reproaches, and passionate appeals for justice,
about the only thing he had learned so far was that Oeth and Peryf
stood firmly united against clan Llyr.

During a momentary pause in the hostilities, Lord Gradlon
summoned one of his servants, calling for food and wine. When
the meal arrived, everyone fell to, as though suddenly famished.

Tryffin took advantage of the lull that followed to observe the
antagonists. Teign of Peryf was dark and dignified; his cousin,

Gradlon of Oeth, solid and muscular, with an elegantly trimmed beard and a commanding presence. Dalldaff Llyr, in contrast, was a tiny man, rather wild-looking, with restless black eyes, nervous hands, and thin grey whiskers.

All three men were amazingly angry, particularly considering how *trivial* the complaints they had advanced so far: livestock strayed or stolen and a questionable claim to a very few acres of stony ground. Had these been common folk, thought Tryffin, farmers or herdsmen scraping a bare subsistence out of the soil, the loss of a sheep or a goat, a horse, or even a pig, could mean utter ruin. But for two pretty lords and a clan chieftain to be shouting and gnashing their teeth . . .

The Governor shook his head. There had to be more to this quarrel than any of that, something which reflected so badly on all three families that nobody liked to mention it. He accepted a goblet filled with perfumed wine that Garth handed him, and addressed the Lord of Oeth. "You were telling me, Gradlon—or was that your son?—that a horse had been stolen."

"Your Grace, it was a very fine stallion," said Lord Gradlon angrily.

"And an excellent stud," added Teign. "We had hopes of improving both our herds. As it is . . ."

And so the discussion began again, going on and on with pigs and goats and boundaries and a great deal more, until someone mentioned the name "Bronwen" and everyone fell silent.

"And who," said Tryffin, into the sudden hush, "would Bronwen be?"

"Lord Gradlon's sister," said young Ewen Llyr, Dalldaff's grandson and heir to the chieftainship. He resembled his grandfather, being slender and dark-eyed with that quality of intensity which always marked the pure-blooded Mochdreffi. "Gradlon and Lord Teign and a troop of men murdered my Uncle Hywell on Bronwen's account. I do say *murder,* for they surrounded Hywell and killed him by treachery, and that was a black deed if ever I heard one!"

The Governor looked around him for confirmation. "A woman of Gradlon's house wronged? If that is so—"

"That is not so!" exclaimed Dalldaff, tugging at his long thin whiskers.

"And they never even claimed it was," Ewen added indignantly. "Mother of God, they never even *pretended* it was. They killed Hywell just for looking at her, just for smiling at at her with his heart in his eyes, because he wasn't good enough to even think of her! Yes, that's what they said in their wicked pride: not good enough to even think of her.

"And Prince Tryffin," the boy continued earnestly, "we are an ancient family. And perhaps we haven't such lands or a title as the houses of Peryf and Oeth, maybe we haven't held positions at court or distinguished ourselves in time of war, but—"

"All very true," sneered Kemoc fab Gradlon, whom Tryffin privately considered an overdressed puppy. He was a sallow youth with colorless eyes and hair, and an air of bored dissipation quite at odds with his meager years. "In fact, you are hardly more than peasants tilling the soil, for all that you hold your heads so high." He might have said more, but Gradlon silenced him with an angry glare.

"So," said the Governor, curling his fingers around the stem of the goblet on the table before him. He was relieved to be finally getting somewhere. "It is not a matter of goats or sheep, but a true blood feud in every sense of the word. And just when did this blood feud actually commence?" He looked to young Llyr, who had impressed him more favorably than any of the others.

"It happened six years ago. Yes, it began the year that Lord Cado stayed with them at Castell Peryf, and I, of course, was in my twelfth summer, about to become . . ." Ewen shot a meaningful glance at Gradlon. ". . . Lord Gradlon's squire. Because whatever Kemoc says about our clan now, the families were friendly before that, and nobody called us 'peasants' then. As God is my witness, Kemoc and Drwst and Dirmyg and I played together as children!"

Tryffin turned to Dalldaff Llyr. "As the murder occurred so many years ago, will you accept compensation in the form of—"

"We have not yet admitted any wrongdoing," Gradlon interrupted, pounding his fist on the table. "It is true that Hywell was never alone with her, but it was perfectly plain that he meant to seduce her."

"He meant marriage and you know that," Ewen retorted, flushing darkly. "And that was why—"

Tryffin silenced them all with an upraised hand. "I merely asked Dalldaff if he *would* accept compensation. I have yet to inquire if any of you are willing to pay." He turned to Dalldaff Llyr. "What blood price would you set on Hywell's murder? And if it were paid, would you be willing to forget these other grievances and make peace with your neighbors?"

The old man shook his head stubbornly. "No, Prince Tryffin, I would not. There was a time I might have done so gladly. But seven months past, Kemoc fab Gradlon stole Ewen's cousin

Cigfa—a virtuous girl and a faithful wife, until Kemoc abducted her and kept her by him an entire night, ruining her completely. Yes, and Dirmyg fab Teign and his brother Drwst helped Kemoc to steal her away!''

"For the love of God," said Tryffin, feeling disgusted. "Not *another* female supposedly wronged. Why must you people insist on sleeping with women you aren't married to? Why will you cause your families so much grief, all for the sake of a single night's pleasure?"

The others only answered him with looks of wounded reproach.

"Aye, well . . . anyway," said Tryffin, suddenly remembering he was in no position to speak, having slept with so many women before he was married. "At least we shy away from adultery in the Hill Country, having too much sense of family to permit it."

Kemoc smirked at him across the table. "In Tir Gwyngelli perhaps. But I hear, Prince Tryffin, it's the custom for men of your house, when looking for sport, to go into Mochdreff or Perfudd . . .''

There were shocked faces all around the table. The Governor put a hand on the hilt of his sword, and his squires and Captain Meligraunce shifted in his direction. "If you desire to insult me, Kemoc," he said softly, "I wish you would do so directly. Then we might settle the matter at once."

"As to that, Prince Tryffin—" the foppish youth began huffily, rising from his chair. But his father reached out with a strong hand and pushed him back down again.

"Hold your tongue," thundered Gradlon, with his hand still on Kemoc's shoulder, "before some better man forces you to swallow it."

Then, with an apologetic glance at the Governor: "Your Grace . . . Prince Tryffin. I ask pardon for my son's behavior. No offense was meant, that I can assure you. I beg you will forgive him his hasty words."

"They are already forgiven," said Tryffin, disturbed by his own loss of temper. He had no real wish to engage in armed combat with a weedy youth no older than Garth and Conn.

He turned toward Drwst and Dirmyg, two young men who had been recently knighted, who still wore their white belts and golden spurs with a kind of self-conscious pride. Only three years past his own knighting at the age of eighteen, Tryffin knew exactly how to handle them.

"Am I to understand that the pair of you actually joined Kemoc in abducting an innocent girl?" he asked sternly.

Teign's two sons stirred uncomfortably. "It wasn't an abduction, it was a seduction—or so we thought at the time," said Drwst. "And I will tell you one thing: Dirmyg and I were with them the whole night long and he never raped her. They just sat and talked and drank wine and he said pretty things to her. It was very courtly and elegant, even if she did cry a little—I think because she was frightened what would happen afterward. And then in the morning she agreed to go to bed with Kemoc, rather than return to that old man she had married."

"God forgive you. And what do you call it but *rape*," said Ewen, grinding his teeth, "when a man disgraces a girl so that she can't ever go home again, and she has no choice but to throw herself on his mercy and beg for his protection?"

Drwst and Dirmyg exchanged a guilty glance. "Well . . . yes. But if she had asked for *our* protection instead, at the very beginning, we would have seen that she was returned unharmed long before Mwrgen missed her," said Dirmyg. "You know we would have done that, Ewen, you know it is true."

Ewen laughed mirthlessly. "Maybe *I* know that, maybe I do—but what of poor Cigfa?" Teign's sons were silent. It was plain to see they were both having second thoughts, beginning to reconsider their actions in a far less favorable light.

Kemoc, however, remained as cocky as ever. "Well, if you want Cigfa back again, you can certainly have her for all of me, because I've grown sick of her. And seeing that old rooster she was married to died of an apoplexy, you might even find it amusing to bed her yourself."

Ewen Llyr turned a dull shade of red. "Thank you, Kemoc, but I have the key to your sister's bedchamber, where I get all the amusement I need."

There was an uproar after that, not easily quelled. Kemoc's elder sister was another young widow, one who took full advantage of her present unmarried but no longer virginal state. However, as Ewen eventually admitted with a shamefaced look, no man of Llyr had ever slept with her. He even apologized for implying that he had.

Then it was back to the pigs and the horses, a cottage mysteriously burned down, some insulting words spoken one Sunday after Mass, and a great deal more. But when the Governor said: "Somebody mentioned Cado Guillyn some time since. What part had he to play in all of this?" there was a general shaking of heads.

"He had nothing to do with anything," said Ewen. "He was just *there* at the time, the way he sometimes is."

65

"He spent his time at Castell Peryf quietly," added Teign. "Reading his books of wizardry, or wandering in the forest, collecting herbs and other strange plants that grow there."

At last, Tryffin grew weary of this fruitless discussion. "We will meet again tomorrow after dinner," he said, with a sigh. "And speak of this quarrel again."

He woke early the next morning, when the door to his bedchamber flew open and Meligraunce came striding in from the anteroom. Garth and Conn (both half dressed) came tumbling after the Captain into the room, curious to discover what the crisis might be.

"My apologies, Lord Prince. But Gradlon's young cub has apparently tried to murder Ewen Llyr."

"By All the Saints and the Assembled Hosts of Heaven!" said Tryffin, sitting up in his bed, instantly awake. "What can you tell me about this?"

Meligraunce spent a long moment staring down at the toes of his boots, gathering his thoughts, in order to present a coherent report. "Ewen says he was strolling in the courtyard last night, after all the rest had gone to bed—apparently trying to cool his head, after the unpleasantness earlier—when someone attacked him from behind. There was a struggle, and the assassin escaped in the dark, but Ewen *insists* it was Kemoc fab Gradlon, in revenge for something he said yesterday about Kemoc's sister."

Tryffin sent Garth and Conn back to finish dressing. He threw off the fur robes covering him, climbed out of bed, pulled on his shirt, his crimson leather boots, and allowed Meligraunce to assist him into the rest of his clothes.

"Now there is a loud argument going on down below," the Captain continued, as he handed Tryffin a black velvet tunic embroidered with crimson dragons. "Kemoc is defending his sister's virtue (which from all I hear from her father's men is a cause past saving), and Ewen going on that his own people would be just as grand and powerful as Kemoc's, if they'd been as ready to bed down with foreigners for the sake of titles and honors and—" Meligraunce gave a characteristic shrug. "That's enough to give you a idea of what's being said."

"It is," said Tryffin, buckling on his swordbelt. "I've a high opinion of young Ewen, but he has got to learn to curb his tongue. Still, that doesn't excuse an attack from behind—or murder attempted within these walls, after I summoned Ewen and his grandfather here in the High King's name." His heart sank as he realized what that meant. "If Kemoc is guilty, then he has committed treason, and I will have to deal with him accordingly. Before God, I brought them all together with the intention of *avoiding* bloodshed.''

Down in the courtyard, on a plot of ragged-looking grass, the dispute was still going on: Kemoc and Ewen shouting at each other, Dalldaff and Gradlon glowering, and Teign and his two sons watching uneasily, as though they might like to intervene, if they only knew how.

Worse still, there were other observers as well, including women and children, apparently drawn by all the noise. Tryffin ordered the courtyard cleared, which Meligraunce and his men did promptly, leaving only the men who were directly or indirectly involved in the quarrel.

In the sudden silence, Tryffin turned to Ewen. ''You may begin. What reason can you give for taking part in this unseemly row?''

''I said what I shouldn't have said, yesterday, and I apologized. But if Kemoc was reluctant to grant me his pardon . . . still, he had no right to try and knife me from behind. It *was* him, and I can prove it, and Kemoc should suffer for that cowardly act.''

''As to that, I promise you he will suffer, if you can prove what you say. I gave you and your grandfather safe conduct and I intend to enforce it,'' said Tryffin grimly. ''Tell me how you know that it was Kemoc who attacked you.''

''I *know* it was Kemoc because he cut my face with that ugly great ring he wears on his hand. And I can *prove* it was Kemoc because he dropped this brooch in the struggle.'' And Ewen held up a large and elaborate pin, which had certainly fastened Kemoc's clock the day before.

Gradlon's son went white, but maintained his air of cocky defiance. ''He lies. Ewen made up this story and stole my brooch, stinking little peasant swine that he is. I never came near him last night. And I don't even *carry* a knife that is big enough to do him or anyone else serious harm.''

Ewen folded his arms and curled his lip, in a fair imitation of Kemoc's own sneer. ''Not that toy you carry in your belt—I'm not afraid of that, God knows. But what about the dagger that you wear up your sleeve?''

Kemoc gasped and rounded on Drwst and Dirmyg. ''How did he know that? Did *you* tell him?'' His face went from white to red, as he realized he had betrayed himself. ''That proves nothing,'' he said, with an arrogant lift of his head. ''It doesn't prove anything. What if I do carry a dagger up my sleeve? That's not uncommon.''

Tryffin was quiet for a long time, aware that a hasty decision could only make further trouble. "That you spoke a lie before this company tells me a great deal," he said at last. He motioned to Meligraunce, who started across the courtyard. "Arrest him, Captain, but use him gently."

Kemoc's nostrils dilated. "You call me a liar, Prince Tryffin? Well, you would not fight me yesterday, but you will today. I know how to answer an insult, even if you don't." And the youth whipped a long dagger out of his sleeve and lunged at the Governor. Acting instinctively, Tryffin stepped aside and drew his own dagger.

"Do not allow him to provoke you, I beg of you. My son is only—" But Gradlon's intervention came too late. Somehow, Kemoc managed to stumble, and impale himself on the Governor's dirk.

Horrified, Tryffin grasped the boy by the shoulder and pulled out the eighteen-inch blade, attempting to catch him as he fell. But Kemoc landed on the grass, where he lay in a spreading pool of blood.

"—my son is very young, and had a sickly childhood. He knows very little of armed combat," Gradlon finished quietly, as he knelt on the ground and gathered the body of his dying son into his arms. No one else moved, not Teign or his sons, not even Meligraunce or his men, the attack and its consequences had been so sudden and unexpected.

Tryffin still stood with the dirk in his hand, and a sick sensation growing in his stomach. "I do not know what to say, Gradlon, except that I am sorry."

The stricken father shook his head. "I hold you harmless in this matter," he said, very low. "Even I can see that Kemoc brought this on himself."

They took Kemoc's lifeless body indoors, for the women to wash and to lay out for burial. Tryffin tactfully withdrew to the chambers Lord Gradlon had given to him—knowing full well that he thereby offered an opportunity for Gradlon and his kinsmen to whisper and to plot—but he would be damned (Tryffin told himself) before he would intrude on their grief. Yet the day passed quietly without further incident.

In the evening, after a solitary supper, the Governor took a walk in one of the faded gardens. He needed room to move, to walk off his anger and frustration without fear of the breakage that any agitated movement of his outsize limbs was likely to produce. And his mood being so dire, he had no wish to inflict his company on anyone else. He left Garth and Conn up in his bedchamber, and ordered the two guards who had accompanied him to wait outside by the gate. He was still there, pacing the withered garden, when Meligraunce found him an hour later.

"You know, Captain," he said, by way of greeting, "these Mochdreffi must be the most contentious and bloodthirsty folk on the face of this earth. God knows, they have given my own people enough trouble over the centuries. And yet—and yet it seems to me that the feuding and the bloodshed have grown considerably worse over the last decade or so. I've had an idea for some time that there is someone, some one man behind it all, stirring up trouble. Though who he is or what he hopes to accomplish, I confess I don't know—except that he leaves a trail of broken lives, of senseless violence wherever he goes."

Meligraunce fell into step beside him, matching his long stride to Tryffin's even longer one. He was quite accustomed to being used as the Governor's sounding board and knew what was required of him. "You would know better than I, Your Grace. But what is it specifically that makes you suspect . . . an intervention . . . here at Dinas Oerfel?"

Tryffin pressed the back of his hand against his brow. "Only the stupidity, the stupidity and the utter uselessness. What did young Kemoc imagine that he had to gain by killing *me*? Yesterday, when he tried to provoke me into a quarrel, that was just thoughtless mischief on his part. But you can be certain that his father and Teign spoke to him afterward, made it perfectly clear that any harm done to me must certainly bring ruin on his entire house.

"Always supposing," he added wonderingly, "that Kemoc really believed he could best me in armed combat."

Meligraunce cleared his throat. "In fact, I came to tell you that Lord Gradlon is eager to speak with you. Perhaps he can explain his son's motives. He is waiting just outside the garden gate, hoping you will see him."

Tryffin did not want to see Gradlon, but knew that he must eventually. "Yes, send him in." He stopped pacing and collapsed on a stone bench under an oak tree choked by thorny vines, struggled to assume the mask of stolid composure that was his public face.

Gradlon came in with a heavy step. He would have gone down kneeling at the Governor's feet, had not Tryffin stopped him with an invitation to sit on the bench. The older man obeyed, sinking down on the seat with such a poignant look of relief that Tryffin knew at once that he had not come to press any quarrel. It was with genuine warmth that he invited Gradlon to speak.

"Your Grace, I have come to tell you once more that I do not blame you for the death of my son." The Lord of Oeth spoke with an obvious effort. "More than that, I have agreed to pay a blood price for the death of Hywell Llyr, and Dalldaff has agreed to accept compensation. Young Cigfa's honor is to some extent restored by the death of my son; nevertheless I shall dower the girl handsomely. With a good marriage, she will regain her reputation entirely. All other matters in dispute between my house and clan Llyr, I leave for you to settle, and give you my word in advance that everything will be done according to your wishes. Teign makes the same promise—and gladly, too. Truth to tell, he did nothing in any of this, except what he felt he was obligated to do as my kinsman and my friend."

"I do not doubt your sincerity, Gradlon," said Tryffin, gazing at him in astonishment. "But I can't allow you to make such sweeping concessions. Not at this time, when your grief is still new. I don't want you to feel afterward that you had been disadvantaged or ill-used."

"Prince Tryffin," said Gradlon, with a deep sigh, "I am not likely to change my mind. I have seen enough useless bloodshed to last me the rest of my days. And it was all pride and foolishness from the very beginning. You were right when you said that men should seek to spare their kinsmen grief."

He wrapped his cloak around him, against the chill. "And young Ewen also spoke the truth when he said that our families were on friendlier terms before. Clan Llyr is an ancient and honorable house. It is hard for me to remember why we treated them so badly. And Ewen is a fine lad, except for that temper of his. He has noble instincts and is honest to a fault."

Gradlon managed the shadow of a smile. "Dirmyg and Drwst are also excellent young men. They are, as you may know, my sister's sons. Now that Kemoc is gone, one of them shall be my heir, for I am a widower and will never remarry or get more sons. And so you see, if Teign and Dalldaff and I make peace among us, our heirs will honor our wishes."

Tryffin let out a long sigh of relief. "Llyr will be satisfied— how can they be otherwise when you are so reasonable and generous?" he said, dropping a hand on the older man's shoulder. "But tell me Gradlon: Was there not something more at work here than Kemoc's madness? I don't mean to imply that you or Teign influenced him in any way. But who have his friends been? Is it possible that he had fallen in with schemers and plotters, with enemies of mine or with those who rebel against the Emperor?"

Gradlon shook his head slowly. "Your Grace, he had no friends at all. Other young people did not seem to like him. Even Drwst and Dirmyg only tolerated him because he was their cousin, and I think they sometimes went along with him only to curb his more violent impulses.''

Tryffin nodded, remembering that even Ewen had believed the girl Cigfa would have been safe, had she only thought to claim the protection of Dirmyg and Drwst.

''Kemoc was at one time deeply attached to Lord Cado,'' Gradlon went on. ''But that was many years ago, and I do not think they have met since then. Still, I suppose there might have been other companions, friends he met with when he was away from home.''

Tryffin frowned thoughtfully. As always, he felt a twinge of suspicion on hearing Lord Cado's name, even while he recognized how absurd it was to connect an apparently innocent friendship, six years back, with this recent attempt on his own life. ''I would not ask you to spy or inform on your dead son, Lord Gradlon. But if you could discover if such companions existed, and who they were . . .''

Gradlon sat up very straight and proud. ''If Kemoc died serving the interests of some other, if he did have friends who goaded him on to his own destruction, you may be very sure, Lord Prince, that *I* wish to discover who those friends might be.''

The lovers met in the orchard, under the appletrees, when the moon was full and bright. They had arranged a secret meeting, the highborn maiden and the shabby scholar, and they knew what they risked by doing so. Guenhumara went immediately into his arms and clung there desperately. He could feel her trembling, the agitated rise and fall of her breathing.

"I have loved you," she said, laughing and crying at the same time, "from the first moment I saw you: walking in through the gate all dusty and ragged, with your books carried under one arm and your pack full of curiosities strapped to your back, and your

71

way of looking around you as if everything you saw were shining and new, as if the whole world had been freshly created that very same day.''

"And I have loved you," he said softly, against her hair, "from that very same moment . . . when I glanced up and saw you watching me from your tower window, smiling down on me with such a look of ineffable sweetness. My heart leapt in my chest, and I knew that I was lost."

They began to walk together between the trees. And the lady was sad and discouraged. "You have lived in this place for nearly a year: conversing with scholars, amusing the women with fantastical tales, talking philosophy, religion, and mathematics with the wise old men the Lord of Mochdreff has gathered around him. There is no one in this place who does not love and respect you nearly as much as I do. Yet for all that," she said sorrowfully, "I fear we shall never be happy. My uncle would never permit me to marry a man whose rank was so far inferior to my own."

To her surprise, he gave a quaint little laugh. "If that is all that stands between us, then you and I may yet be married. For know this, my love: I am so much more than I have seemed to be. No mere scholar, no base-born scrivener—I am a king's son, and some day shall rule in Tir Gwyngelli."

At first she would not believe him. Yet it was there in his face and his bearing: all the careless grace and the easy confidence and the unconscious nobility of a man born to rule. How else had he won such wide favor at the Mochdreffi court? People had responded to these things without even knowing what it was that they saw in him.

But once he had convinced her, her heart ached, and she was more discouraged than ever. "The son of a poor man mending shoes in Trewynyn has more chance of winning me than the King's son of Tir Gwyngelli," she said softly. "If my uncle wished it, he could elevate such a man, could gift him with lands—but the son of the enemy of my clan will never, never have me."

"Enemies," said her lover, taking her hands and kissing them lightly, "may yet become friends. Whatever grudge your uncle may hold against me or my people, I will labor to make amends.

"It should not be difficult," he added, with his sweet, confident smile, "for as you have said yourself, he is already fond of me."

But Guenhumara shook her head. "You and I are divided by generations of bloodshed and bitter, bitter wrongs. And how could all these things ever be made right again, in a single lifetime?"

7.

The Tangled Skein of History

It was a sad, drizzly sort of day at Caer Ysgithr. Gwenlliant sat on a stool in one of the grand but oppressive state chambers, with her hands in her lap, and her mind far away, as the old women she was visiting chattered and argued.

There were five of them: five ancient dames much addicted to needlework, cards, and gossip, the widows of powerful men who had lived at the castle in days gone by. The wives and the families of Tryffin's own officers and councilors, like Morcant's before him, all had houses down in the town, great stone mansions in the innermost ring. But these five lingered on, determined to cling to the faded remnants of their power and influence.

Because these sharp-tongued, quarrelsome old dames were so bent and so feeble they could not leave their rooms without their sticks to support them, their sturdy little pages to lean upon, Gwenlliant must needs visits *them*, and this she did dutifully twice a week. For all they saw so little company, the women thought much of their finery and spent hours each day stitching busily away, refurbishing their gowns, their veils, and their great horned hennins.

"Too young," Dame Maffada was saying, as Gwenlliant half listened. She was the most cynical of the five and also the least attractive, an uncharitable old creature in a garish silk gown and a truly terrifying headdress. "Hardly past her thirteenth birthday . . . and what was he thinking to marry such an infant?"

As the day was damp, there was a feeble little fire fluttering on the hearth, trying in vain to heat the chamber.

"A love match," replied Dame Clememyl, shuffling through a pile of tattered yellow letters she held in her lap. She had been amusing the others all morning, reading aloud the most shocking passages, gossip about men and women cold in their graves for twenty or thirty years. "Only think how the Governor dotes on her!"

"Which only makes it worse. I never knew of any love match yet that didn't end in tragedy," sniffed Dame Maffada, putting aside her sewing. And Gwenlliant suddenly realized she was the subject under discussion, and all the old ladies were looking at her with their penetrating dark eyes.

So she said the first thing that came into her head. "Do the rooms and the passages at Caer Ysgithr have a habit of shuffling themselves about?"

The great echoing chamber was suddenly very silent. Then Dame Indeg said, in her creaking old voice, "What put that idea into your head, child?"

"Because," Gwenlliant replied, blushing under their continued scrutiny, "sometimes when I go out walking, when I think that I know perfectly well where I am going, I find that the place I eventually reach is another entirely."

"That may be," said Dame Maffada. "One does hear stories." She picked up the gown she had been mending, and started stitching. "For myself, I've never been one to go poking about where I don't belong, looking for trouble."

Gwenlliant bit her lip. This rebuke seemed most unfair, considering that she *was* the Lady of the castle, if not the chatelaine.

But Dame Clememyl said kindly, "She's only curious, like any other young one. And she's got the full use of her limbs, thank God. If you want to know more, you should ask your pages." She indicated Elffin and Cei, where they sat on the stones by the hearth, playing a game of jackstraws by the sickly glow of the fire.

For a moment Gwenlliant was confused, thinking Dame Clememyl alluded to the year the boys had spent with her cousin Teleri. But then she realized that Elffin and Cei knew all sorts of people at Caer Ysgithr: servants and guards and grooms—and any number of other folks to whom Gwenlliant, mindful of her position, never spoke more than a few gracious words.

She might have questioned her pages then and there, but just then Brother Bedwini came hobbling in, ostensibly to hear the old ladies say their confessions, but actually (as Gwenlliant well knew) for a game of cards and a good long gossip. With Brother Bedwini to keep the old ladies amused, her own dutiful visit had come to a welcome end. As soon as she could, Gwenlliant rose, made her curtsy, and swept out of the room. Cei and Elffin jumped up at once and followed after her.

Those dreadful old women, Gwenlliant reflected gloomily, were exactly what *she* would be in another fifty years: idle, vain, and malicious. Yet if she had married a simple knight or a minor lord, how delightfully busy her days might be. *I would bustle about with the keys at my side, and I would have a stillroom for brewing simples, and a garden full of herbs and beehives, and pages to instruct* . . .

She stopped in the middle of the drafty corridor, turned a brightening glance on Cei and Elffin. "Who has been tending to *your* education, all of this time?"

The boys stared back at her, clearly puzzled. "Why, Prince Tryffin, of course. Along with Meligraunce, Conn, and Garth."

Gwenlliant nodded, continuing on her way. Before Tryffin left on his journey, Elffin and Cei spent two hours each day, sometimes with the Governor, more often with his squires or Captain Meligraunce, doing whatever it was that pages were supposed to do, to prepare themselves for eventual knighthood. "But what precisely do the men teach you?" she asked.

Cei took a deep breath. "Horsemanship, swordsmanship, archery, the art of war, the code of chivalry—"

"Yes, I know all that," said Gwenlliant, descending a crooked stairway. "But what about mathematics, Latin, Greek, history, courtesy, natural philosophy—who teaches you *those* things?"

Elffin rubbed his nose. "The Lady Teleri did, when we lived at Regann. But there is no one here who could . . . Unless you were thinking of Brother Bedwini?"

"Nothing of the sort," said Gwenlliant. "I am going to instruct you myself, beginning today. Why should I not? It is nothing less than my right and my duty, and I know very well what you ought to learn."

And her mind was so occupied with this charming notion that she forgot to pay close attention to where she was going. Apparently the boys were also distracted, following behind her in faithful obedience (as they generally did when not under the dominance of Grainne, Faelinn, and Traeth), because the next thing that Gwenlliant noticed, she was wandering down an unfamiliar corridor, in a part of the Keep that smelled horribly damp and musty.

She stopped to examine her surroundings, and the boys did likewise. She had proceeded most of the way down a long passageway, dimly lit by torches set at distant intervals along one wall. At the end of the hall was a great archway, entirely filled by an immense iron gate banded with copper and brass, and incised with what appeared to be a pattern of delicate scrollwork.

Which seemed such a very odd feature to find *inside* a building that Gwenlliant moved closer to examine the gate.

"How exceedingly curious," she said. What had looked to be a pattern of scrollwork from a distance was actually a series of magical symbols of great antiquity: spirals, and solar wheels, and knotted serpents, repeated again and again.

She turned to Cei and Elffin, who were darting glances about them, not so much puzzled, she saw, as uncomfortable and uneasy. "Do either of *you* know what lies on the other side of this gate?"

Elffin cleared his throat, but it was Cei who answered. "We've

75

heard there is an entire wing of the Keep where the Princess Diaspad used to live . . . corridors and chambers where nobody goes.''

"What else?" said Gwenlliant.

"And everyone feared her," said Elffin. "Nobody wanted her things or her people left in the castle after she died. You remember what Prince Tryffin told you: All of her dwarfs and giants and wild woodwoses were sent away. Then some people wanted to burn her books and her clothes and her furniture, but Lord Goronwy said no, that might release the Black Magic into the air." The boy lowered his voice. "So he sent his men to put in gates on every floor where there was a door or an arch leading to the Princess's rooms."

"This isn't the only place," added Cei. "There are chambers and passages all over the castle where the servants and the guards are forbidden to go."

Gwenlliant was silent, remembering the day she had explored the Keep. It occurred to her now that Tryffin had been very careful what he chose to show her. Because Caer Ysgithr was so vast and so complex, so easy to get lost in, she might have lived in the castle for months or years before wandering into this particular corridor—or anywhere else she was not meant to go.

And that being so, she could not help but wonder what *else* there might be at Caer Ysgithr that the Governor was hiding from her. Rooms full of skeletons, rats, and chains? Or a secret bower filled with roses, where Tryffin kept nine fair mistresses in silken splendor?

Tentatively, she put out her hand—palm flat, fingers spread—and lay it against the iron gate. She pulled it back again, suddenly, as though she were stung or burned.

Something was calling to her from the other side, something strong and deep and powerful that roared like the wind, that boomed like the sea pounding on the shore, like great rocks grinding beneath the soil . . .

And Gwenlliant had a terrible feeling that she knew what that something was. It was the old Earth magic, some part of the magic of Mochdreff which the Princess Diaspad had harnessed long years before. *And it knows me,* she thought, with a shudder. *It knows that I am here.*

Tryffin sat in his bedchamber at Dinas Oerfel, playing a game of Chess with Garth. As was his custom, he had given the boy two pieces at the beginning, in order to lend the contest sufficient interest, but his mind was not on strategy, nor on the ebony and ivory chessmen.

He was thinking of the witch Ceinwen and of her prophecies, and of the destiny he now pursued. It had come to him, recently, that it was not to sign writs and to settle petty quarrels that he had been *sent* to Mochdreff. Instead, he must unknot the tangled skein of history—the complex web of love and hate, kinship, murder and betrayal the wise-woman had described to him—and the only way he knew to do that was by seeking to penetrate certain family mysteries.

Glancing down at the marble gameboard, he reached out and absently moved his rukh three spaces forward. "If the game bores you, Lord Prince, we can put the board away," said Garth.

Tryffin frowned at him across the table, coming fully back to the present moment with an uncomfortable wrench. "Why do you say so?"

"Because," said the boy, "you just crushed me in less than five moves, for the second time this morning."

"Aye, well," said the Governor, pushing back his oak chair. "You're a bright lad and you play well enough, but perhaps a bit more practice . . ."

While things were unsettled following the death of Kemoc, he had not wished to disturb Lord Teign, but now he thought it might be the moment to send for the present Lord of Peryf, and learn if he could what the last lord but one had known.

So he sent Conn in search of Teign, and Garth down to the kitchen and the cellar for some wine and fruit, and stood by the fire waiting for his guest to arrive. He did not wait long; Teign came promptly and accepted the chair the Governor indicated.

Tryffin resumed his former seat. While Garth poured the wine, he mentioned the story of Maelwas and Corrig, and his own doubt that the tale he had heard since childhood was entirely accurate.

Teign shook his head. "As to that, Lord Prince, I know very little. Except that there was some dispute between one of Corrig's men and a man attached to the household of Maelwas fab Garan. There was bloodshed, my grandfather told me, in a manner touching on Corrig's honor."

Garth, still rather self-consciously performing his new duties, chose one of the cups, took a sip of the heavy perfumed wine, and then passed it on to Tryffin.

"If you wish to know more," said Teign, accepting the other cup, "you should speak to my kinsman Avallach Mechain, who saw and heard it all."

Tryffin paused with the wine at his lips, sat up a little straighter in his chair. "You tell me there is a man who was there, who is actually living?" The incident had long since passed into legend, taken on something of the aura of myth, and it was difficult to remember, sometimes, that a mere sixty years had passed since that terrible day.

"Avallach was there as Ruan's squire. He lives near Castell Peryf." Teign took a pear from a brass bowl that Conn was offering him, and began to section the fruit with his silver-hilted dagger. "But he is an old man now and, I regret to tell you, not in the best of health."

Tryffin shook his head emphatically. "I'll not send for him. Indeed, why should I disturb a feeble old man? But perhaps you or your sons will take me to visit him tomorrow."

He sat thinking and sipping his wine for a time, before he went on. "Your family, Teign, served the Lords of Mochdreff for many years. Your ancestors were always to be found at the Lord's right hand. Just when did that change—not to mention why?"

A shadow passed over the Lord of Peryf's face. "About twelve years ago, when the Princess Diaspad became regent for her son. It was only the woman's malice, because I had been so close to Lord Corfil. No one ever accused me of any misconduct. In truth, Goronwy would have been glad to send for me when he took the High Seat almost three years ago, but by that time—"

"You had lost all interest in court politics. Yes, I can easily imagine. But you say you were close to Corfil—at the time of Calchas's birth that would have been? Now, what can you tell me about that? More precisely, what can you tell me about these persistent rumors I hear, that Calchas was none of Corfil's getting, but the Princess's bastard?"

One thing Tryffin had learned living in Mochdreff was that Calchas's doubtful paternity—not even rumored elsewhere—was an open secret among the Mochdreffi. Also, that Calchas was a full year older than anyone had known or guessed in Camboglanna.

Teign frowned slightly. "All that I know, Your Grace, is what anyone could tell you who lived at court. That the Princess left Corfil and fled into Perfudd—according to some stories, to live with her lover Manogan fab Menai, who was there prosecuting some business of the King's—and when she returned she was already big with child." The Lord of Peryf finished his piece of fruit and wiped his fingers on a linen napkin. "If you wish to know more, you might ask your uncle the Earl Marshall."

"No," said Tryffin, his fingers tightening on the cup. "No, he is the one man I *won't* ask, having no desire to open old wounds."

He considered these things for a time, drumming his fingers on the arm of his chair. "Now I begin to understand young Kemoc's insulting remark: Mochdreff *and* Perfudd. And you say this was much discussed at court—though years before Kemoc was born. I can only suppose you mentioned these events in Kemoc's hearing, or if not you, then Gradlon."

"No, Prince Tryffin," said Teign, sounding a bit annoyed. "I have no taste for gossip and I would certainly *not* have repeated such a story in my nephew's presence, or to my own sons. Nor would Gradlon do so, either. If Kemoc had the tale—and it would appear that he did—he must have learned it elsewhere."

Tryffin shrugged. "Ah well, I suppose he might have heard it practically anywhere. Though perhaps quite recently, since the details came so readily to his mind."

• • •

The Geometry of Magic is very different from the Mathematics of Common Men, yet a just sense of Number and Proportion is essential. If you would know more, draw a Circle on the ground, and around it a Square, and around that a Triangle. The Square symbolizes the Four Elements, and the Circle and Semi-circle the Phases of the Moon . . .

—*From* The Geometry of Magic
and the Harmony of Numbers

• • •

It was not until much later that same day, when Gwenlliant had recovered from the shock of her encounter with the magic behind the door, that she remembered her own question about the migrating rooms and passages at Caer Ysgithr.

She donned her cloak and made Elffin and Cei walk out on the walls with her, where she told them what she had observed. "You must have noticed it: Anytime that we follow the exact same path we have followed a number of times before, go from courtyard to stair to garden in the exact same order, we never get lost."

The wind came over the battlements in big damp gusts, so Gwenlliant moved closer to the wall. "But sometimes," she said, running a hand over the rough grey stones of the parapet, "like when I decide to choose a different door or gate—though I know perfectly well what we *ought* to find on the other side—then we end up someplace completely unexpected. Do you know how this happens?"

The two boys held a whispered conference, standing in the drizzle, with the wind tugging at their cloaks and their hair. Then

Cei said hesitantly, "We do know, but we aren't quite certain . . . Well, nobody *said* you were not to be told, and maybe since you already guessed—"

Elffin, less cautious, burst out: "What if you were to go from the kitchens to the orchard to the garden with the well, and then through the double arch behind the South Tower?"

Gwenlliant frowned, working that out in her head. "I would find myself between the stables and the kennels."

"No, you would not. Would you like to try it, and see what happens?"

"Yes, I think that I would," said Gwenlliant. So they descended a mossy brick staircase from the walls to the yard, and then followed the path that Elffin had suggested.

Only as soon as they walked through the double arch, Gwenlliant discovered that they were standing in a particularly dreary courtyard crowded with crumbling statues of men and monsters, on the *north* side of the castle.

"It is a kind of magic figure, you see," Cei explained helpfully. "Or maybe I should say: like a wizard's spell where you have to repeat the words—in this case, the courtyards and the buildings and the gardens and the arches—in a certain order, if you want to make the charm work."

Gwenlliant took a deep breath, perfectly enchanted by this novel idea. "How many of these places are there, here at the castle?"

Elffin shook his head. "We only know this one and two others like it—they make wonderful shortcuts. We've heard there are others, in the older parts of the castle where nobody lives, but they don't work for everyone, and not all the time. You have to use them at the right hour and the proper season. *And mind how you go at Caer Ysgithr,* that's a proverb the servants recite. But they aren't referring to broken stairs and tumbling towers as you might think; they only mean that it is all too easy to end up wrong, if you don't take care."

Gwenlliant thought for a moment, standing with her feet in the wet, gazing across the puddled courtyard. "Does the Governor know about this?" Then she answered her own question. "He must. I believe he even said something once, though I didn't understand what it was that he meant. Well then," she added, with a mischievous glance, "do Garth and Conn know?"

Cei and Elffin both nodded. "Conn uses them now and again, for we've seen him. But not Garth." Gwenlliant knew that of Tryffin's two squires, Garth was the most virtuously Gorwynnach, and far more likely to cast a jaundiced eye on anything improper or overtly magical.

"He does know, but he won't use them," added Elffin, leaning up against one of the fallen statues and crossing his arms, in perfect imitation of Garth's favorite pose. "He says, *'Mother of God, I'll not imperil my immortal soul for the sake of arriving a few minutes earlier.'* That's what he said when I asked him."

At that, Cei began to look troubled. "Wizards use magic figures and patterns and all, don't they? And this is much the same. You don't think that this could possibly be . . . witchcraft?"

"No, I don't *think* so," said Gwenlliant doubtfully. "But to be perfectly truthful, I have never seen anything like it before."

Early the next day, the Governor and his men, along with Dirmyg and Drwst, who were acting as guides, traveled from Oeth into Peryf, in order to visit Avallach Mechain.

Teign's kinsmen lived in an ancient crumbling tower, a morning's ride from Dinas Oerfel. As Tryffin and his party arrived just before noon, the old man insisted the Governor join him for the mid-day meal, and Tryffin readily accepted.

The meal was served in a round room near the top of the tower: roast pig, goat sausages, several cheeses, and a dish of boiled turnips, washed down with good ale. Over dinner, Tryffin questioned Avallach.

"I was told there was some dispute between one of Corrig's men and a man of Maelwas's, and that provoked Corrig's treachery. Now, what might you be able to tell me about that?"

Avallach pulled his beard thoughtfully. "It was a long time ago—and that's God's own truth!—but I'll try to bring it all to mind. Yes, yes, I remember it now. Nefn Elfod played a game of dice with one of Lord Maelwas's warriors. That is—" The old man coughed politely. "In those days we said *King* Maelwas, after your own custom; giving the enemy his due, you see. Perhaps you would prefer that I did so now?"

Tryffin shook his head. "We're not in Gwyngelli. 'Lord' Maelwas will do, if that is how you would usually say it." Yet he was favorably impressed by Avallach's old-fashioned courtesy.

"Aye, well." The old man skewered a sausage on the end of his dagger. "Now, what was the name of Lord Maelwas's man? I don't remember. But the fellow accused Nefn of cheating and successfully proved it against him. What then? Ah yes! Lord Corrig broke up the fight between them and promised to see that Nefn was punished. Only your hotheaded Gwyngellach—I've forgotten his name—he thought that wasn't enough, so he killed

Nefn the next day in a duel." The old man waved his sausage-laden dagger expressively. "Then Lord Corrig was offended, of course. Had he not taken personal responsibility for young Elfod himself and vowed that justice would certainly be done? He wanted Lord Maelwas to hand over his man to be executed on account of the insult to Lord Corrig's honor."

Tryffin looked up from his meat. "I can guess the rest. Maelwas would never have done what he asked, so Lord Corrig was insulted again. How else to restore his honor but to wash it in Maelwas's blood?"

"Well, it wasn't that precisely," said Avallach, between bites of sausage. "He was going for the other man. He took out his knife and went for to cut that impertinent fellow's throat but Lord Maelwas intervened. In the fight that followed . . ." Avallach spread his hands and heaved a great sigh.

"Before God," said Tryffin, pushing back his chair, suddenly too interested to remember that he was hungry. "You are saying that Corrig fab Corrig stabbed Maelwas in the back—in the midst of a *fair* fight?"

"In the back, Prince Tryffin? I would have said it was more in the side. But yes, it was maybe *toward* the back. But however it was, in God's own truth, the two men were facing each other when it happened. I was there and I saw it all."

The old man caught up his tankard of ale and took a long drink. "Well then, what was I saying?" He put down the tankard with a thump. "In comes Menai fab Maelwas almost at once and he sees his father lying on the floor with—with the knife in his back, as it might seem. And there was nobody able to convince him, not even Lord Maelwas's men that were there, that Corrig had not attacked Menai's father treacherously from behind."

Tryffin stood up and began pacing the room. "No one says anything like this in Tir Gwyngelli. Not that I doubt you, Avallach. Your story makes better sense than the way I heard the story before."

Yet this was hardly a satisfying end to his quest for the truth. "Ah God, to think that so much anger and misery and suffering—so many wrongs done by my people against yours and by yours against mine—should have originated in a petty dispute over a game of dice!"

Avallach shook his head. "Prince Tryffin," he said, with a great show of dignity. "That feud was old long before that. The first cause of dispute between the Mochdreffi and the Gwyn-gellach is said to have been a matter of wild pigs. Though what *that* means . . ."

Tryffin smiled faintly. "Yes, I've heard that old legend, and I know no more about those wild pigs, or why they were in dispute, than you do. I only know that the Mochdreffi and the Gwyngellach supposedly lived like brothers before that time. But I wasn't speaking of that ancient feud," he said, continuing to prowl. "I meant the more recent feud between my house and Corrig's."

"Nevertheless, Prince Tryffin, that story I just told you, the death of Maelwas the Ingenuous, I don't believe that was the beginning of *any* feud. Because truth to tell, your grandfather Prince Menai was against the treaty from the very beginning. He had a grudge against Corrig. What was it he said during all the shouting over Lord Maelwas's body? *I know how the earth moves. We are accustomed to earthquakes and landslides and falling stones in the Gwyngelli Hills . . . and I know what comes naturally and what takes a man to start the earth and the stones sliding.* Perhaps not his very words, Your Grace, but something very like them."

"And what did that mean?" asked Tryffin, pausing in his course, leaning his arms on the chair he had occupied earlier. This story, like the mystery of Calchas's birth, was growing more and more complex. He was beginning to wonder how he was ever going to keep all of the details straight. It was true that the witch had warned him it was a tangled history, but just how tangled he had never guessed.

"Well now, I'm trying to remember. There was something about a lady killed in a landslide near Ifarion, when she was coming down from Mochdreff. A lady your grandfather meant to marry—not being affianced, as yet, to your grandmother. That would have been a good few years before the time I am telling you about, because truth to tell it was the first I ever heard of the woman, when Menai started making his accusations. What was her name? It was Guenhumara—little chance I would forget a thing like that!"

Tryffin stared at him. He had come here to solve one riddle, only to be presented with several more, equally obscure. "Guenhumara—but that is a name I never heard outside of Mochdreff!"

The old man nodded. "The more usual form is Gwenhwyfar, is it not? But that was the way Prince Menai kept saying it: Guenhumara. I remember because it struck me as odd that he should use it—a Mochdreffi name, and often bestowed on the daughters and the granddaughters of the Lords of Mochdreff."

The Governor was shaking his head, thinking of Gwenlliant's grandfather, Menai's brother, whom he had known all his life—

who had never said a single word about any of this. But then, making a swift mental calculation, Tryffin realized that Meredydd fab Maelwas must have been very young when his older brother loved the mysterious Guenhumara. "But then it would seem . . . it would seem that my grandfather once actually considered sealing an alliance with Mochdreff, by marrying a woman of Corrig's house!"

Old Avallach nodded again. "That is how I reckon it, Prince Tryffin. Though when I asked my kinsman, Ruan of Peryf, he just told me to leave the past to bury its dead and not stir up trouble seeking improper questions. I was only his squire at the time, you know."

"Holy Mother of God," said the Governor, starting to pace again. "And here is another story that nobody tells in Tir Gwyngelli. I wonder if my father knows it." He gave a rueful laugh. He was well aware there were a great many things known to Maelgwyn fab Menai which Maelgwyn had so far declined to pass on to his sons.

"Ah well, what can it hurt to write him a letter just as soon as I return to Caer Ysgithr and see how my father replies?"

Of the Generation of Monsters much has been said, much more conjectured, but here I shall relate the whole truth as it was known to the Ancients . . .

That there are Monsters that live in the Sea: mermen, sea-lions, and hippocampi, which are generated without copulation when a man or a beast of the land falls into the Ocean and is devoured by fishes, and the sperm is exalted within. In the Air, also, are Monsters generated, for the seed of many living creatures may be carried on the Wind, and the sperm of toads, spiders, scorpions, vipers, and other Venomous Things being resolved in the Air, worms, grasshoppers, flies, and fleas are begotten of one parent and not of two. Likewise, there are Monsters generated in and upon the Earth. For the sperm of a man spilling upon the ground and finding in that element a fertile womb, a mandrake will grow, containing such essence of Vitality and Human Spirit that it will shriek both loud and piteously should it ever be torn from the place where it gestates. Also, there are Monsters which are generated by Sodomy, as in the case of the hyaena, which is born of the adultery of a dog and a cat.

Lastly, there are Monsters which are made by Art. For if the seed or the egg of any living creature should be placed inside a glass vessel and allowed to putrefy in horse dung for a period of Forty Days, a marvelous creation, with many heads, many limbs, many tails, or many bright and Variegated colors (as with the cameleopard and paradise bird), will be found growing within the glass.

> *—From a letter written by*
> *the mage Atlendor to his pupils*
> *at Findias*

8.

All the World in a Vessel of Glass

Gwenlliant was in her solar, seated on a cushion on a broad window sill, with the illuminated bestiary lying open in her lap, when Tryffin returned to Caer Ysgithr. He came striding into the room with Garth and Conn in his wake, looking so big and fresh and healthy that her heart turned over in her chest. She had felt, these last few days, that something was amiss, that he might even be in some danger; to see him so hale and hearty was a profound relief.

"What is this?" he said, his eyes moving from the book in her lap to Cei and Elffin, who were sitting on the floor at her feet with papers and quills and inkwells before them, and a great deal of ink on their fingers and their faces.

"I am instructing my pages," said Gwenlliant a bit defensively, because she had no idea how the Governor would take it.

"An excellent plan," he said, moving past the boys. "You are very lucky, Cei and Elffin, to be able to study with such a notable scholar as the Lady Gwenlliant."

She put aside her book, gave him both her hands, pleased by the compliment. "Did you have a pleasant journey, Cousin?"

"An eventful journey," he said, kissing one hand and then the

85

other. "Meligraunce killed a great beast from the Mochdreffi Woods. You must ask him to tell you all about it."

"Well I will," she answered. "But you . . . you look capable of slaying dragons. How many monsters did *you* kill between here and Oeth?"

His face went still, his eyes clouded. "I am afraid that my part in the adventure we shared was rather less noble than the Captain's. I killed a boy in the presence of his father. But you'll not wish to hear about that—it's a story that makes very poor telling."

Gwenlliant might have asked what he meant, but Garth was silently shaking his head and Conn looked troubled. So she changed the subject, tried to speak cheerfully of inconsequentials. Yet it hurt that Tryffin would not share his problems, that he never allowed her to soothe and to comfort him—which was a wife's privilege as much as her duty.

With Tryffin's return, life at Caer Ysgithr continued on at a tedious pace. Only now Gwenlliant wrestled with temptation: an urge to return to the corridor where she had heard the Earth magic speaking. By night, the deep, resonant voice troubled her dreams; by day, the noise and the activity around her helped her to forget . . . except when there came a silence in her thoughts, and the memory rushed back stronger than before. For a time, the lessons she taught Cei and Elffin served as an agreeable distraction, but the boys could not spend the whole day studying, and neither could she. She required something more to occupy her mind.

Finally, desperate for amusement, she decided to spend an entire day down in Trewynyn. This would not be her first visit. She had already paid two visits before, escorted by her handmaidens and four armed guards, but progress through the town had been painfully slow, and her guards and attendants had hemmed her in. Gwenlliant decided it would be much more interesting, this time, to make the trip with Cei and Elffin her only companions.

She announced her intentions after breakfast—or rather, she declared she would go out walking. She did not say *where* she was going, for fear that someone would send for an escort. Grainne brought her a pair of leather shoes, to replace her satin slippers, and Traeth produced a thick grey cloak, the hood beautifully lined with miniver. Autumn was progressing and the weather was dry but increasingly cold.

Fortunately, none of the older girls offered to accompany her. In cold weather they were perfectly content to spend the entire day sitting by the fire, allowing Gwenlliant to walk in the safety of the castle gardens with only her pages for escort.

Feeling rather nervous, and therefore deciding to go quickly, before she had time to lose her nerve, Gwenlliant swept from the room, her green gown and her long grey cloak trailing behind and her pages scurrying after her. She descended two flights of stairs in a rush, and made her way swiftly through the myriad courtyards between Melusine's Bower and the front gate. It was not until she was sailing across the outermost courtyard, with goats, chickens, and other small fowl scattering before her, that the boys became suspicious.

"Lady," said Cei, running to keep up with her. "Lady, where are we *going*?"

"We are going down to Trewynyn, just the three of us." And when both boys began to protest, she replied firmly: "Nobody ever forbade us to do so, and *I* say that we may."

Which, in the absence of the older girls to say otherwise, effectively silenced them.

Just before she came to the outer gates, she put up the hood of her cloak. With her hair covered and her pale skin shadowed, the guards should not recognize her, so rarely had she approached these imposing portals of iron and stone.

She passed through the gates unhindered, and the boys followed after her without any challenge. And she was halfway down the road to the town before she even realized: Elffin and Cei were dressed in livery—scarlet and gold and black, their surcotes adorned with Tryffin's alchemical blazing dragon—a fact that *might* be registering with the gate guards just about now. With that thought, she quickened her steps until she and her pages arrived safely at the foot of the hill.

From there, she proceeded at a more leisurely pace, from the inner wards to the second ring. Then she stopped, pushed back her hood, and glanced eagerly around her.

The streets were filled with people: craftsmen and merchants and fishermen and housewives, mostly in simple garments of russet, green, or grey, as worn by the common folk anywhere—though perhaps these men and women were not so prosperous, so tidy and bustling, as their Camboglannach counterparts.

Since she had no place particular to go, Gwenlliant selected a direction at random and headed down a long winding lane. People stared as she walked past, at her fine clothes, at her pages in their distinctive livery, but no one approached her.

In that part of the city, there were few signs of the poverty gripping such a large part of Mochdreff. Certainly, there was no shortage of trade goods to be had in Trewynyn. Gwenlliant passed carts and stalls where cloth merchants hawked worsteds, kerseys, and friezes, motleys, stammels, and "felts in divers colors." Old women sold butter and eggs, turnips and custard apples. Craftsmen displayed boxes, drinking horns, and combs made from horn; fine steel daggers, bodkins, needles, and pins; or ropes, pots, hourglasses, leather pouches, pipkins, scissors, lanterns, bottles. And besides all *that*, there were pastry shops, and chandlers, and cobblers, and butchers . . . Gwenlliant could identify most of these by scent as she walked along.

There was no plan to this part of the town at all, it was all haphazard; the taller houses leaned precariously over the streets, there were few sign posts, and the lanes and the alleys all met at odd angles. As a result Gwenlliant soon became hopelessly lost. And though it was possible to see the castle at all times, perched as it was at the top of the hill, whenever she tried to head back in that direction, the streets always twisted her back around, so that she was soon moving away from the inner ring, away from Caer Ysgithr.

At first, this bothered her very little; there was so much to see and to touch and to admire. But many hours later she was hungry and tired, and so parched with thirst that she thought she might faint. Unfortunately, while there was food and drink on every side of her—pies and cheeses and sweetmeats perfuming the air, ciders and meads and ales—she had not thought to bring any money with her, not even so much as a silver penny.

Gwenlliant sat down on a barrel outside a shop, and arranged her train and her cloak so that no one should tread on them. There was no use appealing to Elffin or Cei, for her pages had nothing but what she and Tryffin thought to provide them.

Gwenlliant sighed, and looked down at the golden rings adorning her fingers. Here she was, the wife of the son of the wealthiest Lord in all of Celydonn, who owned gold mines and silver mines, and mines full of diamonds—a man, in short, to whom money was just nothing—and she might have been a beggar, for all the good that Lord Maelgwyn's riches did her right now.

"I suppose," she said aloud, "I might *sell* one of my rings, in order to buy food and drink. Or to pay some man or boy to guide us back to the castle."

Elffin and Cei exchanged a horrified glance. This was their first inkling that she and they were lost; they had followed her trustingly all this while, and never guessed that anything was wrong. But as young and unsophisticated as they certainly were, they both knew instinctively that the Governor of Mochdreff would never wish his Lady to hawk her jewels down on the street.

Elffin put a hand on the hilt of his jeweled dagger. "I could sell this . . ." he began, and then thought better of it. It was more than a pretty plaything, more than a utensil to be used at mealtimes—it was a weapon, one he might need to bring to his Lady's defense at any time.

Cei gave him a withering look. "Don't be an addlepate, Elffin, you can't sell your dagger. *I* have a ring and it is only silver."

Gwenlliant opened her mouth to protest. It was not right the boys should sacrifice their few possessions, just because *she* had been improvident. Indeed, she was mortified to think that she had failed in her duty to provide her pages with all they required.

But before she could say a word, a deep, cultured voice spoke close to her ear. "The Lady Gwenlliant. Or ought I to address you, instead, as Princess?"

Glancing up, she saw a lean, priestly-looking man in a long blue robe and a white cloak—the lord who had first greeted Tryffin when they landed at Trewynyn. And standing at his side, elegantly attired in black and silver, was the beautiful boy Mahaffy Guillyn. Blushing, Gwenlliant climbed down from her barrel, and offered Lord Cado her hand.

"I am not entitled to style myself as a Princess of Tir Gwyngelli, until the day that Tryffin presents me at Castell Maelduin and places the coronet upon my brow."

The Lord of Ochren took her hand and made a deep bow over it. "The Lady Gwenlliant, then. And may one ask what brings the Lady Gwenlliant into this lowly part of Trewynyn?"

Gwenlliant felt herself blushing again. Though perhaps that was just the proximity of the handsome and arrogant boy at Lord Cado's side.

"I am presently concerned," she said, with all the dignity that she could muster, "to find someone who can take me *away* from this part of Trewynyn. Also—" She hesitated. But then, for the sake of the boys, she felt obliged to continue: "And also, Lord Cado, if you could lend me some small coin, so I might buy my pages something to eat along the way . . ."

"An escort shall certainly be provided. But as for the other: You and your good pages must visit my humble establishment—fortunately, only a step away—and there I shall be pleased to offer you a little refreshment."

Gwenlliant hesitated again, not sure what she ought to do. But then she looked up at the dark-eyed Mahaffy, remembered that Tryffin had asked him to visit at Caer Ysgithr. That being so, it must be equally proper for Gwenlliant to visit the boy and his uncle.

She bowed her head in what she hoped was a dignified and gracious manner. "I thank you, Lord Cado. I shall be pleased and honored to accept your invitation."

As it developed, the Lord of Ochren's "humble establishment" was really quite grand: a tall building made of stone, with a slate roof and many chimneys, and dozens of windows filled with the most beautiful stained glass.

"It looks—it looks more like a church than a house," said Gwenlliant, as Lord Cado led her up the high front steps to the door.

"It was at one time a monastery, the home of an order of gentle white friars. Alas, they were all of them slaughtered in a single night by a group of militant monastics called the Knights of Jerusalem. One of the heretical sects, of course."

He brought her through a set of massive double doors, down a long corridor with a high ceiling, past a number of respectable-looking servants, and up a long wooden staircase. "And what," said Gwenlliant, "happened to the Knights of Jerusalem after they murdered the white friars?"

"They flourished for a period of some fifty years. And then were all tried, condemned, and burned for heresy when another sect came into power."

As Gwenlliant and her pages paused in their climb and instinctively crossed themselves, Lord Cado smiled an austere smile. "I believe it is the custom, elsewhere, for the Church to concentrate its energies on witches and pagans, torturing and burning them. But here in Mochdreff, where there are so many schisms and heresies, our militant clerics are mainly occupied with murdering each other."

Gwenlliant was profoundly shocked by this cynical attitude, but too polite to say so. In her experience, the character of the Celydonnian clergy was such that the majority were pious, unassuming souls—or else, like Brother Bedwini, amiable and a little too worldly for her personal taste—and it was fanatically religious lords temporal, like her kinsman Cuel mac Cadellin up in Gorwynnion, who did most of the torturing and burning.

This was not, however, the first she had heard of Mochdreffi schisms and heresies. Without saying more, she took the arm that Lord Cado offered her, and continued climbing the stairs.

At the top of the steps was another wide passageway, and at the end of that, another set of massive wooden doors, beautifully carved and lovingly polished. A page in blue and silver livery rushed on ahead to fling open those doors. Lord Cado led Gwenlliant into a large round chamber, outfitted, she realized with a shock, as an alchemical laboratory.

There were long tables cluttered with glass vessels—aludels, retorts, pelicans, and alembics—and yards and yards of copper tubing. There were shelves filled with books and papers and colored bottles, and a massive brick furnace standing in one corner of the room. In the middle of the floor, someone had painted an enormous golden pentagram.

"No one told me," said Gwenlliant, "that you were a *wizard,* Lord Cado." The Lord of Ochren led her to a high-backed chair.

"Indeed," he said, with another stern smile. "I take a deep interest in matters philosophical."

Gwenlliant sat down in the offered chair. "But am I to understand," said Lord Cado, "that you also have some small knowledge of that noble science?"

"A little," she answered. "That is, I studied wizardry, at one time, but eventually gave up the idea of becoming a sorceress."

Lord Cado remained standing, but his nephew flung himself down into another seat and regarded Gwenlliant with a moody stare. Meanwhile, Cei and Elffin disposed themselves on the floor at her feet.

"Perhaps," said the Lord of Ochren, continuing to regard her, "the master who taught you was somehow at fault."

Gwenlliant arranged the skirts of her velvet gown. "Oh no, Lord Cado, I was *very* well taught. By my kinswoman Teleri ni Pendaren, who was apprenticed to Glastyn himself and is very nearly an adept in her own right, having mastered two full portions of the *Three Parts of Wisdom.*"

And because Elffin and Cei were there to hear, who must not know the truth—not if she ever wanted to go back to Camboglanna or Rhianedd—she added obliquely: "In the end, my kinswoman decided that I had been born with—with other aptitudes . . . and that it was probably necessary to learn to use *those* before I could ever hope to master the science of wizardry.

"I do not need to tell you that I could not do anything like that when I lived in Camboglanna."

"Naturally so," said Lord Cado, understanding her very well. "I wish that my own people had the wisdom of the Camboglannach. To my mind, there are far too many women meddling in magic and witchery as it is."

He turned to his page. "Bring cakes and wine for the Lady Gwenlliant and her attendants. Or perhaps . . ." He glanced in her direction. ". . . perhaps you would prefer metheglin instead?"

Gwenlliant agreed that a cup of spiced mead would be very welcome. She shot a sideways glance at Mahaffy, still glowering at her from across the room. He did not seem disposed to talk, and she felt an increasing certainty that she did *not* like his uncle. She wondered how she could possibly pass the time until the page returned with the cakes and metheglin. "Lord Cado, perhaps you would like to show me your laboratory?"

"If it pleases the Lady Gwenlliant, then naturally it pleases me." But she had an impression as he said it that it was exactly with some such notion in mind that he had brought her to his house in the first place.

He escorted her across the room and there she was surprised to see that the glass vessels arranged down the length of one table, far from containing the usual tinctures, elixirs, and menstruums, were filled with a variety of unexpected things: a miniature thunderstorm in progress; a brass bird, amazingly lifelike, which flew about inside an egg-shaped vessel; a golden flame tipped with silver that seemed to burn without consuming any fuel; and many other things, equally strange and wonderful.

But as she inspected one after the other, as she murmured the expected words of approval and delight, Gwenlliant grew more and more troubled. Because a *true* wizard might attempt any of these spells one at a time as part of his training, by way of demonstrating certain magical laws, but he would not maintain these magics indefinitely, nor would he show them off to impress his visitors.

She thought: *Lord Cado must be a bad wizard, one way or the other. Either not very wise or not very principled . . . and he must think that I am hopelessly ignorant, if he expects me to admire what he is doing here.*

And then she saw something that helped her to make up her mind beyond any doubt, just what sort of wizard Lord Cado was.

There was something alive in one of his glass bottles. Not an agreeable monster, not some glorious fabulous creature out of a bestiary—this was beyond question an abomination: a sickly-looking thing with great blind eyes, too many twisted limbs, and a rictus of inexpressible torment on its all-too-human features. The creature lay sprawled out at the bottom of the bottle, panting weakly, its pale sides trembling. Gwenlliant could see the fragile bones beneath the skin, the blood vessels where the blue blood moved so sluggishly.

"I think," said Lord Cado, with another of his wintry smiles, "that you have never seen its like before."

"No," she replied, wishing with all her heart that she was back at Caer Ysgithr . . . in her own chambers doing needlework with the hitherto boring Traeth, and Faelinn, and Grainne . . . in the chapel, the garden, or the room where the five old ladies sat quarreling and gossiping . . . anywhere but here, with this thoroughly unprincipled wizard, staring at this terrible thing.

But it took no more wizardry than Gwenlliant possessed to still that fluttering heart, to put the creature out of its misery. Had the monster retained even the slightest instinct toward life, it might have resisted the delicate thing that she did.

Then Gwenlliant turned and smiled at Lord Cado. She had not lived most of her life at court without learning how to dissemble, had not existed as a strange, fey child among powerful adults without learning how to speak and to smile so that nobody guessed what was truly going on in her mind.

"It is quite remarkable—and I daresay utterly unique." And so thoroughly did she charm and beguile him, the wizard never spared a glance for the pitiful creature that lay expiring in the glass.

It was Mahaffy Guillyn who finally offered Gwenlliant the opportunity she wanted, the chance to make a graceful exit.

"It grows late," said the youth, just as she and her pages finished the last of the honey cakes. "No doubt the lady will wish to return to Caer Ysgithr."

"I shall send for a servant," Lord Cado replied, though he made no move to leave his seat by one of the beautiful rose windows.

"*I* shall escort her," said Mahaffy, rising from his chair.

His movements were slow, almost languid, but Gwenlliant read tension in every line of his slender body. She put aside the silver goblet which the page had just refilled with metheglin, and answered breathlessly, "Yes, please. You are very kind."

Under the circumstances, there was really very little that the wizard could say or do if he wanted to detain her. Lord Cado's page scurried to open the door, and Gwenlliant followed Mahaffy out of the laboratory and down the passage.

She felt Elffin tugging softly at her cloak, to gain her attention. "Lady," he hissed. "Lady, this is a bad place. We shouldn't—"

Fearing the wizard's nephew might overhear, Gwenlliant silenced her page with a look.

Halfway down the long oak staircase, they met a haughty-looking damsel in a gown of spangled blue velvet, in the process of climbing up. Gwenlliant could not help but pause and stare, for surely this was the most beautiful woman she had ever seen in her life. Besides absolute perfection of form and feature, the lady had a vast quantity of chestnut-colored hair which she wore elaborately dressed, wide grey eyes fringed with thick dark lashes, and an absolutely flawless complexion.

"My cousin Dahaut. The Lady Gwenlliant." Mahaffy made the presentation with obvious reluctance.

Dahaut smiled, bestowing on Gwenlliant a glance so brilliant that the younger girl was a little dazzled and was about to return that smile . . . when her own glance chanced to fall on the remarkable necklace encircling Dahaut's slender throat, a magnificent golden torc studded with many tiny sidhe-stones.

Not ordinary gold, Gwenlliant knew that at once. The gold that was found in the mines of Gwyngelli was unmistakable, for it came out of the earth with few imperfections and was further refined by processes known only to the Gwyngellach to an incredible purity. Gwenlliant knew of one man only, in all of Mochdreff, capable of bestowing such a priceless gift.

This lady, she thought, *knows Tryffin very, very well.*

The silence between them stretched uncomfortably long. And Gwenlliant knew that she ought to say something. It was for her to acknowledge Dahaut, not the other way around, but she simply could not think of a single thing to say.

So Mahaffy solved the problem for her, by taking her gently by the arm, leading her past his cousin and down the stairs.

"I beg your pardon," he said, releasing his hold when they reached the street.

Gwenlliant shook her head, blinking back tears. Though why she should feel so hurt and shaken she did not know. The world was full of beautiful women who had once been intimate with Tryffin. Probably, it was just meeting one of them so unexpectedly. "It is I who should beg *your* pardon. But I didn't—I truly didn't mean to insult your cousin, under your uncle's roof."

Mahaffy turned those stormy eyes of his back toward the house. "As to that," he said, "some people are *beneath* insult. Nor should you trouble yourself what they think or they do."

They proceeded down the narrow cobblestone street, the Mochdreffi youth striding on ahead, Gwenlliant and her pages hurrying to keep up with him. "No doubt," said Mahaffy, "you thought me discourteous enough back there."

Gwenlliant shook her head again. "No . . . yes. Yes, I did, just at first. But now I see that you were trying to warn me."

Mahaffy slowed his pace. "You had no business visiting Lord

Cado. The more so because you went to his house without Prince Tryffin's knowledge or permission." He took a deep breath. "It is a wicked house, and my uncle is a wicked man."

"Yes," said Gwenlliant. "But if you know that, why do you *live* there?"

"Because I have no real choice in the matter," he answered, with a bitter little laugh. "It's either that, or beg in the street."

They rounded a corner and started to cross one of the crowded marketplaces. A party of men in light armor and long red cloaks rode into the square, and Gwenlliant saw, with a mixture of relief and dread, that Tryffin was one of them. Catching sight of her, the Governor pulled in at once, swung out of the saddle, and handed the reins over to one of his men.

Gwenlliant stood very still, awaiting her husband's approach. He came striding across the square, looking uncharacteristically grim, and when he recognized the youth standing at her side, he gave Mahaffy a withering glance.

"Cousin . . ." said Gwenlliant, suddenly the recipient of a careful but nonetheless passionate mail-clad embrace, ". . . Mahaffy Guillyn has been so kind to rescue me when I was lost."

"Then I am mightily obliged to you, Mahaffy," Tryffin said, against her hair. "But if you will excuse me—" And he swept Gwenlliant off her feet and carried her, before all those people, over to the place where his men were waiting.

"I am very sorry," she managed to say, as he put her up on Roch's broad back and took back the reins.

"So you should be," he said softly, wrapping the leather lines around his arm. "Before God, Gwenlliant, I have been searching for you ever since morning, when the guards at the front gate recognized your pages and sent a man to your rooms to ask questions." For all that he spoke so low, she could tell that he was still very angry.

"Anyway," she said, as he took the bridle and started to lead the roan gelding back through the winding streets, back toward Caer Ysgithr, "I did take Cei and Elffin with me, just as you said I should."

"Yes," he said, under his breath, "but I think that you knew very well what I meant when I said it."

The King's expression was troubled as he gazed down at his step-sister.

"And so," he said wearily, "you have come here to Caer Cadwy, you have waited these many weeks to speak with me, all so that you may ask me to dissolve your marriage, which was no marriage at all . . . seeing that you contracted to marry Corfil fab Corrig without my consent, that you lived with him all of these years against my wishes . . . and I am expected to grant what you desire, simply because you ask it?"

Diaspad, kneeling at his feet, her aspect unusually meek, uncharacteristically humble, started to speak, but Cynwas interrupted her.

"And what will you do, if I grant your desire? No, I will say it myself: You will marry Manogan fab Menai, a good man and my best friend—who is far, far better than you deserve—and then you will devote the rest of your life to making him utterly miserable."

"No," said Diaspad, her voice very low. "No . . . Lord . . . you misunderstand me." She held her hands crossed in front of her, over her belly, as if by doing so she might ward and protect that which she secretly carried. "I have come to you to ask that you recognize my marriage to Corfil of Mochdreff . . . that you grant your consent as well as your blessing . . . so that any children which come of that union may be legitimate issue in the eyes of the law."

9.

A Great Golden Beast, Like to a Lion

The weather turned wild and blustery the next day, and black storm clouds loomed on the eastern horizon. By afternoon, the wind tasted of snow. Or so thought Tryffin, as he crossed the frosty courtyard where the stables and the kennels were located, heading for his own rooms in the square tower. Garth and Conn went on ahead of him, to light the candles and build a fire.

Only six weeks until Christmas, he was thinking. At Caer Cadwy or in any other proper household, the coming of Advent would bring masked balls and pageants and other celebrations, amusements enough to keep his restless little bride wholesomely occupied until the end of the winter. But how to keep Gwenlliant both happy and safe, here at Caer Ysgithr?

He was so caught up in these thoughts, he was scarcely aware of his surroundings—until Garth called out ten paces ahead of him, in a voice that was tinged with panic: "My lord, stay *back*!"

Tryffin glanced up just in time to see the chickens and the geese scattering, and an enormous snarling mastiff, all tawny fur and flashing teeth, charge across the yard, then hurl through the air in a mighty leap. The dog hit Garth squarely, causing him to drop the sword he was attempting to draw, and knocking the boy off his feet.

By the time the Governor had covered the distance between them, Garth was down on the ground, curled up in a ball, trying to protect his face and his throat. Conn had one arm wrapped around the mastiff's thick neck, struggling to hold the furious beast off his brother, while with the other hand he fumbled his dagger out of the sheath and plunged it into the animal's heaving flank again and again.

Tryffin whipped out his own dirk, grabbed the mastiff by its rolled scruff, and with all his strength, thrust the blade in hard between the dog's ribs. The mastiff stopped snarling and suddenly went limp.

Tryffin put the knife in a few more times, to make certain the dog was dead. Then he rolled the corpse off Garth and helped the boy to sit up. "For the love of God, you might have been killed. Why didn't you run?"

"I am supposed to protect *you*," Garth said shakily. "And I was worse than useless . . . at Dinas Oerfel, at the inn in Pwll Gannon . . ." His voice faded away.

Relieved that the lad could at least speak, Tryffin knelt down and made a quick examination. The mastiff had mostly worried at Garth's clothing, but one arm was badly savaged, was torn and bloody. Conn was still on his knees, but staggered to his feet when Tryffin spoke to him.

"The brute hit me in the face with that great head of his," Conn explained, wiping a copiously flowing bloody nose on one satin sleeve, insisting that the rest of the blood staining his doublet had belonged to the dog.

By now, there were shouts and footsteps coming from all directions, and a crowd of grooms and stableboys milling around. But Tryffin waved them all back, intent on the two boys.

"You are both fine brave lads, and it's likely you saved my life by standing your ground," he said quietly. Though thinking what might have happened if the incident had occurred a day earlier, when Gwenlliant and the little boys were crossing the yard, he broke out into a cold sweat.

He ripped open what remained of Garth's ragged shirtsleeve, baring the wound for a close inspection. "Ah God . . . I don't think you will lose the use of this, but a dog's bite is often unclean. The wound will have to be cauterized."

"I know," whispered Garth, and promptly fainted from shock, which was far and away the most merciful thing that could have happened.

They loaded the unconscious boy onto a hurdle and carried him into the forge. Tryffin wrapped the hilt of his dirk in a piece of ragged cloth, thrust the blade into the blacksmith's fire until the metal began to glow. Garth was still blessedly oblivious when Tryffin took the dagger out of the fire and applied the heated blade to the wound.

Poor Conn started gagging, with the blood still running down the back of his throat and the stench of burning flesh. Only by a supreme effort was Tryffin able to prevent himself from doing the same, to force himself to hold the blade steady until he thought he had burned out all the poisons left by the dog's bite. Garth gasped once or twice, but did not come around.

"Your Grace," said a voice, rising above the general babble. "My apologies . . . Lord . . . I do not know how the beast escaped from his pen. I was in the kitchen, eating my dinner, but I swear to you . . . the catch was secure when I left the kennel."

Tryffin shifted his gaze upward and saw the master of Morcant's kennels standing in the door of the smithy. The man was green and wobbling on his feet, likely expecting a beating or even worse punishment. Tryffin resheathed his dirk and called for bandages.

He forced himself to reply calmly, as he rose to his feet, wiping his sweating palms on the skirts of his long tunic. "We will think about assigning the blame later. For now, will you just tell me: Was the dog mad?"

Conn, who had apparently not considered that possibility before, went a shade whiter, looked ready to pass out. Tryffin put an arm around the boy to steady him.

"Your Grace, no!" The man sounded offended at the idea he

might keep a diseased animal in his kennel. "The beast was extraordinarily fierce, likely to attack anyone whose scent was unknown to him, and we had orders to keep him a bit hungry and ill-tempered. For the bull and the bear baiting, you see."

"Ah yes," said Tryffin, remembering that Morcant had favored those sports. "And tell me: Would there be any more dogs of the same sort, caged up in your kennel?"

The man shifted uneasily from one foot to the other, perhaps beginning to catch the Governor's drift. "There are other mastiffs for the baiting, but none quite so ferocious as this one. It was—it was Lord Morcant's favorite. Dogs of such mettle and such strength are difficult to come by."

"Aye, no doubt," said Tryffin, one arm still supporting Conn. He could feel the boy shaking with reaction. And poor Garth was still lying, as pale as death, on the hurdle at their feet.

His gaze hardened. "Nevertheless, you will take those mastiffs, every one of them, and see they are mercifully destroyed."

Tryffin sat back in his chair, surveying the pile of papers and parchments heaped on the table before him, the letters and writs and warrants which had already kept him occupied for so many hours. Yet these were the last . . . if not the last he would ever have to read and sign, at least the last that were required to put things back the way they had been before Morcant's death.

Somewhere in the castle, a chapel bell tolled the call to Lauds. Just as though, he mused wryly, anyone at all in that Godforsaken place went to prayers between midnight and dawn. Yet it had been his own idea, to institute the practice of marking the canonical hours, simply because it reminded him of home.

There was a scratching sound on the half-open door, and one of the Mochdreffi servants came into the room. "It is Mahaffy Guillyn, Your Grace, still waiting to speak with you."

Tryffin ran a hand through his hair. "I forgot that I sent for him. Send him in at once."

The servant slid past the door, and a moment later Mahaffy came into the audience chamber, slender and graceful in black velvet and mulberry silk. "Prince Tryffin, I don't wish to interrupt your labors."

The Governor waved him toward a chair. "Aye, you do right to rebuke me. I should never have kept you waiting so long. The more so, because you've been so reluctant to accept my invitations in the past."

Mahaffy deposited himself in the indicated chair and assumed a negligent pose. "I meant no reproach. I was only remembering how tiresome and how endless Lord Morcant always found the signing and sealing of official documents. I was his squire, you know.''

''Yes, I remember,'' said Tryffin, and saw a spark of something ignite in Mahaffy's eyes. ''I haven't summoned you here to ask questions about Morcant—or about the men who murdered him—if that is what you are thinking.'' Apparently it was, because the boy looked vaguely disappointed.

Now, what was the lad so eager to say about *that*? Tryffin found himself wondering. But now was not the time to ask.

He gave Mahaffy his sweetest and blandest smile. ''Neither did I call you here to account for abducting my lady wife, since she tells me you were the one responsible for removing her from your uncle's house.''

Mahaffy returned his smile with a frown, clearly not disarmed in the least. ''She took no harm there, that I can promise you—though maybe she saw considerably more than she wanted to see. And more than you wish her to know.''

While he thought about that, Tryffin reached into his tunic and drew out the seal that he wore on a chain around his neck. He slipped the chain over his head and began sorting through the documents yet to be sealed.

''Maybe you can tell me,'' he said, taking a stick of sealing wax and holding it over a convenient candle, ''why it was that your uncle invited Gwenlliant to visit him to begin with.''

Mahaffy appeared to consider. ''I think no more than a momentary impulse to mischief, an attempt to win your lady's friendship, which he knew very well you would disapprove.''

Tryffin glanced up, his eyebrows rising sharply. ''Lord Cado *knew* that I didn't want him to make a friend of my wife?''

The boy laughed scornfully. ''Seeing that Your Grace has been at some pains to keep my uncle from visiting Caer Ysgithr, I would imagine that he *did* know.''

Tryffin shook his head, went back to the business of sealing documents. ''I've not responded to Lord Cado's continued hints for an invitation—is that what kept you away? Did you imagine my displeasure extended to you? But so far as I know, your uncle has never actually been turned back at the front gate.''

Mahaffy made a soft sound of amusement. ''No need for that, is there? Caer Ysgithr isn't like other places, you know. A wizard like Cado Guillyn requires a direct invitation from the Lord of the castle before he can enter. Though perhaps a word from your lady would work just as well.''

Tryffin put down his seal and his stick of wax, leaned back in his chair. "Now, there is an interesting piece of information." And he had a fair idea where Mahaffy had picked it up. Which was as good an introduction to the subject he really wanted to discuss as any he could imagine.

"I met a servant of your uncle's some months back. Your old nursemaid, I believe she is—the witch Ceinwen."

Now it was Mahaffy's turn to look surprised, to stiffen and sit up in his chair. Then he relaxed again, and a slight smile played around the corners of his mouth. "Old Ceinwen, was it? I hope, for your sake, you weren't discourteous."

Tryffin shook his head, folded his arms across his chest. "I was not. I believe she even commended me for my pretty manners."

Now Mahaffy laughed out loud. "I suppose she would at that. I had forgotten you had such a way with the common folk. Fortunate for you, in this case."

He seemed to regard the Governor in a friendlier way after that, and his manner became almost confiding. "She isn't really a servant, you see, but a distant kinswoman. It suited her fancy to play nursemaid when Dahaut and I were small, just as she had the care of my Uncle Cado when he was young . . . in whatever age of the world *that* was . . . just as it suits her now to dress in rags and go about the countryside pretending to be a poor old peasant woman. Not many emerge from an encounter with Ceinwen unscathed, that I can tell you."

Tryffin nodded, for Mahaffy's words only confirmed what he had already guessed. "I take it, then, there is an element of risk in meeting this woman? That she is as likely to dispense curses as blessings?"

Mahaffy shrugged. "So I have heard, but she has always been very good to me. I was her favorite, you see."

"But not Dahaut? And not your Uncle Cado?" The fact that Mahaffy declined to answer was answer enough. The Governor decided it was time to change his approach. "Well then . . . tell me what you know of Calchas fab Corfil. You were about the same age, you used to be one of his mother's pages, you must have spent a fair amount of time in his company."

A faint flush came into Mahaffy's cheeks; he shifted uneasily in his chair. "We weren't friends, if that is what you mean. And I was page to the Princess for a year only."

Knowing Diaspad's habits, her fondness for pretty youths and handsome young men, Tryffin could easily guess what had precipitated Mahaffy's sudden departure from the Princess's household. But that was a matter he had no wish to pursue.

He took a moment shaping his next question. "There are

rumors I've heard since coming here that have made me wonder if there might not be some mystery surrounding Calchas's birth.''

"Well, if you mean that everyone knows he was Diaspad's bastard, that's true enough. Corfil was the only one I ever knew who was willing to believe that he was the father. But what man wishes to think he is incapable of getting children? Yet there was Corfil with all his mistresses, and only the women who were already married ever seemed to quicken. Oh yes,'' Mahaffy went on, warming to his theme, ''there were one or two brats that Corfil chose to *think* were his, and the little beasts were willing to lord it over the rest of us—but not a one of them looked anything like him.

"Calchas came the closest, truth to tell, and that was just the hair and the eyes . . . common enough in these parts. And they say your uncle was a dark—'' Mahaffy stopped suddenly and turned scarlet.

"You needn't try to spare my feelings. God knows, nobody else has attempted it. I've heard that story before, that my Uncle Manogan was Calchas's father.''

Mahaffy scowled at him. "Then why do you ask me what you already know?''

"Ah well, it's always wise to ask more than one person,'' said Tryffin. "And that part about Corfil's bastards—or lack of them—that I did not know.''

It was beginning to look more and more like the story was true. Tryffin sat staring down at his hands, flexing and unflexing them. He was remembering his own words, spoken impulsively, as he stood facing the horrified question in Fflergant's eyes, after Calchas was dead: *"Ah God, he had to die! He would have used the same story back at Caer Cadwy, to save his miserable skin. It wouldn't have saved him, but Manogan would have suffered for it. Don't you see. Calchas had to die, and you or I had to be the one to kill him!''*

Tryffin shook his head. He had murdered Calchas to protect a secret that half of Mochdreff already knew or suspected. It was bad enough to commit the one unpardonable sin, the crime of kinslaying that no Gwyngellach could ever excuse, but to do the thing and discover afterward that his reason for doing it was all a sham . . .

Tryffin took in a deep breath and expelled it slowly. "So that is why no one here blames me for Calchas's death: It was never anything more than a family quarrel, the sort of thing that might happen in any Mochdreffi clan, given sufficient provocation—and

102

none of their business anyway, since foreigners were the only ones involved."

"Yes," Mahaffy agreed cheerfully. "Nobody's business outside your family. Though it may not be true, of course. The Princess was promiscuous enough after Calchas was born. Who is to say she hadn't a number of lovers even before that?"

By now, Tryffin had forgotten the warrants entirely, and the stick of sealing wax was melting away in a dish on the table. "Now, who, do you suppose, would be able to give me the most accurate account of the entire story? Who would be able to do more than repeat rumors? Your uncle?" he suggested, just to see how Mahaffy reacted.

But Mahaffy remained unmoved. "Not likely. He did live here in those days, but I doubt he was ever in the Princess's confidence. He was Corfil's friend and advisor, you know. And Uncle Cado's magic was less in those days, as was Diaspad's . . . I believe there was even some rivalry between them."

"Brangwengwen, then?" Tryffin suggested, still watching him closely.

This time, Mahaffy registered considerable surprise. "If one could find her, if the creature is still alive."

The Governor put his hands on the table and pushed back his chair. "The Lady Gwenlliant thought she saw Brangwengwen walking in the orchard."

The boy squirmed uneasily in his chair. "Aye, she used to do that. Still . . . they are bad luck you know, dwarfs and hunchbacks. The Princess kept so many of them, after Corfil died, simply to make the rest of us uneasy—to flaunt her power. But if any of her creatures tried to return, her dwarfs or her lame giant, why, your guards at the gate would refuse to admit them. And Brangwengwen: Some people thought she was more deeply involved in Black Magic than even the Princess herself."

The Governor sat thinking again. "What do you know about Kemoc fab Gradlon?" he asked suddenly.

Mahaffy blinked. "I'm not certain what you mean. I don't know anyone by that name, though I am vaguely acquainted with Lord Gradlon of Oeth. His son, would that be?"

Tryffin left his chair and came around to the other side of the table. "Yet you lived at Castell Peryf with your uncle, did you not? And there is considerable intercourse between Peryf and Oeth."

"Perhaps there is, but I never lived there. The year Cado and Dahaut were in Peryf, I was the Princess Diaspad's page. You can ask anyone, if you doubt me."

The Governor smiled faintly. "I would never call you a liar," he said mildly. "You are far too transparent, and I think you know it."

Mahaffy stifled a yawn, reminding Tryffin that the hour was late. "You ought to be in bed. My apologies for keeping you here so long. If I want you again, I will send for you."

The youth rose gracefully from his chair and started for the door, but stopped when Tryffin called him back.

"You are how old, Mahaffy? Nineteen? Aye, I thought so. You'll be ready to be knighted before another year has passed, or would be, if you were any knight's squire. Why didn't you attach yourself to anyone after Morcant died? Or was it . . . that having expected to be knighted by the Lord of Mochdreff, you don't care to receive the accolade from any lesser man?"

Mahaffy smiled bitterly. "That is what everyone seems to think, anyway."

Tryffin perched on the edge of the table, which being of sturdy oak was able to support him. "But not the actual truth?"

"No knight has *asked* me to serve in his household," said Mahaffy, with a painful little laugh. "I think they must suppose, as you do, that my Guillyn pride would forbid it. And the truth is: I *am* too proud to go begging for a place, if no one sees fit to offer me one."

Tryffin regarded him thoughtfully. "You may have heard, I'm in need of a squire. At least for a few months, anyway."

Mahaffy suddenly lost all the color in his face, as though he had been wounded—or else offered something he wanted so much that the wanting hurt. "I heard about Garth. A terrible misfortune, that dog getting loose. But Prince Tryffin . . . there is no reason on earth why you should want *me* to replace him."

"I don't see that. You were Morcant's squire, and that certainly makes you fit to be mine. And I stand in your debt, for your kindness to Gwenlliant. Unless this is your way of saying you would rather not serve me?"

Mahaffy's color went from white to red. "I have no wish to decline your generous offer, Prince Tryffin." Then, suddenly and surprisingly, the boy went down on one knee.

"Make me your squire and promise to knight me with your own sword," he said quietly, "and I will give you my entire devotion."

Now the Nature of our island is this: the Matter of Celydonn is composed of nine parts of the Mundane elements—earth, air, fire, and water—to one part Magic. For this reason, the rain, winds, mist, and snow are not regulated in our Kingdom, as they are elsewhere, by the Weather of the World, but are principally influenced by other factors. And among these: the state of the Realm, the virtue and the strength of the King (and of the Lords who rule under him), and the fortitude and prowess of his Warriors.

—*From* The Three Parts of Wisdom,
attributed to Teleri ni Pendaren

10.

A Question of Virtue

Gwenlliant woke early one morning. Early and alone in her big bedchamber, which was a thing that seldom happened. The door to the smaller room where her handmaidens slept stood ajar, but there was no sound of movement on the other side.

A pale gold beam of sunlight coming in through one of the upper windows illuminated the room. It was a little past sunrise, but in such harsh weather, when it was difficult to keep the vast drafty chambers heated, when it was bitterly cold outside, the castle would not be stirring to life for some time.

In spite of that, Gwenlliant slid out from under the sleeping furs. Barefoot—actually barefoot, because there was no one to make a fuss or insist that she put on a pair of satin slippers—and rather chilly in her thin cambric shift, she walked across the room and quietly opened one of the shutters that covered the lower casements.

A walled garden with a frozen fishpond lay directly under Gwenlliant's windows; beyond that was the apple orchard with its mournful trees. Snow had fallen during the night, and there was something tragic about the stark shapes of the trees as they stood silhouetted against the smooth white drifts. But there was a single spark of color: a tiny crooked figure in gaudy orange and scarlet, doing a queer little hopping dance, which took her from one end of the orchard to another.

"Brangwengwen," whispered Gwenlliant, on a long sigh. As if in response to her name, the dwarf woman stopped under a twisted limb and glanced up at Gwenlliant's window.

Gwenlliant knew that the dwarf could not see her. The window where she stood must look dark from below. Yet for all that, she *felt* that the dwarf was aware of her, that Brangwengwen somehow recognized her—that there existed a curious bond between them. *I have been an oddity all of my life, and so has Brangwengwen.* The dwarf put up her arm and made a gesture, oddly imperious, as though inviting her younger counterpart to join her down in the snowy orchard.

Without stopping to question what she was doing, Gwenlliant turned, tiptoed back across the room, dressed herself in a wool gown, a warm cloak, and squirrel-trimmed boots, and crept out into the antechamber.

The room was chilly and dim, its windows facing west. There was a branch of stubby candles on a table, drowning in their own tallow, and the ashes on the hearth had probably been cold for hours. Feeling her way in the gloom, moving lightly in her soft leather boots, Gwenlliant tripped over someone who was sleeping on a straw mattress near her door.

It was Cei, who immediately threw off his blankets and jumped to his feet. His fair hair was rumpled, he wore only his shirt and linen breeches. Even in the dim light she could see that he was considerably flustered.

"Lady, forgive me. If I had known you had need of me—" She silenced him, holding a finger to her lips.

"It is I who ought to apologize for stepping all over you," she whispered. "But do not wake Elffin or the others, for I don't want them."

He sat down on the mattress, began pulling on his long parti-colored stockings, tying them to the points on his breeches. "There is no need for that, Cei. I don't want *you,* either."

She wished she had remembered that Cei and Elffin slept so near her door. The boys were generally up and about, their lightweight bedding usually bundled away, long before she emerged from her bedchamber. If she had known they were there, she would have moved more cautiously.

Cei bounced to his feet, snatching up the rest of his clothes as he did so. "Lady, you can't. That is, I *have* to come with you. Prince Tryffin would have my hide if I—"

This time she silenced him with a hand over his mouth. "Prince Tryffin would do nothing of the sort," she whispered. So far as she knew, Tryffin had never raised a hand to a servant or an attendant in his life.

Nevertheless, there were dozens of ways that boys were disciplined in a noble household: short rations, and dirty or demeaning tasks assigned to them, and quite a bit more. It was all part of the discipline that would prepare them for knighthood. She suspected that her pages had been kept fasting for a whole day after her visit to Trewynyn, and she did not want to get Cei into any more trouble. "Very well then, if you fear the Governor's displeasure. But please hurry. And do not wake Elffin or anyone, whatever you do."

She waited impatiently while the boy pulled on his tunic, belted on his jeweled dagger, and fastened on his cloak. Then they both crept out of the room, along the dimly lit passageway, and down the front steps to the long lower corridor where the vengeful brass mermaids held guttering torches.

Cei held open the door, and Gwenlliant stepped out into the frosty morning air. But such was her luck that who should she meet crossing the courtyard, but Tryffin, Meligraunce, and Conn?

The Governor took her hand and kissed it. "And where were you going in such a terrible hurry?" He looked almost impossibly big and bright in scarlet and gold, contrasted against the cold drifts of snow and the grey stones of the courtyard.

And standing there with her hand enfolded in his large warm one, with her cousin smiling so kindly down on her, she did not have the heart to lie to him, for all that she feared he was going to be displeased. "I thought I saw the dwarf again, down in the orchard."

The smile went out of his eyes. "So you came down to meet Brangwengwen, though I warned you against her. And was this the first time you saw her since that day with me?"

"No," Gwenlliant said softly, shaking her head. "I thought I caught a glimpse of her yesterday morning and two days before that. But I didn't go down, because—because then I remembered that you told me not to speak with her."

Tryffin sighed deeply. "I wish you had remembered that today. I wonder if you can tell me: How on earth am I to command the respect of my squires, my servants, my guards, or my officers, if I allow my wife to flaunt my authority?"

Gwenlliant looked away from him, feeling ashamed—but also frustrated and resentful. She shook her head again.

"I have no wish to play the tyrannical husband," he said wearily, releasing her hand. "But for the love of God, Gwenlliant, you are hardly more than a child . . . and I'm your only kinsman here. Don't do anything that forces me to act more like your father than your lover or your friend. Don't do *anything* that forces me to punish you."

Later that day, Tryffin sat in the audience chamber trying to listen patiently, while the Mayor of Trewynyn (a chandler by trade) enumerated a seemingly endless series of petty complaints against two of the Governor's minor officials. Though the man had been talking since just after noon, he showed no signs of stopping, though the light outside was beginning to fade.

It was, therefore, a fortunate coincidence—to the Governor's way of thinking, though not to his visitor's—that brought Meligraunce striding into the room at the exact same moment that the candlemaker paused for breath.

"It is plain that you are a man who has endured much," Tryffin said, before the fellow could start up again. "I will speak to these men, demanding that they account for all of their actions. If I find they cannot justify them, I shall know what to do. But for now . . ." The stout tradesman was opening his mouth to speak, but Tryffin forestalled him with a gesture toward the door. ". . . you can see Captain Meligraunce is eager to see me. A matter, perhaps, of some importance."

Reluctantly, the Lord Mayor made a stiff bow and withdrew, though not without directing a venomous glance at the inconvenient Captain as he passed by.

"And if you haven't come to tell me that the castle is under siege, or of any other disaster, I will say that I've rarely been so happy to see any man before." Tryffin left his chair and wandered over to the long line of mullioned windows overlooking the town and the sea.

"It is that matter you asked me to discover," replied Meligraunce, crossing the room to join him. "I now know the name of the man that you killed at the inn in Pwll Gannon."

Tryffin felt a surge of interest. "And what have you learned? You've been so long about it, I was beginning to think the identity of the man—or more to the point, the name of the lord who sent him after me—would never be known."

"Ah well, it wasn't just the easiest thing, to make these

inquiries without arousing speculation. I had to be subtle and I couldn't be too pressing, and that's what took me so long.''

Meligraunce struck a dramatic pose. ''I made up a story, and a fine piece of work it was, too: I said that I played a game of Cyffle with the man, here at Caer Ysgithr, about the time the petty lords and the clan chieftains came together to write their petition to the King. I lost and he won, a considerable sum of money which I did not happen to have on hand at the time. *'You mean to rook me, you filthy foreigner,'* says he. *'I'll never see the silver you owe me, that's certain.'* So naturally (I've been telling everyone that I speak to) it's a matter of some importance to find the fellow and pay him his money in order to cast off the slur that he put on my name.'' Meligraunce shook his head. ''And here he never told me his own name, nor which lord he served, as though he was certain that I never meant to do the right thing at all.''

Tryffin smiled appreciatively. ''A fine story, very convincing. And what did you learn by it?''

''I was beginning to fear I would never learn anything by it, that the man might not be known here at all,'' said Meligraunce. ''Then I chanced to talk with a fine fellow who walks the north wall. The poor man was confined to his bed with a congestion in his chest through most of September and October, which is why I never had the pleasure of meeting him before. He said he played dice with the other man last spring, and found him just as surly as my story made him out to be. *'Him with the two great scars on his cheeks, like twin bolts of lightning, and the short sword he wore in his belt, with a black hilt banded with silver.'* To make a long story short: The assassin was named Urien Glyn, and he served in the bodyguard of the Lord of Clynnoc.''

The Governor picked up a thick wax candle, carried it over to the fire, and applied it to the flame, frowning thoughtfully. Efrei fab Ogryfran, Lord of Clynnoc, was a quiet man of little apparent ambition, and he had no reason at all, so far as Tryffin knew, for wanting to murder him.

''Efrei of Clynnoc was one of the few petty lords at the council who bears no relationship at all to one of the two remaining heirs, Peredur and Math. And as for any personal grudge against me or my kin . . .''

''No, I had forgotten. There is no relationship by blood, but his brother Rhys is married to the Lady Essylt, mother of young Peredur.''

Meligraunce whistled softly under his breath. ''And perhaps this Rhys wishes to see his step-son sitting in the High Seat, and his brother is merely lending a hand.''

But Tryffin shook his head. "No, that's the very thing that makes it all so improbable. Rhys of Eildonn—that's a small piece of land he inherited from his maternal grandfather—has nothing to do with his step-son at all. The boy has lived with his father's people all along, and Peredur is entirely estranged from his mother and step-father."

He stood the burning candle upright on the mantel, and began to pace the room. "Rhys is so far from anyone's idea of the doting or ambitious step-father that no one gave him or his brother so much as a suspicious glance when all the accusations and recriminations went around after Morcant was murdered."

"Very convenient for the Lords of Clynnoc and Eildonn," commented Meligraunce.

"That, certainly, but also entirely consistent with everything I know of them both." He stopped walking and stood staring at nothing, playing idly with the hilt of his dagger. "Rhys of Eildonn and Efrei of Clynnoc have been notable by their absence these last months. Unlike most of the petty lords of this land, neither one has written or paid me a visit, to bid me welcome or curry my favor, or to enlist my support in any matter. And they were rarely here in Morcant's time or in Goronwy's—preferring, so far as I know, to govern their own lands and leave the ordering of Mochdreff to the rightful Lord."

He stood thinking that over, sheathing and unsheathing the dirk at his side.

"There is something else I learned," said Meligraunce, and Tryffin shifted his gaze upward to the Captain's face. "This man I spoke to, from the north wall. He said, *A pity you didn't speak to me before. Two men of Clynnoc were here four days past, on some business or the other, and you might have given them the money to carry to Urien, had you only known.*' And four days ago, Prince Tryffin, if you've not lost track, is the day poor Garth was savaged by the dog."

"Aye," Tryffin said slowly. "I've not forgotten the day. But there remains the chance that the dog escaping had nothing to do with an attempt on my life. After all, the men who tried to kill me in Perfudd did so quite openly, they didn't try to arrange any so-called accident. And Morcant died with an arrow through his heart—no one pretended that was an accident, either."

"As to that," said Meligraunce, his lean face all shadows and angles in the fading light, "from all I hear, most people in these parts are very concerned no ill should befall you. Morcant and Goronwy were murdered, but each was Lord of Mochdreff in his own right. But you are the King's own kinsman, and it was the

110

King himself who sent you here to govern. That being so, everyone believes your cousin will come down with fire and sword, lay waste to the land, and slay men by the thousands, if anyone harms you."

Tryffin smiled and shook his head. "That hardly sounds like my cousin Cynwas."

Meligraunce folded his arms. "Yes, but it *does* sound exactly like your cousin, seemingly. Because the King sent a letter, before you arrived here, addressed to the petty lords and clan chieftains, making all manner of horrible threats about what he would do, should anyone take it into his head to assassinate you."

Tryffin sat down in his chair again, giving that idea his full attention. Cynwas fab Anwas had not ruled Ynys Celydonn in peace and in plenty for so many years by indulging in the sort of royal temper tantrum that involved the slaughter of innocent people. Yet Tryffin could see that it might be useful, sometimes, for Cynwas to allow his more recalcitrant subjects to *believe* that he might be capable of acts of sweeping retaliation, given some particular provocation.

"Well, it was a kindly thought on the part of the Emperor. And I am grateful for his care of me. Not that his threats did much good so far as young Kemoc was concerned. But even in the case of wiser enemies, who might feel obliged to act in secret, at most this causes them a slight inconvenience."

Meligraunce unfolded his arms. "An inconvenience that could save your life. Easy enough to send a fool with a knife or a bow to kill you, but much more difficult to arrange something that appears to be mischance. Also, if one of their attempts fails to finish you off or claims the wrong victim, as it happened with the dog, they dare not arrange another too soon, for fear of giving their game away. If you suddenly become accident prone, people will begin to ask questions."

"True enough." The Governor leaned back in his great oak chair. "And the longer it takes my enemies to destroy me, the more opportunity for me to ferret them out and put an end to their mischief."

• • •

But when there should be no heir by direct male descent within seven generations, then Primogeniture should give way before the ancient law of Mother Right . . .

In this way, Cynfelyn sought to perpetuate the advantages of both systems: that a youth born and bred up to display the same extraordinary qualities as his fathers before him should also

111

succeed them, but in the event that such an heir should not exist,
a man of similar descent and of proven superiority over other men
of his own generation should be chosen.

And this law has continued down to the present time. By it,
many wise and noble men have come to power, but also much
bloodshed and many bitter rivalries have resulted.

—*From* The Laws of Celydonn,
with Commentary on the Code of
Cynfelyn the Emperor

• • •

When Meligraunce entered the Governor's bedchamber just before supper, he found Prince Tryffin sitting on a sturdy three-legged stool by the fire, with a big book lying open on a small table in front of him.

"I heard an interesting bit of gossip today. From Dame Clememyl that was." Meligraunce did not fail to detect the note of excitement in Prince Tryffin's voice. "Did you know that the Lady Essylt is about to bear her lord a child—in fact, may have done so already?"

"No, I did not. But I assume it must be a matter of some importance, or you would not be so pleased to hear of it."

The Governor shook his head. "Not pleased, but I'll admit that I find the news enlightening. There was an important something I forgot to consider earlier. Young Peredur holds his place in succession to the High Seat by reason of Mother Right, in the absence of any heirs by direct male descent—that we knew. But it has occurred to me, since the time we last spoke, that he must have inherited that right through his mother the Lady Essylt, and *not* through any of his father's maternal ancestors. That stands to reason," he added, "or Peredur's uncles and perhaps half his clan would be heirs as well. So it must be the orphaned and brotherless Lady Essylt who carries the blood of the Lords of Mochdreff."

Prince Tryffin pushed the massive volume across the table for the Captain to see. "This book of the lineage of the Lords of Mochdreff confirms all that. Essylt is the great-granddaughter of Corrig the Elder."

The book smelled of mice, and the parchment was crumbling around the edges. Meligraunce cast a wary eye over the family tree diagrammed in faded brown ink on the open page. He recognized some of the names, but he had never seen a genealogy laid out before, and he could make no more sense of the figure than if it were a magic square or pentacle. "I will have to take your word for that."

"Aye, very well then." Prince Tryffin motioned his henchman to be seated. "Now let us suppose that Peredur should become Lord of Mochdreff by the Grace of Cynwas and his right of election, passing over young Math fab Madawg, the other presumptive heir—but let us also suppose that Peredur dies a year or maybe two afterward, long before he can get any sons of his own. Who would succeed him as Lord of Mochdreff?"

As there was no other stool in the room, Meligraunce pulled up a chair, and feeling rather embarrassed to be better accommodated than his princely patron, lowered himself into the seat.

"Ah," he said, with dawning comprehension. "Any son the Lady Essylt might produce in the meantime would displace young Math, because that boy would be half-brother to the previous Lord. Rhys of Eildonn would be the father of Peredur's heir."

"He would at that," said the Governor, taking back the book. "And I wonder I was so dull that I never thought of these things before."

Meligraunce smiled and shook his head. "Nothing wonderful in that, nor were you particularly dull, since Rhys had done nothing to attract your notice before today."

"There is that. But now that he does have my attention, I find myself asking: Is it merely marriage to the Lady Essylt and the impending birth of an heir which brings out this sudden raging ambition in the formerly mild and unassuming Lord of Eildonn— not to mention his equally self-effacing brother, Efrei of Clynnoc? Or are there other, more sinister influences at work?"

Prince Tryffin closed the book, sat staring at the calfskin cover. "I have an idea, Meligraunce, that I would like to take a troop of men and pay a visit to both of those noble gentlemen, in order to determine if all is exactly as it should be in Eildonn and Clynnoc."

Meligraunce frowned. "Are you certain, Your Grace, that would be wise? If those are the men who are trying to murder you . . . ?"

The Governor gave a careless shrug. "As you said earlier, whoever has been laying traps for me, they have to be careful. They are hardly likely to call attention to themselves by arranging anything unpleasant during my visit.

"Truth to tell, I can think of no place safer, at this moment, than the lands of the men who wish me harm."

Gwenlliant was propped up in her bed, her handmaids clustered around her, when Tryffin appeared on the threshold, later that evening. Traeth froze at the unexpected sight of the Governor, let an ivory comb fall from her hand, a strand of pale hair slide through her fingers; Faelinn put down the silver cup containing wine

113

and spices, which she prepared for Gwenlliant each night before retiring; and Grainne stopped fussing with the bedding and the pillows. All three young women dropped hasty curtsies and promptly withdrew.

Gwenlliant caught her breath and tried not to be nervous, thinking he had come to lie down beside her, as he had done a few times when they were first married. Though little had happened beyond some touching and kissing, those occasions had been awkward and intensely humiliating.

Tryffin closed the door behind her departing handmaidens. "I am sorry we quarreled," he said softly. There was something tentative in his voice, and his face was strangely vulnerable.

Gwenlliant flushed, staring down at her folded hands. Her palms were damp and she felt sick inside, and her voice sounded brittle and spiteful though she never meant it to. "*Did* we quarrel, Cousin? I didn't notice."

He crossed the room slowly, sat down on the edge of her bed, and put out a hand to touch her face. When she flinched, he drew back again. "I have an idea that we did. You had nothing to say to me during supper tonight."

Gwenlliant sat quietly, neither agreeing nor denying. After a long silence, she glanced up curiously. "What would you do, if you meant to punish me?"

He released a long sigh. "So it *was* that, as I suspected. Mother of God, Gwenlliant! What do you suppose I would do?"

She thought a little longer, her fingers twisting the silky white fur covering her bed. "You couldn't send me down to work in the stables or in the kitchen, as you might with Cei or Elffin. And I don't *think* that you would beat me, unless I had done something particularly wicked."

"I don't expect I would beat you, whatever you had done. I suppose the only thing that I *could* do would be to put guards outside and confine you to your chambers." He made a hopeless gesture. "But I don't wish to make you a prisoner, Gwenlliant. Wouldn't it be better if you just behaved yourself, without any threats or punishment?"

I already feel like a prisoner, most of the time, thought Gwenlliant. She did not say it aloud, because that would be cruel.

Yet he seemed to know what she was thinking anyway. He smiled so sadly it was painful to see him, rose slowly to his feet, and walked out of the room without another word.

Things were *not* well with Clynnoc. And as Tryffin and his men rode through Efrei's lands, he doubted he would find conditions any better in neighboring Eildonn.

It was a poor region to begin with, existing as it did in that nebulous zone between the comparatively populous coastal provinces and the grim north-eastern barrens. This was that part of Mochdreff where every year a few more acres of land lost fertility to the spreading sickness that was sucking the life out of the entire dominion. Farms and villages were small and scattered; what people there were in Clynnoc had a lean, hollow-eyed look. Moreover, early winter was not a kindly season anywhere in Mochdreff.

Yet Tryffin, quite as much as his older brother, had been raised to lead and to rule men. He knew the difference between a land where *conditions* were bad and a land that was poorly governed. Everything and everyone in Clynnoc had a weary, disheartened air. And when the Governor and his troop rode into a village, all the ragged children who were out playing on the snowy village green ran for cover, as if terrified by the sight of a company of armed men.

But when they came to Caer Clynnoc, Efrei's fortress, things had a different aspect. Banners were flying from every tower, a new curtain wall had been recently erected, and the guards who minded the gate were spruce and jaunty looking.

Meligraunce demanded entry in the Governor's name and in the King's, the usual formalities were conducted, then the portcullis rose, and Tryffin and his men rode into the castle. They dismounted by the stable.

Tryffin glanced around him. A groom came out of the stable leading a pair of horses: The beasts were sleek and pampered. The buildings in the courtyard showed evidence of recent whitewashing and thatching, and delicious smells were issuing from a series of kitchens and bakehouses. All these things should have been welcome signs of prosperity—but not in connection with the widespread poverty he had seen outside the walls.

As for the Captain of Efrei's household troop, striding across the courtyard to meet the group by the stables, he was a dark little man with a springy gait and a definite look of someone: Add two jagged scars and an aggressive nose, and he would be the image of Urien Glyn. If the two men were not brothers, thought Tryffin, he for one would be amazed.

"Lord Prince. I beg your pardon, but you were not expected. Perhaps the messenger you sent ahead . . . ?"

"The roads are difficult this time of year," Tryffin replied evasively. There had been no messenger, because he wished to arrive unannounced. "But if you will kindly escort me to find Lord Efrei—"

"My apologies, Your Grace, but the Lord of Clynnoc and his brother went out riding this morning and have not yet returned. Yet we expect them at any time. Perhaps you would wish to see the Lady Essylt . . . ?" The Captain left the question hanging in the air.

"The Lady Essylt," the Governor said, under his breath. Then his manner became genial and expansive. "Already recovered from her lying in, has she? I am pleased to learn that she feels so well she is making visits."

"Lord, she gave birth to a son five weeks past, right here at Caer Clynnoc," replied the Captain. "There is wasting sickness in Eildonn, and Lord Rhys thought it best to remove her from all danger of infection."

Tryffin removed his crimson leather gauntlets. "Very well, Captain—" He paused with a look of polite inquiry. "I don't believe that I know your name."

The wiry little man bobbed his head respectfully. "Llefelys Glyn, if it please Your Grace."

"Very well then, Captain Llefelys," said the Governor. The fellow had such an obliging manner about him, Tryffin felt a vague regret for killing his brother. "You may take me to the Lady Essylt."

With Meligraunce ahead of him, two guards to either side, and Conn and Mahaffy following behind him, Tryffin followed Llefelys Glyn into the Keep, up two flights of stairs, and into a large firelit chamber. There they discovered the beautiful Lady Essylt, softly playing on a harp of gold. On the floor at her feet sprawled Efrei's two motherless sons, boys of eight or nine by the look of them, playing with a set of dice. In a cradle by the fireplace an infant was sleeping, wrapped up in a rabbitskin blanket.

It was a scene of charming domesticity, but Tryffin did not allow himself to be moved by it—just as he did not permit himself to stride across the room and take a closer look at the baby, lest concern for the infant's welfare affect his dealings with the parents.

The lady put down her harp, swept the heavy golden tresses away from her face, and came to meet him. She sank down in a deep curtsy.

"You are very welcome, Prince Tryffin, though unexpected," she said, in her rich pleasant voice. But the fact was, her face was white and terrified, her dark eyes wide, and her breast heaving with some deep emotion.

116

Tryffin replied as was proper, took the seat she offered him, and watched her leave the room—in search of servants, she said, to prepare rooms for the Governor—though not without an apprehensive glance over her shoulder, at the infant sleeping in the cradle by the fire.

The Governor glanced moodily around him. Bright woven tapestries adorned the walls, equally fine carpets were scattered on the wooden floor; jewels glinted red, blue, and green, on the Lady Essylt's abandoned harp. Besides the fire on the broad stone hearth, the room was lit by dozens of wax candles in gold and silver holders. And the two boys, Efrei's small sons, looked like miniature courtiers, so exquisitely were they dressed.

"Ah God, it's a sad thing to see these people living in such wanton luxury," Tryffin said, under his breath,

Mahaffy gave a visible start. "Do these things strike you as luxurious, Lord Prince? I always thought that your father—"

"The Lord of Gwyngelli lives more splendidly than all the Emperors of Christendom, but his people are not *starving*. If men died for want of food in Tir Gwyngelli, you may be sure that my father would be hungry along with them, giving up his own bread to feed the widows and the orphans."

He realized Mahaffy was looking back at him with patent incredulity. "You may wonder that I can be so certain of this, when neither my father nor his fathers before him have ever been put to the test. But isn't that proof enough? It is the love of the Lord for his subjects, his subjects' love for him, that keeps the land fertile and the people prosperous."

He might have said more—that the time had been when Efrei fab Ogryfran was a plain man of simple and becoming habits—but just then there was a commotion in the passage outside. The Lords of Clynnoc and Eildonn came hastily into the room, both looking flustered, both obviously apprehensive. If Gwenlliant were here, thought Tryffin, she would smell their fear. He could practically smell it himself.

Efrei went immediately down on his knees at Tryffin's feet, seized the Governor's hand, and kissed it passionately. And that was out of character, too, for a man who had never been a sycophant or courtier. "Prince Tryffin, we are honored . . . we are overwhelmed. But what brings Your Grace into Clynnoc?"

Tryffin waited a long moment before replying, let the silence stretch out almost to the breaking point. Then he gifted the man with his sweetest and sunniest smile. "Why, what *should* bring me here, Efrei, but your nephew's christening?"

117

And Myfanwy, the daughter of Rhiwallon, went riding one day. As she proceeded along the road, she met a poor woman walking with a newborn infant in her arms. The woman's feet were dusty, and her face was lined with many cares, and as she walked she keened softly to herself, so that the Lord's daughter took pity on her and asked what ailed her.

"I was not always as you see me now," said the woman. "Less than a year ago I was as fair and as sleek as you, and many men sought after my favor. But I gave myself to Lord Rhiwallon, who soon grew tired of me and cast me out. And this child I hold is his son that he will not acknowledge. You can see quite plainly by looking at him that my boy has a lordly brow and greatly resembles his father, but for all that, he will live and die like a beggar, scraping his bread from the dust of the earth in spite of his noble blood."

"Shame on me," said Myfanwy, "if I allow this child, my half-brother, to starve. Give him to me and I will take him to my father and pretend that the boy is my own. For though the child will then be raised as a bastard, yet there will be no denying he is of Lord Rhiwallon's own clan and lineage, and in that way the boy will gain all that is due to him."

So Myfanwy took the infant, and wrapped him in a mantle of gold, and brought him to the place where Rhiwallon was staying, and presented the child to her father when he sat eating and drinking with his men. Rhiwallon blushed a fiery red, because the lady had approached him in the presence of his warband. Also, though he had not seen his daughter in many months, he could not help but wonder how she had gotten this baby, for she had never seemed to favor any of the men that she knew.

He said to Myfanwy, "Woman, I will swear a Destiny on this child. If there is anything of me in your son, he will have this peculiarity: He will run with the stags and he will run with the hounds, and no man will be able to match him, whether on horseback or on foot. So swiftly and lightly will he travel that never a blade of grass nor a slender reed will bend beneath his feet.

"If there is one drop of my blood in his veins, your son will have

118

*another peculiarity. He will never want for meat or for drink, yet
he will never be satisfied. His horses, and his weapons, and his
houses, and his servants will all be extraordinary, yet he will not
care for a single one of them.*

*"Woman, if this child was born of my clan or my lineage, he
will have a third peculiarity. When the battle rage is on him he will
be terrible: His voice will be louder than thunder, his gaze more
deadly than serpents, his touch more fiery than an iron sword
which has been heated in the forge, and he will revolve like a
whirlwind inside his skin. When the battle fury is on him, he will
not hold his hand neither for love nor for charity before he takes
a life."*

*And Myfanwy bowed her head to hear the Lord speak so
harshly, and she went from the place where Rhiwallon was staying
and lived in a house nearby. But as the boy, Rhongomynyad, grew
older he displayed all these peculiarities, and in that way soon
came to be a favorite of Lord Rhiwallon.*

— *From* The Black Book of Tregalen

11.

The Governor's Dignity

After the evening meal, the Lord of Clynnoc personally
escorted the Governor to the rooms allotted him, rooms so
spacious and so well furnished, Tryffin realized they must be
Efrei's own quarters, hurriedly vacated.

"I regret the christening took place before you arrived," said
Efrei, as he led Tryffin into a luxurious bedchamber. As elsewhere
in the castle, there was an abundance of gold and silver, crystal,
fur, tapestry, and silk. The Lord of Clynnoc was bleeding his lands
and his people dry in order to provide himself and his sons with so
many fine things, that much was plain.

Lord Efrei made a motion in the direction of the door, and a
little red-headed girl, Gwenlliant's age or a little younger, came
into the bedchamber carrying a harp. The girl made a brief curtsy
and said in a clear sweet voice: "I shall play for the Governor, if
it should please him."

Tryffin eyed her with considerable approval. By the neat
simplicity of her dress, she might be the daughter of some lesser
clan chieftain; by the color of her skin and hair (too fair and
brilliant for any of the old families), she might well be some

by-blow of Efrei himself, or another nobleman. Yet she was the first fresh, innocent thing, not including the Lady Essylt's unfortunate newborn, that Tryffin had seen since he arrived in Clynnoc.

He removed his heavy black cloak and handed it over to Conn. "Yes, Sweetheart," he said, taking a chair. "It would please me very well to hear you play."

At Caer Ysgithr, the temperature dropped. The water in all the fishponds and fountains froze solid, and a light powdery snowfall continued for two nights and two days without stopping.

The animals felt it most, though provision was made for them: tubs of steaming mash brought to the kennels and the stables for the hounds and the horses, bonfires lit in the outer courtyard to keep the ducks and chickens, the sheep and goats, from freezing. The falling snow was not enough to put those fires out. But they did smolder and sputter and make great clouds of steam in the frosty air, so that it looked, from a distance, rather as though a party of gigantic washerwomen had descended on the livestock with their equally gigantic iron washpots, and were boiling the animals clean.

Or so it seemed to Gwenlliant, standing at one of the windows in her solar, watching the snowflakes fall, and the clouds of steam rise over the grey stone walls of the outer courtyard.

She smiled, delighted by the whimsical notion. It was unusual, these days, for her thoughts to be so quick or lucid; more often than not, her head ached and her mind whirled. The castle had become so *noisy:* all the ancient secrets clamoring to be heard, the heartaches, the hatreds, the unfulfilled desires . . . and the magic calling to her from the sealed rooms.

She looked over toward the fireplace, where her pages and handmaidens had gathered in chairs and on satin cushions, in order to stay as warm as possible. They all seemed cheerfully and productively occupied. Traeth and Grainne were working on a tapestry, Faelinn mending a silk gown, silver needles flashing in the light of the fire. Elffin was cleaning the shoes Gwenlliant had worn earlier that day, and Cei was down on the floor with Garth, helping to polish some bits of armor Tryffin had left behind.

Gwenlliant turned away from the window and moved to join the others by the hearth. She put a hand on Garth's shoulder. He looked up at once, with a bright inquiring glance, instantly eager to be of service. "Lady? Is there anything you need?"

More than a fortnight had passed since the mastiff had savaged him. Garth looked well: clear-eyed and vigorous, except for the way that he held his arm so stiffly, as though it might still pain him. Yet he had only recently recovered from the shock and the fever which had kept him confined to his bed after the attack. That was why Tryffin had loaned his squire to Gwenlliant, to be her equerry, until the boy should be well enough to assume the more strenuous duties, the exercises, and the discipline of a knight-in-training.

"Garth, would you like to go walking with me?"

"Yes, certainly," he said, putting aside the vambrace he was working on, rising immediately to his feet.

None of the others left their seats. Perhaps, thought Gwenlliant, they were beginning to realize how they all worried her, how they all plagued her with their constant attentions. Or perhaps, with Tryffin gone, the threat of instant reprisals should anything happen to her so conveniently removed, none of them felt any particular urge to look after her.

It was Garth who obligingly caught up the grey cloak and draped it around her, then helped her to fasten the clasp—leaning so close that she could feel his breath tickling her ear, smell the light scent of the soap that he used to wash with in the morning.

"Where shall we walk?" he asked, throwing his own scarlet cloak over his shoulders, then pinning it in place with a large silver brooch. He really was a nice-looking boy, with his broad shoulders, and his fine northern skin, and the wavy brown hair he wore long at the back like a page.

Gwenlliant liked the way he was always so polite and so scrupulous, so eager to do right, so painfully disappointed in himself when he did wrong. He put her in mind, sometimes, of her brother Garanwyn, who would be about the same age if he were still alive. Though there were other times, and this was one of them, when Gwenlliant was acutely aware that she and Garth were not related at all.

"I think I would like to walk in the orchard. The trees speak so softly, I find them restful." But she wondered why her heart was beating so hard, why she felt so weak in the knees.

"You've a fine imagination," said Garth, smiling indulgently. And even though she liked him so well, there was something a little superior in his manner—seventeen years old to her thirteen—which she did not like to hear.

But perhaps if I act a little older, he will realize I'm no longer a child. Perhaps something will happen to make *him see.* Gwenlliant lifted her hood to cover her hair, gave him a sidelong glance. There was really no telling what might happen in a weird old place like Caer Ysgithr.

121

• • •

Tryffin sat in the Hall at Caer Clynnoc, under the bright array of banners hanging from the beams, and he listened to the harp girl sing and play. Two days had passed since he first arrived at Efrei's fortress, two days in which he had seen and heard much to disturb him, yet he had learned nothing of real value.

He sighed and ran a hand over the intricate scrollwork carved into the arm of his chair. "Prince Tryffin?" said Mahaffy, as though the movement signaled some need that his squires could accommodate. The Governor shook his head.

On a stool at his feet, Conn sat raptly listening to the music, his gaze fastened on the little harpist. Tryffin had seen Conn and the girl sitting with their heads together the night before, talking for hours. Cianwy, that was her name, and curiously enough—with that fiery hair, several shades brighter than Rhys and Efrei's dull auburn, and that milky complexion—she appeared to be closely related to the assassin Urien Glyn.

"She is not any man's bastard," Conn had related, a bit defensively. *"That was her mother, who was a cousin of Lord Efrei. She is the legitimate daughter of a clan chieftain, and Captain Llefelys is her uncle."* It appeared that Conn and Cianwy were already exchanging confidences.

Tryffin did not know if Conn was still a virgin, but suspected that he was; the straitlaced Gorwynnach usually were at that age. He also suspected the lad was sufficiently enamored to consider altering his virgin state.

So now, when the girl finished her song, made her curtsy, and left the room (Conn's eyes following her every movement), the Governor felt obliged to warn him. "I can see that she is a taking little creature. But don't do anything foolish, even if she should be willing. The girl can't be more than twelve, if so old as that, and you're certain to feel like a brute afterward."

Conn and Mahaffy both turned to stare at him, then immediately looked away. Tryffin smiled ruefully, realizing what he had just said.

Yet both boys must know the truth about him and Gwenlliant. How could they not know, living as close as they did? Chances were, everyone at Caer Ysgithr knew the Governor had been living like a monk, like some pious canting northerner, for the last six months.

Tryffin stared down at his hands. What alternative had he, so long as Gwenlliant continued to repulse him? He had never liked to make use of servant girls, who had no choice but to do what he asked, lending any liaison an unpleasant air of coercion. And he

122

refused to keep a mistress down in the town, where Gwenlliant might hear of it. A pity there was no suitable female here in Clynnoc, but he was not about to touch Conn's girl or seduce another man's wife.

But thinking of the Lady Essylt, he began to wonder: Where had that lady and her precious husband gone to? He had seen neither of them for hours, nor anything of Efrei fab Ogryfran, now that he thought of it.

Tryffin stood up and walked over to a narrow window set into a nook in the wall. Gazing down at the enclosed courtyards below, he spotted Efrei and Rhys over by the stables, apparently engaged in a furious argument. Both men gestured wildly, and Rhys kept shaking his head.

"Prince Tryffin," said a low voice behind him. And turning around to see who spoke, the Governor saw that Mahaffy had followed him into the alcove. "Your Grace . . . might I speak with you privately?"

Tryffin glanced around him; there was no one close to overhear what either of them said, so long as they kept their voices low. "This is private enough—and not so likely to attract attention as a retreat to my chambers certainly would."

The boy made a restless movement. "This is something, perhaps, that I ought to have said before. But I didn't know we were *coming* to Clynnoc, until we actually arrived. You said nothing, and before we left Trewynyn, Meligraunce told everyone we were heading south."

Tryffin nodded. "Aye, those were his orders. But it was never a matter of not trusting you or Conn, if that is what you are thinking. Before God, I never doubted either of you for a single moment."

Mahaffy shrugged. "There is no reason why I *should* stand high in the Governor's confidence. And regardless of that, I should have told you, just as soon as we came here, everything that I knew."

Tryffin folded his arms, leaned up against the rough grey stones of the alcove. "Which was . . . ?"

The Mochdreffi youth hesitated. "Perhaps you already know that I was there when Lord Morcant was murdered? Only he didn't die as soon as the arrow pierced his heart, the way some people say. He died in my arms and he was several minutes doing it."

Mahaffy's eyes went dark with remembered pain. "I was never particularly attached to him; no one could be, he was so damnably cold and meticulous. But I respected him and admired him and—and it was ghastly kneeling there on the battlements, with

Lord Morcant's head on my shoulder while he gasped out his last. And there was noting I could—nothing anyone could . . . I don't believe that I was *entirely* in my right mind, you see."

"No shame to you if you were not," said Tryffin. "And so?"

"And so, there were a great many men who came running, because the guards on the walls started shouting that Lord Morcant had been assassinated." Mahaffy ran a hand through his wild dark curls. "And the lords of Clynnoc and Eildonn were there with the rest, all of them exclaiming what a terrible thing it was and speculating who was to blame. And I *think* I remember that Rhys fab Ogryfran said: *What a cowardly deed, to lie in wait and strike from a place of concealment.*"

Tryffin shook his head, not yet understanding what Mahaffy meant him to make of that.

"But how could he *know* that? No one saw the arrow while it was still in flight, no one but me and one of the guards—and neither of us said anything up until then. So for all the others knew, the archer stood in plain sight on the roof of one of the houses down below, and fired from there. Why should anyone think otherwise? I still don't understand how he managed to shoot from a window, a long shot at a bad angle, unless—unless some sort of sorcery was involved."

"Now that you mention it," said Tryffin, "I remember wondering that myself. But why didn't you ever tell anyone about Rhys before?"

Mahaffy made that restless gesture again. "Because I've never been quite certain that I heard him say those words. And because—because I was just a boy, while Rhys was a man that other men respected. And I didn't want anyone to call me a liar." He smiled ruefully. "My Guillyn pride again."

"Aye," said Tryffin, with a sigh. "Well it happens that I do believe you; so you can rest easy about that. But in the name of God: If you learn anything else that might incriminate Rhys or his brother, don't hesitate to tell me at once."

Meals in the Hall at Caer Clynnoc, at least since Tryffin had first arrived there, were generally forced and uncomfortable affairs. The Governor sat at the High Table between a faded lady with nothing to say and the fair Essylt, whose uneasy efforts to offer amusement were painful to see and hear.

And the strange thing was, the way that Rhys and his wife and his brother acted so guilty *almost* argued for their combined innocence. Because how could people so obviously ill-suited to play at conspiracy be involved in a plot so monstrous and wicked as Tryffin suspected? Every now and again, he found himself wondering if they might not be hiding something entirely different, some minor transgression that need not concern him . . . and it was only because they felt so wretchedly guilty, they imagined he had come to uncover their secret.

But then he would catch a glimpse of Captain Llefelys standing guard by the door, wearing a face so like the man who had tried to murder him at the inn in Perfudd. Or of Mahaffy, kneeling to present him a dish of eels floating in a sauce colored with saffron—that boy who was so proud and so transparent in all his emotions that he was virtually incapable of deceit. And then nothing made any sense unless Efrei and his brother were plotting treason.

"You are recently wed, Prince Tryffin," said the Lady Essylt, as the meal wore on that second day. "I wish you would tell me about your bride. A sweet child, so they tell me, and a cousin of yours, is she not?"

"Yes," said Tryffin, staring down at the bones on his plate. "We are related on both sides of the family, being second and third cousins at once."

Meanwhile, young Cianwy was serving the wine, moving about from table to table with a silver flagon, sometimes pouring, sometimes (in the case of Efrei, who grew impatient) handing it over to be poured. This duty brought her often into proximity with Conn, and the two were so intensely and burningly conscious each of the other, it was amusing to watch them . . . but also a little painful.

"Second and third cousins," said the Lady Essylt, nervously brushing her hair from her brow. "I did not know the Rhianeddi married so close in the family."

"You confuse them with the Gorwynnach, who are indeed very strict," Tryffin replied. He thought of his kinsman, Cuel mac Cadellin, who had fallen in love with a second cousin, overcome his scruples in order to marry her—and then spent the next seven years tormenting himself with a crippling sense of guilt.

"The Rhianeddi and the Gwyngellach marry their cousins quite freely, unless they should happen to be born or fostered under the same roof." Tryffin accepted the silver goblet that Mahaffy handed him, raised the cup to his lips. "That relationship we consider incestuous, although the Church—"

"Prince Tryffin, *don't* drink that wine. There is venom in the cup!" Conn spoke in such strangled tones that just for a moment Tryffin thought Conn had swallowed the poison himself—before he remembered the goblet had come from Mahaffy.

"It can't be," said Mahaffy, going white with shock.

Tryffin put the cup down on the richly embroidered linen tablecloth, regarding the goblet with a suspicious frown. And then gripped it again, just in time to counter a nervous movement from the Lady Essylt, which must certainly have toppled the cup and spilled out the contents, had his hand not been there to prevent an accident. Meligraunce, who had been standing with the other Captain in the arch by the door, took several steps in Tryffin's direction.

There was a long silence. Then Efrei rose clumsily to his feet. "It was the girl—she poured the wine. She was ever a sly one, and I was a fool to trust her in my house."

Now Cianwy went as white as Mahaffy. Gazing down at the empty flagon in her hands, she began to stammer. "My lord, I *never* . . . ! Lord Efrei, how can you—" She choked on the words and could go no further.

Over by the door, the dark-eyed Captain Llefelys spoke out in protest, declaring his niece's innocence. People at other tables began babbling and gesticulating. And up on the dais, poor Conn gripped the edge of the High Table, pleading in agonized tones: "Prince Tryffin, no! No, it was never her doing. How *could* it be, when she has no reason. Your Grace, I beg you, who have always been so fair and generous . . ."

Gazing at those two anguished young faces, Tryffin was suddenly furiously angry, so angry that the world went black for a moment. And even when his vision cleared, he felt sick and shaken.

He forced himself to speak steadily. "There is no reason to suppose that this child would attempt to poison me. Not unless Lord Efrei had commanded her to do so. And even then—"

Lord Rhys sprang up to support his brother. "There is no reason to suppose that the cup *is* poisoned, except for your squire's word. Your Grace, this may be nothing but mischief on the part of the boy."

Which would have left Tryffin wondering how he would test it—whether Rhys or Efrei should swallow the contents—except that Mahaffy conveniently provided all the proof that anyone needed, by collapsing to the floor in a fit of violent retching.

The two guards standing behind Tryffin's chair moved closer. Meligraunce went down on his knees beside Mahaffy and held his head, while the boy heaved out the contents of his stomach, then collapsed, shivering, in the Captain's arms.

"If this boy dies," said Tryffin, ignoring the pressure that was building behind his eyes, "I will cut out the heart of the man who poisoned him, and fry it for breakfast." And as he was a man who invariably spoke the truth, he meant what he said.

Nor did anyone doubt him. The Gwyngellach were slow to anger, as everyone knew, but if you wronged them, their revenge could be shatteringly complete.

It appeared however that Mahaffy was not going to die. He stopped vomiting and shaking, and a little of the color returned to his face. Tryffin pushed back his chair, walked around the table, down the steps from the dais, and knelt on the floor beside Meligraunce and the boy, just to make certain.

When he was satisfied that Mahaffy was not in any danger, he glanced up at Rhys. "I believe we may be certain that the cup was unwholesome."

Rhys opened his mouth, then suddenly discovered he had nothing to say. But Efrei made a swift angry movement, reaching past the faded lady, to sweep the goblet off the table, spattering the contents across the dais. "Then no one shall drink from it."

"Prince Tryffin," said the Lady Essylt, speaking very low. "You might ask your boy Conn how he knew the wine was poisoned, if it was not a plot between him and the girl."

That was an excellent question, and even in his anger, Tryffin was curious. "Conn? How *did* you know the wine was poisoned, when it was Mahaffy who tasted the cup?"

Conn, who had grasped Cianwy's hand some time previously, suddenly dropped it, apparently realizing that *he* was suspected, and so might implicate *her*. "I didn't know. I just remembered . . . it came back to me all at once. It was a dream I had at the old woman's house, when we were lost on the marshes."

"Ahhhh." Tryffin let out a long breath. "You are telling me that it was a vision sent to you by the witch, Dame Ceinwen?" He asked the question loudly, so that everyone might hear, and he would then be able to judge their reactions.

Rhys sat down again, very suddenly, as though the name were familiar to him, and his lady flinched.

"It was all the girl's doing—a wicked, spiteful little creature she always was," said Efrei. "We only permitted her to live in this house because her mother was a bastard cousin."

The pressure was in Tryffin's chest now, as well as behind his eyes. "I wonder if you realize, Lord Efrei, that the penalty for attempting to poison a Prince of the Blood is death. And if Cianwy is guilty, her youth will not save her."

The girl began to weep. Conn put an arm around her, cradling her head against his shoulder, stroking her fiery hair with his other hand. But Efrei spared hardly a glance for the child he was condemning. "She shall die by my own hand, if the Governor wills it."

And that was too much for Tryffin. Something vast and powerful uncoiled inside him. He knew what was happening now, he knew that someone was about to die violently and bloodily, and that it was going to happen very soon. The best he could hope for was to choose his victim—and attempt to carry the whole thing off in such a way that no one guessed the Governor fell victim to occasional bouts of madness.

"Mother of God," he heard himself saying. "What sort of man would seek to poison another and then place the blame on a child of his own blood, base-born though she may be?"

Efrei cringed. "Do you accuse me, Lord Prince? I protest my innocence. And surely, as it is you who accuse me—"

"As you say. Since I accuse you, I can hardly sit in judgment." One square hand moved toward the hilt of his sword. "That being so, and because I would settle this swiftly, we are forced to determine your guilt or innocence by trial of combat."

The Lady Essylt made a tiny sound of protest. "Prince Tryffin," said Efrei. "You are my guest. We can hardly engage in combat, here in this house. In truth, I have no desire to fight you at all."

"If you do not," said Tryffin, stepping out into the middle of the Hall, away from the tables and the other people, "you will be hanged in your own courtyard. To refuse a challenge to judicial combat is to admit your guilt, according to the law."

Efrei glanced desperately around him, as if seeking support. But he could see just as well as Tryffin could, that the number of his men and the Governor's was approximately equal, that none of his guards had made a move, and that Captain Llefelys, still standing in the doorway, was *not* running off to fetch reinforcements. It may have occurred to him, just about then, that accusing a child of the same clan and lineage as most of his men was a fatal error.

"Well," said the Lord of Clynnoc, still sweating profusely as he moved around the table. He held his hands out, so the Governor could see that he carried no weapon save the silver-hilted sword hanging harmless in the scabbard at his side. "I believe that I may invoke the right to name a champion in my place."

"You might," Tryffin said, less steadily than before, so great was the fury building inside of him, "were you not a man still in his prime, in good health, and a belted knight into the bargain. But as you are all those things, Efrei fab Ogryfran, you are going to have to fight or be hanged."

The Lord of Clynnoc turned away, as if he would appeal to his brother for support. But in the moment he had his back to Tryffin, he found the hilt of his sword, drew it out with a horizontal slash, and spun around in what he fondly hoped would prove to be a surprise attack.

But Tryffin had been expecting some such treachery, and threw himself aside in time, drawing his own sword as he did so, and grasping it with a two-handed grip.

Recovering, Efrei turned his wild stroke into a continued attack, by bringing his sword around and back over his head, to slash down from the left at the Governor's head. But Tryffin's blade was there to turn the blow aside, and the battle was met with a clash of steel.

The two men circled, taking each other's measure. Even through the red mist that obscured his vision, Tryffin could see that Efrei moved like a seasoned fighter, a man who made up in years of experience what little he might have lost in the way of youthful strength and speed. The Governor parried another blow. Taking advantage of that instant of proximity, Efrei kicked out, striking Tryffin in the shin with a booted foot and causing him to stagger back, momentarily off balance.

Another blow came slashing down, but Tryffin recovered in time to block, meeting Efrei's blade with such force that the Lord of Clynnoc was forced back instead. Now that he had the advantage, Tryffin pressed the attack with a series of swift, powerful blows, which his opponent was hardly able to parry.

Somewhere behind him, Tryffin heard someone call out a warning. He spun around and stepped aside, just in time to avoid a treasonous blow from Rhys, who had drawn his sword and entered the fray on his brother's behalf.

Rhys went skittering past, and ended up fighting the Governor at Efrei's side, rather than retaining the advantage he had hoped to gain by striking from behind. Enraged by this treachery, Tryffin gave himself entirely over to the battle madness.

Efrei swung and caught him on the arm just above the wrist, a more than glancing blow. Tryffin hardly felt it. Moving with incredible speed now, he recovered, struck a blow of his own, which the Lord of Clynnoc blocked—though in the process, Efrei's sword was knocked aside, allowing Tryffin between countering one stroke and another from Rhys to finish him off with a crushing blow to the head.

Taking advantage of that moment of recoil, Rhys lunged and somehow missed, recovering just in time to block an overhand cut. But the next time their swords clashed, Tryffin smashed the other blade out of his way, and the blow continued downward, slicing through Rhys's shoulder and lodging in his ribcage.

There seemed to be blood everywhere, and people were weeping or shouting on every side. Down on the floor, Mahaffy struggled in the Captain's arms, perhaps with some belated idea of coming to Tryffin's defense. Up on the dais, the Lady Essylt gave a despairing cry and covered her face with her hands.

But the Governor, suddenly back in control once more, simply pulled out his sword, stepped to one side . . . and allowed his opponent to topple at his feet.

When the time came that Rhongomynyad was old enough to take arms, he went to Lord Rhiwallon and asked for weapons. "For I believe," said the youth, "I came into this world to win fame and perform mighty deeds."

"Well," said Rhiwallon, "since it is you that ask, I will give you the weapons my father gave me when I was a boy, and we will see what you can accomplish with them."

So Rhongomynyad went into battle, and so great was his strength and so terrible his rage that all who challenged him fell before the fury of his onslaught, and the field of battle was red with blood. Nor could any man wound him, not with the edge of a weapon or the point, for he was invincible when the rage was on him.

But when the battle was over, Rhongomynyad's fury had not diminished, and he came home carrying the severed heads of his enemies, boasting loudly of his victories and brandishing his sword, so that all who saw were startled and afraid, his friends and his foes alike. And indeed, he slew a great many men along the way, just with the fire and the venom of his glance.

So they sent Lord Rhiwallon's swordsmith out to meet him, and they prepared, also, a great wooden vat filled with cold water. And when Rhongomynyad approached him, the smith took the young warrior between his two hands and he plunged the youth into the *water of the vat. So great was Rhongomynyad's fury that the water begun to boil, and the hoops and the staves of the vat burst apart with the heat.*

Then the Lord sent his bards and his magicians out to reason with him. But the young warrior would not listen. He cracked the heads of all the bards, with their harps and their crwths, and beat the magicians with their own wooden staves, and killed a great many of them.

Finally, when there was nothing else to be done, Lord Rhiwallon sent for Ailinn, who was betrothed to the youth. They put her naked in a bed of white linen with crimson hangings, and invited the hero to sleep with her.

As soon as Rhongomynyad touched his side to the smooth side of the woman, his fury abated, and he had no more desire to work any harm on the people of Rhiwallon.

—From The Black Book of Tregalen

12.

Debts Fairly Paid

"Fool that I was, I thought it was Efrei I ought to be watching for signs of treachery," said Meligraunce, as he bound up the wound on Tryffin's arm. "And after Rhys moved in . . ." The Captain shrugged. "I wasn't so certain you wanted me there to hinder your movements."

"You were wise," Tryffin replied wearily. He was sitting on the edge of the big bed in the vast bedchamber Efrei had given him. "If you had entered the fight, I might have killed you."

Meligraunce looked him over with considerable interest. "I thought as much. But will you tell me this, Lord, of your goodness: Does this sort of thing happen to you often?"

The Governor sighed. The worst was over, he felt exhausted and a little sick, but his nerves were all on edge, and the pressure inside him had not entirely subsided. "A cold fury comes on me now and again, and when it does I am capable of deeds of shocking violence. But if you are asking about the battle madness you just witnessed, this was the third time I was unable to stop it from overwhelming me, though it has threatened to do so from time to time."

The Captain tied a final knot in the linen bandage. "And how many men did you kill those other times?"

131

Tryffin shook his head. "The first time it happened I was just a lad. A wild boar came down into the little rocky valley where I was playing with some of my cousins and the other children from Castell Maelduin. We all ran, but the beast cornered two little girls. I don't remember what happened next, but they say I tore the brute to pieces with my bare hands. The second time, that wasn't a battle in the usual sense. My brother had fallen into quicksand, and I pulled him out."

"Ah," said Meligraunce. "Well, it was a fine thing to watch, and I am glad to have seen it. But it wasn't much like they describe it in all the old tales."

The Governor grimaced. "If you mean that my eyes didn't turn backward in my head or shoot flames, and that I didn't begin to revolve inside my skin, I am glad to hear it. Do you suppose that anyone else noticed I wasn't entirely myself?"

Meligraunce considered. "I think not. Of course they must all be marveling at your strength and your speed. There wasn't much left of poor Efrei's skull, the last I looked. But the only reason I recognized what was happening was because I had been watching for something of the sort. You told me once to never get too close to you in the midst of a fight, and I heard you repeat the same advice to Garth and Conn. It was the way you said it that started me wondering."

Tryffin ran a hand through his hair. "I don't remember very well—were Efrei's two sons there in the Hall when I killed their father?"

When Meligraunce did not answer, the Governor sighed. "They were, then. A great pity. I should have managed things better but for this wretched temper of mine!"

Meligraunce, who had been sitting on a stool by the bed, rose to his feet. He stood regarding his master with a thoughtful frown. "If you don't mind my saying so, there is a difference between a show of bad temper and righteous indignation. I have seen you display the one, but never the other."

The Governor shook his head. "I have a brutal temper, though I admit I take great pains to hide the fact."

Meligraunce smiled suddenly. "Aye, and you do very well, hiding that and other things—especially for a man who never utters a single false word."

Tryffin returned his smile ruefully. "You're a clever man, Meligraunce. I am ashamed I hadn't the sense to heed your words back at Caer Ysgithr. It seems that Rhys and Efrei *were* foolish enough to try and murder me, right here at Caer Clynnoc."

There was a scratching at the door, and Conn came into the

room. "My lord, she wishes to speak to you, the Lady Essylt. They say she is nearly hysterical, weeping and talking wildly. It seems she fears for the safety of the children."

Tryffin groaned softly. "I suppose I should speak to her before she has time to concoct any lies to explain her behavior." He rose with a weary sigh. "Take me to the woman, then. I would as soon get this over and done with."

It was necessary for him to go to her, since the lady had been confined to her own bedchamber, with guards outside the door and beneath her windows.

She was alone when Tryffin arrived. All of her servants and her women in waiting had abandoned her; whether out of fear of the Governor and his men, or because clan Glyn, to which most of them belonged, had withdrawn all fealty, it was not quite clear. But the men and women of that clan were not serfs and could shift their allegiance given sufficient cause.

As the hour was growing late, the lady had been preparing for bed, in her shift and a loose dressing gown of wine-colored brocade. Her fair hair was hanging free, a rippling mantle of gold falling past her waist. Her eyes were wet and she was pale and wild-looking—but also very beautiful, being the sort of woman who could weep for hours without spoiling her complexion. At the sight of Tryffin standing just inside her door, she threw herself down on her knees at his feet.

"Lord Prince, I beg of you, have mercy on me and my fatherless child," she whispered hoarsely. "I knew nothing—nothing of any plot to poison you."

Tryffin gazed down at her, and his stomach knotted up as though he were about to be physically ill. "Your son is not in any danger, Lady. As for you . . . since I killed both of your fellow conspirators, there is not much chance that either one will incriminate you."

Evidently, she did not believe him, failing to understand the nature of the Gwyngellach—who knew seventy-seven different ways to kill a man, but would never stoop to the torture of a woman and a mother. She just went on weeping and clinging to the skirts of his crimson velvet tunic.

Tryffin detached her, using his good hand. He walked further into the room and flung himself down into a seat. "I wish I knew, Lady, whether it was you who seduced Rhys and Efrei with your wicked ambition, or whether they corrupted you."

Lady Essylt rose slowly to her feet, fixed him with a pair of tear-drenched brown eyes. "I do not know what you mean, Prince

Tryffin. I do not know what . . . ambition . . . my lord and his brother hoped to fulfill by destroying you.''

Tryffin ground his teeth. ''Spare me that lie at least. I could smell your guilt along with your husband's the moment I arrived here. Tell me the truth if you can, and I may deal with you mercifully. Why did Efrei send men to kill me eight months past, and what part did Rhys play in Morcant's death?''

The lady appeared to consider. Then she swept across the room and knelt again at his feet. ''That I cannot tell you. If I knew all, I would reveal all—that I swear. But I knew only a little of my husband's plans.'' She took Tryffin's hand and kissed it. ''Rhys was not so wicked when I married him; he was a good man then. But he and Efrei both changed and they began to speak of things that—that frightened me at first, though in time I began to share a little of their ambition. What mother would not wish to see her son sit in the High Seat at Caer Ysgithr? And I felt some loyalty to my husband, after all. I could not betray his plans, no matter how reprehensible, not if I wished to keep my faith with him.''

These were arguments calculated to soften him, to appeal to that deep sense of family loyalty that was bred into his line, blood and bone. Yet even knowing that the calculation was there, he felt his anger and disgust begin to diminish a little—until he remembered something else, and the fury began to build in his chest, the mist to rise before his eyes. ''What kind of a woman would sacrifice one of her sons, even plot to have him murdered, to advance the interests of the other?''

Essylt looked up at him, her eyes wide with shock. ''But no, Lord Prince. I do not know what you can possibly mean. The son I gave to Rhys was to become Lord of Mochdreff in his own right and by the King's grace. Peredur was not to suffer at all. How should he?''

''Because the succession is likely to be settled long before your infant son is of an age to be considered,'' said Tryffin coldly. ''Someone must be Lord of Mochdreff in the interim, someone that Rhys and Efrei intended to remove when the time was right.''

The lady opened her eyes even wider. ''That was to be young Math. He was to be Lord of Mochdreff, allowed to rule for a time, then discredited or murdered. I am not certain which. Peredur was to be passed over entirely. He was ever the tool of his father's family; they have taught him to hate me, ever since I married Rhys fab Ogryfran.''

Essylt hung her head, and she spoke in a ragged whisper. ''They did not wish me to have sons that would stand in the way of an heir of their blood. They reviled me before my own son, and Peredur

134

believed their lies, said no word in my defense. I felt . . . not much compunction at robbing him of his rights, but I would never have been a party to any scheme that would take his life.''

Tryffin continued to study her face, uncertain whether to believe her or not. He was inclined to credit her story a little, to believe that she had been in some sense Rhys's dupe, simply because the alternative was practically unthinkable. ''Very well then,'' he said, between his teeth. ''Tell me something of this change you mentioned, this change in the Lord of Eildonn and his brother.''

She was still holding his hand, as if her very life depended on it. ''They went to Caer Ysgithr one time and stayed for many weeks. When they came back, Rhys said strange things: that he had gained a powerful friend, that he saw what a fool he had been not to understand his own destiny, which had a grandeur and an elegant simplicity he had never suspected before. And after that, neither Rhys nor Efrei seemed to care for his lands or his people, or for anything but living well and plotting, plotting. But neither one of them ever spoke the name of the friend who had put such ideas into their heads.''

The Governor was quiet for a time, attempting to weigh her words—but it was hard for him to think, with his heart still pumping so furiously, and the blood pounding in his head. And much to his self-disgust, the proximity of this beautiful, desperate woman was beginning to affect him.

The smell of her fear, the way that she clung to his hand, the little sounds of distress that she made, these things aroused him, made him long to feel her smooth skin against his skin, her sweet woman's body moving beneath him. He had been celibate far too long.

''What will become of me? What do you intend to do with me, now that I have told you all these things?'' she moaned, kissing his hand over and over, only now her kisses were passionate rather than pleading.

''What *should* become of you, Lady?'' he asked, forcing the words out. He was not entirely a fool; he guessed that she had summoned him here in the hope that she might seduce him, and so gain some hold over him, some claim that would force him to treat her less harshly than she deserved.

The thing that appalled him was his own realization that she was going to succeed.

He woke in the morning with the woman's hair in his eyes, and just for a moment he thought it was Gwenlliant. Then he remembered where he was and who he was with, and a bitter taste flooded his mouth.

One-handed, Tryffin disentangled himself from the net of her hair. He sat up, swung his legs over the side of the bed, and glanced back over his shoulder. Essylt was still asleep, lying on her side with her face hidden by one shapely white arm, and that golden hair her only covering. She was a woman to bring out the carnal instincts in any man, but this morning the sight of her sickened him.

"God help me," he said, under his breath. "I have betrayed my sweet innocent wife, and taken instead this bitch who devours her own young." He climbed out of bed and started searching for his clothes, which were scattered around the room.

Yet he thought as he dressed: *Not one moment of tenderness, not one instance of kindliness or affection the whole night long . . . just two animals rutting. I have given this woman nothing that belongs to Gwenlliant.*

It also occurred to him that he might be judging Essylt too harshly. It was possible she had been just as ignorant as she claimed, had gained only a glimpse of her husband's true intentions. He had no reason to suppose her a woman of any considerable intelligence. And what she said about Rhys and Efrei changing, about a powerful and mysterious friend—these things rang true, with all that he already suspected, with all that he knew of those men before, with their *obvious* ineptitude as conspirators.

Say that someone, some wizard or woman of power, had robbed those two of their moral sense. A comparatively simple task that might be, as easy as cutting off an arm or a leg. But to change the entire tone of a mind, to teach a man to think in a more devious fashion than he had ever done before, to bestow on him the cold hard logic that would allow him to succeed at such schemes: That would be rather more difficult, like making a new limb to grow in the place of one that was lost.

Once dressed, Tryffin left the room immediately. He found Meligraunce waiting for him in the corridor outside, leaning against the wall with his arms folded and a sardonic look on his face. "Before God! Don't tell me you have been standing there since last night, Captain?"

Meligraunce gave a characteristic shrug. "I thought it best to send the others away, in case there should be consequences afterward. No need for everyone to know that you spent the night."

"Consequences?" Tryffin was startled and more than a bit

136

appalled. "Ah God, I never thought about that. But if she conceived, I would hardly deny responsibility."

"That possibility had not occurred to me, Lord Prince. The lady is so recently a mother. No, I was thinking she might wish to cry rape. It sounded like rough work, most of the night."

Tryffin stared at him. "Mother of God. What do you take me for?"

"For a man who was badly over-wrought, bedding a woman who was equally distracted," said Meligraunce, unfolding his arms.

The Governor went back to his bedchamber, pausing along the way to speak to some of his men and send them to relieve the Captain at his post. He found Conn and Mahaffey waiting in his room.

"Your Grace," said Mahaffy, very pale, very stiff. "Your Grace, I was at fault; I was unpardonably careless. But I swear to you, I noticed nothing—nothing when I tasted the wine."

Tryffin waved him aside. "For the love of God, Mahaffy, how could you taste anything, under all that honey and orris root?"

The boy gnawed on his lower lip, clenched his fists tight. "Because," he said miserably, "assassins *always* choose the wine for that very reason. I was taster to Lord Morcant all those years, and twice I detected poison in the wine: once by the color, and once by the bitter taste."

The Governor sighed. "And this time the poison was something sweet and flowery, and much too swift to act. Unless I had been unusually thirsty, I don't see how I could possibly have swallowed a fatal dose before you showed signs of poisoning."

"I was at fault," Mahaffy insisted, determined to blame himself. And Tryffin had neither the energy nor the inclination to argue the point.

He lay down on his bed and stretched out, and Conn brought a rough grey fur to cover him. "How does your little Cianwy?" Tryffin asked, wishing he had thought to inquire before.

"She was well enough when I saw her but her uncle has taken her away," said Conn. "Her people have served the Lords of Clynnoc for—for hundreds of years, and then Lord Efrei betrayed their trust and their fealty . . . !" The boy's eyes filled with unshed tears. It came to Tryffin that he was not the only one who was badly over-wrought. Most likely they all were.

"And Lord . . . Lord, you were very good to take her part. What you did was splendid. But it was like your goodness, your wisdom and compassion. You have always been kinder to me than my own father."

137

Tryffin smiled faintly, wondering if he liked that comparison, coming from a lad scarcely five years younger than he was himself. "Aye, well, I feel old enough to be your father, just at this moment," he said, closing his eyes. "But see that my breakfast is waiting when I wake up again."

The next morning, as the Governor was preparing to leave Caer Clynnoc, the Lady Essylt was allowed to speak with him one last time.

She came into his room flanked by two guards. She had dressed in a gown of dull green silk and a dark cloak, her beautiful hair was braided and carelessly pinned in place, and her eyes had a bruised and weary look.

"Prince Tryffin, I wish to know what punishment you have decided for me, what will happen to my child and to Efrei's two sons."

Tryffin barely glanced at her, being much too absorbed in putting on his cloak, pulling on his gloves. "You will be escorted to a suitable place of retirement, a convent I know, where the nuns live in strict seclusion. There you will be treated in a manner befitting a woman of your rank—and if you do not wish to endure some closer confinement, Lady, you will not show your face beyond the walls of that convent while I remain Governor of Mochdreff."

"And the children?" she asked.

"I have persuaded Captain Llefelys and his brother the chieftain, whom I believe to be honest men, to look after things here and in Eildonn until I can find a suitable regent for Efrei's eldest boy. As for your infant—" He paused, suddenly reluctant to say the words which must certainly cause her great pain.

"As for your son, Lady, I do not find you a suitable guardian. I intend to make him my ward and raise him at Caer Ysgithr. I would not wish to see him made the pawn of unscrupulous men ever again."

She made a tiny sound in her throat. "And so I lose another child. It is a wicked world, a cruel world. But you . . . you will treat him kindly? For my sake, remembering the comfort we shared between us that terrible night?"

He looked at her then, and his face grew hard and still. "I cannot imagine what you suppose I owe you, Essylt. But I am not in the habit of mistreating children. I shall care for your son, and learn to love him if I may, not for your sake, but for his own."

Meligraunce and the rest of his troop were waiting with the

horses, down in the icy courtyard, when Tryffin and his guards arrived. Young Mahaffy was already mounted, still looking like he carried the weight of the sins of the world on his slender shoulders. Conn stood at Roch's head, holding the bridle.

But Tryffin walked to the end of the line, where a dark-haired girl sat on a sturdy grey pony. She was the wet nurse who had suckled Essylt's infant since he was born. The girl held the baby now, shielded from the cold by wrappings of fur and sheepskin, tightly and protectively in her arms.

The Governor had so far stood by his decision not to allow himself a close look at the child until his fate should be decided. But now he took the infant carefully on his good arm, and the nurse pulled back the hood covering the upper half of the baby's face.

Rhys's son had soft white skin and red hair, a shade brighter than his father's rusty auburn. His eyes were tightly closed against the light, and his tiny hands were clenched into fists.

"Now, here is a precious thing," Tryffin breathed. "And perhaps if he were mine . . . perhaps I, too, would wish to move Heaven and Earth on his behalf." He glanced up at the wet nurse. "What names did his parents give him?"

"He was christened Rhys for his father, and Efrei for his uncle," said the nurse.

The Governor shook his head. "I will not allow him to bear a traitor's name. He will be Grifflet, which is a name I had thought to give my own son."

Suddenly he smiled, cradling the infant against his chest. "A fine gift this will be for my lady wife . . . and entirely appropriate to the season."

The cold spell continued and December came in. At Caer Ysgithr, the Mochdreffi servants poured fragrant oils on all the fires to make the wood burn hotter. Gwenlliant gave up walking in the orchard or in the gardens because the air pierced like a knife. And even on days when the chill abated a little and she ventured as far as the chapel, the courtyards were bleak and deserted. The folk of Caer Ysgithr were holed up indoors, like badgers in a snowbank, trying to keep warm.

She grew weary of waiting for Tryffin to return. He never sent word when to expect him, so there was no use at all counting the days, which crept slowly past, with a dreary sameness. Even Faelinn, Grainne, and Traeth grew bored of sitting in the solar, chattering and sewing. And Cei and Elffin were so restless and sullen when it came time for Gwenlliant to teach them, she was ready to abandon the scheme—but Garth spoke to the boys and made them behave, and the lessons went a little better from that time onward.

Christmas was coming, but promised to be dull. It would be impossible even to deck the halls, evergreens being so scarce, and there would be no pageants, no processions, no feasts or other entertainments.

"Well, we *might* arrange a masque of our own, to amuse the Governor when he returns," Grainne suggested, one day when the young ladies were bemoaning their sorry plight.

At her words everyone felt a stirring of interest, until Faelinn pointed out a single flaw in the plan. "But there aren't nearly enough of us. Especially as someone must provide the music."

They all sat and thought for a moment.

"We might do *The Death of Goewin*," ventured Grainne, wrinkling her nose. "Not precisely suited to the season, but there are only the three main parts." Her face brightened. "The Lady can dance Goewin, which is entirely appropriate, since it is a story of her own family. And Garth can do the Selkie lad. Cei is just tall enough to play the cruel father if we make him a mask with a long beard, and Elffin can do the other parts—they are none of them very important."

"Yes, and we can come in for the Dance of the Seals, which we will make very pretty but also very brief," chimed in Traeth. "That will leave most of the dancing to the Lady and Garth, and *we* will be free to work on the costumes."

All three girls turned expectantly toward Gwenlliant. She sat staring at her hands folded in her lap, thinking that Goewin was hardly the story she would have chosen. The end was so tragic, with the lovers parted and Goewin dying in exile. Yet it really seemed such an excellent arrangement, in the end Gwenlliant agreed to take part.

After that, everyone was excited and happy. The older girls set to work designing and making up the costumes, choosing the music. Gwenlliant and Garth arranged the dances, trying out the steps, then practicing together for hours at a stretch. Gwenlliant became so thoroughly absorbed in this new pastime, she forgot to listen for the voice of the castle, or the clamor of the magic in the Princess Diaspad's abandoned rooms. And Elffin and Cei, eagerly embracing this new diversion, were soon very busy: running errands, down to the town and around the castle—for needles and thread, for harp strings, for horsehair for beards—and helping to paint the masks.

The young ladies began with Gwenlliant's gown, surely the

most important, and that took several days, even with Faelinn, Traeth, and Grainne all stitching enthusiastically away. They had decided on crimson velvet, low on the shoulders, the neck trimmed with white rabbit and tiny crystal beads, to be worn over a kirtle of gold brocade.

"And of course there must be a crown, as Goewin was a royal princess," said Grainne. Fortunately, Gwenlliant had her golden circlet, and the spangled veil she had worn at her wedding.

On the day they finally tried the completed costume on her, Faelinn gave a sigh of satisfaction. "How well it becomes you! Prince Tryffin will be perfectly enchanted."

Even Gwenlliant, catching a glimpse of her reflection in a bit of polished silver, thought she looked very nice. And when Garth came into the solar and saw her in the bloodred gown, with her hair down and her shoulders bare, he stared for a long moment, then abruptly turned and walked out of the room, looking like a young man who had just experienced a troubling revelation.

But the long days passed, and Tryffin and his troop did not return. It began to look as if Gwenlliant and her partners would dance their masque without anyone to watch them.

The Governor and his party were crossing a rocky heath, empty save for drifts of wind-driven snow, when the crone appeared out of nowhere, standing atop a slight rise in the land, her ragged gown and even more ragged cloak fluttering in the breeze.

She held a walking staff shod with iron in one clawlike hand, as though she had trudged far to reach that place, and the red vixen and the grey wolf, no longer cubs, were her only attendants. Tryffin rode out to meet her, taking Mahaffy with him, signaling the others to keep their distance.

"And so we meet again, son of Maelgwyn," she greeted him. She looked older than he remembered her: older than stones, older than wind, rain, stars, or snow, like the first living thing summoned out of the void. "In Mochdreff, where you never thought to return."

"And exactly where you thought to find me," he said, swinging down from the saddle. "But I believe that I stand in your debt, Lady Ceinwen—for more than shelter and water."

Mahaffy dismounted also, and embraced the old woman, who managed to hug him and kiss him and box his ears, all at the same time. "And no thanks to this fosterling of mine that you still live."

She fixed the Governor with a beady black eye. "I am an old woman, Prince Tryffin. All my lovers, all my friends and playfellows, have been dead for many years. Even this boy that I

141

raised from the day he was born has left my care. And I find that I am lonely. If you wish to reward me for saving your life, then give me the child that you took from the Lady Essylt.''

Tryffin felt a sinking sensation, a sense of dread inevitability. Yet he could not give up the infant so easily as that. "I cannot barter the life of a child, no matter how heavy a debt I owe you.''

"Well, and will he not be happy and well cared for—and a good deal safer than you could keep him at Caer Ysgithr? He has a destiny, this Grifflet, but not as Lord of Mochdreff.'' This close, the crone smelled musty, like earth and old leaves.

She nodded in Mahaffy's direction. "Ask this boy, if you doubt my ability to raise this child and provide for all his requirements.''

Tryffin shook his head. "There is no need for that. It is easy to see that you would make an admirable nursemaid. But I—I have a fondness for children, and this one I am already learning to love.''

"The more reason why you should give him to me,'' said the witch. The breeze ruffled her white hair; the fox and the wolf sat at her feet, panting softly. "For the Governor of Mochdreff, the High King's kinsman, must not seem to favor one heir over the others.''

Tryffin felt his throat tighten. He knew what she said was true, but he had set his heart on taking the baby to Gwenlliant, on raising the boy as his own.

"Lord Prince . . . perhaps it is not for me to say,'' said Mahaffy, very low. "But if Ceinwen says the child will be safer and happier in her care, then you ought to believe her.''

The Governor passed a hand over his eyes. "Before God, do you suppose I don't know that perfectly well?'' His voice came out harsh, like the voice of a stranger. He took a deep breath. "Go fetch the wet nurse, then, and tell her to bring the child.''

He stood without speaking, his dark cloak blowing in the wind, while Mahaffy went down and came back leading the grey pony. Then he took the baby out of the nurse's arms and pressed a kiss on the infant's brow.

"It is a cruel world,'' he said, unconsciously echoing Essylt's words, "that would take this child from those who would love him.''

"It is a cruel world,'' agreed old Ceinwen, handing her iron-shod staff to the young nurse, stretching out her arms to receive Grifflet. "Yet there is also kindness to be found, and honor, and debts fairly paid.''

"So I have always tried to believe,'' he said, as he put the child into her arms. "But now . . .''

The wind was rising, was beginning to keen and wail across the rocky heath. Tryffin had to raise his voice in order to be heard. "I married my cousin Gwenlliant, as you no doubt intended that I should, and she is still very young. It may be many years before she gives me any sons of my own."

The old woman kissed the infant and cradled him snugly in her arms. "You will have sons, Prince Tryffin, and beautiful little daughters as well. And because you have done the right thing today, I can give you these words of comfort: The time may come when Grifflet will return to you."

"May that day come soon, then," said Tryffin, swinging back up into the saddle. He headed down the hill, to the place where his men were waiting, and Mahaffy followed after him.

But when he looked back again, hoping for a last glimpse of the infant . . . the two women, the pony, the tame beasts, and young Grifflet were already gone. There was nothing there on the hill where they had been but rocks and wind-driven snow.

Corfil was dead. He had collapsed at dinner, just as he sat down to eat, and all efforts to revive him had failed. Diaspad shuddered at the thought of her narrow escape—had Corfil taken so much as a bite of food, a sip of wine, there would have been talk of poisoning, and the suspicion must surely have fallen on her. But now she had slain him and no one the wiser, and the years of misery and torment were ended, all in a single night.

She stood before the mirror in her bedchamber, her auburn hair hanging down in a ragged tangle, her eyes clouded and weary. The dwarf women crowded around her, eager to offer comfort, but she wanted no part of them . . . none but Brangwengwen. "Send them away," Diaspad said hoarsely, and Brangwengwen ushered the others out.

When they were alone together, the Princess looked down at the dwarf, and her hard green eyes grew momentarily soft with tears. "I owe my freedom to you, dear Brangwengwen. Had you not led me to the woman who knew the spell . . . But now my son will be Lord of Mochdreff, and I will rule in his name. I will never forget what I owe you, my best and dearest friend."

"It is late," said the dwarf, "and you are ill and weary. It is time that you went to your bed." Brangwengwen brought a stool and stood on it; began unlacing the back of her lady's gown.

The silk slid from Diaspad's shoulders, past her hips, and down to the floor, and it was followed a moment later by her linen shift. The dwarf made a tiny strangled sound.

Wondering what had startled her, Diaspad came out of her abstraction. As her eyes focused on the image in the mirror, she gasped and put a hand to her throat. Then she began to scream.

Her hoarse cries of distress brought her other attendants boiling into the room. The dwarf women began to weep and to wail, sweeping up her garments off of the floor, ineffectually attempting to cover her. Only Brangwengwen had the presence of mind to jump down from her stool, scurry across the room, and lock and bar the door.

"Lady, Lady," said the dwarfs, "we beg you to be silent, lest others come and see you in this state."

But Brangwengwen approached her, head held high, and spoke to Diaspad with a note of triumph in her voice. "Do not be distressed, Lady. For this thing which seems to be a tragedy to you, only brings you that much closer to us. And we shall love you and serve you, and hide your secret from the eyes of the world, so long as you live."

13.

A House of Strange Sorceries

With the costumes nearly completed and the dance steps all worked out, it was time to search the Bower for appropriate props and scenery. This task had been assigned to Elffin and Cei, but Gwenlliant insisted on joining most of their forays and Garth came, because: "The floors may be rotten or the stones loose in rooms where nobody goes anymore—someone should be there to watch over the Lady."

But the way that it happened, the boys grew so absorbed in the task, rummaging through dusty storerooms and wardrobes on all three floors, turning up all manner of interesting and curious items which had belonged to previous inhabitants of the square tower, they quickly forgot to keep an eye on Gwenlliant. Soon, she was digging through chests and cabinets with the rest, exclaiming at each new discovery, or running from one room to the next, searching for some particular item.

One day, when they were turning the top floor upside down in an effort to find a length of fabric of suitable magnificence to drape Cei's throne, Gwenlliant suddenly remembered that she had seen some purple velvet bedcurtains, worked in gold and silver, bundled up in one of the storerooms on the ground floor. Taking a candle with her, she went off alone to fetch the velvet. She took the dark back stairs, because that was the quickest way to go, and she was several steps past the first landing when her candle went out.

Gwenlliant stopped with her hand on a newel post, one foot in the air, unwilling to take the next step down. There was something vaguely horrible about descending in the dark, and she had a sudden mental image of the mermaid brackets in the corridor below, coming down from the wall and slithering about on the floor. She could almost hear the rattling of their bronze scales as they scraped against the flagstones.

She decided to go all the way back to the upper corridor and relight her candle on one of the torches, so she turned and started to climb. But the steps went up and up and up. Even moving slowly and cautiously in the dark, it hardly seemed possible it could take so long to reach the landing.

My mind is playing tricks on me. I never went as far as the landing to begin with, and I am just climbing up to the top floor. And sure enough, just ahead and to her right there was a dim smoky light like that of the torches in the upper corridor.

Only when she turned the corner, she found herself in an unfamiliar passageway, this one lit by smoldering rushlights in wrought-iron holders. The ceiling was low, the air was musty and stale, and the floorboards creaked under her feet. Except for the sounds of her own movement, the corridor was oddly quiet, the walls strangely silent. Gwenlliant knew at once that she was no longer in Melusine's Bower, nor in any part of the castle she had visited before.

It must have been another of the mysterious pattern-spells, one that Cei and Elffin had neglected to show her—right there in the square tower where Gwenlliant lived, and no one had ever said anything about it.

Which means that perhaps nobody knows, *and I may use the spell to come and to go exactly as I please.*

She tried to remember what she had done to work the magic.

Along the upper corridor, down one flight of stairs to the landing; five, or six, or maybe seven steps down from there; and then she had turned and started up again. It would be easy enough to figure out the proper number of steps once she got back to the tower again.

Right now, of course, the problem was *getting* back, preferably by such means that no one guessed she had been away. Gwenlliant had learned there was generally a way to make the magic return you to the place you had started from. The spells did not work backward; it was impossible to go back by simply turning around and walking the same way you had come. But there was usually something, a door or an archway not very distant, which served as the final part of the spell, and whisked you back to the place you had started—providing you made use of the door or archway before returning in the usual way.

Just at the moment, there were a great many doors Gwenlliant might choose from, lining the corridor on both sides. She could only hope that the one she wanted was not locked, because then she would never be able to find out which one it was.

Trading her candle for one of the rushlights, she walked up to the nearest door and pushed it open. The hinges creaked loudly, but the door opened smoothly. Though it had been quiet in the corridor, the moment Gwenlliant crossed the threshold the walls spoke out with a great clamor of voices . . . which gradually subsided to a low murmur.

She stood in a minstrels gallery, a small semi-circular balcony overlooking a private dining hall. She moved closer to the carved and gilded railing to get a better look at the floor below. There was a little colored light coming in through a row of jewel-like stained-glass windows along one wall, but much of the hall lay in deep shadow, shadow with such a weight of time and neglect behind it that Gwenlliant's torch did little to penetrate the gloom. Yet even so, it was easy to see this was a truly gorgeous room: The ceiling had been plastered over and painted with flowering vines and figures of fantastical beasts, all working in bright colors and gold leaf, like a page from Gwenlliant's illuminated bestiary or the painted chapel at Caer Cadwy. There was tapestries on one wall, and a great marble fireplace opposite, and running down the center of the room was a long table with magnificently carved chairs arranged on both sides. Everything, without exception, was made of the richest and most expensive materials, crafted with the most exquisite workmanship.

And then she knew where she was: behind the iron gates, in the forbidden wing of the Keep, standing in one of the Princess

Diaspad's abandoned rooms. But where was the magic she had heard calling to her from the other side of the iron gate? And how—if she did not find the final figure of the spell which had brought her here—was she going to get out again?

Gwenlliant looked down at the gallery railing, then moved instinctively away, for there was something troubling about the carvings. When she lifted her torch to get a better look at the figures painted on the ceiling, she again felt that same repulsion. Every man, every woman, every beast, bore an uncomfortable resemblance to the monster growing in a glass vessel in Lord Cado's laboratory. Each and every one looked as if it had been captured in wood or in paint in the midst of terrible suffering.

"And I cannot imagine," Gwenlliant said aloud, "why the Princess chose to surround herself with such misery and ugliness."

"Because she was so miserably unhappy herself," said a cracked old voice. And turning, Gwenlliant saw a tiny hump-backed figure in an elaborate gown and headdress, painfully climbing the narrow steps from the floor below.

"Brangwengwen," breathed Gwenlliant. It had been one of the Princess's affectations to dress the dwarf in exact duplicates of her own fantastic gowns and hennins, except that the materials were always shoddier, and the jewels made of pinchbeck and paste. Gwenlliant recognized the gown that Brangwengwen wore now, for all it had become so ragged and dingy.

Heaving herself up the last steps and achieving the balcony, the dwarf made a deep curtsy. "The Lady Gwenlliant is kind to remember me, after so many years have passed."

"It is not quite three years," the girl reminded her.

"Three years, so little as that? But the time goes slowly when one is old and lives all alone," said the dwarf. "And now *you* are the foreign princess living at Caer Ysgithr, just like my lady who was. But more fortunate than she: for you married the big blond boy who was always so kind—yes, always so courteous—even to the wretched servants of his enemy."

Gwenlliant did *not* like being compared to the Princess Diaspad, but when the dwarf spoke well of Tryffin, she relaxed just a little. After all, it was true, neither she nor the Governor had ever done anything to offend this woman, and unless the dwarf had been genuinely attached to the Princess and Calchas (which hardly seemed likely, considering how cruel and how wicked they both had been), she could have no reason to carry a grudge.

In any case, Gwenlliant needed someone to show her the way back to her own quarters. "I came here by means of the spell in the square tower. Perhaps you can tell me how to return again. If I stay away too long, my attendants will miss me.''

The dwarf laughed harshly and shook her head. ''No, Lady, that they will not. It is a powerful figure written under the staircase in Melusine's Bower. That pattern twists time, like the maze in the Bearded Wood, like the Breathing Mist. You may stay here for hours if it pleases you, and when you return, if you use the right door, you will find that only minutes have passed since you left your own rooms.''

Gwenlliant regarded the dwarf with a thoughtful frown. That was certainly something useful to know; it would make coming and going that much easier. Yet what if she should fall into difficulties and nobody even missed her, until it was far too late to come to her assistance? ''Even so, I think I should go back again. Will you show me the way?''

''In good time,'' said the dwarf. ''But first there are many strange and marvelous things here, things that no one has seen for many years now. Let me show you one or two of them, and then I will lead you to the door that you want.''

Gwenlliant sighed. And yet . . . she was just a bit curious. In truth there was really no telling how long she might wander through these rooms without finding the proper door. It would be so much easier, she decided, just to go with Brangwengwen and see what she had to show.

The girl followed the dwarf out of the dining hall and down the corridor. The brackets containing the rushlights, she realized, were all set low on the wall.

''This was done so that the dwarfs might light the torches,'' Brangwengwen explained when Gwenlliant questioned her. ''The Princess would only have small misshapen creatures like myself to serve her. And the giant could not come into this wing at all because the ceilings in the passages are all so low, while the woodwoses, of course, were only for show.''

Brangwengwen opened a set of double doors and ushered Gwenlliant into a vast bedchamber. The big bed had been stripped of its curtains and all its bedding, giving it a skeletal look, but someone had set up a tiny pallet in one corner of the room, and that showed evidence of recent use.

There was a great deal of heavy carven furniture besides, and several leopard-skin rugs on the floor—but the strangest thing in the entire room was a great mirror of polished bronze covering most of one wall. Gwenlliant walked closer to inspect the mirror. It was set in an elaborate frame of the same material, though less highly polished, cast in a pattern of lizards and snakes, and venomous toads, each with a jewel set into its head.

Gwenlliant made a tiny sound. Something moved in the mirror, a dim image where her own reflection should be, but it was taller and so badly distorted she could not make out the features—though everything else in the room, including the dwarf, was faithfully reflected, with only the faint distortion one might logically expect from irregularities in the metal.

"What does the Lady see?" asked the dwarf. Her voice was eager, her eyes bright. "The Lady is gifted, that I know. She has the power to see what others cannot. What does she see in the Princess's mirror?"

Gwenlliant shook her head. "Nothing. I don't see anything . . . out of the ordinary. It is a very poor mirror," she said, turning away from the disturbing image. But then she could not help asking, "What did Diaspad see?"

"She saw a woman who had grown into a monster. Indeed, what *else* was there for the Princess to see?"

And Gwenlliant remembered what Tryffin had told her: *"We buried the bones, Fflergant and I. They were scorched and cracked by the flames which had consumed her. But it was still possible to see . . . well, that the shape of the skull was not right—though you would never have known when the skin was still there—and we found something attached at the base of her spine, and dozens of tiny bones scattered among the rest. She had a tail like a great cat, and if it hadn't been for the trains on all her gowns, everyone would have known it!"*

Remembering this, staring at the hand that had touched the iron gate when she heard the magic calling from the other side, Gwenlliant had a sudden vision of that hand covered in velvety dark fur, or was it black feathers? "Was—was it dabbling in witchcraft that changed her, that made Diaspad into a monster?"

"It was the mark of her sin. The mark of her terrible sin," said the dwarf, while the girl continued to stare at her own black velvet hand. When she flexed her fingers, she could feel the cunning little claws unsheathe and retract. "A sin that *you* would never commit, sweet Lady, your husband being so handsome, so kind."

Gwenlliant blinked her eyes and the vision faded. Her hand was just a hand again, pale and smooth. Yet the dwarf's words troubled her, reminding the girl that she was disobeying Tryffin, who had forbidden her straitly to speak to Brangwengwen. "My husband, you know, does not want me to be here. Please show me the way back, as we agreed."

"But there is one more thing, sweet Lady, sweet Princess. You promised I might show you one thing more,'' said the dwarf, growing strangely agitated, dancing about in her gaudy rags.

Gwenlliant did not care for this form of address, not under the circumstances, but she did not wish to take up time arguing the point . ''You said one *or* two more things, and you have shown me one already,'' she reminded the dwarf, as patiently as she could.

''If you go now, then you will just have to come back again and fulfill your promise.''

''Well . . . perhaps,'' said Gwenlliant. But she did not think she would ever return. It was one thing to come here by accident and cajole the dwarf into showing her the way back again, but to visit Brangwengwen a second time, and that intentionally, would be very, very wrong.

Bad weather and worse roads delayed the Governor's return to Caer Ysgithr. And the loss of the child he had hoped to bring home to Gwenlliant weighed heavily on Tryffin's heart, making the journey seem even longer than it was. Catching his mood, his squires, Meligraunce, and the other men all grew silent and morose as well.

Yet the time passed, however slowly, and the day finally came when they rode through the streets of Trewynyn and up the hill to the castle gate. Tryffin dismounted in the outer courtyard and left Conn and Mahaffy to look after Roch.

He hurried up to his own room in the square tower, where he changed out of his leather and mail and into something more suitable for calling on a lady. Then he climbed the steps to the next floor two at a time. But as he walked down the corridor toward Gwenlliant's sitting room, his pace slowed. He had been gone a month, and he was suddenly afraid that he would find things terribly changed.

It was late afternoon and the shutters were open, allowing shafts of winter sunlight to stream into the solar. Someone was playing on a harp, someone else plucking on a crwth. At first he was aware of nothing but the music and the light. Then he saw Gwenlliant in a green gown, dancing a measure with Garth.

They made a pretty picture, the two of them, dancing there in a beam of sunlight, intent on the steps yet clearly enjoying themselves. And though he knew their enjoyment of the dance and each other was entirely innocent, he felt a momentary twinge of jealousy.

Then Gwenlliant caught sight of him standing in the doorway, dropped Garth's hand, flew across the room, and flung herself into Tryffin's arms.

"Before God, it would seem that you missed me," he said, as lightly as he could. Though he held her tightly and stroked her hair with one hand as he spoke.

"I thought you were never coming back, you were away so long. Where *were* you, Cousin, for such a long time?"

"I went to Clynnoc," he said. As the others were already discreetly filing out of the room, without even waiting for his signal, he sat down on the nearest chair and pulled her into his lap.

"But that's to the north," she said. "Garth said—that is, he had it from Conn, that you were going south."

"Aye, that's what I let people think. I didn't want Efrei and Rhys to know that I was coming to visit them." He dropped a kiss on the top of her head. "I suppose I should have told you, but I never thought you would worry. But traveling south—yes, I might have gone to Perfudd and back a dozen times during the month. And even riding from Clynnoc I should have been back a week ago, were it not for the snow and the damnable roads. No wonder you thought I was never coming back."

He reached into the breast of his tunic and pulled something out: a velvet bag tied with a silver cord. "I did stop a day in Penhalloc, a large town on the coast, in order to buy you a gift, but it's a poor thing beside the one that I meant to bring you."

She opened the bag and examined the contents: a dozen ivory hairpins carved in the shapes of birds, a veil of sheer, opalescent silk, and a number of other pretty and amusing trifles.

"Do they please you, then?" he asked.

"How could they not please me? I thought you had forgotten you had a wife waiting for you at Caer Ysgithr, but now I see that you thought of me, after all."

He took one of her hands and kissed it, felt the pulse flutter like a bird: "Forget you, Dear Heart? I thought of you nearly the entire time I was gone." He kissed the palm of her hand and each of her fingers. As Gwenlliant seemed to like what he was doing, he captured her other hand and raised it to his lips.

"No, please," she said breathlessly, snatching the hand away, holding it behind her.

He frowned, afraid that he had somehow betrayed himself, that she somehow knew he had spent one night with the Lady Essylt. With Gwenlliant's intuitive gifts, there was no way of telling how much she knew.

"I burned that hand," she said, with a false little laugh. "I dripped wax from a burning candle."

151

"Was that the way of it? Then you had better take care after this. Your hands are so soft and white, it would be a pity to spoil them." Yet he had seen her hand quite clearly before she snatched it away, and he knew very well there was not a mark on it.

Tryffin was in the castle chapel, kneeling in the incense- and beeswax-scented dimness, when Meligraunce found him later that afternoon. "I had word that you sent for me, but I do not want to disturb your devotions."

Tryffin shook his head "You don't disturb me. I have said my prayers and composed my mind, and I was just about to leave." He crossed himself, rose to his feet, and joined Meligraunce at the chapel door. "I have something to show you, Captain."

Meligraunce followed him across the courtyard, into the Keep, and up several flights to the firelit audience chamber. The bells had yet to toll the hour of None, but the winter night was already descending outside the mullioned windows, and the Mochdreffi servants had already come into the room to kindle the torches and place a silver branch of lighted candles on the long table.

"The business of government is apparently endless," said the Captain, indicating the piled documents and letters on the table.

"The business of government is just as tedious and trivial as it was when I left." Tryffin removed his cloak and draped it over the back of a chair. "But while I was gone a letter arrived from my father. You may recall that I wrote to him right after our visit to Oeth, asking what he knew of the woman Guenhumara and whatever she once meant to my grandfather."

"And how does Lord Maelgwyn reply?" asked the Captain, beginning to look interested.

Tryffin picked up one of the letters, stared at it for a moment, then gave a deep sigh. "He says that I have stumbled on a riddle he has been attempting to solve for more than forty years. From which I can only guess that he has not been giving the matter his full attention, or all hope is lost. What Maelgwyn fab Menai could not solve by a concerted effort during his entire lifetime is not likely to yield to any pitiful efforts of mine."

He handed the letter to Meligraunce, who gave it no more than a cursory glance before passing it back again. "I think you give yourself too little credit, Prince Tryffin. Everyone says you are a remarkably clever man."

"Those who say so have not met my father. Compared to him, we are all half-wits. Not that he is in the habit of flaunting his intelligence or his vast knowledge; rather the opposite. But . . . what was I telling you? Ah yes, he offers me this one

152

piece of advice: *Ask the intimates of Bron the dwarf.* Which brings me full circle, and no closer to a solution than I was when I first arrived in Mochdreff as deputy to the Lord Constable."

Meligraunce nodded thoughtfully. "That would be the Princess Diaspad's Bron, the man you suspected of being your father's spy —the fellow we tried to learn more about, nearly three years ago, with so little success."

"Aye," said Tryffin, folding the letter and slipping it into the rabbitskin pouch he wore on his belt. "That is the man. I wrote to my father back then, asking him the question: Was Bron a spy in his service? His reply was somewhat evasive. He said there were a number of things he would tell me when I was older. It would seem that I have gained enough wisdom in the interim—or as he puts it, *'knowledge of the means a man must occasionally employ if he wishes to govern wisely'*—enough worldly wisdom, let us say, to accept the truth without suffering a grievous blow to my youthful idealism. Bron was a spy, and his mission was not only to keep an eye on the Princess Diaspad, but also, as a secondary task, to see what he could learn about certain family secrets which had been troubling my father for many years."

He sat down in the chair behind the table, gave the chair an impatient hitch forward. "I wrote to him telling what I learned about Maclwas and Corrig, Diaspad and Manogan, and he replies yes, he has heard these stories himself, but he cannot vouch for the truth of any of them. These tales, he says, have a way of growing more interesting each time that someone repeats them." He began sorting impatiently through the piled documents. "As though I did not *know* this, having been the subject of a few stories myself. Have you heard what your men say about the deaths of Efrei and Rhys?"

Meligraunce laughed, moving toward the fireplace. "I have. The last I heard, you had cut poor Rhys in two neat halves, and spattered Efrei's brains throughout—" He stopped, noting how the Governor frowned. "You do not find the story amusing?"

"There was nothing about the fight or the aftermath that amuses me in the least," said Tryffin, putting his hands palm down on the table. "For all their treachery, I should not have killed them, I should have kept them alive to answer my questions. My madness cost me very dearly, Captain. I may never learn what was really afoot at Caer Clynnoc, any more than I can fathom what inspired young Kemoc to goad and attack me when we were in Oeth. Or didn't you notice that *everything* was wrong—wrong and utterly false, without reason or sense—from the moment we set foot in Efrei's courtyard?"

"Well I did, now that you mention it. My teeth were on edge the whole time." Meligraunce held his hands over the fire, which scarcely repaid his effort, the flames were so sickly.

Tryffin laughed mirthlessly. "It had a slightly different effect on me. It made my teeth *ache,* though it was a long time after before I realized the nature of my discomfort."

Then realizing the Captain did not comprehend: "What I mean to say, Meligraunce, is that I believe I sensed a certain misuse of magic, of wizardry. And as it just happens to be—I know of one man only in all of Mochdreff who claims to practice that particular philosophy."

Meligraunce nodded. "I'm acquainted with no other myself. Yet I suppose there *may* be someone else, that neither of us knows about." He threw a few sticks onto the grate, and the fire revived a little.

"Yes," said Tryffin. "But I think I will begin with the man that I already know." After months of suspecting Lord Cado for no other reason except that he disliked him, it was a relief to finally have *something*—something a reasonable man like himself could accept—if only the merest shadow of an excuse to confront the wizard. "Have the men and the horses ready tomorrow morning. We'll go down to Trewynyn and pay a call on Cado Guillyn."

The Governor climbed the steps to Lord Cado's house a little before noon. Meligraunce, Conn, and two guards accompanied him, but it was Tryffin himself who knocked on the oak panels with an iron-clad fist. One of Cado's most trusted retainers, a dark man with a long beard and greying hair, answered the door.

"Ah, Sennan, I am here to visit Lord Cado," said the Governor. He stepped past the servant and entered the house without waiting for an invitation. "You will oblige me by escorting me to your master at once."

Sennan frowned fiercely as Meligraunce and the others followed Tryffin into the house, but his voice as he addressed the Governor was gentle and respectful. "My apologies, Your Grace, but Lord Cado is not here. If you will return another time—"

Tryffin continued down the passageway, heading toward the stairs to the upper floors. "And when," he asked, over his shoulder, "might another time be? Where is Cado Guillyn, how long has he been gone, and when is he likely to return?"

Sennan scurried to keep up, to the great detriment of his dignity. "Where he has gone, I do not know. As he left more than a week ago, we may suppose a journey of some length. These wizards, you know, have a habit of wandering."

Tryffin stopped at the foot of the steps, standing with one hand on the railing. "Some wizards, certainly. But Lord Cado was never a wanderer when *I* knew him. Just when did he develop this habit?"

Sennan opened his mouth, was about to reply, when a high sweet voice coming from the top of the stairs prevented him. "Prince Tryffin . . . it is good of you to call on me, though you arrive much later than I might have expected."

The Governor looked up to see Lord Cado's beautiful niece coming down the steps, the train of her blue velvet gown trailing behind her, and the golden torc he had given her glittering at her throat. "Dahaut," he said, on an indrawn breath.

Indicating with an abrupt gesture that he was not to be followed, he swiftly climbed the stairs and met her on the first landing. "I believe you know very well why it was not fitting for me to visit you here." Tryffin spoke very low, lest Meligraunce and the others waiting down below should hear what he said to her. "Nor could I send for *you* to visit *me*."

The lady gave a bitter little laugh. "Oh yes, I know. Though you never told me when you wooed and won me that you were already betrothed. And then to hear from the gossips, not from your own lips or from a letter, that you had married your cousin! I never expected such cruelty, in truth I never did."

Tryffin sighed. He knew from past experience that Dahaut was inclined to over-dramatize the events of her life. She was one of those women who looked especially well with their eyes sparkling and their bosoms heaving—and unfortunately she knew it.

"I have a desire to view Lord Cado's laboratory," he said, raising his voice for the benefit of the others. "Perhaps you will be so good as to take me there." And when she shrugged and led the way up to the next floor, he added under his breath: "Mother of God, Dahaut, if never occurred to me that I owed you any particular courtesy in the matter. Not when we had parted by mutual consent so many months before. And you, so they told me, had already taken another lover."

She turned to bestow a melting glance from those magnificent grey eyes. "When a man makes it clear that he is tired of her, what can a woman who wishes to retain her pride do but consent?"

As no servant was by to open the laboratory door, Tryffin did it himself. "And admit another man to her bed before the week was out? That hardly suggests a broken heart."

Dahaut walked past him and into the laboratory. "Oh, if you would speak of hearts: Did I ever have yours, Prince Tryffin? I believe I did not."

Tryffin stepped into the room, shaking his head. "You had my friendship, anyway. You are very beautiful, Dahaut, but I wanted more than your lovely body. When I found that you had nothing more to offer me, I lost interest."

Turning away from her, he glanced around the laboratory, surprised to find it so empty. Even from Gwenlliant's brief description, he had expected to see the room crowded with a sorcerer's paraphernalia. But the tables and the shelves had all been cleared, and the only remaining signs that a wizard and alchemist had once occupied this chamber were the brick furnace in one corner of the room and the golden pentacle painted on the floor.

"This room is no longer in use?"

"My uncle has another house; I am not certain of the location." In the act of sitting she suddenly remembered who he was and straightened up again. "Perhaps he has set up his laboratory there."

"For the love of God, be seated if you wish," said Tryffin, taking a chair for himself. "And tell me why your uncle has done this."

Dahaut dropped gracefully into the chair opposite him. "I do not know, unless it should be as Sennan says. It is the nature of wizards to be restless," she replied, folding her hands in her lap. "You have not known Lord Cado so very many years—even I have known him but a small part of his considerable lifetime. And while it is true that he has never been a great traveler, it is also true that we lived in many different places when I was small."

She sighed and gave him a wistful smile. "Perhaps that is how I learned never to grow too attached to anything or anybody. Yet I think you might have claimed much more of my affection, had you been willing to make the effort.

"You think me light, no doubt," she continued, the wistful smile fading. "But I have always known that an honorable marriage was not for me. What man would marry a woman of whom such vile things are whispered, a woman who has since childhood . . . consorted with her own uncle?"

Tryffin leaned forward in his seat. He had caught wind of those ugly rumors through whispers and innuendoes, but had never heard the stories spoken aloud. "Ah, Dahaut, I never believed that wicked gossip, not even for a moment. If I had, I would never have come near you."

Again she gave that bitter laugh. Her hands fluttered up to the gleaming golden necklace at her throat. "Then the more fool you.

Oh, I don't say that I ever consented to anything, nor did it ever go so far as rape. But there was truth behind those stories."

The Governor frowned, shifting uneasily in his chair. "Do you mean to tell me that Cado Guillyn persecuted you with unseemly attentions? But what of Dame Ceinwen, who raised you? What of your cousin, Mahaffy? Did neither of them make any effort to protect you?"

Dahaut passed a hand over his eyes. "Ceinwen! That hag always hated me, and chose to believe that I brought my troubles on myself. A woman of my sort suffers not only by the lewd appetites of men, but also by the envy of other women."

A dry little sob escaped her. "As for Mahaffy, I believe he wished to defend me, but he was only a boy. And now, of course, he has turned against me. In his eyes, I am little more than a whore. And that was your doing, Prince Tryffin. It was one thing when I took Mochdreffi lovers, but he never forgave me for bedding with a foreigner."

Tryffin studied her face carefully. Her distress seemed real, and to be perfectly honest he *knew* nothing at all to her discredit, aside from her eagerness (he had once thought it charming) to share his bed. Also, he remembered quite vividly the way her young kinsman had behaved at the time of their affair, the affront to Mahaffy's Guillyn pride. If Mahaffy had since forgiven *him*, it might well be that the boy had shifted his displeasure to Dahaut.

"But why, if you do not encourage his attentions, do you continue to live in Lord Cado's house under his protection?"

"And where else should I live?" she flung back at him. "Who will maintain me? Despite all appearances to the contrary, we are not a wealthy family, but live by the favor of great men like yourself. As for me, I have *nothing* of my own. And shall I live with a man unwed and be his whore in very truth? I have my share of Guillyn pride. If a man sleeps with me and he gives me gifts afterward, I may tell myself: These are tokens of his affection. But if he *keeps* me, I know full well that I am nothing more than his drab—and he knows it, too!"

Suddenly, she left her chair, crossed the room, and threw herself kneeling at his feet. It was a posture that reminded him most forcibly of the Lady Essylt. And because he still felt a guilty regret about separating Essylt from her child, the comparison affected him profoundly. "Lord Prince, my uncle persecutes me still, with his sly caresses and his vile suggestions. Until now, I had no means of escape. But now Lord Cado is gone, and you have arrived in good time to rescue me. Take me into your household and place me under your protection. If I must humble myself before any man, let it be a man as great and as worthy as yourself."

He put out a hand, brushed his fingers against her cheek. "I wish you had told me these things before, Dahaut, when I might have done so much to help you. But I can't take you for my mistress now, I won't humiliate Gwenlliant." He wracked his brain for some better solution. "I will buy you a house somewhere, *not* in Trewynyn, and hire servants to watch over you. You will be perfectly safe, I will see to that."

She gave another dry sob and buried her face in her hands. "Safe? How can I be safe when Lord Cado is so powerful? There is only one place in all of Mochdreff where I can be safe, and that is Caer Ysgithr, where a sorcerer like Cado is unable to enter without an invitation."

He shook his head in denial, yet he knew that she spoke the truth. How could he hope to ward her against a determined assault by the wizard, unless he offered her the safety of Caer Ysgithr? To make matters worse, he had as much as *promised* her his protection, and he did not dare to think what supernatural penalty would befall him or those close to him, should he violate his geas and be foresworn.

"Aye, very well," he said at last. "You may come and live at Caer Ysgithr—but not as my mistress. You will be handmaiden to the Lady Gwenlliant and enjoy *her* protection. That is an arrangement with some claim to respectability, since it happens that your cousin is already a member of my household.

"We will hope that other people see it so," he added, with a sigh. "Because truth to tell, I do not see any other way that I can protect you."

Now the infant in the womb is as much under the Influence of his mother as the bear cub being licked into shape by its dam. Both are infinitely Malleable and subject to molding, though in the case of the infant it is the woman's Imagination which is the principal

Influence. For the Thoughts of the mother are so active after she receives the seed into her body and so strongly directed toward the foetus, that they produce a powerful Impression. Thus it sometimes occurs that dwarfs, pygmies, giants, and other Prodigies are born, when there are no physical deformities in the parents.

While all Monsters are hateful to animals begotten in the usual way, even more are Monstrous human growths despised by men. Indeed, the more remarkable they are, the more extravagant in their deformities, the less likely they are to grow and thrive in human Society, and are therefore often carried away at an early age to some Secret place, which if it were not done they would surely Perish.

> —From a letter written by
> the mage Atlendor to his pupils
> at Findias

14.

A Garden of Gargoyles

Tryffin lost no time informing Meligraunce and Conn that Dahaut would be joining their household at Caer Ysgithr. Each accepted his decision without comment. Even when he brought the news to Mahaffy, the boy was silent, though he looked like he had something on his mind and meant to speak eventually.

In fact, Mahaffy was still behaving as though he had disgraced himself by failing to detect poison in the Governor's cup at Caer Clynnoc, and in that state of mind he was not likely either to confide in Tryffin or to state any reason why Dahaut should not be welcome at Caer Ysgithr.

When the Governor walked into the solar with Dahaut on his arm and presented her to Gwenlliant, he was unprepared for the glance of painful inquiry which greeted him. He had never imagined for a single moment that Gwenlliant knew anything about Dahaut—she was acquainted with so few people, and the gossip had been stale for more than a year—and he had made very certain that Dahaut put away her golden necklace before stepping through the gate.

When he came into the solar, Gwenlliant and Garth were sitting on a bench by the fire, a game of fox and geese laid out between them. Puzzled by her look of wounded incomprehension, Tryffin went down on one knee at her feet, and said very low, "Sweetheart, this is Mahaffy's kinswoman, and so has a claim on our protection. As she has been most bitterly wronged, I rely on your generosity to offer this lady a home."

Gwenlliant turned away from him, pretended to direct her attention back on the game which had engrossed her a short time before. "It shall be however you please," she said, in a stifled little voice. Yet she said nothing at all to welcome Dahaut.

Christmas Eve came and Gwenlliant and her household danced their masque, though with considerably less enthusiasm on the part of the principal dancers than might once have been expected. Gifts were exchanged, a feast prepared and eaten on Christmas Day—but the holidays otherwise came and went with no festivities to mark them.

"When spring comes, we will ride out into the country for a picnic or some hawking," Tryffin suggested, just after Twelfth Night, hoping to raise Gwenlliant's spirits. When he took her hand and raised it to his lips, her skin was cold. Once she had trembled a little whenever he touched her, but now she was unresponsive.

"Yes," she said. "Whatever you wish—whatever pleases you." Which was the way she replied to all his suggestions, and sorely disturbed him, it was so unlike her.

What would please him, he realized, was a wife who might age three years in a single night, grow from child to woman, a woman he could love so tenderly and so passionately, there would be no room in her heart for doubts or jealousy.

Meanwhile, Gwenlliant went through the last days of winter in a blur of misery. *It is very hard,* she reflected gloomily, *to be a good person and an obedient wife, when your nights are so restless and your days so dull, when the husband you love has brought his mistress to live under your roof and expects you to be kind to her.*

When she remembered that it was only to keep faith with Tryffin she had never gone back to visit the dwarf, the temptation to seek out Brangwengwen became positively intense.

At last it was too much for her. She slipped away from the others one day and headed for the back stair. Running down to the first landing and seven steps beyond, then back up again, up and up, for what seemed like flights and flights, she found herself once more in the musty corridor lit by smoking rushlights.

She paused for a moment, wondering how Brangwengwen came by the torches, or anything else that she needed to live. *I daresay she knows every pattern and figure in the castle, and she uses them to go secretly about. She undoubtedly lives by theft,*

*poor creature. If I come again, I will bring her something—
something she can't easily get for herself.*

"Brangwengwen," she said softly, but there was no reply. So
she took down a rushlight and went down the corridor, opening
each of the doors and looking inside.

Most of the rooms were empty and dusty, abandoned long
before Diaspad's time. Then Gwenlliant wandered into a chamber
that had once been a nursery. The windows were barred, and there
were two small beds—one for a child and one for a dwarfish
nursemaid—and every sort of a toy that could possibly appeal to
a very small boy: a castle made out of wood with dozens of carved
and painted figures to live there, a charming hobby horse with a
real horsehair tail, a puppet theatre with a vast array of handpup-
pets and marionettes, short wooden swords and painted wooden
shields. Whoever had occupied this room had been a fortunate and
remarkably pampered child.

Gwenlliant went down on her knees in the dust to get a better
look at the castle. It was outsize for a plaything, filling up a good
portion of the chamber, and she soon realized it was a miniature
version of Caer Ysgithr.

"These were his things, they belonged to Calchas," said a
familiar voice. The dwarf Brangwengwen, as gaudily and shabbily
dressed as ever, stepped into the room. "Such a dear little boy he
was, so bright and so eager to please."

Gwenlliant, still on her knees, scowled up at the dwarf.
"Calchas fab Corfil was the wickedest boy, the wickedest person,
I ever knew. He tried to make me do terrible things."

Brangwengwen nodded her head sagely. "Oh yes, he was a bad
one by the time that you knew him. His mother had ruined him by
then, ruined him with her anger and her spite. I speak of before,
when he was still very small and the very image of the man that
she loved. Though that, of course, was what turned the Princess
against him in the end. He reminded her too much of her terrible
mistake." The dwarf smiled brightly and nodded her head. "But
after all . . . a boy must have a father, he must have a name,
don't you agree?"

"I really don't know what you are talking about," Gwenlliant
said crossly. Thinking of Calchas made her palms damp and her
stomach twist into knots. Rising to her feet, she brushed off her
skirts. And she thought the old dwarf woman might not be entirely
right in her head, she rambled on so.

"Then, listen," said Brangwengwen. "Listen to what the walls
have to say to you."

So Gwenlliant listened, and the walls spoke: with their own dry voices, like stones crushing mortar into dust, and with the faint sad echoes of all the voices that had ever sounded in these rooms before. It was not a coherent tale, of course, but Gwenlliant heard enough to grasp the sense of their story. A proud passionate girl had run away with a man she did not love, and had suffered under his many cruelties for years and years. Gwenlliant could hear the man laughing, hear him say with a sneer in his voice, *You are not my wife, only my whore, for the King never acknowledged our marriage.* Yet he had never been willing to send the girl away, because she was the King's step-sister, and it pleased Lord Corfil to keep her by him. At last, unable to bear the violent arguments or his cruel mockery, the Princess had run away from him.

But the stones of the castle could only relate the scenes they had witnessed. Gwenlliant was curious by now, and she wanted to hear more. "Yes, Brangwengwen, and then what happened, after the Princess left Lord Corfil?"

"Why, what *should* she do but go straight to the man she had loved all along and only married Corfil to spite him? Such a kind man he was—do you know?—he took her right back, for all she had lived three years with another man. He was willing to forgive and forget, to offer her honorable marriage."

Brangwengwen turned and went out the door, and Gwenlliant trailed after her. "And what was the name of Diaspad's lover? Was it Manogan fab Menai?"

"Aye, you have it," said the hunchback, closing the door to the nursery behind her. "Him with that great Gwyngellach heart of his. But he had business to attend to, very pressing it was. He was the Earl Marshall of Celydonn and he had a duty to perform up north in Perfudd. So Manogan sent the Princess on ahead to Caer Cadwy, to petition the King to make the pronouncement he had threatened all along, but never made—to set aside her marriage to Corfil fab Corrig."

Gwenlliant followed Brangwengwen down the passageway, around a corner, and through chamber after dusty chamber. "But she was married to Corfil in the end, that much I know."

The dwarf shrugged a crooked shoulder. "By the time she arrived in Camboglanna, by the time the King had recovered from his pique and allowed her an audience, she knew that she was carrying a child. Who was the father? Only once had Manogan slept with her during the week they spent together. But Corfil had her a dozen times during the fortnight before she left him. The more she loathed him, the more Corfil wanted her, and he was willing to use force to have his way."

Brangwengwen shook her head sadly. "Two men and only

162

three weeks between them. What was she to suppose? And Manogan was generous, but would he consent to raise Corfil's bastard, and love the child as though it were his own?''

Gwenlliant considered that. "You know, he was a very different man by the time I was acquainted with him, but they say he was very like Fflergant and Tryffin when he was young. I believe he *would* have accepted the child, and I think he *would* have married her.''

"You think it . . . I think it . . . but the Princess Diaspad, with her injured pride, her wounded spirit, would not allow herself to believe it. She asked the King to make her marriage legal, went back to Corfil, bore him a ten months child as she supposed at the time, and then watched her son grow in Manogan's image.

"After that," said the dwarf, pausing outside a low wooden door with iron hinges, "after she was legally and truly his wife and had no way of escaping him, Corfil began to beat her and the little boy, too. He beat her and abused her until she used her magic to kill him." Brangwengwen gave a nod of satisfaction. "That was her sin, the one that changed her. She murdered her husband by the use of Black Magic. God might forgive her, for He knows all. You or I might pity her. But the magic knew only her wicked intent and marked her accordingly."

"Oh, Brangwengwen, that is a terrible, terrible story," said Gwenlliant, standing with her hand to her heart, there in the smoky light of the flaring torches. "And it hasn't even ended, because Calchas hurt me and Tryffin killed him, and we are still paying the price, because Tryffin and I can't—we don't . . .'' She blinked back sudden tears.

"Blood guilt," said the dwarf, "has a way of claiming its own price."

"Yes," said Gwenlliant, very much shaken. "Yes, it does. But I feel I should go back now. I need to go back to my own rooms and think about all of these things."

"No, no," said the dwarf, reaching for her hand and clasping it between her dry old fingers. "I have not shown you anything yet, and you said that I might the next time you came. That was a sad story I just told you, but the thing I wish to show you is far more pleasant. I am sure it will delight you."

"Very well," said Gwenlliant, remembering she had disappointed the old woman once before.

The dwarf opened the door. There was a shadowy staircase on the other side. She pulled Gwenlliant over the threshold (the girl had to duck to avoid hitting her head on the low lintel), then dropped her hand and started to climb. The steps were so steep, it took a great effort for Brangwengwen to mount them, stumping ahead, huffing and puffing, pausing every now and again to speak.

"She kept a menagerie of sorts up on the roof, a regular garden of gargoyles and stone monsters—but not like the terrible creatures you see down below," said the dwarf. "It was her favorite retreat, where she liked to go walking when the weather was fine. It was something she had made for her, during the first days she lived here."

They came out on the broad flat roof of the Keep; a stiff breeze was blowing that smelled of the sea. "We are higher than the highest tower, and if we are careful not to walk near the edge, no one below can see us."

Stepping out of the shadows into cold winter sunlight, Gwenlliant glanced delightedly around her. Despite what Brangwengwen had said, she had expected a garden of horrors worked in marble, but the gargoyles on the roof were gregarious monsters: a lion-fish, a graceful winged stag, an unusually benevolent manticore. She spent a long time wandering from one to another, for there were certainly a great many of them, and each one different. "But how does the roof support such a weight of stone?"

"It is magic," said the dwarf, in an offhand way. "Magic like so much else you see at Caer Ysgithr. It is one of the great magical sites on Ynys Celydonn, this castle we live in."

One statue in particular, the figure of a sweet-faced girl with feathery wings worked in pale pink marble, was so attractive and appealing that Gwenlliant reached out to touch . . . only to draw back with a soft cry of dismay, as she caught sight of great hooked talons where the feet ought to be and a long scaly tail coiled about the base of the statue.

"I thought it was an angel, a nicer one than the brass cherubim down below," Gwenlliant whispered. "Is she meant to be a demon?"

"She is the harpy, a heraldic device much favored by the Princess," said the dwarf. "You will find images of the creature everywhere in the rooms below. The early statues and paintings are all as beautiful as this one, but the later ones changed as *she* changed herself, becoming more and more monstrous.

"But it was not the physical deformity that she saw in her mirror that she meant to portray," said Brangwengwen. "Because that of course was very, very different. It was the ugliness inside."

As Gwenlliant stood gazing into the beautiful, gentle face of the statue, for the first time she felt her heart soften toward the woman she had feared and hated. "But then, if the harpy was Diaspad, she must have thought she was beautiful and good when she first came here.''

''Not *good*,'' said the dwarf. ''She was far too honest for that. But she knew she had some goodness in her. As when she brought me here, poor miserable creature that I was, forever being cuffed and kicked and reviled. She gave me a home and such lovely things to wear, and she even called me her friend. So when she turned cruel, as she did much later, I always remembered her kindness at the beginning, and I forgave her everything.''

Gwenlliant turned away from the statue. ''And how old was Diaspad when she first came to live at Caer Ysgithr?''

''Sixteen or seventeen, I do not remember exactly,'' said the dwarf. ''Older than you, Princess, but not by very much.''

''Is that why you kept calling me down to the orchard? Is that why you wanted to show me her things?'' said Gwenlliant. ''Because you think I am . . . like her?''

''Oh no,'' said Brangwengwen. ''It was because I was lonely, hiding here all alone. And I must have a lady to serve, a lovely princess to love and to serve.'' The dwarf glanced up with a pitiful smile, small and harmless beneath the statue. ''You *will* come again to see me—please say you will.''

By now, Gwenlliant was thinking hard. She knew that Tryffin wanted to learn about Calchas, to uncover old secrets, though she was not exactly certain what he expected to accomplish. It had something to do with Diaspad's dwarfs, that much she knew, because she remembered what Tryffin once said about trying to locate the Princess's servants.

But I can learn it for him, I will learn it all from Brangwengwen. And perhaps we may go home again that much sooner—home to Camboglanna without Dahaut. Tryffin would never risk scandal by taking her with him.

''I will visit you again,'' said Gwenlliant, coming to what seemed like a sensible decision. ''But you must promise to tell me more about the Princess and Calchas.''

''That I will promise gladly,'' said Brangwengwen, beginning to dance about. ''But there are so many things I might show and tell you, it may take a very long time.''

Meligraunce was in the stable, feeding an apple to his horse, when Prince Tryffin came in with a purposeful stride, his red cloak swirling around him. ''There you are, Captain, I've been looking for you the entire afternoon.''

''My apologies,'' said Meligraunce, giving the big rangy black a final pat on the nose, then opening the gate of the stall. "I had no idea that you had need of me. How may I serve you?"

"You can choose some men to accompany me to Peryf," said the Governor. "And you can prepare yourself for the journey as well."

"Certainly," said Meligraunce, stepping into the aisle, fastening the gate behind him. "But if I might ask . . . ?"

"I grow weary of waiting for Lord Cado to return to Trewynyn," said Prince Tryffin. He had assigned men to watch Lord Cado's house and bring word to the castle the very moment that Cado appeared, and other men to search up and down the coast, but so far the wizard had managed to elude him. It was frustrating to think of all those months when the wizard had been close at hand, months when it would have been easy enough to call on him and question him . . . except then there had been no questions to ask, only some nebulous suspicions. Now Lord Cado's protracted and mysterious absence seemed to confirm those suspicions, yet the nature of the threat he presented remained obscure and would probably remain so until the wizard was found.

"I keep thinking what his niece said: that her uncle has another house somewhere in Mochdreff. You will remember Lord Cado spent a year in Peryf, where the Mochdreffi Woods seemed to exert a powerful fascination. Perhaps he has returned there now, perhaps that is where he has set up his laboratory, and perhaps I will find him there.

"Or if not," he added, "at least I might ask questions of Teign and his sons, and perhaps learn precisely how the wizard occupied himself when he lived at Castell Peryf. Which might possibly throw some light on his present activities. Now that the year has turned and the weather improved, I am eager to ride out and see what I can discover."

"Of course," said Meligraunce, following him out of the stable and into the open courtyard. "And yet . . ."

The Governor scowled darkly, which was much in keeping with his current temper, but not with his former good nature. "You were about to say, Captain?"

"It is not for me to say," Meligraunce demurred. "It is no business of mine."

"Yet since you began I would have you finish," said Prince Tryffin.

"I was only thinking that the Lady Gwenlliant might take it much to heart, were you to leave at this particular time," said Meligraunce quietly.

The Governor shook his head. "My lady wife has little use for me, Captain." Because Prince Tryffin spoke so coldly and so formally, Meligraunce knew he was hiding some powerful emotion. "Try as I might to regain her, she simply grows more and more distant. It is like living with a ghost or a wisp of fog."

"Perhaps," ventured Meligraunce, "since you had so little time for her in the past, and so much now, she believes you seek . . . not her own company, but that of Dahaut."

"Yes," said the Governor, with a sigh. "That has occurred to me also. But since Gwenlliant denies me those private moments that a man and his wife usually share together, I see no way to convince her otherwise."

Meligraunce had already noticed that some of Prince Tryffin's brightness had faded, that almost palpable glow of health and self-confidence that distinguished him from lesser men. The Captain's heart ached to see his friend and patron so unhappy and bewildered.

"Ah well," said the Governor, with a shrug and a wry smile. "She always seems to miss me when I am gone, to appreciate me more when I am far from home. Perhaps if I spend a fortnight or so in Peryf, I may even revive her affection."

As it was plain that Mahaffy had *still* not forgiven himself for his supposed failures in Clynnoc, Tryffin took care during the journey into Peryf to show the boy all the favor he could—all the favor he might without slighting Conn. So the Mochdreffi youth rode by his side most of the way, poured his wine, brought up his morning wash water, and helped him into his armor afterward . . . which was the most eloquent demonstration of confidence the Governor could possibly devise. Fortunately, it seemed to have the desired effect. As the journey progressed, Mahaffy grew noticeably more cheerful.

They arrived at Castell Peryf three days after setting out. "Prince Tryffin, you are very welcome," said Teign, looking flustered though not displeased when the Governor and his men walked into the torchlit Hall. "But we did not expect you."

"I did not think it wise to let my plans be generally known," said Tryffin. While he had not elected to keep his household in the dark this time, he had not sent a messenger ahead to announce him. "I hope this causes no great inconvenience?"

"No, no," said Teign, springing up from his chair by the fire. "Suitable arrangements will be made at once. The best rooms in the castle shall be at your disposal."

But Tryffin shook his head. "Quarter us in any style that gives

167

you the least trouble. Unannounced guests should not be particular.''

For all that, a large comfortable chamber was given him, and the rooms directly below turned over to Meligraunce and his men. A great feast was prepared that first night, at which the Lord of Peryf insisted that Tryffin's squires be treated as guests, and Teign's sons claimed the honor of waiting on the Governor personally.

Perhaps Lord Teign felt that he and his family should be on their best behavior in order to make up for the treachery of his nephew Kemoc, or perhaps word had spread of the disgraceful incident in Clynnoc. However it was, the Lord's own sons tasted every dish, every goblet of wine, before it reached Tryffin—which task they performed with somewhat excessive enthusiasm.

"You're a good lad and I appreciate your willingness to die in my place, but I wish you would leave a little something in the cup for me," Tryffin said, under his breath.

"Lord Prince?" Dirmyg inquired politely, standing with a half-empty goblet in one hand. In his zeal, he had drained the rest.

Tryffin reached out and took the goblet. "It was of no great importance. But perhaps you or your brother or father can tell me: What influence did Lord Cado have on you and your kinsmen during the feud with Llyr? Surely he must have said something while he was here, either encouraged you to take your revenge or counciled you against it.''

"He said nothing, did nothing," Drwst insisted. "Except . . . well, you know how haughty and superior the Guillyns can be. And it just somehow seemed, with him looking on, that we *had* to be proud and accept no insults, or be shamed forever in Lord Cado's eyes.''

Dirmyg nodded his agreement. "It was a kind of moral force that he exerted over us," the youth tried to explain.

"Or an immoral one," Tryffin suggested, staring moodily down at his plate, moving the food around with his knife.

"Yes, I believe you are right," said Dirmyg. "Only it seemed very different at the time.''

The Governor stayed up late that night over wine and conversation, and went to bed well after midnight. As usual, he fell into a deep restful sleep as soon as his head hit the pillow.

But he woke up several hours later, with smoke in his eyes and his throat, to find young Drwst kneeling by his bed, shaking him by the shoulder and hoarsely exclaiming, "Prince Tryffin, for God's sake, wake if you can. There is a great fire raging down below, and most of the rooms beneath yours are already ablaze.''

Tryffin climbed out of bed and felt about in the swirling smoke, searching for his sword and armor. Drwst had carried a torch in with him, but it was hard to see much in the smoky gloom.

"Lord, I swear to you, there is no attack." Teign's son was gasping, could barely force out the words. "Leave by your arms and come with me, before the fire and the smoke—"

"You are right," said Tryffin, coming to a swift decision. He left off searching for his armor and picked up his sword and his boots instead. He had known too many midnight incursions during the last year to feel comfortable sleeping naked, preferring to lie down in his breeches, shirt, and hose . . . but he had better sense than to be caught outdoors in winter in his stocking feet. "God of Heaven, Drwst, where are my squires?"

"We are here," said Conn, from the other side of the room. The four of them left the chamber together, but the smoke was even worse out in the corridor, and the air was as hot as an oven. Everyone began to cough and wheeze.

"Meligraunce and my men," Tryffin said, directly in Drwst's ear. It was the most he could manage.

"They were awake . . . Trying to put out the flames—" The young man's reply died in a fit of coughing.

They hurried down two flights of stairs, along a corridor, and emerged in the courtyard a short time later, where they promptly collapsed on a plot of damp earth.

All around them, Teign's servants and guardsmen were running from every direction, bringing buckets and tubs and jugs full of water to douse the flames. But the Governor and his companions needed time to regain their breath, to draw in great drafts of fresh air, until their lungs stopped burning and their eyes stopped watering, before they could offer to help.

Meligraunce appeared out of the smoke near the building. "No accident," he said. "There are fires in several places: floors, beams, furniture, wherever there is wood to burn. And not only near our rooms, either. Lord Teign and his lady barely escaped with their lives."

Tryffin glanced around him. Conn and Drwst sat on the ground looking pale and ill by the light of the burning castle, but someone was missing. "Where is Mahaffy?" he asked sharply.

Conn shook his head, trying to remember. "He was with us, there on the stairs, but I don't remember seeing him after that. Ah God, he may still be—"

Without a word to anyone, the Governor turned and headed back toward the burning building, and Meligraunce followed only a few steps behind him.

169

"There is a creature called Salamander," said the wizard Glastyn, "because it endures the fire. I have known magicians and philosophers to keep a salamander in the furnace. Indeed, the beast may remain in the flames indefinitely without being burnt or consumed. The creature can do this because it is composed of the element fire—and just as a viper cannot be infected by its own poison, so no living thing may be destroyed by its native element. But to keep one in the laboratory is a dangerous practice . . . for let the salamander but escape from the philosopher's furnace for even a brief span of time, and it will cause the most terrible destruction.

15.

Of Fallen Magicians and Imperfect Philosophers

"Your Grace, no! The smoke . . . you can't—" Tryffin heard Drwst shouting behind him as he went in through the door. There were running footsteps close behind him, but he had no need to glance back. The Governor knew without looking that would be Meligraunce.

Already, the flames had reached the far end of the corridor, lighting the way with their lurid glow. He leapt up the steps two at a time, and was fortunate enough to find Mahaffy lying unconscious at the first landing.

"Lord Prince, let me help you," shouted Meligraunce, over the roar of the flames. They picked up the boy, one at each end, and started to carry him down the stairs.

But the smoke was so thick by then, it drove them back up the stairs and along an upper corridor. "There may not be another way out," gasped Meligraunce, as they hurried along with Mahaffy between them.

But by moving toward a draft of cooler air they finally came into a passage that was free from smoke, and there they discovered a window on the courtyard. "We're but one flight up. You go down first and fetch a ladder or a rope so we can lower the lad," said Tryffin. "I'll stay with Mahaffy."

Knowing better than to argue, the Captain swung his legs over the window sill and pushed himself off into the air. He landed undamaged on the ground below, because Tryffin heard his voice a few moments later, shouting reassurance.

While he waited for Meligraunce to return, smoke started creeping into the passage. Tryffin was considering a leap of his own, no matter how dangerous a jump might be with Mahaffy in his arms, when the top of a ladder appeared in the window, followed a moment later by the Captain's head and shoulders.

Tryffin passed Mahaffy to Meligraunce, and the Captain handed the boy down to the men in the courtyard below. Tryffin waited impatiently as Meligraunce climbed down the ladder; the heat was painfully intense by now and smoke was billowing out the window. As soon as the way was clear, Tryffin jumped.

By daybreak, most of the fires had been extinguished, but more than half of Castell Peryf lay in smoking ruins. Mahaffy had yet to revive, causing Tryffin considerable worry. The apparent cause was a blow to the head when he fell on the stairs; a great purple lump the size of an egg formed on the side of the boy's head, and his breathing continued shallow though not labored.

"That such a thing should happen while you slept under my roof!" said Teign, haggard and wild-eyed by the dawn's first light. "Your Grace, I am ashamed. You will think—God alone knows what you will think of us, after Kemoc's treason and now this . . ."

"I am the one who should apologize for bringing disaster on you and your family," said Tryffin, clenching a big fist. "It seems to follow me wherever I go. And while those who have tried to kill me in the recent past have not shown any marked degree of wisdom, yet I can't imagine you would burn down your home in order to destroy me—or having set the fire, send your own son at the risk of his life to bring me to safety.

"Although," he added thoughtfully, "there may be someone who is hoping right now that I will think just that."

"But who?" said Teign. "I have no enemies, nor have my sons. We settled our quarrel with Dalldaff Llyr. And even if he still harbored some secret resentment, neither Dalldaff nor Ewen would be capable of such a wicked act."

"My enemy, not yours," said Tryffin wearily. "The man or

171

men I mentioned when we met in Oeth. Perhaps the enemy of anyone who seeks to bring peace and order to Mochdreff.''

As the sky grew brighter, Teign sent those of his guards and his servants who had escaped without injury to sift through the ashes for the bones of the dead. A half dozen people were missing, had undoubtedly perished. Tryffin could only hope they had died of the smoke before the flames consumed them.

Lying on a thin patch of grass with a blanket over him, Mahaffy began to stir and moan. They carried him into the gatehouse, which was still standing, and put him to bed in the barracks there.

"These rooms shall be at your disposal, Prince Tryffin," said Teign, as his servants began to bring in water and wine and food. The kitchens and many of the storerooms had also survived unscathed.

"And what of your men whose quarters these are?" The Governor was wearing a sheepskin cloak and a russet tunic, borrowed from Teign's largest guardsman. It was a fortunate thing that the man had a fondness for long, loose-fitting garments, or the tunic would never have fit Tryffin at all.

"They will sleep in the stables; the horses can graze in the courtyard," said Teign.

Tryffin nodded. "Very well then. But I shall send some of my men into the nearest town to buy provisions. It would be wrong to impose on you at a time like this."

• • •

But the True Wizard shall always be known, because above all else he values Equilibrium, Balance, Symmetry, and Proportion, seeking always to work in Harmony with the Natural Order. For who that understands the Universe in all its Elegant Complexity— Moon, Sun, Clouds, Angels, the Spinning Stars, the Immovable Earth, Tides, Planetary Conjunctions, and all—who would risk the Ruin of all this Glory and Splendor, only for the sake of a Momentary Gratification?

—*From* The Geometry of Magic
and the Harmony of Numbers

• • •

In the days that followed, the Governor and his men scoured the countryside, searching in vain for any sign, listening for any word, that Cado Guillyn had set up residence in the vicinity.

"If he is here," said Meligraunce, "then I think he must be living in the forest. It would be difficult to get my men to venture beyond the margin of the woods, but if you require it—"

"No," said Tryffin. "I'll not ask that of them, particularly when I have no powerful reason to suppose that Cado is living there."

Five days passed before Mahaffy fully recovered his wits and revived enough to sit up in bed. When the Governor went up to see him in his room over the gate, the boy flushed painfully at the sight of him. "I can't think how I came to be so stupid as to stumble on the stairs."

"I don't reckon that you did stumble," said Tryffin, pulling up a rude bench and sitting down beside the bed. "More likely, you passed out from breathing so much smoke."

Mahaffy only looked mortified. "None of the rest of you passed out."

Tryffin laughed. "As to that, I have lungs that a horse might envy. Drwst was walking ahead where the air was better, and Garth and Conn . . . ah well, you know the Gorwynnach, they're bound to be accustomed to a certain amount of fire and brimstone."

Mahaffy did not even smile. "You are kind to excuse my weakness," he said stiffly.

"No, I am making a clumsy attempt to ingratiate myself," said the Governor, "because I want you to answer some questions."

Though he still had no satisfactory proof, his suspicions about Lord Cado were growing. The fire, for instance, had been too widespread to be accidental, and the circumstances were sufficiently mysterious to warrant an assumption that magic was involved. To set fire to so many places, a man would have exhausted himself running about with a torch. And why go to such effort anyway, when a single blaze close to the room where the Governor slept would more likely finish him? All this suggested the flames were ignited by sorcery, and by someone outside the castle.

"Mahaffy," said the Governor, "you told me once that you spent a brief time as Diaspad's page, six years past, when your uncle lived in Peryf. But you also told me that you were at Caer Ysgithr when Corfil was alive."

The boy nodded. "I lived at Caer Ysgithr when I was very young, but then I was with my great—that is, I was with Lord Cado's household. I always lived with my uncle until the year he spent in Peryf."

"And where was your kinswoman, your nurse, Dame Ceinwen?"

Mahaffy settled back on his bed. "In Trewynyn, looking after

173

me the best that she could, or else wandering off on her own the way that she does."

Tryffin leaned forward. "Not here in Peryf with Dahaut?"

"Saints in Heaven, no!" Mahaffy laughed. "Dahaut was fourteen or fifteen at the time, quite the young lady and in no need of a nursemaid. Let alone, she and Ceinwen never got on. Possibly Lord Cado poisoned Dahaut against her. He is afraid of Ceinwen, you know. Otherwise, he would never let her set foot over his threshold, as much as he hates her."

Tryffin moved the bench a little closer. "So only Dahaut could say what his activities were at the time."

"I believe," said Mahaffy, "they were much the same as ever. Magic and politics, those were always his great interests."

The Governor thought about that. "But he had to do without politics when Calchas was Lord, because the Princess refused him a place at court."

"Yes," said the boy. Five days in bed had increased his natural pallor, and his big dark eyes were bright with fever. "But truth to tell, he was in and out of favor, in and out of a position at court, for just as long as I can remember."

Tryffin nodded thoughtfully. "I know Corfil and Goronwy generally favored him, but what of Morcant?"

Mahaffy shrugged. "Lord Morcant thought he was clever and often sought his advice, but I don't think that he ever *entirely* trusted him."

"And where did he live, where did *you* live, when your uncle was out of favor?" asked Tryffin. "At his house in Trewynyn, or at Castell Ochren?"

"We lived a great many places," said Mahaffy, fiddling with the rough wool blankets. "But not ever at Castell Ochren. You've never been to Ochren, have you? As God is my witness, it's the most blighted spot on the face of the earth. Nothing lives there, nothing grows there."

Tryffin began to suspect that he was about to learn something. "Do you know any reason why your uncle would wish to cause strife among the petty lords and the clan chieftains?"

Mahaffy was silent, his brows pinched together, his fingers continuing to play with the blankets. The Governor said, very gently, "When we were in Clynnoc you had something you wanted to tell me. Because you delayed you regretted it later."

"There are any number of things I would like to tell you, but . . ."

"But why won't you tell me, then?"

A tinge of color rose in Mahaffy's cheeks. "Because I did

everything wrong that I possibly could when we were in Clynnoc, and because I don't think you will think well of me now, if along with everything else I should happen to tell you that I was born of a wicked and treacherous house. Because if I do that, you will either distrust me on account of my blood, or else condemn me for disloyalty to my own clan.

"But then," he added, with a twisted smile, "you probably don't think we care much about family loyalty here in Mochdreff, anyway."

Tryffin sighed, because that came uncomfortably near the truth. "Aye . . . well. But I wish you *would* confide in me, for all that."

"Well," said Mahaffy, thinking it over, "perhaps I will. You took me in, offered me a place in a noble household when nobody else would have me, and you did save my life at the risk of your own. I owe you something for that . . . if only the sacrifice of my abominable pride."

"As to that," said Tryffin, "I was growing more than a bit weary of watching my attendants chewed and slashed and poisoned and all. I was damned if I was going to allow you to burn. But if you feel sufficiently obligated that you are now willing to tell me something of your uncle's motives, believe me, I won't think the worse of you."

Mahaffy lay back and closed his eyes, heaved a great weary sigh. "He calls himself a wizard, my Uncle Cado, and he has the laboratory and the wands and the pentacles—even a great sidhe-stone he uses sometimes as a crystal for scying. But I don't believe for a moment that he strives for harmony, order, or proportion. I can't tell you anything he has actually done to contribute to the trouble existing in Mochdreff, if that is what you are asking, but I can say that the feuding and the discord have always pleased him mightily."

"But why?" said Tryffin. This fit very well with everything he suspected, but offered no explanation. "Why does he want this? He has no place in the succession."

"I can only guess. But as I have known him all of my life, I believe that my guesses are good ones. If there is disorder throughout Mochdreff, why, that offers more scope for a man of his talents. And it isn't the role of Glastyn, the kingmaker, the peacemaker, he has selected for himself. I believe that he fancies himself another Gandwy of Perfudd. He wants to become an adept and he wants to become the greatest man in all Mochdreff, and if he ever gains the upper hand here, why then, like Gandwy, he will soon go looking for power beyond his own borders."

Mahaffy opened his eyes. "The reason I believe this is that I happen to *know* he is making animals."

Tryffin permitted himself a faint smile. "I think you mean breeding animals. Though what that could possibly—"

"I mean he is making them in his laboratory. He tried summoning a few out of the depths of the earth, as Gandwy and his cohorts did at the beginning, but that was a failure, so he started making them. Monsters, hybrids, like Gandwy's dreadful creations. The Lady Gwenlliant saw one of my Uncle Cado's more pitiful attempts when she was there in his laboratory. I don't know if she told you. It was a sickly creature and we found it dead soon after. Most of them do die eventually, or else Cado puts them out of their misery. They never have the vitality of Gandwy's monsters.

"You know of course," the boy went on, "that the Princess Diaspad actually kept two hybrids for a time: a griffon and a small manticore from the Mochdreffi Woods. It was your kinsman, Ceilyn mac Cuel, who killed the griffon at Caer Wydr, and they say you were on hand to view the deed, so you probably know more about the creature than I do. But I can tell you this: Cado was not best pleased when he learned the griffon had been killed and burned. Very taken with it he was, when it first came to Caer Ysgithr, back when Corfil was alive. The hours he spent studying the monster! And I always wondered how the manticore died before that. It was all so sudden, and the very same day, my uncle had the carcass in his laboratory, opening it up to see how the creature was made. I believe that he poisoned the poor beast, just so that he could take it apart."

"He always had an interest in monsters," Mahaffy added bitterly. "Why do you think he was after Dahaut?"

The Governor frowned and shook his head. "I don't follow you."

"They were too near related for marriage—and some people say the children of incest are abomination. He wanted to father his own little race of monsters: dog-headed boys and little daughters with webbed feet." Mahaffy's breath was irregular now; he clenched and unclenched his fists at the disgraceful memory. "In the beginning, she encouraged him. She liked all the special attention and favors, and she thought he was madly in love with her. But when she realized she was to be nothing but a brood mare for his unnatural offspring . . . well, that was too much, even for Dahaut!"

Tryffin was startled. "You say that she encouraged his attentions at first? Are you certain of that? God knows, it is always easy to blame the woman, when most of the time the poor things have no choice in the matter at all.''

''Yes, I know that,'' said Mahaffy. ''I do know that, Prince Tryffin. I've seen servant girls forced, and the men who took them revile them afterward for behaving like sluts. I'm a bit too young not—not to be shocked by such things. That is why I always wanted to believe in Dahaut. Only even for me, it became too difficult. Because she wasn't a child and she wasn't an innocent. She was seventeen years old and she had already taken a number of lovers. And if she was afraid—well, for all they weren't friends, she knew that Ceinwen would never allow my uncle to rape her.''

''God of Heaven,'' breathed Tryffin. He got up from the bench and began to pace the room. ''And this is the woman I made handmaiden to Gwenlliant. You might have warned me, Mahaffy.''

Mahaffy shrugged. ''I thought you were sleeping with her. If Dahaut was your mistress, I didn't think you would want to hear a word against her.''

The boy laughed, without much humor. ''Do you despise me for playing the complaisant kinsman? But Dahaut had entertained any number of lesser men in her bed; why should I take offense if she was sleeping with you? The time was it sent me absolutely wild, Dahaut and her affairs. When you had her two years back, I was ready to cut out your heart, though truth to tell, you weren't the first. You knew that, I suppose: Dahaut not being a virgin, and me hating you?''

''Yes,'' said Tryffin. ''I've been wondering these last few months why you decided to forgive me. And why *didn't* you cut out my heart, or at least try to?''

''Ah well,'' said Mahaffy, with a bright despairing glance. ''I was too young for anything like that. Though I kept a list of men I was going to kill as soon as I was old enough. But as the time drew near, the list grew so long, I knew I could never hope to kill so many. I thought I would do better to kill Dahaut, or else kill myself. Eventually, I decided she wasn't worth it.''

Two days later, Tryffin decided that Mahaffy was well enough to make the journey home—and he had already abandoned hope of finding the wizard if he was living in Peryf. The journey was uneventful, and the Governor's party reached Trewynyn in good time. Yet Tryffin barely had time to dismount, to set foot in the courtyard at Caer Ysgithr, before a crowd of people came out and surrounded him, all of them eager to claim his attention.

The Seneschal, it seemed, had quarreled with the Steward; and the Steward was at war with the Mayor of Trewynyn. Lord Dyfan and Lord Caradoc were disputing some minor point of precedence; the five old dames who lived in the Keep were ailing, but no doctor would attend them, they had such a reputation as difficult patients; and the Cook was at odds with the Butler. Besides that, two nearby clans were threatening blood feud . . .

Tryffin nodded his head, spoke soothing words, and promised to see to the more important matters just as soon as he possibly could. He had supposed before his journey that he left the government of Mochdreff running smoothly. But not so smoothly, he reflected gloomily, that the wheels kept turning despite his fortnight's absence. And the worst of it was that the journey into Peryf had been nothing more than a wild-goose chase, from beginning to end.

Looking over the heads of the crowd, he caught sight of Conn and summoned the boy to his side. "Go up to the Lady Gwenlliant immediately, and tell her I will visit her sometime tomorrow." He stripped off his gloves, tucked them into his belt. "After supper, take Mahaffy with you and spend the evening with the ladies. I am sure they will be heartily sick of their own company and of Garth by now, and very glad to see you. Convey my apologies that I can't visit her today, and tell her how it was that I was prevented."

"Yes," replied Conn, but his expression said as plainly as words that he wanted to say more, and did not know how to begin.

Tryffin was troubled, too. Standing suddenly undecided there in the courtyard, with the activity swirling around him, he wondered if he might be intentionally delaying a meeting that he was reluctant to face, a meeting that he genuinely dreaded.

Because supposing Gwenlliant should be as listless and remote now as she had been on the day he left her? Supposing she made it painfully obvious that she had not missed him at all?

And as she had done when each of her grandsons and grand-daughters came of an age to choose, the woman took Goreu up to the highest tower at Caer Ysgithr, and bade him look out upon the land below.

When he did as she instructed him, Goreu was struck by a marvelous vision, and the vision was this: Caer Ysgithr was a great silver wheel ceaselessly turning, and the tower where he stood was the hub of the wheel, and the walls and courtyards were the spokes. And beyond the castle was the town of Trewynyn that was likewise a wheel, only that wheel was far greater and it was made of gold. And beyond that, Goreu saw all the kingdoms and the principalities of the earth spread out before him, and they, too, formed the figure of a vast wheel, which was made of the same material as the stars of the firmament. And for each of these wheels, the place where he stood at Caer Ysgithr was the hub, and all these wheels were turning together, as though one mighty hand had set them to spinning at once, so that ever afterward what affected the motion of one wheel must likewise affect the others.

Later that day, when Goreu was alone in his room, his father's mother came to him, and she offered him the choice. In one hand she held an apple that was made of the purest, most shining gold, and in the other was a silver bowl, and the rim of that bowl was set with many sparkling jewels. She said to him: "One of these objects represents power and glory, and dominion over lesser men to the end of your days. The other represents Salvation. Now is the time for you to choose."

But she did not tell Goreu which object was which.

—*From* The Nine Sorrowful Tales
of the Misfortunes of Mochdreff

16.

The Castle of the Silver Wheel

Gwenlliant sat in the solar, feeling dreary and cross, only barely listening as Conn and Mahaffy recounted the story of their journey

179

and the fire in Peryf. Tryffin had returned virtually unscathed, and for that she was grateful, but it was plain *she* was not the woman who had drawn him back, and that thought was exceedingly painful.

She sat curled up in one of the great carven oak chairs, with her feet tucked under her skirts, her elbow on the arm of the chair, and her aching head supported by one icy hand. Whenever her eyes chanced to fall on Dahaut sitting by the fire sewing a seam, the heartache and the headache both grew worse.

The only bright spot, in what promised to be a dismal evening, was that Garth had arrived along with the other boys and promptly sat down on the floor by her chair, where he had remained ever since, silent but somehow companionable. Out of sheer idleness, without really thinking what she was doing, Gwenlliant reached down and absently stroked the back of his neck, at the place where his soft chestnut hair curled so appealingly.

Garth stiffened as though she had struck him. "Lady . . . don't ever do that!" he said, in a furious whisper.

"I thought you would like it," she whispered back. And then on an impulse—because she was cross and because he had hurt her feelings—she bent down and kissed the nape of his neck.

The boy made a strangling sound, deep in his throat, and turned to glare up at her. "Holy Mary Mother of God! What do you think you are doing?" he whispered indignantly.

Gwenlliant shook her head, blinking back tears. "I thought you were my friend," she said. "My *one* friend in this Godforsaken place."

His eyes softened at her apparent distress. "Well I am your friend," he replied. "And if you weren't such a child and—and an innocent, you would understand what a very good friend I am trying to be."

Much later, when her visitors had returned to the floor below, when her handmaidens and pages were all asleep, Gwenlliant slid out of her bed, dressed in the dark, then crept softly through the antechamber and along the corridor, until she came to the back stair.

As it had happened twice before, the magic took her instantly to the forbidden rooms in the Keep. And this time, Brangwengwen must have been expecting her visit, because the dwarf was already trotting down the hall, nodding her head and clapping her tiny hands together, as if in anticipation of some special treat.

"Ah, Princess, sweet Princess, I knew that you would come at last." The hunchback wore a tattered gown of mulberry silk and an immense headdress with curving horns like sickle moons, adorned with tiny pearls and sparkling glass jewels. "If not tonight, I told myself, then another time soon, for she has not been back in more than a fortnight."

"I can't come too often," said Gwenlliant, taking a rushlight down from one of the brackets on the wall. "Yes, I know that the pattern in the tower can twist time, but even during the short span it takes to go between the back stairs and my own room, someone might miss me."

"Well, you have come at last, however that might be," said Brangwengwen, in her creaking old voice. "And what would you like me to show to you tonight?"

Gwenlliant thought for a moment, though she had really made up her mind in advance. "I wish to see the chamber where the Princess worked her spells, where she kept her tools and her books of magic."

"And so you shall," said the dwarf. "And a very fine chamber it was and is. I will take you there gladly."

The girl followed the hunchback down the passage, through several dim, cobwebby rooms, and into a great circular chamber. It was like no room that she had ever seen before, and Gwenlliant, who knew quite a bit about wizardry but very little about witchcraft, glanced eagerly around her.

"How very odd," she said, placing her torch in a bracket by the door. "What is this on the floor?"

Where Lord Cado had a golden pentagram—very similar to the one in the Wizard's Tower at Caer Cadwy, where Gwenlliant's kinswoman Teleri practiced her craft—someone had painted on the floor of Diaspad's sanctum a great silver wheel with twelve long spokes radiating from a ring of gold stars at the center.

"It is the wheel of the year," said Brangwengwen. "Each spoke represents one of the twelve months. If you watch very closely, you may see it move."

So Gwenlliant watched, she stared very hard at the ring of stars at the center . . . and the wheel began to turn, slowly at first, then spinning faster and faster. Gwenlliant felt giddy watching it, for the silver wheel seemed to grow larger as well, so huge that the room could not contain it, so vast that it carried the entire castle with it, around and around.

And the wheel hummed as it turned, first very low and then increasingly louder, until it spoke with a great booming voice, the storm voice, the tide voice she had been listening for ever since she first stumbled into the forbidden rooms: the voice of the magic of Mochdreff.

181

But when she blinked her eyes, the wheel grew smaller and stopped spinning, the chamber grew silent, and she was staring at nothing more than a picture of a wheel that someone had painted on the floor of the room. And it was only her imagination, perhaps, that caused her to think she smelled lightning and rain in this musty stone room.

The dwarf took Gwenlliant by the hand and led her around the wheel to the other side of the chamber, where a large bronze brazier stood on three legs. "But watch, Lady. If I touch these coals and say the *word*, you shall see a wonder," she said, quite as though Gwenlliant had not already seen something marvelous.

At Brangwengwen's touch an eerie purple flame sprang up, perfuming the air with the scent of roses and lilies.

"I can make a fire, too," said Gwenlliant, not much impressed. "Though not nearly so pretty."

She had already seen that there was a broad brick hearth in another part of the room, piled high with dried branches waiting to be kindled. She stepped across the room, made a pass over the wood, and spoke the name of fire.

A thin plume of smoke rose up from the pile, and a pale blue flame, sickly even for a fire fed by Mochdreffi wood, began to lick the branches. Yet Gwenlliant felt strangely excited, because this was a trick she had never performed in anyone's sight but Teleri's.

The dwarf snorted derisively. "A Wizard Fire is not much." She knelt down beside the hearth and blew the fire out. "Bring me that light you brought in from the passage, and I will show you something more marvelous still."

Her curiosity aroused, Gwenlliant ran back to the bracket, drew out the rushlight, and brought it back to the hearth. Brangwengwen took the torch out of her hand, thrust it into the pile of branches, and ignited the wood. Then, as the girl knelt down on the hearth beside her, the dwarf said some words and made some gestures, and the flames blazed higher and took on many different colors, as though the wood had been doused with oils.

Gwenlliant was disappointed. "Pictures in the fire—I can do that. Though truth to tell, I'm not much of a wizard."

"But can you make the pictures come *out* of the fire?" Brangwengwen asked, with an arch smile.

When Gwenlliant shook her head, the dwarf did something else, something small and intricate, and the tiny glowing men and women inside the fire divided themselves from the flames and came tripping out across the hearth, where they stood quivering expectantly in their brilliant garments, their shining faces upturned, as if they were waiting for further orders . . . until a *word* from Brangwengwen snuffed them out.

"Shall I teach you how it is done?" asked the dwarf.

"No," said Gwenlliant. Her heart was pounding painfully in her chest, the pulse leaping in her veins. "You don't have to show me. I *felt* how you did it." And she repeated the dwarf's gesture, made the proper pattern in her mind, and another troop of tiny flame people came dancing out of the fire.

The dwarf drew in a sharp breath. "Ah, Lady, you have a great gift, a tremendous gift. Not as a wizard, to be sure, but for witchcraft. To think that you were able to learn that spell just by watching me! I have never seen such a natural aptitude in all my life."

"Yes," said Gwenlliant. "I know all that." Though the truth was, up until this moment she had scarcely grasped the extent of her power. "But I may not use my gift because—because an untrained gift is far too dangerous, and there was never anyone—not anyone but vile old hags and black warlocks dabbling in dirty little spells they did not understand—not anyone in Camboglanna who had the wisdom and the power to teach someone like me."

Brangwengwen was staring at her with shining eyes. "But you have come to Mochdreff, where the wise-women have mastered the art. And *I* could teach you a little, a very little, as I did just now." Suddenly, she leapt to her feet and ran across the room to a shelf crowded with books and the devices of magic: willow wands, and strange squat candles, and leathery bat wings, and weirder things besides. "And look, here are books, ancient grimoires, each one filled with mighty spells of magic that you could teach to yourself."

The dwarf pulled out a thick volume bound in black leather stamped in faded gold, sealed with great iron bands. Staggering a little under its weight, she carried the book across the room, where she placed it reverently in Gwenlliant's lap.

"I do not know what names she used to seal these books, but I doubt it would take you long to discover what they were. Shall I tell you something? These spells were too great for the Princess to master. She had only a small gift, after all. She paid a great price for these books, she studied and she studied, she practiced and she practiced, but she could only do little things, with fire and water, with smoke and mirrors, potions and love charms; only mists and illusions, and tampering with the minds of men; only small hurtful things, like itchings and burnings, and snatching a person's breath away—the sort of magic you mentioned just now, the province of dirty old hags and black warlocks. The great spells were always beyond her.''

Gwenlliant put out a hand to touch the grimoire, then pulled it away. The very walls reverberated with the names Diaspad had used to seal the books—how could she have imagined they would remain secret? "And what makes you think that *I* can do the great spells?''

The dwarf laughed merrily. "I do not think; I know. You made the silver wheel spin. The Princess could rarely cause it to move, and then only slowly. And you know it yourself, Lady, you feel it in your bones, in your blood. You were born to work such potent magics.''

By now, Gwenlliant's heart was pounding so hard she thought she might faint. She wanted to open that weighty mysterious volume, more than she had ever wanted anything in her life.

But she shook her head. "No, no, I must not do it. The greater the gift, the greater the danger. If I could find a—a wise-woman capable of training me, of guiding me every step of the way, then I might dare to open this grimoire, explore its secrets. But as things stand now, I must not even think of it.''

She gave the dwarf a pleading glance, pushed the volume from her with a repulsive gesture. "Take this book away, Brangwen-gwen, please take it away. I dare not even touch it.''

Tryffin was waiting for her in the morning, when she left the chapel. Gwenlliant was just handing her book of devotions over to Elffin, about to take the arm that Garth offered her, when she felt a shadow fall over her. She looked up through her misty silk veil, to see Tryffin standing beside her.

"Will you walk with me, Cousin?'' he asked, so coldly that Gwenlliant could only nod wordlessly.

He started out so swiftly across the yard that she had difficulty keeping up with him, nor did he look back even once to see how she fared. She had a horrible feeling that someone had seen her kissing Garth, that Tryffin had been told and was furiously angry. He did not stop until he reached the foot of a staircase leading up to the wall walk, and then he paused long enough to offer her a hand, to aid her in climbing the mossy steps.

His clasp was hard and cold, like holding hands with a stranger, and between that and attempting to manage her skirts with her other hand as she climbed, Gwenlliant was barely attending as he spoke.

"I own a house in Treledig, a very fine house . . . you could live at Caer Cadwy with your friends and relations, spend one

184

night a year under my roof, and we would still be married by the Laws of Celydonn, whether we live together or not.''

She had reached the top of the wall before she even realized that Tryffin was talking about sending her away. And then all the air went out of her lungs at once and the world went grey for a moment, and she might have fallen if he had not put an arm around her waist to steady her.

''You mean to put me aside, because I no longer please you.''

''Ah God, not anything of the sort at all. I'm just thinking of sending you home, where you will be happy and safe. For a year or two at most, until I am free to come and fetch you.''

Gwenlliant was glad of the veil that hid her face. She thought that perhaps he had good reason to be tired of her, as poor a wife as she had been, and she thought that perhaps she ought to do as he said and just go away. But something resisted the notion. ''Is that—is that what you truly want, Cousin?''

There was an icy wind blowing across the wall, and she began to shiver, as much with the shock as the cold. Tryffin drew her into a more sheltered spot, beside the parapet. ''It is not what I want at all. But neither do I wish to keep you here, breaking your heart and your spirit—''

''Because I won't go,'' she said, feeling suddenly quite stubborn, though she was uncertain whether it was Tryffin or the castle and its secrets she did not want to leave. ''Not unless you send men to carry me away by force.''

''No?'' he said, on a rising inflection, and he sounded so relieved she thought she might have misheard him.

She shook her head. ''I belong here with you, and I won't go away. Not if you bring a dozen mistresses one after the other, and set each one in my place.''

Now there was no mistaking his profound relief. ''Ah well then, we'll not speak of it,'' he said. Gwenlliant began to breathe a little easier, and her eyes stopped stinging. ''But I haven't any mistresses,'' he said, drawing her into his arms, ''not even one.'' Even through layers of clothing, the hard muscles of his chest, she could feel his heart pounding strongly.

She relaxed against him, inhaling his clean, sunny scent, while Tryffin continued on in that soft Gwyngellach lilt that made even the sweetest blandishments sound utterly believable. ''Even if I had, if I wanted to be foolish and cruel, I could bring a woman here and take her into my bed, sit her at my right hand on state occasions, even take her to Gwyngelli and present her to my father. But I could never put her in your true place, because that is in my heart, and that is where you will remain as long as I live.''

It was very pleasant being held so close and warm, but Gwenlliant sighed and slid out of his arms, so that she could look up into his face and study his expression. "Is that true? Is that really so?"

"You should know by now," he answered, drawing her back again, "that I would never say so, unless it was God's own truth."

Winter was over but spring was reluctant. The first week of February was all rain and mud, yet the sky finally cleared and a hint of spring softness crept into the air.

Those apparent disasters that had greeted the Governor on his return had all been resolved, and with surprising ease. Tryffin was beginning to realize that his councilors and his officers had a flare for the dramatic (or else desired to impress him with the vital importance of their offices and their duties) and were therefore inclined to make much out of little. Accordingly, he put his own duties aside every evening before supper, that he might spend an hour or two with Gwenlliant, before retiring.

But there was a marked coldness between the Governor and Dahaut—which from Gwenlliant's viewpoint was all to the good. Whether he and Mahaffy's beautiful cousin had quarreled, or whether Tryffin had merely shifted his affections back where they belonged, she did not know. Gwenlliant was content to devote each evening to keeping him happy and amused with bright conversation—and spend the rest of the day seeking her own amusement, solely to keep herself occupied until he arrived.

She was searching for something to do, one fair, breezy day, when Dahaut, who had spent most of the morning wandering listlessly from one room to another, suddenly conceived a desire to go out riding, and surprised Gwenlliant by asking for her company.

"Do please come with me, Lady. It will do you good after living so confined the whole winter long," said Dahaut—with a pretty show of regard that was just as unexpected as it was unusual.

Gwenlliant felt sorry for her and inclined to be generous. Dahaut had lost whatever attraction it was she had exerted over Tryffin; Conn, Garth, and Mahaffy plainly wanted nothing to do with her; Grainne, Faelinn, and Traeth admired her beauty but could not endure her temper; and of course Dahaut herself had little use for such young and negligible persons as Cei and Elffin. Small wonder, then, if Mahaffy's cousin was feeling lonely and miserable, and looking to make friends with the Lady of the castle.

And while the evenings were pleasant, Gwenlliant sometimes

found the days intolerably long. Even an outing with Dahaut would provide some distraction.

"But where would we go?" Gwenlliant asked. "It is not very good exercise riding through the town, because the horses can only go poking along.

"I wish that we knew someone to visit *outside* of the town," she added wistfully. In fact, she had never ventured beyond the gates of Trewynyn, not in all the months she had lived in Mochdreff.

"But *I* know someone—or at least someplace," said Dahaut. "There is a sweet little wayside chapel a mile or two from the West Gate, and I am longing to go there. I haven't been inside a church in weeks and weeks."

Gwenlliant favored Dahaut with a skeptical glance. "You might have come with *me*. Why have you not, if it means so much to you?"

Dahaut made a restless, scornful gesture. "A *Rhianeddi* Mass: all candles and incense, all show and little piety. I am accustomed to a very different service, that I can assure you."

Gwenlliant shook her head. Brother Bedwini (when he did not garble the whole thing) followed the southern rites of worship. About all that Mass in the chapel at Caer Ysgithr could boast of pomp and ceremony was a dozen or two wax candles set up behind the altar, a massive gold crucifix, and a liberal sprinkling of incense, every now and again, in the course of the celebration. These things—presumably—as Brother Bedwini's concession to the Governor's lady, her northern birth and her southern upbringing.

This being so, Gwenlliant was frankly curious to learn how the true Mochdreffi, the proud old families like clan Guillyn, actually worshipped. Yet she had heard of Mochdreffi schisms and heresies all of her life. "Dahaut, this isn't a *heretical* church you wish me to visit?"

Dahaut looked positively horrified. "Oh, Lady, how can you think it? It is nothing at all like that. Just a plain service, very simple and very holy. Being so sweet and simple yourself, I feel certain you would appreciate it."

Gwenlliant was not so certain that was meant as a compliment, but Dahaut had aroused her interest by now, and she was very eager to go. "It ought to be safe, even outside the town, if we take one or two men to guard us. And my pages of course—I have to take them."

But then she thought of something that caused her to hesitate. "Dahaut, do you dare leave the castle?" Gwenlliant had only the haziest idea why Lord Cado's niece was supposed to be living up at the castle, but she knew it had something to do with escaping her uncle.

Dahaut shrugged her beautiful shoulders. "I had a letter from my uncle just last week, brought up from Trewynyn. He is somewhere to the north and has no idea that I left his house and accepted your protection. As he'll not be back for a month at least, I intend to enjoy my freedom while I may."

As soon as she passed through the gates of the town, Gwenlliant started to look around her with intense interest. It was too early in the year to get much sense of the land. Fields were still grey and mostly barren, bushes were leafless. But the trees Gwenlliant and her companions rode past, in orchards and little copses, were straighter and more comely than the appletrees up at the castle, and here and there, along the road, she spotted boys and girls minding their flocks: pigs, or geese, or shaggy slant-eyed goats.

"Dahaut," said Gwenlliant, after a considerable time had passed. "I think we have traveled much more than two miles."

"It is just ahead," said the young woman. "Just around that rise in the road . . . or perhaps the one after that."

The church was not over the next rise, but it did come soon after: a place that Gwenlliant might have mistaken for a poor sort of cottage with a thatched roof, except that the building was longer and higher, with a large wooden cross nailed up over the door.

That cross, Gwenlliant noticed with a certain distaste, had been carelessly placed—or perhaps some of the nails had rusted and fallen out, so that it tilted to one side in a drunken manner that struck her as slightly sacrilegious.

"I am not quite certain—" she said, when they had dismounted by the door. But Dahaut had already taken her by the hand and was leading her into the church. Cei and Elffin and the two guards sent by Meligraunce trailed after them.

From the very moment that she passed through the door, Gwenlliant was sorry she had come. The church was bare and unlovely: tallow dips on the alter instead of candles, a rough wooden floor, a number of crude benches arranged in straggling lines. As Dahaut led her to a bench at the front of the church, she could see that the cloth up on the altar was plain white linen, rather dingy, and that the cup and the plate were old, cracked wood.

Yet it was not the poverty or even the dirt that was so distressing. When Gwenlliant, following Dahaut's example, knelt on the floor, turned her eyes toward the alter, she saw for the first time a second wooden cross, a crudely made crucifix with a saturnine Christ (he reminded Gwenlliant of Rhun of Yrgoll) sneering down at the congregation. And that congregation—a mixture of rich and poor, common and noble—she could actually *feel* the evil radiating off them in dark smothering waves. The place fairly reeked of heresy, a rank spiritual malaise so strong there was no mistaking it, and Gwenlliant thought she was going to be sick if she stayed much longer.

Without a word to Dahaut, she crossed herself, rose to her feet, and hurried out the door, her guards following after her. Once she was out in God's pure air, Gwenlliant sat down on a mossy rotting log, about twenty feet from the church, and tried to compose herself.

"Where are Cei and Elffin?" she asked, after a considerable time had passed.

"Here we are," said Cei, from somewhere behind her. The boys came around and sat down on the log to either side of her. They both looked just as pale and shaken as Gwenlliant felt.

"What kind of a church *was* that?" Elffin asked indignantly. "And why was Lord Jesus so—so ugly?"

"Because," said a gentle voice, "some men create God in their own image."

Gwenlliant looked up at once, and was surprised to see that a strange friar in a dusty black habit was standing over her. She had no idea who he was or where he had come from, but he had a mild and saintly demeanor that inspired confidence.

"Oh, Father," she said unsteadily, "if that is true, then the men who carved that crucifix must be exceedingly wicked."

"That is entirely possible," said the cleric. "But then it might follow that men who make beautiful images must be saintly indeed. And that as we know is not always true."

Gwenlliant managed a faint smile—until an unpleasant thought struck her. "Father, you aren't in any way connected with that church over there?"

"Daughter, I am not," said the friar, returning her smile with a peculiarly radiant one of his own. "Except that I often pass this way, hoping to meet someone like yourself, someone who is not past saving, and turn them aside with words of gentle piety before they make the mistake of going inside."

He sat down at one end of the rotten log and crossed his sandaled feet. "I see that I have arrived too late, this time. Too late to spare you and your poor pages from a terrifying experience— for which I am sorry. But perhaps I can offer some words of comfort. A pure heart can withstand any temptation, and innocence provides a shield that is stronger than steel. Unless . . ."

His radiance dimmed just a little. "I hope, dear child, that you did not take Communion?'' Gwenlliant shook her head. ''That is fortunate. They mix goat's blood with the wine, you know, and bone dust with the flour to make the bread. If you had touched either one, you might be in some danger.''

''In—in danger of what?'' Gwenlliant asked, suddenly remembering that Dahaut was still inside. But then, Dahaut had already been to this church before, and had probably been drinking blood and swallowing bone dust for years and years.

The gentle friar crossed himself. ''In danger of succumbing to the lure of evil. What greater danger could there be? If a man loses his life, what does it matter? But if he should lose his immortal soul!''

''Yes,'' said Gwenlliant, plucking at her skirts. ''Yes, that would be much worse. But Father . . . I do not know your name,'' she suddenly realized.

''I am Father Idris. And you, my daughter?''

Gwenlliant told him who she was, and also presented Cei and Elffin. The truth was, she was much attracted to this kindly cleric. Brother Bedwini was so vague and forgetful, so lacking in piety and so given to idle gossip, he hardly seemed to be paying attention when she made her confession. And as for telling him anything *serious*, like her temptation to open the Princess Diaspad's books . . .

''Father Idris, if I wished to visit you, if I wanted to make a confession, where would I find you?''

''My dear child,'' said the friar, ''if you should need me, I will gladly come to you.''

But Gwenlliant was strangely reluctant to extend Tryffin's hospitality, for all that she felt so drawn to this man. ''No, it would be better to visit you myself than to send a servant after you, and then have to wait while he travels both ways.''

The friar shrugged and smiled sweetly. ''I have a humble hermitage a mile down the road. You cannot miss it, for there is a ruined church and an ancient oak tree, and a beautiful little well which is a natural spring. You are welcome to visit me anytime,'' he said, rising to his feet. ''Indeed, I should be going back there now, since I arrived here too late to save any poor souls.''

Gwenlliant gave him permission to go, and he walked down the road, soon disappearing over another rise. Deprived of his comforting presence, she began to feel sick and disturbed all over again.

In fact, she wanted desperately to go home, but could not bring herself to take the guards and abandon Dahaut, as little as she felt that she owed her. Fortunately, she did not have long to wait. The church door opened and the congregation came swarming out, Lord Cado's niece among the rest.

The service had strongly affected Dahaut, though not, so far as Gwenlliant could see, for any good. Dahaut looked more beautiful and more arrogant than ever, walking with her head high and her eyes sparkling. She even laughed at the sight of Gwenlliant's troubled face.

"So you did not care for it, after all," she said, abandoning the friendly pose she had assumed earlier. "I should have taken your foolish northern prejudices into account before I invited you."

Allowing one of the guards to help her up into the saddle, she threw Gwenlliant a defiant glance. "Shall you cast me out—now that you know I practice this 'heretical' faith?"

Gwenlliant shook her head sadly. "No, I can't do that, or I would have done so a long time since. Prince Tryffin has brought you to stay at Caer Ysgithr, and he has been acquainted with you so long and so . . . well . . . he must already know this thing about you."

Dahaut laughed. "But of course he knows. What does it matter to Tryffin? You know the Gwyngellach, they are all of them pagans or the next thing to it. Why should one form of Christianity be more to them than any other?"

Gwenlliant sighed. Dahaut's familiar use of the Governor's name had not passed unnoticed. And if the things she said of Tryffin's people were not precisely true, they were still uncomfortably close to the truth. Like Gwenlliant's own Gwyngellach mother, Tryffin and his family were devoted to the Church, but many of Lord Maelgwyn's subjects practiced the Old Religion openly—which freedom they owed to a tolerant attitude on the part of Maelgwyn and his two sons.

An attitude, Gwenlliant thought, which probably embraced people of Dahaut's sort as well.

"No," she repeated, "I can't send you away. But it would please me very well, so long as you remain at Caer Ysgithr, if you would keep yourself just as far from me as possible."

Dahaut laughed and tossed her head. "As to that . . . the farther from you and the nearer to your lord, the happier I shall be."

"I will speak with my father; I will gain his consent," said Menai. "Then I will return here before the year turns, and make you my bride." Taking her by the hand, he led her across the garden. They sat down, side by side, on a bench under a tree. Through all this he continued to hold her hand tightly—as though (for all his hopeful words) he feared to lose her.

Guenhumara smiled at him, but that fragile smile did not go so far as her eyes. "Dear Heart," he said, "do you doubt I will return? My love for you is not so small a thing that I could forget you while I am gone. You and I shall be wed. Has not your uncle consented, who vowed he would oppose us to his last breath. And when we do marry, all the old wounds will be healed, and your people and my people will live as brothers ever afterward, as it was meant to be from the beginning."

"Then go swiftly and return soon," said Guenhumara. "I have bad dreams and my heart aches me, and I cannot banish this terrible fear that someone will come to snatch away our happiness, just when we think we hold it secure."

17.

Riddles Wisely Expounded

"You looked tired," Tryffin said to Gwenlliant, that evening after supper. "How far did you ride?"

Gwenlliant glanced up from her hand of cards. She and Tryffin sat in his bedchamber, on opposite sides of a small table, playing a game of Cyffle. As the hour was growing late, and Gwenlliant's pages and handmaidens had gone up to bed, the two of them were quite alone together—if you did not count Garth, Conn, and Mahaffy, who were out in the antechamber just the other side of a half-open door.

Gwenlliant gave a slight shake of the head. "Not very far," she answered, a little abstracted. She had not been thinking of that unpleasant outing, but of the magic books up in Diaspad's rooms.

There was still so much that Gwenlliant wanted to learn from Brangwengwen, but she was afraid to return to the Princess's rooms, for fear the dwarf might attempt to convince her to read some of the spells.

"But you know, it is a long time since I had so much exercise." She put her last card down on the table: the Knave of cups. Tryffin trumped it with the two of staves, and took the trick, winning the hand at the same time.

"Another game?" he suggested, but Gwenlliant shook her head again.

They had hit on the idea of of using Gwenlliant's ivory hairpins for counters, and most of these were already piled on Tryffin's side of the table. "As you can see," she said, with a movement of her hand, "you have practically beggared me."

He laughed, reached out and captured a lock of winter-gold hair, and carried it to his lips. "We might play for different stakes. We could play for kisses, or . . . ?"

Gwenlliant blushed and pulled away, so that the lock of hair slipped through his fingers. "I think it is growing late, Cousin, and I should go to bed."

"Aye," he said softly, not trying to conceal his disappointment. "But not with me, it seems."

She pushed back her chair and rose to her feet, made him a curtsy, and waited to be dismissed.

"Good night, then," he said, with a sigh. "Sleep well, Dear Heart." But he did not get up and open the door for her, as was his usual custom, nor did he escort her up the steep flight of stairs between their rooms.

Gwenlliant went up the private staircase alone, wondering how badly she had offended him. It was not until she reached her own bedchamber that she remembered she had left all of her hairpins down on the table below.

"If I go back to get them, he will naturally think I have changed my mind," she said, under her breath. "And perhaps I *have* changed my mind. It is absurd for me to be frightened, for he is not at all like Calchas, and he would never hurt me."

Yet she continued to hesitate. "But if I do go back, and he tries to kiss me, and I get frightened again, then perhaps he will despise me for teasing and provoking him. And if I go back and *he* has grown cold . . . No, there would be no reason for me to feel humiliated then, because I was only going back to fetch my hairpins." She sat down on the edge of her bed, with her hands clasped tightly in her lap. "Only he may think it was the hairpins, anyway, and I won't know which one it is: whether he doesn't want me or is just trying to be kind.''

She wrung her hands, trying to decide what she ought to do. While she thought she might like to return, she was horribly afraid she would make matters worse, and the more she thought, the harder it was to reach any decision.

Down in his bedchamber, Tryffin stood staring into the fire, cursing himself for a clumsy fool. Why had he suggested they go to bed together, when he knew perfectly well how Gwenlliant would react? Why say anything, when a few gentle kisses might have pleaded his case better than any words?

The door to the antechamber opened wide, and Garth came into the room. ''Your Grace, it's Dahaut. She insists on speaking with you privately.''

There was disapproval in every line of the boy's body, and Tryffin could not blame him. The situation did conjure up an unflattering (though inaccurate) picture of the way he conducted his affairs: supper and cards with his trusting little wife, and then bed with his beautiful, sensuous mistress. Let alone, a man would have to be blind not to see that young Garth was growing much too fond of Gwenlliant.

''For the love of God, send her away. Do you imagine that I sent for her?'' Tryffin asked impatiently.

Garth's expression softened slightly. ''Ah well, I didn't know. I mean—I mean it's not for me to say, is it? But she seems very urgent. Will you come out and dismiss her yourself?''

Tryffin considered that, but decided against it. ''No, send her in. But don't you and the others go to bed yet. I will be needing you soon to help me undress.''

But Garth did not take the hint. He brought Dahaut into the room and then closed the door firmly behind him as he left.

With an effort, Tryffin kept his face blank, his voice soft. ''Lady, if my regard for your reputation forbids me to invite you, surely you should have more pride than to come here uninvited.''

She advanced several steps, speaking in a low, throaty whisper. ''Pride? What use have I for pride, now you have grown so cold and cruel? When you brought me to Caer Ysgithr, at least I had your friendship. Now I have even less than that. Yet what have I done to offend you? Tell me my fault that I may amend it.''

Tryffin made a futile gesture with his hands. ''You have not done anything, not anything to me, that requires either amendment or forgiveness.

''No, Dahaut, let me speak,'' he said, as she moved a little closer. "I brought you here for your protection, but I am afraid I caused a scandal instead. Let me find a place for you in another household. Dame Indeg or Dame Maffada . . . one of those venerable ladies might be willing to take you in. You would still be safe within the walls of Caer Ysgithr, but people would not be so ready to assume the worst of us."

Dahaut laughed, a dry, brittle sound. "You think my good name can be so easily restored? How little you know of the ways of the world. Because you are generous in your own mind, you expect equal generosity of others."

She took another few steps in his direction, came so close that he could smell her musky perfume, feel the heat radiating from her body. And God help him, he knew how soft and smooth and sweet that body was, under her satin gown. "If people will say hard things of us whatever we do, why should we not at least claim the pleasure that goes with the blame?"

And the truth was, it had been far too long since Caer Clynnoc. Without entirely meaning to, Tryffin reached out and took Dahaut into his arms, felt her body yielding to him, her mouth go soft and warm under his kisses. Wanting more, he crushed her against him.

"Ah God, no," he breathed, with his mouth against her throat "If things were different . . . but not here in this place." Yet he was still holding her, still kissing her, when the door at the back of his bedchamber creaked open.

If God is merciful, it won't be Gwenlliant. But he was afraid to look past Dahaut, afraid to find out. *If God loves me, it will be Elffin or Cei come down to fetch something she left behind. It will be Grainne or Faelinn or Traeth, but it won't be Gwenlliant.*

With a heavy heart, he put Dahaut away from him and forced himself to look. And of course it *was* Gwenlliant, standing with one hand on the door and a look of sorrowful reproach on her face.

"I beg your pardon, Prince Tryffin. I did not mean to disturb you," she said softly, sketching a little curtsy.

"Sweetheart, I swear to you, it's not what you think," he said. But he knew as he said it how banal, how commonplace, how utterly unconvincing, that must sound. Men had been saying those same words since the beginning of the world—and how many women had been foolish enough to believe them?

Not Gwenlliant, certainly, for all he happened to be speaking the truth. She slipped out of his room and closed the door quietly behind her. And by the time he had followed her up the stairs, by the time he reached the landing outside her bedchamber, she had locked her door and barred it against him.

Early the next morning, an hour before dawn, Gwenlliant left her bed, threw a cloak over her nightgown, and tiptoed down the corridor to the back stairs.

She went directly to the circular chamber where the Princess Diaspad had once worked her magic, lit a fire on the hearth, and selected a thick volume from one of the shelves. She sat down on the floor with the grimoire in her lap. Taking a deep breath, she spoke the name that opened the iron bands, lifted the cover, and started leafing through the brittle parchment pages.

Sometime during the long, dark, tearful hours following her discovery of Tryffin and Dahaut, Gwenlliant had come to a terrible realization. Dahaut was not only proud and disagreeable, she was actively evil. *I have no mistress,* Tryffin had said. Yet Dahaut went into that Church of the Damned, came out virtually glowing with infernal energy, and a few hours later Tryffin was holding her in his arms, kissing her as though he never meant to stop. Could it possibly be that Tryffin was under the influence of some evil spell, the victim of Dahaut and the powers of Darkness?

Sitting on the floor of the circular chamber, with the big grimoire lying open in her lap, Gwenlliant shivered at the thought. Having been the victim of a so-called love charm, she knew what a horrible experience that could be. It was *because* Calchas had raped her mentally and emotionally when she was still very young that she could not love Tryffin in the way that she ought.

Gwenlliant felt her stomach turn over, her hands go damp and clammy. Even remembering all the repulsive, dreadful, *perverse* things she had thought and felt, even recalling the whole sordid incident so many years later, the degrading sense of violation was still strong. And while Tryffin was a man and not . . . inexperienced . . . he must still hate what was happening to him, must despise himself as much as he loathed Dahaut.

Yet if there are love spells in these books—and considering they belonged to the Princess Diaspad, I think there must be—then there may be counterspells as well. Staring sightlessly ahead of her, Gwenlliant stiffened her spine. *If there is a way to save Tryffin, then I should be the one to find it, I should be the one to save him. Because nobody else can begin to guess what he must be suffering.*

The Governor was standing at an open window near the top of the Keep, staring moodily out to sea, when Meligraunce found him the next afternoon. ''Ah, Captain, you look like a man with something important to relate," Tryffin said, as he turned away from the window.

"I have," replied Meligraunce. "At least, in light of your former attempts to locate the Princess Diaspad's servants and Lord Maelgwyn's more recent advice to seek the intimates of Bron the dwarf, I think you will find my news of great interest. Pergrin the giant has been found."

Meligraunce reached into the front of his doublet and extracted a roll of parchment. "But here, I believe you might wish to read Cradawg's report yourself."

Tryffin accepted the parchment, opened it up, and scanned it briefly. "At Castell *Ochren*? The giant has been living at Castell Ochren these last three years?"

"So it would seem," said the Captain.

"In that case," said Tryffin, setting his jaw, "I think it is time I had a long talk with young Mahaffy." It seemed to him that the boy had been less forthcoming than he previously supposed, and that some explanation was in order now.

"Certainly, Your Grace. I believe you will find him in the South Tower, polishing your armor," offered Meligraunce, moving aside so Tryffin could go past him. "At least he was heading that way when last I spoke to him."

Half an hour later, Tryffin found Mahaffy seated on a bench in the armory, vigorously buffing a piece of plate armor with a bit of rag. At his approach the boy started to rise.

"No, continue on as you were." Tryffin pulled up a stool and sat down, and the youth resumed his task, though not without an apprehensive glance at the Governor's stony countenance.

"Mahaffy," said Tryffin, rather more sternly than was his wont, "why didn't you tell me that Diaspad's giant was living at Castell Ochren?"

Mahaffy furrowed his brow. "Because you never asked me. Did you wish to find him? I remember that you wanted to know about Brangwengwen and the other dwarfs, but you never said a word about Pergrin."

Tryffin released a long sigh, and his manner grew slightly more cordial. "No more I did. Yet I remember that you did tell me, once, that nothing lives in Ochren."

The boy shrugged. "I meant to say that no wild birds or animals live there. There apparently remains just enough fertility in the soil of Ochren for a single garden, capable of supporting one enormous man and a small flock of chickens. But except for the garden and the chickens, Pergrin lives entirely off the bounty of my Uncle Cado."

Tryffin thought that over. "But why should it happen, if you don't mind my asking, that your Uncle Cado of all men should take compassion on poor Pergrin and give him a place to live?"

"For a number of reasons," said Mahaffy, continuing on with his work. "It suits my uncle's fancy to have *someone* live in Ochren, else the Lord of Ochren is lord of no one . . . and no one but Pergrin is willing to live there. And dwarfs and hunchbacks and giants, they all bring bad luck, but how could ill-fortune possibly come to Ochren, which is Hell's Back Country to begin with? Also, my Uncle Cado would like to learn certain of the Princess Diaspad's secrets and he imagines that Pergrin is the man to tell him. And lastly, it is rare for these freaks of nature to live to any great age. When Pergrin dies, my uncle wants to know where he is, so he can boil off the flesh and examine the bones.

"The rest I just told you is just me guessing," added the boy, holding the piece of leg armor up so that it caught the light, and he could examine his handiwork. "But Lord Cado told me himself that he wants Pergrin's body after he dies."

Tryffin grimaced. "Now I wonder if that might be considered a fortunate or an unfortunate circumstance for Pergrin?"

"As to that," said Mahaffy, beginning to polish again, "I believe that Pergrin might be as dead as Diaspad's manticore by now—and of the same causes—but the great oaf is so incredibly stupid and inclined to wander in his conversation that it has taken all this time for my uncle to glean what few bits of information the giant has to offer.

"Though now I come to think of it," he added, with a wry smile, "Pergrin may not be so stupid, after all. Maybe he has good reason to play the half-wit. And what Lord Cado has learned from Pergrin, I don't know. That's not the sort of thing that Cado would tell me. I can only say that he always appears dissatisfied whenever he returns from a visit to Ochren."

Tryffin picked up a stray piece of harness and examined it absently. "I wonder if I can learn anything more from the giant than your uncle has—supposing I went into Ochren in order to meet with him."

Mahaffy shook his head. "I don't know. But the giant seemed a timid sort in the days when I knew him. I think he may be afraid of my uncle, and that makes him even less coherent than usual. But you, Prince Tryffin, have a way with the common folk, which might stand you in good stead in the case of the giant."

"Aye," said Tryffin, glancing up at him. "A journey into Ochren, that hardly sounds pleasant, but it may prove of value— yes, it may prove valuable.

"And considering that I seem to invite disaster wherever I go, when it doesn't come seeking me here at home, there is some comfort at least to be had in the thought that even *I* can't bring ill-luck to a place like Ochren."

With the fine weather continuing, Tryffin was eager to begin his journey into Ochren, but he had one or two items of personal business he wanted to attend to first. He began with Dahaut, when he found her alone in Gwenlliant's solar, embroidering a piece of fine linen.

She had settled herself on a velvet cushion in the window seat, where the light pouring in set her chestnut hair aflame—a sight which could not fail to move him profoundly, as much as he hardened his heart against her.

"You must do as I suggested and find yourself a place, and that in the next week, before I go. You know how to make yourself agreeable when you choose. Go to the old women who live in the Keep and ask one of them to take you in."

"And what if I *won't*," retorted Dahaut, rising to her feet, her bosom heaving and her grey eyes flashing. "What if I won't serve as waiting woman to some half-blood hag, whose birth is inferior to my own? I am a Guillyn, after all, and there is no clan of purer descent. Will you cast me out into the street to starve, or leave me at the mercy of my lecherous uncle?"

"I will not cast you out, but neither will I keep you," he said. "If you cannot or will not find a household that will take you, then I will have to find a place for you—and you may not like the place that I choose."

Rather than argue with him, Dahaut turned suddenly thoughtful. "Prince Tryffin," she said, after a moment of deep concentration, "you said once that you would give me a house of my own, hire servants to wait on me, provide all else that I might need. Why should you not do so now? The castle is large. I can set up a household all of my own, and live as befits my birth."

He had meant, of course, a residence elsewhere. But he was eager to get her out of Gwenlliant's way, had not the heart to evict her by force, and so he was willing to compromise. "Very well, Dahaut, find some rooms for yourself—as far as possible from Melusine's Bower—and two or three servants who please you. But you are not to attempt to rival my lady's household or live in a style that attracts attention."

Having got her way, Dahaut sat down on her velvet cushion and took up her fine embroidery once more. He was turning to go, when another thought struck him.

"Would you like your cousin to come and live with you? I don't know that Mahaffy is comfortable sharing quarters with Garth and Conn, and you might wish to have your kinsman near you."

Dahaut gave a nasty little laugh. "Oh yes, that would be a splendid idea, considering the proclivities of the men of my house."

Tryffin frowned at her, considering the joke in questionable taste. "I think you do Mahaffy a great wrong comparing him to your uncle. From all I have seen, he is an honorable lad and perfectly trustworthy." Gazing down at her, Tryffin began to feel a deep disgust. "I never guessed it before, but you have an evil mind."

The lady gave a careless shrug. "And I suppose you will also accuse me of an evil mind, if I say young Garth has been sniffing around your innocent little bride, like a dog after . . . Ah, but I see that you know already. Well, I hope you have sense enough to take him with you on this journey of yours."

"I do," said Tryffin. "Though not because I mistrust either one of them."

Dahaut found rooms for herself and moved out before the week was over. Unfortunately, during those same seven days Garth went to bed with a severe chill, a chill which swiftly descended to his lungs, making him desperately ill for several days. Though he was mending by the time Tryffin was ready to depart, there could be no question of subjecting the boy to a two- or three-day journey.

"Lord, I will ride at your side, if you ask," said Garth, lying on his narrow bed, looking utterly miserable. "I missed all the excitement in Clynnoc and Peryf, and I don't mind a little discomfort in order to be there when I am needed."

Tryffin shook his head. "If you come on this journey, the only excitement that is going to occur will be a dangerous relapse on your part, and the rest of us scurrying to find a healer capable of saving your life. Stay at home and stay in bed, Garth. I will take you with me on my next journey."

He might have postponed the trip, but that would be much too pointed—especially with Dahaut still in the castle, eager to draw conclusions that others might miss and eager to spread those conclusions abroad.

And if he allowed Gwenlliant and Garth to believe that he doubted them . . . well, he knew something of young people, after all, and expected they were perfectly capable of getting into mischief merely for the sake of proving him right.

• • •

Now there are some Secrets which would be Perilous indeed if Common Men were permitted to Bruit them abroad, for which reason our Philosophers conceal them through the use of Paradox, Contradiction, and Enigma, dipping their pens in Obscurity and writing out their precepts in Riddling Words and Cloudy Clauses. Yet there are other Mysteries so Profound they may be mentioned openly, for only a very Wise Man or an Exceedingly Foolish one could possibly Explain them.

—*From* The Magician's Seventh Key

• • •

If Clynnoc had been a grim place to visit, Ochren was even worse. The land was bare and ugly, harder than iron, colder than stone, and dryer than weathered bones. As Mahaffy had said, nothing grew there. Yet from the number of ruined castles, the remnants of once fine roads, it must have been one of the most pleasant and populous regions in all Mochdreff four or five centuries past.

This was the place where it all started, Tryffin thought, as Roch carried him down the long dusty road. This was the heart of the blight. He had never in his life encountered such a harsh, unforgiving landscape.

Castell Ochren was bleak and proud, as might be expected, a mass of black stone piled up on a rugged eminence. When the Governor and his party rode into the courtyard, Pergrin limped out from one of the gloomy towers to greet them. Ten feet tall, or perhaps a bit more, the yellow-haired giant looked just as lanky and awkward and genial as Tryffin remembered. At the sight of the Governor, he smiled broadly.

"Tryffin fab Maelgwyn, that was a squire at Caer Cadwy," said Pergrin, apparently forgetting he had seen Tryffin and his brother knighted.

"Aye, that's right," said Tryffin, swinging down out of the saddle. It had been a long time since he and the giant had met, almost as long since he had encountered anyone who exceeded him in height, so it was an odd sensation looking up into Pergrin's grinning, childlike face. "But I have been living in Mochdreff for some time now, at Caer Ysgithr."

The giant grinned more broadly than ever and nodded his head. "Now, there's a strange thing . . . there's a wonder for the world. A Prince of Gwyngelli living in Mochdreff."

Mahaffy made a face and a hopeless gesture, as if to apologize

201

for his uncle's henchman, but Tryffin thought Pergrin spoke good sense. "I must admit that it surprises me, too."

What Tryffin was doing at Castell Ochren the giant declined to ask, apparently concluding that the presence of Lord Cado's nephew explained the whole thing, or perhaps not considering the question at all. It was not until much later, when the Governor, his squires, and Captain Meligraunce were sitting in the ruined dining hall sharing the giant's rude but hearty meal—boiled turnips, coarse bread, roast capon, and ale—that Tryffin first mention the reason for his visit.

"I have come to talk with you, Pergrin, because you were a friend of Bron the dwarf."

Pergrin's face clouded. "Bron. Aye, he was a friend of mine. The best friend I ever had, Brandegorias Corynaid, God love him. But he went away some years past. He went north with the Princess while the rest of us went on to Caer Ysgithr, and I never heard word of him afterward."

Tryffin felt his heart sink. Whether Pergrin had forgotten or had never known, it was no welcome task informing the big man that his friend was dead.

He broke the news as gently as he could. "Bron was killed, but he died like a hero. In truth we gave him a hero's burial, wearing a golden torc like a prince of the south."

As Tryffin had hoped, the giant set his mind on the grand burial rather than on his friend's death, and was mightily taken with the notion. "Like a hero, you say? Poor old Bron, Bron the dwarf? There's another wonder, that is. Though mind you," he added, gnawing on half a roasted chicken, "I always thought he had it in him to become a great man."

And Pergrin began to speak of his friend, a long, foolish, rambling discourse which soon had Mahaffy and Conn yawning behind their hands, and even Meligraunce, though he tried to hide it, close to nodding off. But the Governor listened to it all with great interest, fortifying himself, every now and again, with the giant's ale and turnips. Bron had saved Fflergant's life at the cost of his own, and even now, when Tryffin knew the dwarf had been his father's spy—not Mochdreffi at all, but true-born Gwyngellach—there was much about Bron that remained a mystery.

About an hour into this lengthy recitation, Pergrin sighed deeply. "It's the grand storytelling I miss the most. Aye, he would have made a fine bard, if he hadn't been so little and funny-looking."

At this, Tryffin put aside his tankard, sat up straighter in his chair, and even the others began to revive a bit. "He told you stories, did he?"

The Gwyngellach were often remarkable storytellers, possessing excellent memories and the gift of eloquence, but Tryffin was not so much interested in Bron's abilities as in the sort of information he might have passed on to this hulking friend of his. "And among those stories . . . did there happen to be a tale about a girl named Guenhumara and the King's son of Tir Gwyngelli?"

The giant nodded his head delightedly. "Guenhumara, lovely Guenhumara, a fine tale. Do *you* know that story, Lord Tryffin? I'd be pleased to hear you recite it."

The Governor leaned back in his chair. "No, I don't know that tale, though I confess I would like to hear it myself. Now, how much of that story do you think *you* remember?"

Pergrin frowned thoughtfully. "Likely, I remember it all. Though I can't do it justice as Bron would, as a bard would. You find yourself a bard to tell it, Lord Tryffin, or else ask Brandegorias himself."

"I would," said Tryffin patiently, "if I was ever likely to meet him. And I never met the bard yet who could tell me that tale—not so far as I know, anyway. I would like to hear you recite it, if you will oblige me."

The giant sat for a time, perhaps gathering his scattered thoughts. "Aye, well . . . I will, then," he said at last. "She was the niece of the Lord of Mochdreff and she fell in love with a simple scholar. Only he wasn't an ordinary scholar, really—he was the King's son of Tir Gwyngelli, just as you said. He pretended to be a scholar that he might travel from place to place and learn everything there was for a man to learn."

"He was my grandfather, Menai fab Maelwas," said Tryffin. He had not known this about his own grandfather but could certainly sympathize with the curiosity that drove him.

"Aye, that was the name: Menai fab Maelwas. He said he would marry her, but her uncle said no." Pergrin sat nodding his head for a long time, apparently off in some world of his own, causing Tryffin to prompt him: "And was that the end of it?"

The giant started, then shook his head emphatically. "The end of it? No. He had the silver tongue, Prince Menai did. He talked her uncle around, and the old man gave his consent. So Menai went home to Gwyngelli to speak to his father and make the arrangements, only it was winter and bitter weather, and he was gone many months." Pergrin sighed deeply and sat staring at the bones on his plate. Finally, he spoke again. "While he was gone, the old fellow died that was Lord of Mochdreff, so naturally his younger brother was the Lord after him.''

"That would be Guenhumara's father?'' asked Tryffin, trying to remember all the Mochdreffi genealogies he had studied. But the truth was, there were so many ladies with the same name, he was still uncertain exactly which girl they were talking about.

"No,'' said Pergrin, "that was her other uncle, Corrig fab Corrig. He went into a rage when he heard that his niece was to marry a man of Tir Gwyngelli. But there was nothing he could do, because the marriage contract had already been signed. And so they were married, Menai and Guenhumara.''

Tryffin let out a deep breath. "My grandfather married a Mochdreffi lady, and nobody knows it in Tir Gwyngelli? That virtually passes belief.''

"Yet it may have been a private ceremony,'' suggested Meligraunce, "meant to protect the lady from scandal while she traveled with him into Gwyngelli. Prince Menai may have planned a more formal wedding when he arrived home, just as you intend with the Lady Gwenlliant.''

"Yes,'' said Tryffin, taking the flagon that Conn had placed at his elbow earlier and pouring himself another tankard of ale. "That's entirely possible, of course. But what happened then? Did they marry again, when they came to Castell Maelduin?''

Pergrin shook his head. "The warlock made the rocks fall down, and they all died,'' he said morosely.

The Governor paused with the tankard at his lips. "I don't quite follow you. Who was the warlock . . . and who died?''

"He was a page that Lord Corrig gave her, meaning to work her destruction. When they were riding through the Gwyngelli Hills, the witch-boy made the ground move and the rocks fall, and the Lady Guenhumara and all her attendants were killed. Only Prince Menai survived . . . and the warlock, of course. He went back to Lord Corrig to claim his reward.''

"God of Heaven,'' said Tryffin, under his breath. "That's a tragic tale. I wonder how much of it's true.'' He put down his tankard and looked at Mahaffy across the table. "You have lived in this land all of your life, and your uncle has been deeply involved in the politics of Mochdreff. Did you never hear—did Lord Cado never say *anything* to you about any of this?''

Mahaffy shook his head, ran a hand through his tumbled black hair. "Never, Lord Prince.'' He turned to the giant. "I wonder: Did you ever tell this story to my uncle, Pergrin.''

To the surprise of all, the giant began to shake with laughter, to guffaw loudly and slap his thigh, apparently enjoying some private jest.

"You have a pretty wit, my lad, a very pretty wit," wheezed Pergrin, when he could finally speak again. "Now, why should I tell Lord Cado a story he already knows so well?"

Mahaffy gave him a puzzled glance. "But if you never spoke of it between you—then how do you *know* he is familiar with the tale?"

"Because," said the giant, beginning to chuckle again, "he was in the story himself, Lord Cado. He was the witch-boy who called down the rocks."

So Goreu, not knowing how he should choose, selected the apple, for the love of the gold. And when he had done that, the woman began to laugh as though he had pleased her.

But all that she would say to him was, "Take the golden apple and keep it hidden in a secret place. And when nine days have passed, you may take it out and look at it. Then you will know whether you chose wisely or not."

When the witch left him, he did as she said. But because he was troubled in his mind, Goreu went to a friend of his, who was a man of great knowledge and wisdom, and he told the man all that had happened and what his father's mother had said to him.

The friend was very sad, but also very angry that Goreu had not come to him before. "The woman tricked you by appearing to offer you two choices only. Also, she lied to you, because both choices were equally sinful. Why were you not thinking? You need not have accepted either the golden apple or the silver bowl, or anything that she wanted to give you. There was a third choice that you did not consider, which was to take nothing from her at all."

Then Goreu knew that he had been very foolish, and trusted one who wished only for the destruction of his immortal soul.

—From The Nine Sorrowful Tales
of the Misfortunes of Mochdreff

18.

A Dish of Bitter Herbs

Gwenlliant put a hand to her head. Her mind reeled with all that she had read this night, enchantments of every description, though most were cruel and hurtful: spells to hold and spells to bind, spells to make a man cry out in the night from evil dreams, or to fill his veins with the venom of loathing for every creature he met in the waking world, spells to burn and spells to blast—yet among them all not one single counterspell of the kind that she sought.

Gwenlliant felt stiff and cold from sitting on the floor with the great heavy book in her lap. This was the third time in ten days she had slipped away from her own quarters, made the magic take her to the forbidden rooms, and spent the entire night poring through one of Diaspad's grimoires. Because the pattern under the stairs played tricks with time, she could spend most of the night leafing through these dusty volumes and still sleep for three or four hours before her attendants rose in the morning.

Just *when* she had stopped glancing over the pages, reading the names of the spells, perusing the curious figures penned in colored inks, and started actually reading the spells themselves, she was not certain. She could not remember, but it seemed like many hours had passed since then. She had said to herself: What could be the harm in reading a few of them? A spell once read could be easily forgotten, and she would never be tempted to make use of them anyway.

But now, rubbing her forehead, Gwenlliant knew that was not so—because the spells were *there* inside her mind, were as much a part of the way she thought and the way she felt as if they had been written there at the moment of her birth. She remembered every single word she had read this night and knew beyond doubt that she could use the magic at will, could call it up with a thought or a wish to do her bidding, the same way she had known how to use the fire spell after Brangwengwen ignited the wood.

It seemed it was the nature of her gift that these things should come easily, that she should absorb the charms and the chants, the cantrips and the pishogues, like summer rain on the thirsty earth. Yet she had been taught all her life that knowledge of that sort gained at such little cost must demand a heavy price eventually.

And many of those spells were dangerous: She could pull down the castle, cause the mortar to crumble between the stones and all the towers to come crashing down; raise up a windstorm, whip up the sea; stop a man's heart or boil away his blood. She could make the fire turn to ice and the milk turn to gall; water to wine and wine to water. She could not restore the dead to life, but she could make them walk, call them rotting and worm-eaten out of their graves, to come shambling up the road to Caer Ysgithr.

It took her breath away, it made her shudder, to think of all that power in her own inexperienced hands, and no one to prevent her from using it at the slightest whim.

Until she remembered her meeting with the friar, the saintly cleric whose words had moved her when she sat sorely troubled outside the heretical church.

She thought: *Father Idris said that innocence provides a shield that is stronger than steel. But I—I am not so innocent, not so pure. Though still a virgin, I am not inviolate, and I do not think that I can claim the shield of* true *innocence.*

And yet, if not in the arms of the faith which had sustained her through so many troubles in the past, where *could* she be safe, where find consolation?

Searching through the ruins of Castell Ochren for a suitable room to accommodate the Governor, Meligraunce finally discovered a large drafty chamber at the top of a tower. It had walls and a floor and a ceiling, and wooden shutters to all the windows (which was a great deal more than could be said of the other rooms), and it had, in addition, a great oak bed in good condition, and a mattress filled with straw that was comparatively fresh. This room, so Pergrin informed the Captain, had been often occupied by Lord Cado himself, during his infrequent visits.

But when Tryffin came in with his squires to retire for the night, he was immediately drawn to the brick fireplace rather than the bed. That was an ordinary chimney piece except for one thing: There was a small iron cage suspended from a bracket by an iron chain, positioned so that whatever the cage contained would rest in the heart of the fire.

"Before God," said the Governor, bending down to examine the cage. "This is a nasty little device. Does your uncle burn birds and field-mice as an amusement?"

Mahaffy shook his head. "He is a hard man, Lord Cado, but why waste his time tormenting mice or birds? He isn't cruel—just abominably ruthless."

"It looks like a cage to keep a salamander," Conn volunteered unexpectedly.

The Governor eyed him with considerable surprise. "Now,

where would *you* have seen such a thing?" he asked, rising to his feet.

The Gorwynnach lad gave a shrug of his shoulders. "I never have. But young Cei described something of the sort, one time or the other, something he had seen at your kinswoman's house in Regann . . . though I have an idea the Lady Teleri's creature was considerably larger."

"Aye, well, this one grew larger, too," said the Captain. "Or Lord Cado kept them in different sizes. There's a large cage of the same sort, down in what used to be the kitchen, inside a great stone furnace."

"Is there so?" said Tryffin, thinking of the fire in Peryf. "And just how big would that other cage be?"

Meligraunce indicated the size with his hands. "Big enough for a creature the size of a goat or a large dog—though with shorter legs, of course."

Tryffin stood staring at the cage in the fireplace, thinking that over. "That would explain it, then: a salamander let loose at Castell Peryf, climbing the walls like any lizard, then running rampant until the wizard summoned it back."

While Meligraunce went down to assign the watches and Conn went out to check on the horses, Tryffin prepared for bed.

"Could it possibly be true, what Pergrin told us?" he asked Mahaffy. "Your uncle is a wizard, not a warlock—and even Pergrin should know the difference."

The Governor sat down on the side of his bed, so Mahaffy could help him out of his boots.

"Well, I believe Lord Cado *did* have some talents in that direction when he was younger. Only they say the old women refused to teach him, and that was the beginning of the trouble between him and Ceinwen. It was the same with the Princess Diaspad—though *she* found ways to get around Ceinwen and learn some witchcraft all on her own—but my uncle cursed the wise-women for their *damned interference* and decided to take up wizardry instead.

"Only," said the boy, "it was impossible to find a master to instruct him, here in Mochdreff, and he had a difficult time learning by himself. That is the reason why, for so many years, he was really a very inferior wizard."

Tryffin stood up and unbuckled his swordbelt, placed it close by the side of his bed, where he could find it at need even in the dark. "But the tale Pergrin told, the events he described, that was a long time ago. Is it possible your uncle was already alive? I know it is

208

difficult to guess at a wizard's age, but Lord Cado is your uncle . . .''

The boy began to look uncomfortable. "Your Grace, I never meant to deceive you. Dahaut and I aren't much in the habit of referring to Lord Cado as our *great*-uncle, but the fact is he was our grandfather's brother. Yes, I think he might have been alive at that time—though he takes great pains to conceal his age.''

In his stocking feet, Tryffin began to pace the bedchamber. Many things began to make sense now: mocking references Mahaffy and Dahaut had made to their uncle's great age, a sentence begun and not finished. "But why should Lord Cado *wish* to conceal how old he is?''

Mahaffy turned back the fur bed coverings. "Ah well, it's a fine thing to be a wizard and live for a century or more, but it happens Lord Cado is vain. I believe he wants people to think of him as young and brilliant, rather than old and crafty.''

Pausing by the fireplace, Tryffin made a swift mental calculation. "But if Cado Guillyn was a boy eighty years ago—Mother of God! How old does that make Dame Ceinwen, who raised him?''

Mahaffy sat down at the foot of the bed. "I don't think that anyone knows. I have heard it said she is the oldest living thing on Ynys Celydonn, but that may be an exaggeration.''

The Governor was very quiet and grim for a long time after that. "And so I have followed the feud all the way back to the beginning," he said at last. "And I find Lord Cado there working mischief, as I believe he has been working mischief right up to the present day. Could it possibly be that the destiny I follow has brought me into Mochdreff . . . for the sole purpose of destroying Cado Guillyn?''

The full enormity of Lord Cado's wickedness was beginning to dawn on him. Not only the deaths in Peryf and at the inn in Perfudd; not only the men Tryffin had killed in Mochdreff, or Essylt bereft of her child; but generations of wrong, generations of sorrow. Guenhumara crushed by a rock slide on the way to her wedding. Diaspad and Manogan's separation and heartache. Gwenlliant—yes, even Gwenlliant's violation and the mental and emotional scars she might still carry. The blame for all of it, directly or indirectly, could be laid at Lord Cado's door.

Thinking of these things, Tryffin felt the blood begin to course in his veins, saw the red mist rising before his eyes. But he could not give in to the madness now, must suppress it if he could, because there was no suitable object on which to wreak his vengeance.

When his vision cleared and the desire to tear someone to pieces had passed, he glanced up and caught Mahaffy watching him.

"What is it?" he asked, unknotting his fists, wondering how much the boy guessed, to what extent he had betrayed himself.

"I was thinking, Lord Prince, of the Lady Essylt. She and young Grifflet must be descended from one of Guenhumara's brothers."

And that made sense as well, because Essylt and Grifflet must be part of the pattern the witch had mentioned. "Ceinwen said the child might yet return to me. Perhaps I must first revenge Guenhumara's death."

Mahaffy nodded his head. "That may be. It is just the sort of task that Ceinwen might set you. But of course you will have to find my uncle first—and that may prove to be very difficult."

"I know that," Tryffin said, with a deep sigh. "How do you find a wizard, when there is no way of knowing what face he might be wearing?"

Father Idris's hermitage was located in a spot of great natural beauty. In Rhianedd or Gorwynnion or anywhere in the north it would have been scarcely remarkable, but here in Mochdreff it was strange to find a place so picturesque, or so peculiarly suited to the contemplative life.

The ruined church the friar had mentioned had long since been reduced to a pile of grey stones at the top of a rocky hill, but the first green of spring was beginning to show in every nook and cranny. A venerable oak tree, rooted halfway up the slope, sheltered the hermit's neat little white-washed cottage, and a spring bubbled up through a fissure in the rock and pooled in a marble basin.

Gwenlliant dismounted at the foot of the hill, leaving all but one of her guards to mind the horses. She knocked on the door of the cottage, but there was no answer. Thinking the friar might still be somewhere in the vicinity, she decided to search for him.

At the top of the hill she called his name, and this time there came an answer from inside the ruined church. "My daughter, do not be afraid to enter," said Father Idris.

Gwenlliant stepped under a crooked lintel and came out in a kind of cave among the fallen stones.

The stones made a circular room with a low ceiling. Light came in through gaps in the rock and through a window made of green glass, which was miraculously intact amidst so much destruction. "This is my chapel," said Father Idris, appearing out of the shadows at the back of the cave.

The glass in the window was a peculiar shade of green, bathing the chapel in an eerie light. Gwenlliant had seen glass like that once before, although then it had been combined with other, more brilliant colors, at Lord Cado's house in Trewynyn.

"Was this a church of those gentle friars who were murdered by the Knights of Jerusalem?"

"It was," said the cleric. "That is why I like to come here, because that order and my own are nearly related. Have you come to make a confession, my child?"

"Yes," said Gwenlliant, very low, remembering what trouble had brought her here. She turned and signaled her guard to wait outside, then knelt and covered her face with her veil.

The whole story came pouring out: the books, her inherited gifts, all the warnings she had received about the dangers of untrained talents, Tryffin's danger, her own past suffering at the hands of Calchas, the spells she carried in her mind. She told it all, with tears and self-recriminations.

Father Idris was thoughtful for a long time after she had finished, his face solemn and strangely austere as he considered her situation. Then he sighed. "This is a heavy matter; these are terrible things you tell me. To even approach those books was very, very wrong. You must know that even here in Mochdreff, where no attempt is made to punish the offenders, even here the Church does not condone the use of witchcraft."

Kneeling on the rocky floor, Gwenlliant blinked back tears. "But—but, Father, where do these gifts come from if not from God? Saints work miracles and so—and so do the King's knights, sometimes. My cousin Ceilyn had a vision in the chapel the night of his Vigil. And even in Gorwynnion and Rhianedd, no one claims that *wizards* gain their power from the Devil."

"Are you a saint, my child?" he asked sternly. "Are you a knight who has gained strength and wisdom through discipline and self-denial? Or a wizard who has come into his power by following much the same path? No, you are only a poor, weak woman—less than that—a wicked and confused child, without even the innocence and purity I thought I saw in you the first time we met."

By this time, the tears were flowing copiously. Seeing how distressed she was, he spoke more kindly. "Yet you are not, I think, entirely beyond redemption. Will you perform such acts of penance and contrition as I advise you?"

Gwenlliant nodded wordlessly. "Very well then. You will mortify your flesh by fasting from this time until tomorrow at sunset. You will purify your spirit by an hour of prayer each evening, and—"

"Father," she interrupted him tremulously, "I already attend Mass practically every day. Is that to count toward the hour, or should—should I pray an additional hour on those days?"

"You are not to enter a church or any place of worship until you are fit to do so," he said coldly. And when she gasped and made a tiny sound of protest: "Yes, that seems hard, I know. But you must be prepared to suffer. Tell me, my child—considering that you were introduced to the horrors of perversion at such an early age, do you have lustful thoughts toward any man besides your husband?"

Under her veil, Gwenlliant began to tremble, and her clasped hands went cold and clammy. "There is someone—someone who sometimes makes me feel . . ." she replied faintly. "But I try never to think about that."

Father Idris loomed over her, more terrible than she had imagined the gentle cleric could ever be. "So it always begins, child, so it always begins. Your state is very bad. Yet take comfort. I will give you some holy relics; meditate on them during your hour of prayer. Think on your own wickedness, examine these feelings of yours. You will know if your efforts to improve are successful when these sinful thoughts and temptations begin to fade from your mind. When they are entirely gone, you may go to church again. But if you find that these thoughts begin to intrude at other times, you will know that your sins are more deeply ingrained than you thought, and must increase the time you spend meditating on the relics. Perhaps you will wish to pray in the morning as well as the evening."

He fixed her with a penetrating glance. "Will you promise to do all these things?"

"Yes, Father," she whispered. Something in this advice of his was vaguely troubling, but she could not work out what that something was. "I will do exactly as you say."

"Then I shall absolve you, child, and all will be well."

Gwenlliant left the hermitage an hour later, with a sackcloth bag clutched in her hand, a bag containing the holy relics Father Idris had given her: a piece of bloody veil worn by St. Niamh, a bit of bone from the tomb of St. Teilo, a scrap of parchment from a missal which had belonged to St. Sianne, and a dusty wreath made up of bitter-smelling herbs that had grown on the grave of an unknown martyr. It might be wise, Father Idris had advised her, to sleep with the relics under her pillow at night.

And when she arrived at Caer Ysgithr, Gwenlliant went

immediately up to her own rooms without a word to anyone. Once there, she sent her attendants out of her bedchamber, locked the door behind them, and spent a long tearful hour in prayer and meditation.

At Castell Ochren, there was a great commotion, a clash of steel and much shouting, during the night. Tryffin had his sword in hand within moments of waking, and he and his squires were already clattering down the long staircase from the tower bedchamber, when they met Meligraunce coming up to inform them that matters were well in hand.

The Captain held a torch in one hand, a bloody sword in the other. "A half dozen fighters came over the walls. We killed three and the others escaped."

Tryffin decided to put off viewing the bodies until daylight. "But call me at once if there is any further disturbance." Then he went back to bed and back to sleep, and the rest of the night passed peacefully.

He made a hearty breakfast in the morning, then went down to the courtyard, taking Mahaffy with him. Meligraunce and his men had arranged the bodies in a line on the ground: men in armor and plain dark surcotes, bare of any heraldic device. But for all that, Mahaffy gave a cry of recognition. "This man and the one next to him, they were Lord Cado's men. Yes, Prince Tryffin, I am certain of that. I remember seeing them both at the house in Trewynyn."

The Governor nodded slowly. "So now he has taken to attacking me with his own men. The questions we asked in Peryf, my journey here—Lord Cado must know that I am looking for him.

"Although," he added thoughtfully, staring down at the bloody corpses, "he can hardly guess what brought me *here* in particular. Perhaps that worries him."

They left the castle as soon as the dead were buried, traveling cautiously. The Governor sent out scouts before and behind, to make certain the road ahead was safe. Fortunately, the land of Ochren was so flat and empty, it offered few opportunities for an ambush, and Tryffin and his troop rode for many hours without any incident.

"Everywhere I go—everyplace but Clynnoc, where I was not expected—Lord Cado sets traps for me," Tryffin mused, as he and his companions traveled across a rocky plain. "And some of these traps were clearly the result of careful planning. It seems obvious that Lord Cado has a spy in my household."

Riding at his side, Mahaffy went white and stiff. "By my

213

confession to God," said Tryffin, "I don't suspect *you*. If you wanted to kill me, you've had plenty of opportunity to do so and make a neat escape afterward. Almost certainly, the spy is Dahaut. I wonder I was so foolish not to realize that a long time since."

"Not foolish," said Mahaffy, relaxing a little. "You don't wish to be like those other men we spoke of: men who seek to excuse themselves for sleeping with a woman by painting her just as black as possible afterward. Only in Dahaut's case, you may be carrying the principle a bit too far.

"For myself," the boy added, under his breath, wrapping the leather reins around one hand, "I should be the last to deplore your good nature."

The Governor looked at him wonderingly. "My good nature? Mahaffy, do you have any idea how many men I have *killed* in the last year?"

"I do. But as all of them were trying to kill *you* first, I don't see why that should trouble you."

"Aye, but it does," said Tryffin, with a sigh. "Ever since I was a young lad, ever since I started to grow so much faster than the other boys, I have struggled with the temptation to settle everything by the use of brute force. When a situation arises that calls for a violent solution, I always wonder afterward whether there might not have been some better way, if I only had the wit and the patience to find it."

They passed out of Ochren and into neighboring Penafon. They were riding past a scrubby little wood just at sunset, when a hail of arrows came flying through the air.

One shaft grazed Tryffin's cheek, and another caught him in the shoulder. But he was out of the saddle in an instant, standing bleeding in the road, with Roch between him and the next rain of arrows, arrowfire which seemed to be concentrated in his direction.

An arrow with a black shaft and barred fletching hit the gelding in the withers. Two more struck his muscular haunch, before the Governor's guards recovered their wits and went crashing into the brush after the assassins, forcing the archers to throw down their weapons and flee.

"Your Grace, you are hurt," said Meligraunce, when he and the others came back to report that the archers had all escaped.

By that time, Tryffin was sitting on the stony ground, with his back against a leprous ash tree. Mahaffy had already pulled the barred arrow out of his shoulder, and Conn held a folded piece of cloth to the wound, in order to staunch the flow of blood. "I'm well enough, Captain,'' said the Governor, between his teeth. ''But for the love of God, someone should see to poor Roch.''

A quick examination revealed that the roan gelding had not sustained any serious damage, since the arrows had lodged in muscle and not hit vital organs. But he was in no state to carry a rider.

That being so, when the Governor's wound was bandaged, and they were all ready to go again, Tryffin borrowed the Captain's big, bony black (the only horse that was up to his weight), Meligraunce accepted the loan of a muscular grey, and two of the smaller men doubled up.

''I don't understand it.'' Meligraunce ground his teeth in frustration as they started their journey again. ''Lord Prince, it is a mystery to me. These men who attack us, we can never catch them. Kill them, yes—but we can never take a single one of them alive.''

''Easy enough to guess what is happening, now that we *know* a wizard is behind it all.'' Tryffin winced as the motion of his mount jolted the wounded shoulder. ''Lord Cado teaches his assassins some simple spell that allows them to move without being seen, so long as they are not actually engaged in battle. I recall a similar spell used by the Lady Teleri, which requires silence and stillness in order to work. Only they can't attack me that way at Caer Ysgithr, and must wait for me outside—because once they have learned even that much magic, they can't pass the wards without a direct invitation.''

''In that case,'' said Meligraunce, ''I would advise you, Your Grace, not to leave home unless you must.''

''Well,'' said Tryffin, ''I am thinking about that. I may stay home for a time. But once I get wind of where Lord Cado is hiding, I intend to hunt him down and kill him if I may, though an entire invisible army should lie between.''

There is a devil called an incubus, which troubles the sleep of young virgins. The more pure and virtuous the maiden and the more she seeks to repulse him, the more persistent becomes this evil spirit, filling her nights with lustful dreams, itchings and sweatings, heart-burnings, and vile whisperings, that the virgin knows neither peace nor rest until she yields herself up to his infernal lust.

—*From* Moren Clydno's Book of Secrets

19.

Heart-Burnings and Vile Whisperings

Gwenlliant knelt in her bedchamber, with her hands clasped so tightly they ached, and her head bowed. Her book of devotions lay open on the bed in front of her, and the relics given to her by Father Idris were arranged in a semi-circle around the illuminated prayer book: the bloody scrap of cloth, the bit of stained parchment, the splinter of bone, and the garland of bitter herbs. She had been praying and meditating all of the morning; her eyes were dry and her throat was scratchy, because she had wept all her tears away hours before.

Someone knocked softly on the door. "Yes?" she answered, with a weary little sigh. The door opened and Garth walked in.

"Lady, we are on our way to Mass now, Cei and Elffin and I. Will you be—" He paused with his hand still on the door, shocked by the sight of her strained face, crushed gown, and tumbled hair. "Will you be accompanying us?"

Gwenlliant shook her head. "No . . . no, I can't go with you. I must stay here and pray by myself. But you should go, Garth, and the little boys. You shouldn't stay away on my account."

Garth hesitated on the threshold. "Are you quite well? Is

something troubling you? Have—have *I* done something to offend you?''

Gwenlliant began to gather up the relics, to put them back in the sackcloth bag. ''No, you haven't done anything to offend me, nor anything else that is wrong. In fact, you have tried very hard to help me be good, but I am just too wicked to benefit by your example.''

''Mother of Mercy! It *is* my fault.'' He moved swiftly across the room, knelt down on the floor beside her. ''I thought it might be. Lady, I had no right to—to say anything that would upset you. I had no right to speak so reproachfully.''

He captured her hand and clasped it in both of his. He was as pale as she was, and very much in earnest. ''But it was always my own weakness I feared, never any sinful intent on your part.''

Gwenlliant tried to pull her hand away, but he refused to release it. ''Yes, but *I* am sinful. You don't know. I never *intended* to do anything wrong where you were concerned, but sometimes—sometimes when we are together, I feel . . . I feel that I might like to do bad things.''

''Oh, as to that,'' he said, sitting back on his heels, forcing a smile. ''There is nothing extraordinarily wicked in that. Even up in Gorwynnion, we know that people—'' He seemed to lose the thread of what he was saying, caught between the dictates of his own fiercely virtuous upbringing and a desire to offer as much comfort as he could. He began again. ''It is wrong to even *think* a sin, of course, but the flesh is weak and will have its yearnings. So long as you don't yield to them or allow your mind to dwell on them, then you are all right.''

''Yes,'' she said mournfully, ''I used to think so, too. If I put a bad thought out of my mind as soon as it came to me, I would not be harmed by it. But someone much wiser than I am said that—that in my case, those thoughts were there because I was introduced to sin at an early age. I'm not like other people. And I can't go to Mass again until I purify my thoughts. Only they just keep getting worse and worse, until I can hardly think of anything else!''

She retreated inside the pale curtain of her hair. ''Also, I have bad dreams.''

Garth caught her other hand and held it. ''Nightmares, you mean?''

''Wicked dreams, evil dreams. About—I cannot say what they are about. The things that men and women do together, only horrible . . . horrible.''

That gave him a moment's pause. He had heard the rumors

about her and Calchas, had been at Caer Cadwy at the time, serving as page to the Earl Marshall; having been a little acquainted with her, he was reluctant to believe the stories. Yet he knew that sin often wore a fair face, clothed itself in the garments of innocence. But no, it was impossible for him to look into her wide, terrified eyes, hear the anguish in her voice, and still believe she was capable of genuine evil.

"Lady, it *can't* be right what you have been told to do. If you sit here brooding on your sinful thoughts, then you won't be able to summon up anything better. And that will make things horribly difficult for both of us, because . . . God knows, I could be very, very wicked where you are concerned, if I forgot what I owed to Prince Tryffin, to you, and even to myself."

He raised her hands and kissed them, one after the other. She shivered and drew them away. "Do come away," he said. "Do come down and hear Mass, Lady, and see how much good it does you."

Gwenlliant shook the white-gold hair out of her eyes. "What you say sounds—sounds very reasonable. But, Garth, I *have* to pray and meditate alone, and I can't go to Mass. It's a penance Father Idris gave me, and I have already been absolved. I can't relapse, or my soul will be in worse case than it was before."

He ran a nervous hand through his own chestnut curls. He had never before faced such an impossible dilemma: Of *course* one had to perform the penance one was assigned, to do otherwise would be unthinkable—but what if the penance was just as wrong and wicked as the original trespass?

"Yes, I see," he said at last. "But were you told that you have to meditate on those—those particular sins specifically or can you just pray and meditate?"

"I don't know," whispered Gwenlliant. "But you are right— the harder I try not to think about them, the less I am able to think of anything else. Not only when I am here trying to pray, but all of the time!"

Garth rose to his feet. "We will just have to find something better to occupy your mind when you aren't here. We will just have to find some pleasant distractions."

Tryffin was just as shocked as Garth had been, when he caught his first glimpse of the white, terrified face Gwenlliant turned up to receive his kiss on his return home from Ochren. It was hard to believe that a few days had worked such a startling change in her.

His first thought was: *What have those children been doing to themselves and each other while I was gone?* But when Garth came into the room a short while later, Tryffin realized he had been wrong about that. The boy from Gorwynnion was clearly sick with worry, but he bore none of those signs of devastating guilt that must have accompanied any transgression involving Gwenlliant.

Tryffin thought it might be best to allow Garth a chance to confide in him, rather than put him on the defensive with any immediate questions. Accordingly, he put off speaking to the boy and went to see Dahaut instead.

The rooms that Lord Cado's niece had chosen for herself were airy and spacious, and she had ransacked the uninhabited parts of the castle for the best furnishings she could find. Tryffin found her standing before a mirror, gazing with considerable satisfaction at her lovely reflection, while a maid servant dressed her thick chestnut hair.

His eyes went immediately to the golden torc set with tiny glimmering sidhe-stones that she wore at her throat. "I thought that I asked you not to wear that necklace."

Dahaut shrugged. "While I was a drudge to your lady it was clearly inappropriate, but why should I not have the pleasure of wearing it now? It is extremely handsome, and God knows I earned it. Besides, I have nothing else nearly so fine."

The smile he gave her was not a pleasant one. "The necklace was a gift. If I had meant it for payment . . . I fear, Dahaut, you reckon your worth a bit too high. And however that may be, you are not to humiliate my lady by wearing it here. That necklace was wrought of Gwyngelli gold, and a glance would tell Gwenlliant exactly where it came from."

Dahaut returned his smile with a predatory one of her own. "As in fact, I believe she did, the first time she saw it." Then she laughed to see how his face suddenly changed. "You didn't know that, did you? It never occurred to you, great fool that you were, that your bride had met me *and* the necklace the day she paid a visit to my uncle. She saw the torc, knew who it came from, and exactly what it meant that I should have jewels of your bestowing, while she . . . not so much as a silver brooch!"

"Sweet Jesus," he said, under his breath. Things were beginning to make sense now: Mahaffy saying Gwenlliant had seen more than the Governor might intend her to see, Gwenlliant's look of shocked surprise when he first came in with Dahaut on his arm. Yes, and it was true what Dahaut had implied, because for all the things he had given Gwenlliant, gowns and elegant little trifles, and books and playthings—all the natural gifts of a loving brother, an indulgent father, an affectionate kinsman—not once had he

219

bestowed on her the one gift that men had been sending their wives and their mistresses since time out of mind: a gift of precious metals and costly gemstones.

It was not even that he had forgotten. He had meant from the beginning to shower her with such gifts as soon as they journeyed to Tir Gwyngelli, where she could choose from the best works of his father's goldsmiths, or from the family heirlooms Lord Maelgwyn kept in his treasury. But now he saw he had left it too long—allowing Gwenlliant to measure her worth against an inferior piece of work he had picked up one time in Pengaren, just over the border from Mochdreff.

Yet that was one mistake he could easily rectify. "I thank you, Dahaut. You have done me a service, though I doubt you meant to. And it is a pity you have made yourself so comfortable here, because you will be leaving immediately. I have good reason to suppose you have been spying for your uncle, and telling him everything I do and I plan."

Dahaut bridled at the accusation. "And why, even supposing I was willing to play such a degrading role, would Cado Guillyn take such a particular interest in your actions, Lord Prince?"

The Governor folded his arms and looked her over with a searching glance. "I think you know that as well as I do, or better."

Dahaut sent the serving girl out of the room. She sat down in a chair (without asking leave to do so) and smoothed her skirt. "Well, I suppose I can guess. You imagine that he is behind these recent attacks on your life. I would scarcely put it past him; he never did care for foreigners meddling in Mochdreffi affairs. But why believe that *I* would betray you? That is your faithless young bride's idea, I think, poisoning your mind against me."

He felt a strong urge to break the habit of a lifetime and strike this woman across her face. With an effort he restrained himself, knowing how much damage he might do once he started. "If you truly believe that, you know nothing of Gwenlliant. She never mentions your name at all. But I have been a gullible fool. I see now that you came to Caer Ysgithr for the purpose of causing just as much mischief and dissension as you could."

Dahaut flushed angrily. "Very well, then: Accuse me of spying on you, put me in chains, cast me in prison, see what it gains you. The castle is full of servants who have been here from the time you arrived, servants who knew my uncle very well during the years that he lived here. Any one of them might be in Lord Cado's pay. If you wish to find your spy, you should be persecuting them, not me."

"I have no intention of persecuting anyone," said Tryffin, continuing to control a murderous urge. He was all but convinced she was guilty, but what she said could not be denied. And even as angry as he was, there remained that part of him that was too fair minded to imprison the woman while any doubt of her guilt remained in his mind. "But you will leave this place and you will leave today."

"And what is that, if not persecution? Throwing me out to starve in the streets?"

"Lady, you can live in your uncle's house in Trewynyn. If you really do fear him, as I very much doubt, you need not worry that he will bother you there. Under the circumstances, he must know very well that the very first moment he is seen to set foot in Trewynyn I will have him arrested."

The Governor turned and walked toward the door, but he paused on the threshold and glanced back at her. "At need, you can sell the necklace," he said. "You could live off its price for many years in considerable luxury."

She ignored that, and answered instead, "You may seek to arrest my uncle, but first you must find him. And I think you are not nearly so clever as that."

Tryffin remembered that Mahaffy had said something of the same sort. But having thought the matter over, he was not so certain. "I believe Lord Cado is just as much a prey to frustration as any man. His schemes to murder me being so far unsuccessful, I believe the time may soon come when he is just as eager to meet with me as I am to meet with him."

He awoke that night, sometime between midnight and dawn, to a light fall of footsteps across the floor and a glimpse of something pale and slender moving in the shadows. His first thought was of Dahaut, until he remembered how he had personally escorted her to the castle gate and then watched her ride down the road to the town. And the intruder—who was still moving softly around his bedchamber—was too small and light to be one of his squires.

Then she stepped into a shaft of moonlight coming in through one of the windows, and Tryffin saw it was Gwenlliant, poised in the frosty moonglow, trembling in her thin nightdress. He was out of bed in an instant, taking her hands in both of his. "Ah God, you're like ice. Are you ill? Has something frightened you?"

Gwenlliant did not answer, but continued to stand there, wide-eyed and shuddering, with the cold tears pouring down her face. It was a moment before he realized she was walking in her sleep, and could neither see nor hear him.

He had heard it was dangerous to wake a sleepwalker, but her dream was so clearly causing her distress, he was uncertain how to proceed. Finally, he caught up one of the fur robes from his bed, wrapped Gwenlliant in it, and carried her over to a chair by the fireplace. The fire had been banked, but a poker and a few sticks of wood brought it back to life. He knelt down beside her chair and spoke quietly and soothingly, until the tears stopped flowing and she seemed to know him again.

He touched her face, wiping the tears away. "It was a bad dream. Are you awake now?" She nodded wordlessly. He remembered she had been prone to such dreams as a small child. "Was it the old nightmare, then?"

She shook her head, wiped her eyes with the back of her hand. "Did I dis-disturb you? I'm sorry. Why did you bring me here?"

"You came here yourself; you were walking in your sleep," he said, and saw her expression change to one of stark terror. "It's all right. There was no harm done, and Faelinn or Grainne or Traeth can sit up with you after this, to keep you from hurting yourself."

"What did I say to you . . . what did I do?"

"Nothing," he said gently. "You said nothing, not anything I could understand. But you looked so tired and ill earlier today— did you have nightmares while I was gone, has your sleep been disturbed?"

As the night was not cold, he had gone to bed in his breeches only. He was reaching for his shirt, when she began to shiver and to weep again. "Please, Cousin, I'm not ill. Please don't send me away."

He dropped the shirt, took her hands in his. "Now, why should I want to do that? Ah . . . you are thinking of before. But that was when I thought you had grown tired of living with me. Of course I'll not send you away." He rose to his feet, gathered her up in his arms, and carried her over to the bed. "You can stay here with me for the rest of the night. I'll make certain you don't go wandering off, and I will wake you up at the first sign that the nightmares are returning."

He was laying her down on the bed, when she surprised him by turning in his arms, pressing her body against his, and giving him a long, passionate kiss. For a moment he responded hungrily, one knee on the bed, straining her slight figure against him, aroused by the feel of her skin through the thin cloth, devouring her mouth with his. Then he realized that something was very, very wrong.

He released her and drew back, leaving her kneeling on the bed, flushed and breathless. He was breathless, too, and more than a little confused. "God save us both! What brought that on?"

She shook her head. "I wanted—I wanted to see what it was like. Was it—was it very wicked of me to do that?"

"Not wicked for you to try that with me. But a shade provocative . . . unless you had something more in mind." Tryffin picked up the discarded shirt and slipped it on, then sat down on the bed beside her. "I think you had better tell me something more about these dreams of yours."

She shook her head, averted her eyes. He pulled the fur robe up and wrapped it around her shoulders. "If you don't tell me, how can I help you to make things any better?"

"You can't," she said, flushing more painfully than before. "No one can make things any better. I am wicked and sinful, and I am going to burn in Hell."

"Mother of God! You'll do nothing of the sort—not if I have a thing to say about it. You had better tell me about your dreams, Gwenlliant, for I'll not see you tormented in this life or the next and consent to stand by doing nothing."

He looked so fierce when he said that, she gasped and started to cry again, but she obeyed him nevertheless. "A black man with a cloven hoof comes into my room at night. He lies down beside me and holds me very tight until I can hardly breathe, then he sucks on my fingers and my throat and my—no, I can't say—and he makes me do vile things. When he is through with me, he takes a long knife and cuts out my heart, and he eats it while I look on. Then Calchas comes in, and he sees me with the blood on my nightdress, and he makes me take off the gown. Everywhere he touches me, there is a black mark like a burn, and then he puts his hand between—"

"That's enough," said Tryffin, between his teeth. "You don't have to say any more, for I've heard quite enough to understand what is happening to you. These are the dreams that Calchas sent you, all those years ago."

She nodded, starting to speak, and then choked on the words. He put his arms carefully around her. He knew now that she had never really forgotten, as he and Teleri had dared to hope, and that her memories of Calchas had been part of the trouble between him and Gwenlliant from the very beginning. The question he had refused to ask her, had refused even to ask himself, came out of Tryffin's mouth before he could stop it.

"Was it only the dreams—or did Calchas touch you with his body? Did he rape you, Gwenlliant?"

She buried her face on his shoulder. "I don't know . . . I don't think so. It is hard to remember, but I think it was only the dreams. But what does it matter? I am spoiled either way."

223

His arms tightened around her. "In truth, it doesn't matter," he said softly. "Because you are not spoiled; you've done nothing wrong."

That was not a lie, because he half believed it, but part of him said that she *had* been sullied. He had been too long from home, had lived too long among foreigners, absorbing their prejudice. He despised himself, that part of himself that was ready to blame her for something that was no fault of hers. It was that part that started him shaking, almost as violently as she did—because he was so angry, and there was nothing he could do to release that anger without frightening Gwenlliant worse than she was frightened already.

When he was in control of himself again, he put her aside and asked quietly, "But what brought the dreams back—do you know?"

She huddled inside the fur robe, refused to look at him. "I thought you were under a love spell. I thought Dahaut had cast a spell over you."

"You thought— Before God, Gwenlliant, the woman means nothing to me. And I've not slept with her in two years," he protested. But then, seeing he had discouraged her from continuing, he forced himself to speak quietly and evenly, "Well, and so you thought I was under her spell, whether I was or not. And then?"

"I found some old books that had belonged to the Princess Diaspad, books of magic, and I—"

He interrupted her again before he thought. "Magic books belonging to the Princess. Where did you find them? Where are they now?"

Gwenlliant shook her head. "I just . . . I found them in an empty room, covered with dust and cobwebs. I can't show them to you, because I destroyed them. I burned them in the fire." There was something in the way she said that, that did not ring true, but he wanted to learn what she had to say next, so he put off the fate of the magic books for some later discussion. "I was looking through those books for—for a counterspell to save you from Dahaut. But there were only spells of the other sort, the kind Calchas had used on me before, and I think that—that reading them, putting them into my head, made the dreams come back."

"Aye, perhaps. I suppose it might happen that way," he said, with a frown. "You know more about magic than I do. But what of the spell Teleri taught you at the time, the one that stopped the dreams before?"

Gwenlliant shook her head mournfully. "That was to prevent

Calchas from sending me thoughts. These are in my head already.''

With an effort he managed a reassuring smile. He reached out and touched her face, spoke as gently as he was able. ''Then we must find a way to drive them back out again.''

''That's—that's what Garth said. Only I don't know that he was able to think of anything that would do any good,'' she whispered.

''Aye, well, we'll give the matter our whole attention, and no doubt we will think of something. I meant what I said, Gwenlliant: I'll not stand back and let you be hurt this way, not for any power on Earth or in Heaven.''

Some years back, there was a man who owned many acres of land in the parish of St. Sianne, and the people called him the Lord of that place, because for many generations the men of his family had been mighty chieftains, and also, the man himself was known for his wisdom and piety which won him the respect of all who met him.

Now there was a priest who came into the parish and began to preach to the people. To all appearances he was a saintly man, and he had the ability to preach powerful sermons. Wherever he went, the people flocked to hear him. But it was a strange thing, because as soon as he arrived in the parish, things began to go ill: Men went mad, and women miscarried, and there were a great many incidences of public drunkenness and debauchery, besides which the crops began to wither and the flocks to fail and die. People thought this had come about because a tribe of tinkers had arrived in the district about the same time as the holy man, and had brought a plague of bad luck with them.

But the Lord of St. Sianne was not so certain of that. Because tinkers had come into the parish before, and things had continued to prosper, just as they ought under the rule of a wise and fair-minded lord. Also, he remembered that something similar to the terrible things that were happening now had occurred a long time ago. So he thought that he would try to get to the bottom of things and solve the problem.

It happened that the new priest had one failing, and that failing was a tendency toward pride. So the lord of that district prepared a great feast in honor of the holy man, and invited the priest to sit with him at the High Table and made much of him the whole time. And in the course of the conversation, the Lord said, "You may be surprised to see how ill things go in this parish." And the holy man said that he was.

"Well, I will tell you, it is not so strange," said the Lord. "Because something very similar happened in the time of my great-grandfather, only then it was even worse. Three strangers had come into the parish, and those men were devils but nobody knew it. Until St. Teilo came to pay the chieftain a visit, and he remarked that the visitors had an evil look to them. So he worked an exorcism, and that exorcism was so powerful that the three devils had no choice but to flee as far and as fast as they possibly could. One of those devils flew up into the air and went flapping away at such a rate he came too near the sun and burnt to a cinder. And another devil went burrowing down into the earth so swiftly he had gone all the way to Hell before he even knew it, and there was no going back afterward. But the third devil was a foolish fellow, and he had no better sense than to leap into the midden and hide himself amidst the stinking offal."

"That is a lie," cried the priest indignantly. "I jumped down a well, as the Prince of Hell himself would attest."

But as soon as he said that, the devil knew that he had betrayed himself, and so lost all his power over the Lord of St. Sianne and his people. So he conjured up a whirlwind to take him away, and he was never seen again in that parish or anywhere near it.

—From A Journey into Rhianedd and Gorwynnion, *by the monk Elidyr fab Gruffudd*

20.

A Circle of Fallow Gold

In the morning, Tryffin left Gwenlliant curled up asleep in his bed, and dressed by candlelight. Summoned by the sound of his movements, Conn and Mahaffy came in to assist him, and a few moments later, Garth, who stood frozen on the threshold, staring at the bed and Gwenlliant's hair spread out across the pillow.

"I wish to speak to you alone, Garth," said Tryffin, as he belted on his tunic. "In the audience chamber at the hour of Tierce." Then, seeing how the boy went stiff with apprehension: "I am not angry with you. In truth, I believe you have done a better job looking after Gwenlliant than I have done myself."

He dispatched all the business that he could before the hour, breaking his fast with oat cakes, sirloin, and ale as he spoke to his Seneschal, his Steward, and the Marshall's deputy. Garth came into the chamber just as the latter was departing and the servants were clearing away the remains of the Governor's breakfast.

"Take a seat, Garth, and try not to look like a man on his way to be hung, or I may change my mind and decide you've been up to some mischief, after all," said Tryffin, indicating a chair. Garth took the seat, but continued to look troubled.

The Governor thought they had better get the worst thing out of the way at once. "Are you in love with Gwenlliant?" he asked bluntly.

The boy blushed a hot shade of crimson. "Yes," he said miserably. "I think that I am."

"Ah well," said Tryffin, glad to hear Garth admit it so freely. "There's no harm in that taken by itself. Truth to tell, it's entirely appropriate." It was expected that a boy of Garth's class would form some such attachment before he was grown, a passionate (but usually chaste) infatuation for a lady of superior rank, who would exert a civilizing influence and so aid the youth in preparing for knighthood. Not that Garth needed moral uplift or further refinement himself. If anything, he was a bit too sensitive, a bit too nice in his requirements. "Although, I think for your sake you might be better off, next time, falling in love with someone just a little older."

"I will try to keep that in mind," Garth said stiffly, sounding a bit miffed because the Governor did not take his grand passion seriously.

Tryffin smiled sympathetically. "My apologies. That was unkind of me. I know that it hurts, Garth. Truth to tell, I have been hurting for quite a long time on Gwenlliant's account. I have loved her since . . . well, since I was not very much older than you, now that I come to think of it. And now I am afraid that she is suffering, too.

"You are as close to Gwenlliant as anyone here," the Governor continued, "and I would like your advice about what I may do to help her recover from her present malaise." The boy did not answer and Tryffin sighed. "Have you nothing to say? Have you nothing to suggest?"

"I have a great deal to say, and a number of things to suggest—maybe more than I ought, you being who you are and I just your squire."

"Then for God's sake say what you have to say, and don't fear to offend me," replied Tryffin. "I never ask for advice unless I am willing to receive it."

Garth took a deep breath and then spoke all in a rush. "You should spend more time at home—she is always better when you are here. And when you *are* here, you should speak to her of important things, not expect her to chatter and be winsome as though she were a child. Well, she *is* a child, but she is remarkably bright, she has a perfectly astounding mind."

Tryffin shifted about in his seat. "You haven't offended me yet. Continue, if you have more to tell me."

By now, Garth was warming to the subject, and he was more than ready to continue. "You need to find her more worthy companions than Faelinn, Grainne, and Traeth . . . or the five old dames over in the Keep. I can see what you had in mind when you brought her here: She is so young that a retired life does suit her in some ways, and she is by no means ready to preside at a court like Caer Cadwy. But she needs the company of people as clever as she is herself."

"Aye, well," said Tryffin, drumming his fingers on the table. "And what of yourself? You're a great deal more perceptive than I ever guessed."

Garth shook his head. "She requires the companionship of poets, scholars, and philosophers. Yes, I do amuse her, for now anyway. But I don't fool myself that I would be able to interest her as she grows older. Which is but one reason, Lord, why I could never be truly a rival for her affection. Ordinary people bore her so badly, she grows frantic for amusement and then does things that—that are not very wise."

The Governor frowned. "*I* don't find ordinary people boring. In truth, I find them endlessly fascinating."

"Oh yes," said Garth, "but you meet a great many more of them than Gwenlliant does, and I suppose they make up in variety what they lack in individual interest."

Tryffin sat silent for a time, thinking that over. "Your advice is good so far," he said, with a wry smile. "What more can you tell me?"

"Her attendants bully her. They tell her what she may and may not do, until she is ready to scream with frustration. When we are traveling here on the ship, she used to play games with Elffin and Cei. Why should she not? I remember the Queen playing Hoodman Blind with her handmaidens, the King playing tag with his squires. But Faelinn, Grainne, and Traeth—being bone lazy themselves for all their apparent industry—would make Gwenlliant an old woman before her time."

Tryffin sat back in his chair, released a long sigh. "That I already knew, as it happens. But I would hardly increase her stature or authority by taking them to task on her behalf. That is a problem she must solve for herself."

"But she doesn't *try* to solve it. She is so concerned to appear gracious, gentle, and dignified, as you are yourself, they have only to say that whatever she wants to do does not accord with her position and she gives in at once," said Garth.

"Before God," exploded Tryffin, "as the Governor's lady she must naturally show a certain circumspection, avoid scandal and not take any foolish risks, but Gwenlliant is not an *ordinary* princess. She is a Princess of Tir Gwyngelli, and her dignity and grace proceed from within; they can't be so easily diminished.

"It is possible," he added thoughtfully, "that she doesn't know that. Perhaps I should explain at some suitable moment. But in the meantime: Have you more to tell me?"

Garth took another deep breath, seemed to steel himself for some unpleasant task. "You are very good, Prince Tryffin—in truth, in some ways much too good. But you give so much of your time and your concern to others, I wonder what is left for you—or for your lady."

"God Almighty," said Tryffin, seriously disturbed by that notion. "I have never believed that the love a man might give was a finite quantity. Maelgwyn fab Menai has an entire nation of people in his keeping and he loves them every one, yet he has still managed to be a kind father to my brother, my sisters, and myself—and an affectionate husband to my mother."

Garth shook his head, as though he did not quite understand it. But after a moment of thought, the Governor answered himself.

"It is possible, of course, that my father's love for his people is rather more detached, more impersonal, than I ever supposed. In truth, Garth, I do sometimes find it wearisome, bearing the burden of so much personal concern. But what do you suggest I do with all my excess time and energy, after I detach myself from the woes of my people?"

"I would suggest," said the boy, plucking up his courage, "that you take up the study of medicine, natural philosophy, and mathematics, in order to be able to discuss these subjects with the Lady Gwenlliant."

Now Tryffin was genuinely startled, but he was not certain if the boy was making a joke or a serious suggestion. "I am no scholar, Garth."

"Well, but you might be if you chose," Garth retorted. "You are clever enough, God knows. I believe she would appreciate the effort on your part, and you might possibly find the study interesting for its own sake."

"Aye," said Tryffin, thinking of his grandfather Menai fab Maelwas, who had left his house and his family in order to travel abroad as a simple scholar. "I might find it interesting at that. It is certainly worth thinking about."

• • •

. . . but the Chemical Wedding is a great Mystery. For if the Brother takes his Sister into his bed, their two Natures being already so Similar (at one moment Yearning, at the next Repulsive) . . . only through the Mediation of a Spirit that is Subtle and Pure, through a Conjunction of the Earthy with the Incorporeal, can they ever achieve the desired Union.
—*From* The Magician's Seventh Key

• • •

March passed, green and showery, and April followed, sunny and cool. The Governor remained at Caer Ysgithr, save for an occasional brief ride into the surrounding countryside with Gwenlliant. He studied mathematics and philosophy, sent his men in search of scholars and poets to attend his court, and discussed with Gwenlliant the problems of government as well as his new studies. At the same time (lest she grew too bookish) he sent for minstrels and dance masters . . . and watched her health and her spirits slowly return.

She would not have Traeth or Grainne or Faelinn sit in her room at night, for fear she might talk in her sleep and say something to shock them, so Tryffin insisted she sleep in his bed. For weeks she woke him in the middle of the night with her nightmares and panics, but gradually the dreams ceased to torment her, and she slept each night peacefully in his arms.

There was nothing more than that between them, and he was no longer certain that dissatisfied him—there was a bittersweet pleasure falling asleep with Gwenlliant lying against his heart, waking each morning to the soft sound of her breathing. They had grown so close, even to think of anything more made him feel like a boy caught peeking at his sister's nakedness. He wondered if that had been part of the trouble between them from the very beginning: not only her age and reluctance, but his own fear of incest. Though they had not been raised under the same roof, the blood tie between them, combined with the emotional bond they shared, brought a quality to their relationship that was almost too fiercely intense.

All this time, his men were riding throughout Mochdreff, searching for the wizard Cado Guillyn. Sometimes, Tryffin grew impatient, experienced a strong desire to go out with them and aid in the hunt, but he controlled that urge and remained at home. He had promised himself not to leave the castle without Gwenlliant, except at the direst need of the people, or for a direct confrontation with Lord Cado.

He lost no time encouraging her to stand up to her attendants. "For the love of God, Gwenlliant," he exclaimed, during the first week of their new life together, when Faelinn chided her for throwing wood on the fire. "You should not allow your women to dictate your actions. You are a Princess of Tir Gwyngelli and my wife—and you can scrub floors if you choose, without any loss of dignity.

"Not that I think you would enjoy it," he added. "My sister Eisiwed tried it once, just to see how people would react, and she didn't care for it at all. But the principle remains: If you dine with the scullions in the kitchen, then that is the High Table, and if you clothe yourself in sackcloth and homespun, those are royal robes."

She considered that quietly before she answered. "Well, I knew that was true for you and Fflergant, but I was not so certain it applied to me."

"It does," he said. "So long as you don't misuse your authority, fail those who depend on you—or frighten your husband by placing your precious self in danger, you may do exactly as you please."

He was gratified several weeks later to find her playing a noisy game of Prisoner's Base, down in the orchard with Cei and Elffin. "Will you play with us, Cousin?" she asked breathlessly, when she caught sight of him standing by the gate.

"Another time, perhaps. For now, I have something to show you, something to give you." He took her by the hand and led her over to a bench under one of the gnarled and knotted trees. When they were seated side by side, he slipped a golden bracelet onto her arm.

She made a tiny sound of delight and surprise, held up her wrist so that the bracelet caught the light. It was made of the pure Gwyngelli gold—though of the pale sort, almost white, like her hair—and the design was very ancient, an intricate pattern of coiling dragons with gemstones for eyes. "It is very beautiful. But why . . . ?"

"It is a betrothal gift, after our custom in the Gwyngelli Hills. I never had the chance to give you one before we were married, the way everything happened so quickly. But I've been thinking: Now we are sleeping together, we had better get ourselves decently betrothed," he said lightly.

"You would have had it some weeks since," he added, "but I had to send to Castell Maelduin. It is an heirloom of my house, and only the bride of a prince may wear it."

She sat looking at the bracelet, turning it around on her arm, thinking of Dahaut and the sidhe-stone necklace—and how jealous she had been of something which had (after all) meant so very little.

"Cousin," she said softly, "you are very good to me. But I fear I don't deserve any of it, because—because I lied to you about the books of spells that I found."

"Well," he said, looking down at the toes of his boots, "it happens that I knew that, but I had faith you would tell me the truth eventually."

She opened her eyes very wide. "You trusted me, even though I was deceiving you all this time?"

"Aye, well," he said. "I regret to say that I have been deceiving you, too. I have been waiting for you to tell me the truth, but I also ordered the servants to search the castle thoroughly in the hope of finding those volumes. You seem to have hidden them very well."

She sat twisting her hands together, wondering how much she dared to tell him. Finally she made a difficult decision. "I don't suppose you sent them to look behind the iron gates, in the forbidden rooms?"

He took in a deep breath and released it slowly. "No, I did not, not knowing there was a way to get into those rooms. Perhaps you will show me how you managed to do it?"

"Yes," she said, with a sigh, thinking how angry and betrayed he would feel when he knew it all. "Yes, I will show you."

Gwenlliant led him to Melusine's Bower and to the back stair, then through the pattern spell, until they emerged in the corridor she had visited before. Tryffin took the candle Gwenlliant had brought to light their way on the stairs, then looked around him with growing surprise: At the brackets on the walls, set at just the right height for dwarfs to light the torches. At the low ceiling, the line of closed doors, and the dust lying thick on the floor.

"Before God, I never thought there might be a spell that led to

232

this place. It never even occurred to me to ask the servants, when I had them all searching the castle.''

It was left to Gwenlliant—who had been there so many times before—to notice that something was wrong. ''No one has lit the rushlights, or swept the floor.''

''And who would light them? Who would sweep this corridor where nobody walks?'' asked Tryffin, turning to fix her with a keen glance. ''Who did you meet when you came here before?''

Gwenlliant blushed painfully. ''I met the dwarf Brangwengwen. She showed me the books and quite a bit more.''

''Mother of God,'' said Tryffin, under his breath. ''Did you pay no more heed to my warnings than that? I begin to wonder if you have any respect for me whatever.''

But his anger soon gave way to curiosity as she led him down the passageway and showed him the rooms she had visited before: the banquet hall with its painted ceiling and magnificent tapestries, the nursery, and the Princess's bedchamber and great bronze mirror, with its design of toads and serpents.

When they came to the circular chamber, Gwenlliant paused on the threshold, speechless with surprise. The weighty spell books were gone, and the bat's wings, wands, and strange devices that had littered the shelves. The brazier, also, was missing, and the hearth was bare. Not even ashes remained to tell of the fires that Gwenlliant and the dwarf had kindled there.

The only sign that the room had ever been used for magic was the great silver wheel painted on the floor.

''The books *were* here,'' said Gwenlliant, when she recovered enough to speak. ''But now you will think that I have lied to you again, though I have no idea where they have gone.''

Tryffin stepped past her and into the room. He circled around the wheel, examining it with great interest. ''I don't doubt you for a moment. If the books were anywhere, they must certainly have been here. This room has been used for witchcraft over the years; I can feel it in my bones even now.''

He glanced up from the wheel, and she could see that he was frowning darkly. ''If you want to learn witchcraft, Gwenlliant, I know a much better teacher than the dwarf Brangwengwen. Before God, I think any Mochdreffi village witch would be far safer.''

''But—but I didn't come here to learn witchcraft,'' she said. ''I came to learn about the Princess and Calchas.'' And she told him all that she had learned from the dwarf and from the whispering walls.

''Aye,'' he said. ''You confirm what I've learned on my own, and added quite a bit more. It is certainly a tragic tale. And I suspect that Cado Guillyn played some part in Diaspad's story, if only by encouraging Lord Corfil in his cruelty. What do the walls tell you about that?"

Gwenlliant shook her head. "Nothing, they say nothing. I don't believe he was ever here. And to go through the castle trying to discover a particular event, a certain conversation, without knowing where it happened, I would have to visit one room after another, listen for weeks or possibly months—and even then I couldn't be sure I would ever hear what I wanted to learn."

He had known before this that things *spoke* to her, but he had never realized until now what a constant barrage of the senses she must endure. "Does it weary you? Do you never long for silence?"

"Yes," she said, with a soft little sigh. "It does weary me. That is why I like to ride out into the country, away from the castle and the town. Trees and bushes and logs and stones, they do speak, but they haven't *nearly* so much to talk about."

He glanced around him one final time. "Ah well, it seems there is no use looking for the books any longer. The dwarf has taken them away."

Gwenlliant was relieved to escape so lightly, to be forgiven for lying and disobedience without even the scolding she knew she deserved. She followed Tryffin out of the room, through the antechamber, and down the dusty corridor.

But when they reached the stairs, he stopped suddenly, and his fingers clamped around her wrist, so tightly she knew there would be bruises the next day. "You are not to come back here again, and you are not to speak with the dwarf if you meet her elsewhere. She has done you more harm than I am willing to allow." Gwenlliant saw that he was furious, after all—more angry, perhaps, than she had ever seen him. "Do you understand, Gwenlliant, will you do as I say?"

She nodded wordlessly. "Very well then," Tryffin said sternly. "You had best remember it."

The Science of Augury, by which the Wizard divines Future Events, is at once more complex and comprehensive than Ignorant People realize. For it is not through one Sign only, but through many Omens and Portents, that the Wizard is able to perceive the Pattern of Things to Come, and among these Signs are: comets, clouds, stars, meteors, winds, spectres, phantasies, tempests, earthquakes, the Deaths of Great Men, the Fall of Cities, and the appearance of Monsters upon the face of the Earth.

> —From a treatise by Atlendor,
> On Celestial and Terrestrial
> Divination

21.

Portents of Terror and Wonder

During the first week of May, strange accounts began to make their way to Caer Ysgithr, tales of weird shambling creatures and miraculous hybrids that walked by night and by day, of men who went out to hunt the beasts and never returned. Meligraunce had been hearing similar stories for years, but these were particularly vivid and there was a great rash of them all at once—nor were these monstrous encounters limited to the villages and settlements nearest the Mochdreffi Woods, but seemed to be occurring everywhere at once. The Captain sent out men in pairs and small parties to see if they could learn what was actually happening.

At the beginning of June his men began coming back. The stories *they* had to tell were disturbing but less colorful than the rumors: Strange beasts had been spotted, and a number of them killed—one of the men even brought back a hide—but they were small creatures, hybrid rats, voles, and weasels, and not particularly dangerous. In fact, many were actually feeble and sickly, and their bodies were discovered on heaths and beside the roads, apparently dead of natural causes.

But one pair of men came back with a tale that Meligraunce felt obliged to carry to the Governor. "A man-eating beast. It left tracks like a great cat but tremendous in size, and the bodies of the slain were found with their heads cracked open and the brains eaten. Men from the village went out to hunt the beast and all were killed—which was hardly surprising since all they carried were bows and scythes and other rude weapons. Their families beg Your Grace to send a troop of armed men."

"I will," said Tryffin, "and lead it myself. If Mahaffy is right and his uncle has been making animals, then the appearance of this creature may well be the invitation I have been waiting for all these weeks, summoning me to do battle with the wizard himself."

Though he was still a little concerned about Gwenlliant, her condition was now so wonderfully improved, it did not make sense to stay behind on her account. He made what provision he could, leaving Conn behind with particular instructions: "Stay by her, do all that you can to keep her in good spirits, and do not allow Faelinn and Grainne and Traeth to plague her with their foolish notions of propriety. If she should fall ill or show any signs of distress or trouble, send word to me immediately."

When Garth heard of this plan, he offered to stay behind instead. "That is, if you trust me to look after her."

"I do trust you. God knows I do, and in many ways it would be an excellent idea. But I don't forget that I promised you the next adventure, and I'll not go back on my word.

"We'll be going to Ywerion, which is not far from Clynnoc," Tryffin added. "You might offer to carry a message from your brother to young Cianwy Glyn."

When he broke the news to Gwenlliant later that day, her response was reassuring—but a little too apt. "Do not worry about me, Cousin. I shall be perfectly well, now there is so much for me to do. And though I feel very sorry for the families of the men who were killed, I think it very fortunate that something should come up and give you a chance to ride out and enjoy yourself."

"Before God, is that how you see me? Am I nothing more than a muscular brute who lives only for battle and strife? I have known such men, but I would not like to think that I was one of them."

"No," she said, shaking her head. "You aren't like that at all. You are simply too big and active to be confined by castle walls, for months and months at a time."

"Perhaps you are right," he said, with a sigh. "Though I have always tried to be ruled by my intellect—perhaps I am just a man of action."

She opened her eyes wide. "Why must you be one or the other? Why can't you be both?"

"I don't know," he replied. "Because other men generally are, I suppose . . . either one or the other."

Gwenlliant smiled and shook her head again. "But you aren't *like* other people. You have been extraordinary all of your life."

The village of Ywerion was located in wild, broken country. There was no man of sufficient importance in that region to be reckoned a petty lord, not even a powerful clan chieftain to attract warriors to him. The folk of Ywerion and the surrounding countryside were clanless men, the descendents of outlaws and rebels. Though they had been respectable and law-abiding for two score years, they owed no fealty, and were unable to claim the protection of any lord save the Lord of Mochdreff—or in his place, the Governor.

Tryffin thought that a troop of twenty men, experienced in battle, fully armed and armored, would be sufficient to hunt down and slay the beast, whatever it was. With that number of fighters (as well as Meligraunce, Garth, and Mahaffy) he traveled to Ywerion. They arrived in the village just before nightfall, and were immediately escorted to the home of the most prosperous family, where the Governor met with the village elders and the family matriarchs.

There were two white-haired old women in particular, women of power in the true Mochdreffi tradition, who made a forceful impression on Tryffin. He asked what they had done between them to combat the beast.

"We can ward the village, we can ward the farmsteads," said the younger of the two, a weathered old creature of eighty or ninety. "And have done so this last fortnight. But people must go out: to hunt, to care for the flocks, to see to the crops. And then we can do nothing to help them."

"And have you not confronted the monster yourselves?" he asked, eyeing them with interest. The two witches seemed as tough as old roots, as hard as stones, and as impregnable as fortresses. Also their magical wards had made his bones begin to vibrate while he was still a league from the village. He thought they might have dispatched the monster easily.

The elder of the two, whose name was Elefedda, thrust out a stubborn jaw. "We do not do the death spells, son of Maelgwyn. We are sworn not to use them, for it was through misuse of those very spells that our forefathers and foremothers came to be outlawed and exiled.

"Even if we were tempted to break that vow in time of great need," she added, "we could not do so. A destiny is sworn on every wise-woman and warlock among us as we come into power, not even to seek *knowledge* of those spells."

Tryffin shrugged and accepted that. And Gwenlliant had spoken truly: He was spoiling for a battle, and was by no means reluctant to take on the monster himself.

In the early morning, the Governor and his men set out on foot, with the crone Elefedda stumping along at the head of the troop, not to assist in slaying the beast, but to help the men find it. Another witch had gone out with the first group of men, to aid them in tracking the beast, and so had been one of the monster's early victims.

"But it seems you have some hope of success," Elefedda told Meligraunce, when she joined the hunting party. "And so I shall risk this, though God alone knows how my sister will ward the entire village if anything should happen to me."

"It may be useful to have a healer on hand, though I hope we won't need one," said the Captain.

But the crone shook her head. "That art, also, we are forbidden. Spells that heal can also kill. I can bind up your wounds—as no doubt any man here could do for a comrade—but more than that I cannot do."

It was a misty morning, surprisingly cool for June, and the breeze carried a tang of peat smoke, a hint of the marshes lying off to the south-east. Tryffin and his men went on foot, without dogs, because dogs (so the villagers said) refused to follow the scent, and horses had only to catch a whiff of the beast to go mad with terror. The men spent hours crossing and recrossing a bit of brushy country, beating the heather and broom, while the mist dissipated and the sun climbed. By noon, they were warm with their efforts and discouraged by their lack of success.

The Governor was about to call a halt and suggest a return to Ywerion for dinner, when Elefedda came up beside him. "The beast is near," she said, gesturing with a scrawny arm.

"How do you know?" Tryffin asked curiously. "We've encountered no tracks, no droppings, no spoor of any sort."

"The earth cringes beneath his feet, the bushes tremble at his passing, and the country is empty in that direction . . . empty of all the small living creatures which ought to be there. The beast is abomination, an unnatural creation, and the natural world shudders."

She led them through brake and through mire for about a quarter of a mile. Tryffin's teeth began to ache in half that distance. But

238

the wind was against them, and the beast—attracted by their scent, by the sound of their passage—came bounding out to meet them without any warning.

It was as big as a horse, and tawny as a lion. It ran on four cat feet, amazingly swift, and was generally feline in appearance, but the mane framed a face that was curiously human, and it carried a barbed tail over its back, like the sting of a scorpion.

Tryffin and his men barely had time to draw out their weapons, before the manticore was upon them, snarling and baring its three rows of teeth. It sent one man flying with the swipe of a mighty paw, swept another off his feet with a swing of its tail (and might have stung him to death, were it not for his armor), clamped a third man between its powerful jaws, and started to drag him away.

By that time, the others had recovered from their surprise. Tryffin struck at a golden flank, somebody else put a spear into the monster, and Garth started hacking at the tail. But the manticore, discovering it was attacked on all sides, simply gathered itself for a mighty leap, sailed over the heads of the men, and went bounding off, with the bloody body of its lifeless victim still crushed between its teeth. Within seconds, the manticore was out of sight.

The air was filled with the stench of blood and heated metal, and Garth stared askance at his broken sword.

"Ah God," panted the spearman, regarding the headless shaft in his hand. "The beast has bones as hard as iron."

"They may well *be* iron," said Tryffin, remembering Diaspad's griffon. Examining his own blade, he was relieved to see that it was barely knicked—the Gwyngellach steel held true.

Meanwhile, the witch Elefedda crouched over the body of the beast's first victim. "His neck was broken. A painless death, anyway."

But when others would have tended their stunned comrade, the man who had been hit with the scorpion's tail, the crone cried out. "Do not touch him. His garments of leather and mail are covered with venom. Throw earth upon him to soak up the poison, then you may help him to stand."

Meligraunce came up beside Tryffin, pale and furious at the loss of two men. "This is a vicious brute. But at least it left a trail for us to follow, a trail of poor Cladauc's blood."

"We will follow the trail with great caution," Tryffin replied, equally grim. "The monster moves so swiftly, I do not see how we can hope to kill it, unless we can somehow corner it." He turned to Mahaffy. "It seems that your uncle gained the knowledge he sought, cutting up Diaspad's manticore to see how it was made."

"Yes," said Mahaffy, looking ill and sounding shaken. "But that one was younger and considerably smaller. My uncle has done a terrible thing, creating this creature, setting it loose—and how will the disgrace ever be lifted from the family name?"

"You will help me to find Lord Cado and bring him to justice," said Tryffin. "And then you will have no reason to feel ashamed."

Three days passed and two more battles with the manticore. Two men were killed, but the survivors harried and wounded the beast so fiercely it fled before them, unwilling to turn and fight. At last the monster took cover in a small copse of trees and bushes, and Tryffin was satisfied he finally had the upper hand.

By this time, they had crossed into Clynnoc, and the Governor sent a message to the men of clan Glyn, requiring they send a troop of men to aid him. He had a plan, suggested by the terrain and the fact that the monster must be hungry and thirsty by now. They had followed the manticore so close, it had not been able to feed since it carried off Cladauc, and there was no source of water in the stand of trees where the creature lay hidden. But to effect his plan, Tryffin needed more men.

"We might set fire to the wood," one of the villagers from Ywerion suggested. "Set the outer ring of trees and bushes aflame, so that the fire moves inward, trapping the brute and roasting him alive."

Though the idea repulsed him, the Governor considered it briefly. The copse was small, perhaps twenty yards across at the widest place, but there was low brush, gorse and heather, growing right up to the margin of the little wood.

"If we do that, and the wood actually ignites, and the wind rises, we might find ourselves with a holocaust on our hands, acres and acres burning before we know it."

The man from Ywerion shrugged. "And what of that? There are men's lives at stake. Would you risk them, merely for the sake of a few poor acres of heather and whin?"

"Yes," said Tryffin. "For the sake of their children and grandchildren—who will starve if this land grows any sicker—I would risk their lives. Mochdreff was put in my keeping, no matter how briefly, and for me to do as you suggest—"

"—would wound this land and leave it bleeding for a thousand years," put in old Elefedda, hobbling up just in time to hear most of the conversation. "You do right, Lord Tryffin, to seek some better solution."

"The land offers me that better solution," replied Tryffin.

"There is no water within many miles, except in that ravine with the stream running through."

The ravine in question was about a hundred yards from the trees, a deep cut in the earth with a single steep path leading down to the water. "If we wait until nightfall, there is a good chance the manticore will come out and drink. If we set a trap and lie in wait, I believe we may corner and slay the creature. Thank God the moon is waxing near to full, because *we* will be able to see as well as the beast does."

When the men of clan Glyn arrived, the Governor disposed them and most of his own men in a ring around the wood, lest the manticore slip out while no one was looking. While that was happening, he borrowed an axe and cut several strong branches from a fallen tree. Then with Meligraunce and two stout fighters he went down to the ravine and began gathering rocks. Between them, the four men soon had selected a number of large stones. With these and the branches acting as braces, Tryffin made a deadfall trap, the stones piled so that a single keystone held them in place, and the whole to be released by one of the branches which he set as a trigger across the path.

After that, there was nothing to do but return to the camp up above and wait until evening—a long wait at this time of year, for Midsummer's Eve was less than a fortnight away.

As the first dusky shadows began to gather, Tryffin divided the men into four parties. One group, consisting of himself, his squires, and eight men, lay belly down in a shallow depression about twenty yards from the ravine. A dozen men, commanded by Meligraunce, went down into the ravine, skirting the trap, and waited around a bend in the stream, in case the manticore should be driven north along the streambed. Another dozen men, commanded by Llefelys Glyn, were stationed in the ravine fifty yards to the south. That left the rest of the men to set up a camp on the far side of the wood, and build a large campfie to discourage the manticore, should the lure of water not prove sufficiently intense, from escaping in that direction.

Then everyone settled down to wait once more.

The night grew blacker and blacker, and the hours passed slowly. In the little copse of trees, the manticore stirred uneasily. In one direction was the smoke of the fire, the maddening voices of the men who had harried and hunted; on the other, the fresh scent of water, sweet and alluring. The beast continued to crouch in the bushes, lashing its scorpion's tail.

Time passed, and the desire to drink became too great. The manticore crept slowly out of the trees, out of the bushes, slunk along the edge of the ravine until it came to the path. There was the scent of men, but that was hours old. Yet the manticore paced restlessly at the top of the cut, looking for another way down. An injured leg prevented a leap down the steep sides of the ravine, but the beast was wary of the path, no matter how stale the scent.

At last, finding no other way, tormented by thirst, the manticore started down the path.

Down in the ravine, twenty-five yards to the north, Meligraunce heard the rocks come crashing down, the scream of the wounded manticore, followed by yowling and a splashing. He and his men had barely time to brace themselves before the maddened beast was on them.

Snarling and squalling, the manticore knocked two men over, managed to sting a third, while Meligraunce attacked with his sword, landing a solid blow on the creature's flank. The manticore turned, retreated, then leapt at the Captain, landing against his shield, and bearing him backward toward the embankment.

Meanwhile, drawn by sounds of combat, the Governor's party, with Tryffin himself well in the lead, came to the top of the ravine above the fighting. A glance was enough to tell them that Meligraunce and his men were getting the worst of the battle. The beast had someone down on the ground between its legs, someone who was desperately trying to fend off that squalling head, those crushing teeth, with a wooden shield, while the other men hacked and slashed with swords and axes.

Tryffin went sliding down the embankment, his sword in one hand, clutching at every possible handhold with the other. Arriving at the bottom, he scrambled to his feet and struck at the manticore's neck. This much he accomplished: The beast stopped worying at the man on the ground and whirled to attack him.

Catching a section of shield in its jaws, the manticore ripped off a large piece of wood. Then it spun once more, whipping its tail around in an attempt to sting. But by now the beast was bleeding copiously, moving more slowly. Tryffin ducked just in time to avoid the poisonous barb.

He remained crouching, met the manticore's next charge with a low thrust, and managed to drive his sword deep into the creature's chest, all the way up to the quillons. The manticore reared, spewing frothy blood, but Tryffin held onto his sword.

Grasping the hilt with all his strength, he gave the blade a hard twist.

The monster shuddered, and fell forward, collapsing on top of him.

And Gandwy, not content with the lands and the title he had inherited from his father, made alliance with warlocks and evil sorcerers, summoned dragons out of the earth, unleashed the Wild Magic, created abominations, devised magical engines . . . and one by one he conquered the lands around, until all the men of Perfudd groaned under the weight of his tyranny, and the women and the children cried out in anguish.

—*From* The Great Book of St. Cybi

22.

A Plague of Monsters

Gwenlliant woke in her big empty bed, to a shuffling in the dark, a smell like sulphur, and a sudden bloom of candlelight over by the fireplace. She sat up in bed, shielding her eyes from the light, and gazed in bewilderment at the tiny hunchbacked figure standing by the hearth, candle in hand.

"Brangwengwen, how did you come here?"

The dwarf smiled slyly. "It is easy enough to come here, when one knows the proper spells, when the rooms down below lie empty." She gestured in the direction of the door at the back of the bedchamber. "I might have come many a time, but I thought it best for you to seek out me."

Gwenlliant was still half asleep. She rubbed her eyes and stretched, then turned an accusing look on the hunchback. "You took away the books of spells. Prince Tryffin was very angry."

Brangwengen chuckled softly. "You did not come back for such a long time, as though something you learned of those books had frightened you, and then I heard and I saw the servants and the Governor's men searching through the castle for ancient grimoires. There is not much that happens at Caer Ysgithr that does not come to me sooner or later. And so I thought it would not be long before you led Prince Tryffin to find them, you being frightened and ill, the Governor so eager to discover the cause. I hid those volumes away that they might be safe—and you would be blameless."

The hunchback moved closer to the bed. "How wonderfully you have improved, Lady. You are well and strong again, ready to take up your studies. And so I have come—faithful Brangwengwen, who knows nothing if not how to bide her time—to take you back to the Princess's rooms, and instruct you in those arts for which you have such an amazing gift."

Gwenlliant shivered and shook her head. "If you know so much, you must also know that I promised Tryffin not to meet with you again. I disobeyed him once, to my cost, and I will not make the same mistake twice. You and those books did me great harm—and might do worse if I opened them again."

"How innocent you are and how ignorant," said the dwarf. "Do you really believe it could be as simple and easy as that? You are like the warlock who kept a demon in a bottle and then released him, imagining he could put the imp back in again. But the demon had no wish to return, and power once sought cannot be denied. If anything happened to frighten you before, that is nothing to what may happen in the future, if you insist on clinging to your ignorance."

"No," said Gwenlliant, feeling under her pillows, in search of the sackcloth bag containing the holy relics. She had not slept with them—and scarcely prayed over them—during all the time that she slept in Tryffin's bed. But now, in his absence, she felt the need to touch and examine them, in the hope they would help her fight off this new temptation. "I made a promise and I intend to keep it. And I do not trust you anymore, if ever I truly did."

"Well," said Brangwengwen, blowing out her candle, speaking in the dark, so it was hard for Gwenlliant to tell where she was at the moment. "You have made a foolish choice, and I hope you may not regret it. But I think the day will come when you *do* regret it, and you will beg then for the very same instruction you scorned to receive tonight."

The Governor sat in the common room of an inn in Penafon, listening to two of the men Meligraunce had sent out months before recount their battle with a great froglike creature which had been terrorizing villages along the river Teinne. "With the assistance of the Lord of Dinas Rhian, who crossed the river and came into Mochdreff to aid us, we eventually slew the creature, but at the cost of many men's lives."

Tryffin nodded sympathetically. The very day after he had killed the manticore, rumors of a giant rampaging two-headed boar had drawn him, his troop, and the men of clan Glyn into Penafon. Within three days they had caught the boar and killed it, though with a terrific slaughter of men in the process.

"Before God," Tryffin said now, under his breath, "it seems that Lord Cado has been generating these monsters for years and years—and more successfully than anyone guessed. Either that, or he has been gathering them in the Mochdreffi Woods and breeding them."

He looked across at Meligraunce. "I recall three years ago, when my cousin Ceilyn killed the griffon. Do you know, he had waited his whole life long to fight such a beast, but having done so he was nearly broken-hearted, because he thought something wondrous, something magical, had gone out of the world, the like of which would never be seen again. If he came to Mochdreff now, I think he would get his fill of fighting monsters."

"Why do you not send for him, then? We could use a hero like Ceilyn mac Cuel just now."

The Governor smiled and shook his head. "I had a letter from him just before I left Caer Ysgithr. The Lady Teleri is soon to deliver their first child. You recall how little and delicate she appears—and though she is stronger than she looks, and a physician into the bargain, yet I do not think we could lure him away from her side, not if we could offer him dragons."

The door opened and Mahaffy came in. He and Garth had distinguished themselves in the fight with the two-headed boar, both striking what must have been killing blows at about the same time, which deed had done wonders for their self-confidence, setting both boys up in their own estimation. And while there was some disagreement whether the great silver-bristled monster had actually grunted a few words before it expired, the general opinion of the men was that it *had*. To kill the first talking swine to be found in Mochdreff in decades was a considerable distinction.

But now Mahaffy looked as though he had seen something that startled him. "Your Grace, men have arrived, the—the Lords of Peryf and Oeth and their household troops. They are most eager to speak with you. Will you come out and see them?"

"Peryf and Oeth, here in Penafon?" After all the strange things

245

that he had seen or heard about these last weeks, he supposed that anything so mundane as the arrival of Teign and Gradlon ought not to have amazed him—yet it was so far from anything he had expected to occur that he was frankly astounded.

Outside the inn, there was a great milling of horses and men. The Lords of Peryf and Oeth had dismounted, stood quietly apart from the rest: Teign as elegant, Gradlon as solid, as Tryffin remembered them. In a world gone mad, there was something so reassuring in the sight of their familiar faces that he strode across the crowded innyard and greeted the two men with hearty handclasps. "My lords, what brings you here? I hope this trouble has not extended so far as Oeth and Peryf. Your families—"

"Our families are well—or were a fortnight since, when we left them," said Gradlon. "These are terrible times, Lord Prince, and the news we bring to you is not good. A message came to Dinas Oerfel, addressed to me and to Teign. Dalldaff Llyr received a similar letter, and so, we believe, have all the petty lords and clan chieftains. Certainly all we have met with along the way have done so." He reached into the breast of his blue velvet tunic and drew out a roll of parchment. "As it concerns you closely, we have carried it here as swiftly as possible."

Tryffin unrolled the parchment and read the contents carefully. While he did so, Meligraunce came up beside him. "What news?" the Captain asked, seeing the color drain out of his face, the twitch of a muscle betraying an urge to rend or crush something.

"Lord Cado is threatening to loose a plague of monsters, creatures more terrifying than any he has released so far, to bring the people of Mochdreff to their knees. He promises to hold his hand on two conditions only: that I should be arrested by the petty lords and brought to him—whether he intends to hold me hostage or execute me, he does not say—and that the council meet and proclaim him Lord of Mochdreff, in defiance of the Emperor."

He looked up at the Captain. "I have been expecting a meeting with Lord Cado for many days now, but I confess that he has surprised me."

A glance around the innyard was enough to tell him that Gradlon and Teign's men outnumbered his own—even if the men of clan Glyn remained loyal. He smiled ruefully. "And so, Lord Gradlon . . . Lord Teign, have you come here to place me under arrest and convey me to the wizard Cado Guillyn?"

"If the Governor means to jest with us, he has an odd idea of humor," said Gradlon. "We have come here to offer our swords and our warriors for your protection."

Tryffin felt a lump rising in his throat. That these two men, men he had hardly counted as friends, should come so far, abandoning their homes and their families in such troubled times, in order to offer him aid . . .

"I hardly know what to say," he answered quietly, to conceal his emotion. "Gradlon, I—I killed your son."

"As I told you at the time, Prince Tryffin, I hold you harmless in Kemoc's death. This letter has convinced me that Cado Guillyn is more truly responsible, and also for the tragedy at Castell Peryf—indeed, the death of many men's sons this last terrible month, and who knows how much grief over the course of many years," replied Gradlon, a martial light shining in his eyes. "In truth, I have a burning desire to see him brought to justice."

"And the other men: the petty lords and the clan chieftains you spoke with along the way?" asked Tryffin, handing the parchment over to Meligraunce, who began the slow task of reading the letter from beginning to end.

Gradlon shook his head. "Lord Prince, your virtues are not such that the Mochdreffi would readily appreciate them. We are far more accustomed to another style of lord. We live in a hard land and so we become hard ourselves—hard and selfish, and secretive and suspicious. And these things make us vulnerable when a villain like Cado Guillyn comes along. Yet this much you have accomplished toward winning the loyalty of the Mochdreffi: The other lords refuse to act at this time, either for you or against you. They wish to see what you can accomplish against the wizard before committing themselves either way. You may not see it so, but this is a marvelous concession on their part—because you are a foreigner and, what is more, Gwyngellach, and it seems that Lord Cado is likely to emerge victorious from any conflict between you."

"But we," said Lord Teign, taking up where his cousin left off, "who have the privilege of knowing you, find the decision easier. We remember how you traveled to Oeth to speak with us personally and settle our feud with clan Llyr, which the previous Lords had considered beneath their notice, for all it was the source of continuing grief to our three families. With my own eyes, I saw you go into the fire and rescue young Mahaffy, who is no kin of yours, and the men of Glyn say that you were equally willing to hazard your own body in the cause of justice for a child of their clan. As we traveled through Penafon, we have heard tales of your exploits against the manticore and the boar." He faltered for a moment, evidently overcome by some strong, unfamiliar emotion. "Prince Tryffin, you have ruled this land as fairly, as faithfully, and with such a tender concern for the welfare of your subjects as though we were your own people. So we have asked ourselves, my kinsman and I, would we rather put our fate and that of our families into the hands of a man like you . . . or in the blood-stained grasp of a palpable villain like Cado Guillyn? As I have said, it was not so difficult a decision.''

Tryffin clasped his hand again. ''But the kinsmen, the families of the two heirs, young Peredur and Math, surely they intend to defy Lord Cado?''

''From all that we hear, those lords refuse to declare themselves, unwilling to pledge support to either side,'' replied Gradlon, his voice tinged with contempt. ''Perhaps they hope to see you and the wizard destroy each other at no cost to them. It is said the two boys have been separately carried out of Mochdreff and into Perfudd, where they may await the outcome in safety.''

Tryffin could only be glad that Essylt's infant was safe in the care of the witch Ceinwen—perhaps hidden away in some other age of the world, or out of the world entirely.

But he was also feeling a little stunned that events could move so rapidly, things could change so drastically—that this land which had been peaceful almost to the point of tedium for nine long months should suddenly teeter on the verge of civil war.

While the other men spoke, Meligraunce had been able to read through the letter twice. ''Your Grace, Lord Cado has said that you must be delivered to him at Castell Corrig. If nothing else, he has revealed his whereabouts.''

''Aye,'' said Tryffin slowly. ''He has at that. And with the council of these two lords, we may yet turn that knowledge to Lord Cado's disfavor.''

The Governor was pacing the floor in the large room under the eaves which he had taken for his own, when Meligraunce joined him after supper. ''You seem troubled in your mind,'' said the Captain. ''And I have been wondering myself: Are the Lords of Peryf and Oeth really to be trusted, Your Grace?''

Tryffin smiled ruefully. ''The wonder is that the two of them are inclined to trust *me,* or that any of the men who follow them should do so. Meligraunce . . . I have a dreadful prejudice against these people, and just at this moment I am feeling ashamed.''

Meligraunce thought that over carefully before he answered. ''I do not think that is entirely true. You have certainly been taught to mistrust the Mochdreffi in general. You will say, 'These people are treacherous and we must be wary of them.' But if a man comes to you asking for justice, you do not say to yourself, 'This fellow is a lying Mochdreffi dog, and he deserves nothing of me.' You hear him out as fairly and as dispassionately as if he were one of your own people. And when Mahaffy Guillyn was in danger at Castell Peryf, you did not say, 'This boy comes of a vicious race, I will not risk myself or my good Camboglannach Captain on his behalf.'

"I think," he concluded, "that this prejudice of yours is merely a habit of thinking, and entirely superficial. It is just enough to make you feel guilty, and that you somehow owe these people a great deal on that account. Your Grace, you do not. Has it not occurred to you that you might do well to follow the example of the two young heirs and flee Mochdreff while you still can? I doubt that anyone would regard such an act as cowardly; more likely, they would commend your prudence."

Tryffin threw himself down into a chair. "I have considered that, yes. By leaving Mochdreff, I might avert bloodshed, for a few months, perhaps for as much as a year. But in doing so I would also leave the Mochdreffi in the hands of a tyrant—and eventually the Emperor would send in his own armies to overthrow Cado. I believe the Mochdreffi would rise against an invading army as they are reluctant to rise against me, and there would be great slaughter and carnage."

He sighed deeply. "It seems whether I go or stay there will be a battle and men will die. But by staying here and facing Lord Cado, I might contain this rebellion before it spreads and becomes a great war. And you know that I feel that my destiny compels me to a final confrontation with the man . . . Ah God, if there were only some other way! I feel that I have failed before I have even begun, because there must be *something* I can do, some decision I can make, some message I can send, that would settle this thing without resorting to violence. I simply cannot think what that something is."

Meligraunce crossed his arms, leaned back against the wall. "I believe that is a riddle which reasonable men have faced since the world was first created: how to prevent the depredations of violent and unscrupulous men without resorting to violence yourself. Your Grace . . . if all the princes and generals and wise councilors who have considered that riddle before you have been unable to discover an answer, I do not think you should blame yourself for being no wiser than they."

"But I do," said Tryffin, clenching and unclenching his fists. "Perhaps that, too, is a failure of logic on my part. All these months, I have truly believed I might redeem this land and her people by careful, meticulous government—and even now, when it seems clear that I must either abdicate my post or *fight* for Mochdreff, and win that battle if I may by the use of brute force, I keep hoping that some better solution will suddenly come to me in a blinding flash of inspiration."

Meligraunce frowned thoughtfully. "It may be that wisdom consists of making a decision when you must—while still keeping your mind open should that better solution appear."

Tryffin quirked an eyebrow. "Do you think so? I had always supposed that wisdom brought a certain . . . serenity. But if this is wisdom, I confess to God, it's a most damnably uncomfortable state of mind!"

"Lady," said Conn, "I am failing my duty. Prince Tryffin left me here particularly to look after you, and I am sure he would not like to see you so languid and pale. Will you go for a walk . . . or perhaps to visit the old ladies in the Keep?"

Gwenlliant, who had been sitting silent and motionless in a chair by the hearth, looked up at him. He was shocked by the difference a few days had worked in her. A week ago, she had been the very picture of health and happiness—now she was haggard. "Yes, Conn," she said, with a sigh. "I suppose you are right . . . I ought to do something besides mope inside. We will pay a call on Dame Indeg and the rest."

She left her chair and sat down on her bed, so that Traeth might change her dainty satin slippers for leather shoes more suitable for walking outdoors. Conn took Elffin and Cei each by the shoulder and pulled them over by the door for a whispered conversation.

"Has the Lady been ill during the night . . . have her night-mares returned?" the boy from Gorwynnion hissed.

Cei nodded his head solemnly. "She woke up *screaming* last night, and the night before."

"It was terrible," added Elffin, in a loud whisper. "Faelinn and Grainne could hardly wake her, and when they did, she held Cei's hand and she cried and cried. She didn't seem to know any of the rest of us, and she thought Cei was her brother who disappeared. She said horrible things, about a man with a hoof, and—"

But there was no more time for further confidences, because Gwenlliant was moving their way. Cei opened the door, and he and the others followed her out.

The Lady was silent and distant, almost as though she walked in her sleep, by day as well as by night. And when Conn offered her a hand to help her down the stairs, she flinched away, as though he had committed some intolerable familiarity.

Yet as they crossed the courtyard, a little color came back into her cheeks, and by the time they reached the chamber where the old women were sitting and gossiping over their needlework, she looked considerably more alert than she had for days.

Unfortunately, all that Dames Maffada, Clememyl, Indeg, and the rest wanted to do was discuss how ill the Lady was looking, and recommend loathsome remedies supposed to improve her health and her spirits.

"Brimstone and treacle," said Dame Clememyl. Gwenlliant sat on a stool and the old women hovered around her, raking her over with their cloudy old eyes, touching her forehead, her hands, and her hair with their crooked fingers. "It always answers."

"If you roast larks and take out the hearts and mix them with cobwebs," said Dame Maffada, "that is a sure cure for any young woman with the green sickness."

"Unless of course," Dame Indeg volunteered, with a repulsive simper, "she should be about to present the Governor with an heir. In which case—"

"No," said Gwenlliant, with a sad smile, apparently oblivious to the liberties they were taking, though Conn's touch had made her shrink. "But I think that a baby would be very nice. Prince Tryffin wants one, I know, and I believe I would like looking after an infant."

Dame Maffada sniffed loudly. "As to caring for the babe after it arrived—that is what nursemaids are for, and a very good thing I can assure you! Whyever should you wish to trouble yourself with the care of an infant?"

"I don't know," said Gwenlliant, "but I think I would like to try it."

The day was warm and humid, but as usual the ladies had a small smoky fire burning. Dame Indeg shivered elaborately. "There is a chill on the air; see how the poor child trembles. You there, lad . . ." She gestured in Elffin's direction. " . . . you must poke up the fire."

Elffin moved obediently toward the hearth, took up a poker, and stirred up the ashes. Then he jumped back as the flames blazed up and a flood of creeping, fluttering horrors came tumbling out of the fire and across the floor: bloodless lizards, hairy spiders, shiny black beetles, and grotesque little birds without any feet or feathers.

"Mother of God!" said Cei, reaching for a silver pitcher of . . . something, it might have been water, it might have been wine, and inverting it over the logs to douse the flames. Only what

251

came slithering out of the flagon was a tangled mass of worms and vipers.

Everyone froze in place, standing or sitting, struck momentarily dumb with horror.

Then Gwenlliant said in a harsh whisper: "I did that. It is all my doing."

"Nothing of the sort," said Conn, recovering the use of his limbs. He took both her hands, pulling her up out of her seat, and Cei and Elffin swarmed around her. Between the three of them they had the Lady out of the room and into the corridor before any of the old women could react. "You mustn't *say* such things," said Conn. "Even—even if they should happen to be true."

"Yes, but they are true," said Gwenlliant, in a dazed sort of way. "I am a witch, Conn, and there is no use trying to hide that fact any longer."

"Well," said the boy, very much shaken. There was a brief internal struggle while his northern upbringing battled with the natural pity he felt for this troubled child and his affectionate loyalty to the Governor. "Well . . . that would be terrible if we were living anywhere else, but it is not—not such a bad thing here in Mochdreff."

Conn turned the Lady over to her handmaidens to be soothed and bundled off to bed, and then went to the Governor's room where he hunted up paper, wax, a quill pen, and ink. He wrote a hurried letter, folded it, and dripped on the red wax. He did not have a seal ring, but he did have a brooch decorated with a Gwyngellach sunburst, that Prince Tryffin had given him, so he used that to make an impression. Then Conn went looking for one of the Sergeants that Meligraunce had left in charge of the household guards. From the wild stories that had been making their way back to Caer Ysgithr during the Governor's absence, Conn had a strong notion that Prince Tryffin had more urgent and important matters to occupy his attention than his young bride's health. Nevertheless, the boy had better sense than to shirk his duty or question the Governor's sagacity. He would send word just as he had promised to do—and leave it up to Prince Tryffin whether to ignore the summons home or not.

He put the letter into the Sergeant's hand. "Send your fastest messenger and instruct him to deliver this letter directly to the Governor, in the village of Ywerion."

"Castell Corrig is a small fortress—indeed, not even much of a fortress, for it was built as a summer residence for the Lords of

Mochdreff," said Gradlon, when he and Teign, the Governor, Meligraunce, Llefelys Glyn, and Tryffin's squires had assembled in the common room at the inn in Penafon, gathered around a long rustic table to discuss their campaign.

"It is perched on a cliff overlooking the sea, and on that side at least it is well defended by its natural situation. Otherwise, however, I cannot imagine why Lord Cado has chosen that spot to make a stand against you. Except that no one has lived there for many years, and he undoubtedly walked in and took over the place without having to contend with any resistance."

"His ability to defend the castle would seem to depend on the number of men he has in his garrison," said the Governor.

"By which you mean the number of mercenaries he has been able to hire," said Teign. "The men of Ochren are scattered to the four winds, and clan Guillyn at the present time consists of himself, Mahaffy, Dahaut, and Dame Ceinwen."

Tryffin looked to Mahaffy. "How many men do you suppose your uncle *could* hire?" he asked, with a frown.

The Mochdreffi youth shook his head. "Not many, Prince Tryffin. Not many at all. Less than you have gathered here right now, with the help of the Lords of Oeth and Peryf, considerably less than you might muster if you sent back to Caer Ysgithr for the garrison there. I think—I think my uncle must have been depending rather heavily on the support of the petty lords."

Tryffin thought that over carefully. "He may have more than men at his disposal," he said at last. "Not only whatever spells of destruction he can summon, but one or two monsters he keeps near to guard him. It only makes sense that he would."

"Yet even taking these things into account," said Teign, stroking his beard, "it seems that Lord Cado has chosen such a poor time to challenge you, has miscalculated the response of the petty lords and the clan chieftains, makes his stand in a castle so ill defended . . . in short, it seems entirely possible you might take Castell Corrig with little difficulty and defeat the wizard at little cost to yourself. Except, of course, for one small circumstance we ought not to ignore."

"That Lord Cado could hardly have been so great a fool, so completely misguided," Tryffin finished for him, his fingers curling around the arms of his chair.

"Indeed, your Grace, it hardly seems likely," the Lord of Peryf agreed. "It sounds very much like a trap to me."

"Yet a trap may be sprung in such a way that the one who sets the snare gets trapped himself, and his prey escapes entirely," offered Meligraunce, entering the discussion for the first time.

"Also," said Gradlon, playing with the hilt of his dagger, "I do not think Lord Cado could ever have imagined—as treacherous and self-serving as he is himself—that Teign and I would declare our allegiance and make common cause with the Governor. That mistake, that miscalculation, I *can* believe Lord Cado would make. And that alone may prove his destruction."

"Yet he may have known—not by his own instincts, but by prescience," said Teign. "He is a wizard, after all, with an ability to see the course of future events."

Again the Governor looked to Mahaffy. "*Is* your uncle gifted with the power of prophecy?"

Mahaffy could not suppress a smile. "I ask you the question right back again, Prince Tryffin. Has Cado Guillyn laid his previous plots with such success . . . that you are inclined to believe him a gifted prophet?"

At this, there was an appreciable lessening of the tension in the room.

"He has shown some foreknowledge of my own movements, but no more than a spy in my household would account for. And other than that, quite the opposite. I would be more inclined to consider Lord Cado a singularly *un*gifted prophet."

Tryffin turned a hopeful glance on Teign and Gradlon. "Perhaps, then, we should attempt an immediate assault—a bold move to impress the lords and the chieftains who are hanging back."

"I think you would be wise to do so," Gradlon replied emphatically.

The Governor pushed back his chair. "Then so be it," he said, with a sigh.

There was a man in the parish of St. Caradoc, who committed some impiety. As a punishment for his sin, he suffered unremitting travail and anguish for nine long years, like the agony of a woman in the throes of childbirth, and at the end of that time was delivered of a monster half man and half ox. The truth of this story

can be attested to by a number of respectable men and women in that district.

There was another incident in the neighboring parish of Holy Saints, where a woman who was extremely avaricious and gross in her appetites, from meditating too long on her desires and growing most furious and savage on account of not being able to get everything that she wanted, grew tusks and bristles like a wild boar.

—From A Journey into Rhianedd and Gorwynnion, *by the monk Elidyr fab Gruffudd*

23.

Harpy in the Mirror

When Gwenlliant woke in the middle of the night, Faelinn was dozing in a chair at the foot of the bed. It was a simple thing to work the spell that would keep Faelinn asleep until dawn; a few words and it was done. Then Gwenlliant slipped out of bed, dressed in a dark gown trimmed with miniver, which was the plainest thing she owned, and opened the door to the antechamber.

Making her way through the anteroom without disturbing the sleepers was more difficult than usual, because now there was Conn, as well as Cei and Elffin, stretched out on straw mattresses upon the floor. She did not want to use the spell on everyone, and leave them helpless if an emergency arose during the night, but when Conn made a soft sound and a restless movement, she worked the magic again.

As always, the pattern under the back stairs immediately carried her to the forbidden wing of the Keep. She started calling to the dwarf as soon as she arrived, but Brangwengwen did not answer. As she walked down the corridor, there was a mysterious rasping sound, like scales or claws dragging across the floorboards—only the terrible thing was, it seemed to have something to do with her own footsteps.

"Brangwengwen," she called, as she opened the door to the banquet hall. There was a muffled answer further down the corridor, and the dwarf appeared out of the shadows, moving in her direction.

"So," said the hunchback, "you have seen the wisdom of what I told you."

"Yes," said the girl. "Or no, but . . ." She lowered her voice.

"Something terrible is happening to me. Do you know what it is?"

The dwarf nodded her head. "I know, but what is the use of asking me, when you do not trust me? No, you must see for yourself. Come into this room and look in the mirror."

Gwenlliant followed her into the bedchamber once used by the Princess, and stopped before the great bronze mirror, with its serpents and jeweled toads. The dwarf came after her, bearing a lighted torch.

The girl put a hand to her mouth, stifled a cry of dismay. Her own reflection, at first clear, was melting, changing . . . great leathery batlike wings grew from her shoulders, stretched out to engulf most of the room, while her shoes split open and enormous hooked talons grew out of her feet.

Gwenlliant shuddered and averted her eyes. "Is *this* what I have become? No, it can't be, because nobody else sees it. Is this what I *will* become?"

The dwarf moved closer. "For now, the change cannot be seen except in a mirror like this one. But soon, soon, Lady, there will come a physical change. Perhaps not the wings and claws, but *something* dreadful, something grotesque and terrifying. You must leave Caer Ysgithr before that happens, before other people begin to guess what is happening to you."

She slipped a dry little hand into Gwenlliant's. "And I know a place—a place where people like you and I can live. The others have all gone there before us, all the Princess's freaks and monsters, all but poor foolish Pergrin and me. I should have followed long since, but it is a long wearisome journey and my legs go queer if I walk too far. And people can be so cruel to a weak, pitiful, twisted creature like me. But I will go with *you* to show the way, and you shall protect *me,* being as yet so beautiful and strong."

Gwenlliant drew away from her. "Oh, but I can't—I can't leave Prince Tryffin. I said I would never leave him unless men came to carry me away, and he would be hurt and angry if—if I broke that promise."

"And what pain and anger will he feel when the change comes over you, when you must always keep yourself covered and concealed in the presence of your servants—or else surround yourself, as Diaspad did, with twisted and deformed creatures who will keep your secret? Will his love not turn to loathing when you are grown to be a monster in his eyes?"

Gwenlliant blinked back tears. She forced herself to look at the image in the mirror, thought of the horrible thing that had happened earlier. Could Tryffin continue to love her, a witch whose touch, whose glance, turned things that were good and ordinary and wholesome into dreadful, squirming, crawling things? Even if he did continue to love her, could she bear to share his anguish as he watched her change?

Is this what the Princess Diaspad felt when she abandoned Manogan and gave herself to Corfil instead? Perhaps it was. She knew that Manogan would marry her despite the child she carried—but what of the years of unspoken reproaches, the growing bitterness, the love slowly turning to pitying tolerance?

"You are right," she whispered. "For his sake and my own, I have to leave Tryffin. But how shall we go? If we wait until morning I will be missed, and I don't think we would be passed at the gate, not at this hour."

"There is a secret way," said Brangwengwen. "A pattern and passage and a hidden door. I have not dared to use them before, because once out I cannot return without an invitation from the Lord or Lady of the castle. If I show you the way, you must swear that you are determined to make the journey. Because *you* can return easily, if you change your mind, while *I* must rely on your good will in order to do so."

Gwenlliant twisted her hands together, heaved a great sigh. "I promise to follow where you lead me—what other choice do I have?"

Castell Corrig was a pile of weathered stones, massed on a cliff by the sea. There was a precarious drop to the east, but a gentler slope led gradually up from the landward side. And as Gradlon and Teign had predicted, it appeared almost ridiculously easy to take: If there had ever been an outer curtain wall it was gone now, and the walls of the castle were ill-fortified. And while armed men appeared, every now and then, walking the battlements, their numbers were far from impressive—leading Tryffin to suppose that either there were few men inside to be spared, or the castle had other, less obvious defenses.

With the help of scouts sent out to determine the lay of the land surrounding the castle, Meligraunce made up a map and brought it to Tryffin in the pavilion where the Governor sat with the Lords of Oeth and Peryf. "There is a narrow path leading up from the beach to a small back gate, and a broad road leading up to the main gate on the west," said the Captain. "If you'll take my advice, you will send men to attack from both directions at once, if only to prevent Lord Cado from using the back gate to make his escape. As for the main gatehouse, I'd not waste an attack there. The walls to both sides are low and I have ordered men to begin building ladders. Once our men are inside, they can open the gate from within.''

Tryffin nodded his head, looking up from the map. "The men who attack on the seaward side will be exposed to the greatest danger. They should not begin to climb until the battle for the gate is well under way, because otherwise they will just be throwing their lives away. I will—''

Gradlon interrupted him with an impatient gesture. "If the Governor will pardon me for speaking so plainly: You should restrain your desire to lead either of these two forces.'' The muscular Lord of Oeth looked grim in his dark armor. "Your previous exploits have been most impressive, and I would be the last to deny that your willingness to risk yourself time and time again has gone a long way toward winning my own loyalty—but I cannot say that I consider such impulsive behavior *wise,* for all its endearing quality. You should certainly be there at the end when Lord Cado is either taken or killed . . . but when the gate is open and the way lies comparatively clear, that will be soon enough to enter the battle.''

Tryffin frowned, because he did not like to send men into greater peril than he was willing to risk himself. "I know very well that I have a tendency to respond to the *immediate* logic of any situation. When I possess the strongest arm and the coolest head available, it never seems to make sense to hold back and leave others to do what needs to be done. For all that, I don't think I make a habit of taking foolish risks. Perhaps unnecessary, because there have always been others to take them for me, but that is not the same thing. I know the limits of my own strength and endurance, and I have never attempted a feat I couldn't perform.''

"Your Grace, in the present circumstances it is *exactly* the same thing,'' said Teign, as elegant as ever in mail and leather. "As a younger son, you may be accustomed to consider yourself expendable—and so you may be to the Gwyngellach. But at this particular time you are the great hope of the Mochdreffi, and must behave accordingly.''

Tryffin released a long sigh, handing the map on to Gradlon. "It is strange to think I may be more valuable to your people than to my own, but perhaps you are right." He cast a wry look in the Captain's direction. "I suppose that would please you very well, Meligraunce, were I to hang back from the worst of the battle.''

The corners of his mouth twitched, but Meligraunce was

otherwise able to maintain a stolid expression. "If you can restrain yourself for the whole of the battle, and behave like a wise leader with a healthy regard for his own safety, I will be the happiest man in Celydonn."

Tryffin watched the assault from a low rise to the west of the castle, fully armored except for the helmet he balanced on the saddle before him, ready to enter the fray at a moment's notice. Lord Teign and his warband, Captain Llefelys and the men of clan Glyn, had already climbed the hill with their siege ladders. Amidst light arrowfire and minor resistance from the guards on the wall, a great many men had succeeded in scaling the battlements.

The Governor shifted impatiently in the saddle. Just about now, Gradlon would be leading a small party up from the beach. The Lord of Oeth (over Tryffin's vigorous protests) had insisted on taking the most perilous task for his own. *"Though I am no longer a young man,"* Gradlon had said, *"yet I am hardy enough for this. And what have I accomplished during my lifetime? I was an indifferent success as a courtier helping to shape Lord Corrig's policy, and this must certainly be my last opportunity to distinguish myself as a warrior."*

As it seemed to mean much to him—and someone must take the risk, after all—Tryffin had eventually allowed Gradlon to do as he wished.

"The battle goes well," said Meligraunce, riding up on his big bony black. "The fighting on the wall has not been fierce, and I believe we may have men already inside."

"Aye," Tryffin admitted grudgingly. "The battle goes well. Yet it might go better if I were there to take part—another strong arm would not be amiss. But you, Meligraunce, do not look as happy as I expected to see you. Here I sit impotent and frustrated, partly at your urging, and yet you appear dissatisfied."

The Captain shrugged. "If you are here, then so must I be. And though I am very glad, Lord, to see you show such admirable discretion, I admit to a selfish wish to enter the battle myself."

Up on the hill, there was a mighty shout. Tryffin drew in his breath. "It seems that we are both about to get what we want," he said, putting on his helmet, adjusting the strapping on his shield as he spoke, and Meligraunce followed suit. "It looks from here as though they are beginning to lower the gate."

A moment later, it was quite apparent that the portcullis was going up, the gate coming down. Tryffin dug in his spurs and Roch surged forward. Meligraunce and the black were only a pace behind, and Garth and Mahaffy followed Meligraunce, carrying

Tryffin's banner and the scarlet standard of Mochdreff. As they rode, a half dozen men, stationed at the foot of the hill, swung into formation in front of them.

Cimbing the hill, Tryffin caught an arrow on his shield, and another skimmed past his helmet, but there was no more resistance than that. The men who had lowered the gate hailed him with shouts and wild ululations as he rode through. As Roch carried him across the courtyard, the Governor glanced around him. There were a few minor skirmishes still going on, but it looked as though most of the wizard's men had already died or surrendered.

Tryffin brought the gelding to a halt near the central building. The windows there were no higher than twelve feet off the ground; Teign's men brought two ladders in from the walls, and a number of men climbed up and disappeared inside the looming stone structure. Tryffin dismounted, stood with his sword in his hand, waiting impatiently for someone to open the double doors to the Keep.

When the doors flew open, Meligraunce and two of his guards went in first, and the Governor, still keeping himself well in hand, followed as slowly as caution demanded.

A long empty corridor stretched ahead of them, lit by torches at irregular intervals. When they came to a door, Meligraunce took down one of the torches, turned the handle, and passed on through. When he called back that it was safe to do so, Tryffin followed him into a large shadowy chamber. A few beams of light came in through some windows high on the wall.

"Look," said the Captain, indicating a trio of bloody bodies lying on the floor. He stooped down to inspect them more closely. "The blood is nearly dried; these men have been dead for hours, long before anyone of ours came inside."

A little further on were more bodies, equally torn and bloody. When Tryffin leaned over to get a better look, his gorge rose. "God of Heaven! Something has been feeding here."

Somewhere, off in the distance, there was an ominous roaring and a moaning. "Whatever killed these men," said Meligraunce, "it may still be running loose in these halls."

The Governor nodded grimly. It was not pleasant to speculate what sort of monster the wizard might keep as a watchdog—or how savage the beast must be to attack Lord Cado's own men and rip them apart.

Yet as he and the others walked through room after room, corridor after corridor, what struck Tryffin most was the silence and the emptiness. "It is Caer Wydr all over again," he muttered under his breath, recalling another assault which had succeeded all

260

too easily—and demanded a greater price for that success than anyone had guessed at the time. In truth, he half expected to encounter Calchas fab Corfil at any moment, dragging a sword that was too heavy for him to wield.

Time passed, and the logic of the moment (as well as the length of his stride) eventually got the better of him. Unwilling to allow the wizard a chance to escape, concerned lest someone else kill Lord Cado, robbing him of his rightful prey, Tryffin gradually outdistanced the others, until only Meligraunce continued at his side.

He was unprepared for the sight which greeted them as they walked into an immense state chamber with a lofty ceiling supported by mighty pillars—and found Lord Cado in a wizard's robe of blue and ermine, sitting to all appearances unarmed and undefended in a throne on the dais.

"Prince Tryffin." The wizard greeted him with a frigid smile. "And so you arrive, exactly as I hoped that you would."

The Governor glanced around him, searching for the guards, the defenses which ought logically to be there. The room was so vast the wizard's words echoed again and again among the pillars, but it was empty of furniture except for the throne on the dais and innocent of tapestries. There was no place for anyone to hide. "Not exactly as you hoped, I think, since you undoubtedly wished to see me arrive bound and helpless. Yet I have come nevertheless."

Lord Cado laughed under his breath. "And far more easily than you had thought. But that is the nature of a good trap, is it not? Easy to go in, not so easy to get out. This room is ringed with mighty spells. If you attempt to leave by any of the doors or windows, you shall die, and painfully, too."

On Tryffin's left, Mahaffy, Garth, and one of the guards entered the room through an immense archway. "If you wish me to spare these others—and among them, I notice, my treacherous young nephew—you will surrender at once."

The Governor put down his shield, removed his helmet. "Yes, but, you see, I don't happen to believe there *is* a spell on this chamber," he said, holding the helm under one arm, casually pushing back his chain camail and leather coif. Even wearing so much iron, he did not see how he could have passed through an enchanted portal without his teeth beginning to ache painfully.

"And how shall you test that assumption—which of these here shall you sacrifice?" said Lord Cado, and Tryffin thought he saw a flicker of doubt come into the wizard's eyes. "Which shall you command to walk through a door . . . and die?"

261

"There is no need for a test. I am perfectly satisfied the doors and windows are safe." In fact, the more Lord Cado protested, the more certain Tryffin became.

The wizard laughed again. "You do not suppose me entirely undefended? You do not think I would lure you to meet me here, unless I meant to work your destruction?"

"No," said Tryffin, who was beginning to see things clearly, "I don't suppose you lured me here at all. You are bluffing now, just as you were when you tried to convince the petty lords and the clan chieftains you had purposely released your monsters—though the truth was, you had simply lost control of them. Your schemes against me have all gone awry, and this plague of monsters was the greatest failure of all, but you hoped to turn disaster to your own advantage by frightening the other lords into lending you their support. When *they* failed you, you had no other choice but to wait like a rat in a trap, for me to come here and kill you." Following his lead, the others unhelmed. It was becoming increasingly apparent that the wizard was virtually powerless, and that his men were all dead or captured.

Again there was the roaring they had heard before, though this time much closer, and more guttural. "You are arrogant," said the wizard. "Foolish and arrogant, and that may prove your undoing. Do you hear that sound? I have one creature left me, and that one more deadly than all the rest. I have summoned it here, and it will arrive very soon—yet it is not too late to sue for mercy."

"Something certainly roams these halls, though whether you command it I very much doubt," said the Governor, putting his helmet on the floor by his shield, moving, with sword in hand, toward the dais. "And it *is* too late to sue for mercy, Cado Guillyn, because I have come here to pronounce and carry out sentence of death, and so put an end to all your crimes."

Yet it was more difficult than he thought. Because as he came closer, he could see that the wizard had changed since their last meeting. Lord Cado's hair and beard were as black as ever, but his face was sunken and wrinkled, his eyes clouded, and his robes, magnificent from a distance, were torn and dirty. Moving still closer, Tryffin could see that the wizard's limbs shook ever so slightly, whether with age and infirmity or pure terror it was impossible to tell. In spite of himself, he experienced a pang of pity.

And something stuck at slaying this helpless old man. It was a dreadful irony, Tryffin thought bitterly, that he had been perfectly able to take the law into his own hands three years since, had willingly exceeded his authority where Calchas was concerned, played judge, jury, and executioner all in cold blood—and now, when he carried the power of the High Justice and the Low, when his destiny had brought him into Mochdreff especially to kill this ruthless and bloody villain and so avenge more than eighty years of wrongs, an inconvenient twist of his conscience should forbid him to act.

He stopped a dozen feet from the dais, unable to go on, and Meligraunce, who had been following after him, came even and then paused, too.

"You cannot do it," sneered Lord Cado, recognizing his impotence.

"But *I* can—and will, to erase the stain of your guilt," said Mahaffy, drawing the dagger from his belt and striding past Tryffin and the Captain. But he hesitated with one foot on the lower step of the dais.

And then a look of horror came over his pale face, as he watched his own hand rise high and point the dagger at his heart. Struggling to regain control of the hand, the sweat started out on his brow, his arm began to shake. "No," said his uncle. "You shall be the one to die a shameful death."

Meligraunce was across the space between them in less than an instant, reaching for Mahaffy's arm, attempting to turn the twelve-inch blade aside. He was too late. The dagger pierced the boy's body, there was a great gush of blood and a strangled cry, and Mahaffy slumped in the Captain's arms, then slid to the floor.

But that was enough to restore Tryffin's power to act. As he climbed the steps and crossed the dais, the red mist rose up in front of his eyes, the pressure exploded inside his chest, and hacking Lord Cado to pieces was the easiest thing he had ever done.

Through a scarlet haze, Tryffin looked down at Meligraunce, who was kneeling beside Mahaffy's body. "Does he live?" It was difficult to speak, because he was trembling with reaction, and there seemed to be blood wherever he looked. He could not even be certain, in the state he was in, if any of that blood was his own.

The Captain nodded his head. "He took the dagger in his side. A dangerous wound, but if we can stop the bleeding, we may be able to—"

There was a thumping and a sort of squishy wallowing in the corridor outside one set of double doors, and again that guttural roaring.

"Mother of God," breathed Tryffin, as the pressure began to build again. "Get the lad up and behind the throne."

The doors crashed open and something enormous came into the

263

room. It had a great, bloated ratlike body and six short legs incapable of supporting that unwholesome mass, though it humped along on its belly with surprising speed, using the long naked tail as a kind of ballast. It had three long serpentine necks, each surmounted by a feral-looking head, and it brought into the room a stench like decaying corpses.

If the manticore and the griffon had been beautiful, each in its own terrifying fashion, this was unspeakably hideous. *"The earth cringes beneath his feet . . . the beast is abomination and the natural world shudders."* That was the manticore Elefedda had meant, so it was a wonder that the earth did not crack, the very stones of the castle come tumbling down, in an effort to blot *this* loathsome thing out of existence.

The governor had little time to think, because the creature was halfway across the room in the space of a heartbeat. Garth and the guard both stood their ground, while Tryffin moved to join them, stopping only so long as it took him to take up his shield and slip it on.

While one head attacked Garth, the others went for the guard, the center head snatching away his shield, while the head on the left caught him by the shoulder, carried him up into the air, and with a whiplike movement threw the unfortunate guardsman against one of the pillars. As the man hit the stone column, there was a loud snapping of bones, and he fell to the floor in an unnatural position, his neck and his back broken. The beast roared in triumph.

Meanwhile, Garth had managed to fend off the other monstrous head with his sword, and hold onto his shield when the center head struck again, though the force of the thing's attack caused him to stumble backward several steps.

By that time, Tryffin had entered the fray. The monster struck with two heads at once, but the Governor dodged one attack and parried the other, cutting a deep gash into one serpentine neck in the process. There was a gush of stinking blood, yet both sets of teeth continued to snap at him, both necks to dodge and weave. Tryffin lifted his shield, slammed it into the left-hand skull, bearing it down toward the floor, while evading a strike from the other head. As the damaged head rose slowly from the floor, Tryffin's sword arced up, down, and connected with a crushing blow. The head groaned, and one pair of dark eyes went dull.

Meanwhile, Garth, who had succeeded in cutting one throat most effectively, moved around to slash at the creature's flank. The remaining head whipped around to strike him, catching his sword arm and biting down until the blood began to flow. But in doing so the beast created the sort of opening Tryffin was looking for. He took his sword in both hands and drove it deep into the abomination's heaving breast.

The creature released its grip on Garth's arm, whipped its head around to strike at Tryffin—but too slowly. Meligraunce was suddenly there at the Governor's side, sword in hand, to deal the ratlike skull a stunning blow.

Before the monster could recover and attack again, Tryffin pulled his blade out of the body, lifted it up, and struck off the ugly head with a single mighty stroke.

They had taken the castle with comparatively few losses, though among those killed was Gradlon of Oeth, who had died in a fall of rocks as he and his men climbed the path from the beach.

"And so Lord Cado's final crime was the same as his first: crushing men to death with falling stones," Tryffin said grimly. Though almost certainly the stones had been dropped by Cado's men using perfectly ordinary means, and not by the wizard's magic.

Tryffin turned to Teign, who had brought the news. "I do not know what I should say to you. You have suffered great losses on my account. I wish there was something I could do to lessen your grief."

"Your Grace," said Teign, with typical Mochdreffi stoicism, "a man endures grief because he must." Nor would he speak of the matter again after that.

They remained at Castell Corrig for more than a week, burying the dead, allowing the wounded a chance to heal. Mahaffy had been less seriously hurt than it first appeared, and was sitting up in bed in half that time. But Garth's sword arm would never be the same again, and his career as Tryffin's squire was almost certainly over. He could not even become an adequate left-handed fighter, because that arm was still stiff from his previous wound and likely to remain so.

"Ah, Garth, you have done such deeds in these last weeks as most men only dream about," said the Governor, when he found the boy sitting dejected in his bedchamber bemoaning his useless state. "You fought the manticore, you slew the talking swine, and God knows I'd never have killed the last creature if you had not been there to help me. You deserve the accolade, if you never carry a sword again in your life." Tryffin drew out his own sword, made Garth kneel, and knighted him on the spot.

"But what use *am* I?" asked the boy, flushed and pleased by his sudden elevation, but still unconvinced.

"Your are bright and conscientious, as I have reason to know, and I think I will make you my Chamberlain and give you the ordering of my household," said the Governor. "God knows, you seem to know better than I do how it ought to be run."

When at last they were ready to leave, their progress was slow, and the road home was long and dusty. They had traveled nearly as far as Penhalloc on the coast, when a rider met them, mounted on a nearly exhausted horse.

Meligraunce and some of the others immediately recognized him as a member of the garrison at Caer Ysgithr, and so he was allowed to pass through their ranks and address the Governor directly.

"Your Grace, I have been searching for you these three weeks, with an urgent message from Conn mac Matholwch. It concerns the Lady Gwenlliant."

Garth went white as death, and the Governor had considerable difficulty maintaining his composure as he opened the letter and read it.

"It is bad but not the worst," he said quietly. "Though it is three weeks since Conn wrote this, and it may take us another week to reach Caer Ysgithr. God of Heaven! Anything could happen in a month."

They urged the horses on as swiftly as they dared, but it was late on the sixth day before Tryffin and his men rode into Trewynyn. They were riding up the hill to the castle when he first noticed that Cyndrywyn's ravens, which had flown with the other standards over the gate ever since Gwenlliant's arrival, had been removed.

He found Conn, Cei, and Elffin waiting by the stables, all very frightened-looking. They had apparently been notified of the Governor's approach and were eager to tell what had happened before he should hear it from anyone else.

"Where is she?" said Tryffin, as he swung down from the saddle.

Conn went down on one knee and bowed his head. "Your Grace, I do not know. She disappeared during the night, and no one can even say how she left the castle. That she *did* leave with the intention of making some journey we are fairly certain. A number of personal items: her plainest gown, a light cloak, her stoutest shoes, and . . ." The boy faltered in what had obviously been a prepared speech.

"She left—she left the same evening that I wrote to you," he continued, with an effort. "And we sent out men to search at once, but no one has seen her in all this time."

"Ah, Conn," Tryffin said reproachfully, before he thought. "I trusted you to look after her, and see what has happened."

Conn flinched as from a blow, Elffin began to sniffle into his hand, and Cei broke down and wept unashamedly. Their distress was so great that Tryffin relented almost immediately.

"Aye, well," he said, putting an arm around Cei, reaching out to pat Elffin on the head. "I doubt there was anything you *might* have done that any of you failed to do."

Garth slipped out of the saddle and came to stand by his still kneeling brother. "Lord, I should have been the one to stay behind with her. I might have prevented—"

Tryffin shook his head. "That was my mistake, not yours," he said grimly. "If it *was* a mistake—your presence might only have made things worse. Stand up, Conn, I was wrong to speak so harshly."

Conn stood, but he still looked so miserable, it was plain to see that he blamed himself, even if the Governor did not. He reached into a pouch at his side, took out a rough sort of bag, and put it in Tryffin's hand. "This was discovered under her pillow after she left."

Tryffin opened it up, took out the items it contained, one by one: the bit of bone, the bloody veil, the parchment, and the wreath.

"We think . . . It has the look, does it not, of some spell or charm?" Conn asked shakily.

"They are holy relics," said Garth. "I have seen her pray over them. They were given her by someone—a Father Idris, I think she said."

"Unholy relics more like," said a flat, discouraged voice. "I suspect that your lady has fallen under the influence of the Black Canons." That was Mahaffy, who had dismounted and moved closer to see what was happening.

Tryffin frowned; he had heard the name before, though he was not certain in what connection. "That is one of the heretical sects?"

"That would be to describe them charitably," said the Mochdreffi youth. "They are evil incarnate," said the Mochdreffi youth. "Anyone who has ever entered one of their churches could tell you that."

"We did—we did go into a church," said Elffin, swallowing hard. "Your Grace, it was the most awful place. Dahaut took us there, but we didn't—we couldn't bear to stay very long. But we met Father Idris *after* we left. He seemed—he seemed very good, not like the others at all."

Mahaffy nodded. "Yes. I have met some of their priests in company with my uncle. As I told you before, Prince Tryffin, he had a desire to rival Gandwy of Perfudd, to become an adept: wizard, warlock, and priest in one. I believe he has been a member of their order for many years now.

"But while those who make up their congregation virtually radiate evil during the Mass, the Canons themselves give precisely

267

the opposite impression," he went on grimly. "It's as though—as though they have so thoroughly absorbed their own evil principles, made a virtue out of vice, and vice out of virtue, that even the most sensitive cannot detect a whiff of evil when they are near.

"It was certainly so with my Uncle Cado. Your lady took an almost instant dislike to him, because of the things he said and the things that he showed her—but I could see very plainly, that day she visited his house, she did not really know quite what to make of him."

Tryffin put the scrap of parchment he had been holding back into the sackcloth bag, and pulled the leather drawstrings so that the sack was closed. "And this Father Idris—might he have been Lord Cado himself in disguise?"

Mahaffy made a hopeless gesture. "Perhaps. I never knew anyone by that name, but I was not acquainted with the entire order."

The Governor drew in a long unsteady breath. "And what power do you think these unholy relics, this Father Idris, might have exercised over Gwenlliant?"

"It is horrible even to speculate," said the youth. "An impulse toward sin, a foretaste of Hell, a despair so deep it might lead her to perform—Your Grace, I do not like to say what she might or might not do."

Tryffin handed the bag to Conn. It was an act of great concentration to keep his hand and voice from shaking as he did so. "Take these things and burn them, before they do more harm." He was determined not to break down, not to show any weakness—not while the boys were all balanced on the fine point of hysteria and looking to him for strength.

"What you are trying to tell me, Mahaffy, is that Gwenlliant may be lost to us—that she may never be found or return."

"Yes," said Mahaffy quietly, "I am very much afraid that may be so."

*It is with the power of Imagination that all magic has its true
beginning and its culmination. There is not one Marvel, one
Prodigy, one Wondrous Thing wrought by magic, whether it
should be through the Science of Wizardry or the Witch's Craft,
that does not owe its existence to the Imagination. For though the
Wizard draws his power from an Applied Will, and the Warlock
draws in a manner quite different on the old Earth Magics, yet
neither could Achieve anything without a lively and vivid Imagination to shape the power and give it form.*

*And for this Reason above all others, magic is not an occupa-
tion for Dullards, or for those who are Selfish, Complacent, or
Callous . . . because people of this sort can do Comparatively
Little, and that little almost Invariably works in their own
Disfavor. But Generosity, Curiosity, Charity, and Compassion,
are all Qualities which proceed from an Excellent Imagination.*

—*From* The Three Parts of Wisdom,
attributed to Teleri ni Pendaren

24.

On the Marches of Otherwhere

The road, which had diminished to little more than a footpath,
wound in wide erratic loops across the stony moorlands. Sunset
was still staining the western sky an ugly crimson, and a haggard
crescent moon hovered just above the horizon, when the two
travelers, grown weary after only a few hours of walking, sat down
by the road to rest.

Already, the night was alive with ominous sounds: a squeaking
of bats as they flew by, a scurrying of tiny clawed feet among the
heather, a whisper of dried branches moving in the wind. And the
wind itself, a rough voice and a cruel one, speaking of hardship
and sorrow.

"How much further have we to go?" asked Gwenlliant,
drawing her cloak around her.

"It is a long way yet," replied the dwarf, just as she had been saying for over a fortnight.

Gwenlliant sighed. She knew their progress had been slow, walking from sunset until an hour or two after dawn, huddling in ditches or under bushes for most of the long summer day. When they did emerge, during the twilight hours, they wrapped themselves in a light illusion: Brangwengwen in the guise of a crippled child, and Gwenlliant as an old woman. Her near-white hair, which hung now in lank, dirty strands around her face, she did not have to change, allowing her to concentrate on her hands and her face, which made the illusion easier.

Never in her life had Gwenlliant been so thoroughly filthy, weary, and footsore. In the beginning, her feet had blistered, for they were very tender and she was not accustomed to so much walking. By the time her heels had grown callused, the soles of her shoes were full of holes. Two days ago, she had abandoned those shoes as useless, and now walked barefoot among the stones.

As for Brangwengwen, she was equally miserable. And even under the best conditions, her short bandy legs could not carry her far.

"At this rate," said the dwarf, "we may walk for another month and still not reach the forest. Yet we are now so far from Caer Ysgithr, it may be safe for you to sell one of your rings. Then you could buy a horse for yourself and a pony for me. If you did that, we might reach our destination very quickly."

Gwenlliant looked down at her hands. Her golden rings were completely hidden under the illusion that twisted and knotted her hands, but she had only to remove one of those rings and hold it in her hand, in order to make it appear. But the dragon bracelet, which she wore under her sleeve, was a different matter entirely. *"Gwyngelli gold,"* the dwarf had informed her, *"cannot be enchanted, except by the smith while it is yet in the fire. They are wizards of a sort, the smiths of Gwyngelli."*

Not that Gwenlliant would sell the bracelet—even if she dared, it was so instantly recognizable—but she thought she must soon sell one of the rings, if only to buy food. The gold and silver pennies (almost certainly stolen), which Brangwengwen had entrusted to her at the start of their journey, were nearly gone.

"In another day or two," said Gwenlliant, "I will sell one of the rings, and then we may ride." Because one thing she had learned about walking: It wore down the talons that she sometimes saw growing at the end of her toes.

After the girl and the dwarf had rested a while, Gwenlliant took up the waterskin she carried at her side, unstoppered the flask, and

270

took a mouthful of bitter water. Then she passed the skin on to Brangwengwen.

When they had both swallowed enough to blunt their thirst, they rose and resumed their journey. They walked for hours, while the withered moon rose high in the sky and the wind died. A long way in the distance, they caught a glimmer of firelight.

"Lady," said the dwarf, "we should head toward that light. There we may find kindhearted travelers willing to share their food and their drink with us."

But Gwenlliant shook her head. "It may be more of the men that were sent to look for me, and we dare not approach them."

"And how if they *might* be men out looking for you? They will not know us disguised as we are," said the dwarf.

For a moment, Gwenlliant considered that. "It might not be wise, out here in the wilderness, to meet up with a group of strange men—even if they should happen to be sent by Tryffin. Fighting men do terrible things to women, sometimes, and the Governor can't know everything that his soldiers do."

"And why should they wish to harm us the way you are thinking, a ragged old woman and a lame child?" asked Brangwengwen. "There are comely women in the villages to please them. Why should they wish to hurt you or me?"

Gwenlliant hesitated, and the dwarf persisted. "It has been such a long time since we ate warm food or tasted wine. Come, Lady, let us at least move in that direction, and see what manner of people these travelers might be."

As she could see no harm in that, Gwenlliant agreed. But it was a long walk to the camp, much longer than it had first appeared, and they were both exhausted by the time they were close enough to see what sort of person had kindled that fire.

It was a solitary old woman, even more ragged than they were themselves, sitting on a large rock near the flames, with a grey owl perched on one crooked shoulder and a great rough-looking dog crouched on the ground at her feet. "It must be another witch to travel so late and alone," whispered Gwenlliant. "We should go back to the road, before she sees us."

But the dwarf scoffed at that. "Your magic is very powerful, Lady. No ordinary witch could pierce your illusions. We have nothing to fear and much to gain, for she will be well-disposed toward another woman, especially one traveling with a little child."

The dwarf continued to limp toward the fire. Rather than be parted from her, Gwenlliant followed. Yet when they had reached the edge of the shadows surrounding the circle of firelight, Brangwengwen hesitated.

Gwenlliant drew in a deep breath. The woman by the fire was doing something truly remarkable, reaching up into the still dark air and drawing out magic: gleaming threads of silver and crimson and purple and gold, which she wove with her hands into patterns like stars and comets, like rainstorms and hailstorms and bolts of lightning, like great exploding suns and burning moons . . . like the aerial magic which had greeted Gwenlliant her first night in Mochdreff.

Beside her, the girl felt Brangwengwen shrink back against her skirts. "What is it—why are you frightened?" she whispered. The dwarf tugged at her gown, so that Gwenlliant bent down. "Do not speak," said the hunchback, directly in her ear. "Only turn around and walk just as quickly as you can, back in the direction we came."

But before Gwenlliant could do as Brangwengwen advised her, the old woman by the fire stopped what she was doing, turned her eyes toward the exact place where the girl and the dwarf were standing, and spoke in a voice that brooked no denial. "You serve no purpose cringing there in the shadows, Brangwengwen. My ears are remarkably sharp. Even if you had not said a single word, I could still hear your heart beating, the pulse of the blood moving in your veins."

The dwarf shuddered, but had to obey. She stumbled into the circle of golden firelight, and fell down on her knees at the crone's feet. Then the witch reached out and whisked away the illusion covering her. It hung in the air for a moment more, like a veil of mist, and then melted away to nothing.

"And you, Gwenlliant ni Cyndrywyn, come out here and speak to me," said the crone.

Recognizing a power far superior to her own, Gwenlliant obeyed, dropping her illusory disguise as she did so.

The witch looked her over with a pair of penetrating dark eyes. "What brings you so far from Caer Ysgithr, and traveling in such deplorable company?"

Gwenlliant took a deep breath. "We are going to the Mochdreffi Woods that we might live in peace—and also that Brangwengwen may instruct me in the art of witchcraft."

The crone made a dismissive gesture in the direction of the shivering dwarf. "Then you will be disappointed. You will not find anyone capable of training a gift such as yours in the Mochdreffi Woods. This pitiful creature has misled you—which is hardly surprising, as ignorant and wicked as the woman is. Even when she means comparatively well, she can only do ill.''

The way the wise-woman said it, there was no doubting the truth of her words.

"Then what," said Gwenlliant, falling wearily to her knees beside Brangwengwen, "what is to become of me? I cannot go back to Caer Ysgithr, or home to Caer Cadwy, or north to Rhianedd. Where *can* I go, Lady, and how may I live there?''

The bright dark eyes examining her so ruthlessly grew perceptibly softer. "That will be for you to decide," said the crone. "Nor will you find it an easy decision.''

At Caer Ysgithr, a dry, scorching August came in. Up in his rooms in the square tower, the Governor paced restlessly night after night. Lacking any clue to Gwenlliant's whereabouts, he did not dare leave the castle in order to search for her, out of fear that he should miss news of her when it finally arrived. Meligraunce, however, was under no such constraint. He went out during July with Prince Tryffin's blessing and spent an entire month scouring the countryside.

When at last he returned, weary and travel-stained, he went immediately up to the Governor's quarters. His first impression, when he walked into the antechamber, was that a stranger, a tall gaunt man with dull hair and eyes, had taken Prince Tryffin's place.

But then the stranger spoke, that soft lilting voice, and Meligraunce knew him. "Your Grace," said the Captain. "If I did not know your habits so well, I would wonder if you slept nights, or ate with a good appetite.''

Prince Tryffin signaled him to take a chair. "I do sleep and eat. Not so well as I used to." He smiled faintly at the Captain's troubled look. "I know, Meligraunce, one would have supposed the world might end before I ever experienced a poor night's sleep. But I do well enough. Garth makes certain that I eat properly, and that I lie down for an hour or two each night. If I had known what a tyrant that boy would become, I wonder if I would still have appointed him to the position of Chamberlain.''

"He has taken to his new duties, then?" said Meligraunce.

Prince Tryffin sighed. "He seems to find some solace keeping himself busy . . . though of course he is broken-hearted about Gwenlliant. Still, it must be a fine thing to be just eighteen years old, a belted knight, and a slayer of monsters. I hear that every time he goes down into the town, the young women come flocking out to see and admire him.''

"Yet I think it will be very hard," said Meligraunce, with a sympathetic smile, "to be nineteen or twenty, no longer a hero, and no way of gaining fame afterward."

"No," said the Governor, with an emphatic shake of his head. "I won't allow that to happen. In another year or two I will send Garth to the High King, with a recommendation that he be given some important post, perhaps under the Seneschal or the Steward. I believe the boy will apply himself to any duties he is given and rise far and quickly."

The two men were silent for a while, then the Governor spoke. "Since you say nothing, I can only suppose you have nothing to report. Do not take it to heart, my friend. I feel certain you made every effort."

Meligraunce cleared his throat. "I do have some news, but so puzzling and obscure I am not quite certain whether you would call it good tidings or not."

Prince Tryffin leaned forward, a curiously hungry look in his eyes, so Meligraunce continued. "I was riding through Oeth when an ancient crone, dressed all in black rags, came up to ask if I would carry a message for her. You may recall that I stood back at a considerable distance when you gave young Grifflet to the witch Dame Ceinwen, but I think this might have been she: an old, old woman with wild white hair, clutching an iron staff in her hand."

"And the message?" said Prince Tryffin, gripping the arms of his chair.

"She said, *'If Prince Tryffin is concerned over something he has lost, he should remember a time when he was lost himself.'*"

The Governor sat back in his seat, heaved a great sigh of relief. "Gwenlliant is with Ceinwen, then—which next to returning home is the best thing that could possibly happen to her. Though whether or not I can find my way to the witch's cottage and reclaim my bride remains to be seen."

Yet his eyes smiled and a little color came back into his face. "Have the horses ready in the morning. We'll begin our journey immediately after breakfast."

"Then I am to accompany you?" said Meligraunce, watching him kindle and begin to glow again. "And how many others?"

Prince Tryffin shrugged his shoulders, gave a delighted laugh. "As many as you deem fit, Captain. It scarcely matters, because I expect to lose all of you along the way."

• • •

There is a place where the Sun and the Moon meet, where the

*Ocean and the Sky are married together, where Divine Mysteries
are commonplace, and the properties of Metals, Minerals, and
Vegetables are all Known. That is the place where Wise-Women
and Sages alike study the Arcana of Earth, Water, Wind, and Fire,
a place as near as your Heart, as far as the Seventh Sphere. There
is no place Like it, yet it is Like to every place you will ever go. As
with every Journey, you begin with a Single step.*
                                —*From* The Magician's Seventh Key

                              • • •

Two days south of Caer Ysgithr, a dense fog came out of the
marshes, dividing Tryffin from his escort. At first he could hear
Meligraunce and the other men calling his name, but eventually
their voices faded and he was riding entirely alone. When the mist
began to breathe around him, the Governor knew he was drawing
near to his destination.

But when Roch ambled out of the fog and into the golden light
of a summer afternoon, Tryffin took a despairing glance around
him. It was not the same place at all. He was riding along a sandy
beach between the sea and a chalky cliff. Gulls and terns wheeled
overhead in a sky of impossible blue, and the sun and the moon
were in close conjunction. Up ahead of him, about twenty yards
from the tideline, he spotted a ruined tower built of white stone.

"Prince Tryffin," said a familiar voice. He looked toward the
cliff, and saw the witch standing precariously balanced near the
edge, her rags and her white hair fluttering in the breeze. "You
have taken your time in coming here."

Tryffin dismounted and trudged across the sand and pebbles to
speak to her. "My apologies. I came just as soon as I had your
message, Dame Ceinwen."

The crone cackled loudly. He could see the moon over her
shoulder like a great silver wheel, and the gulls and the terns
seemed to be describing an immense circle, with the witch at the
center. "As courteous as ever, I see. Yet I think you have aged
considerably since we last met."

Tryffin sighed. That was a strange sort of statement coming
from a woman who might well be older than the cliff where she
stood—if not actually contemporary with the moon shining so
brightly over her left shoulder. "If I have, it is care that has aged
me. But I believe you may be able to set my mind at ease. Can you
tell me where to find the Lady Gwenlliant?"

The crone gestured in the direction of the ruined tower. "You
will find her inside, along with your son. Do not wait for me, but

275

go on ahead. I will look after your horse. I can see you are impatient to greet the young woman.''

He turned on his heel and sprinted toward the tower. But he hesitated a moment on the threshold, dreading what he might find inside. He did not know *when* he was, any more than he knew *where,* and he had a sudden vision of Gwenlliant grown as old and wrinkled as Ceinwen herself. *Was it her pretty face I loved all along? No—though God knows she was always an enchanting child. If she has altered outwardly, she will still be as dear as ever.*

Inside, it was the same cottage he had visited before: the crowded shelves, the mist and cobwebs in all the corners, the packed-earth floor. On her knees by the hearth, stirring a pot of boiling porridge, was Gwenlliant, barefoot in a homespun gown, her pale hair hanging loose about her shoulders. But other than her dress and her occupation kneeling there in the dirt, she was exactly as he remembered her.

A sturdy red-headed toddler in a brown smock stood clinging to her waist. Then Gwenlliant glanced up and saw him standing by the door, and her face lit like a candle.

Striding across the room, he swept up the child with one arm, and pulled Gwenlliant to her feet and into a crushing embrace with the other. ''Dear Heart,'' he managed, around the constriction in his throat. ''I was beginning to believe I would never see you again.''

''I thought that I had grown so wicked and so dangerous that I never *should* see you again,'' she answered, with her face against his breast.

''And now?'' he asked, loosing his grip a little, so that he could read her expression.

''No, I can't go home with you, not for a while yet,'' she said softly. ''Ceinwen says that I learned too much magic far too quickly—and then I fell in with Father Idris. It is no wonder, she says, that everything went so dreadfully wrong. Had I been born in Mochdreff, a talent like mine would have been carefully taught from the cradle up. As that never happened, I must stay here and learn the—the uses and the mastery of my gift.''

Tryffin released her with a sigh. ''I had an idea that might be the way of it as soon as I learned you were here. But it goes very hard to let you go, even for a time.''

''Yes,'' Gwenlliant agreed, moving away from him. ''It is difficult for me, too. But tell me the truth: Can you honestly say that we would have married when we did, if my father had not tried to give me to Rhun of Yrgoll instead?''

''No, I can't say that,'' he answered. ''I always intended to wait

276

until you were older, until *I* had time to make up my mind whether it was a wife or a little sister I was really looking for."

He captured her hand and kissed it. "Yet it can't say that I regret this past year. It was very sweet having you close to me, knowing you were my wife and no other man could take you away. And those last weeks we spent together . . ."

He shrugged his shoulders, smiled ruefully. "Perhaps we *should* live apart for a few months, and then start fresh, with everything as it ought to have been at the very beginning—but it is difficult for me to appreciate the wisdom of that just now."

Much later, when the child was asleep in a wicker cradle, when Gwenlliant was sitting in the chair made of branches, and Tryffin, contented just for the moment to be near her, sat on a stool at her feet, he asked, "Are you happy here? Are you content? Before God, I never thought to see you making porridge, when I don't suppose you had so much as toasted a piece of bread and cheese in your life!"

She smiled, shaking her head. "No, I never had. I learned to mend and spin and do fine needlework, but not most of the things that ordinary girls learn . . . or boys like Garth and Conn. I suppose *you* can make porridge and toasted cheese, if it comes to that."

"I can," he said, stretching out his legs. "And rabbit stew and roasted fowl and one or two other things—though I am accustomed to cooking out of doors and not inside on the hearth."

"I am learning to do everything Ceinwen does," said Gwenlliant. "Sweep the floor and bake bread and look after the baby. I love him already, our Grifflet, and Ceinwen says I am to take him with me when I go. The rest . . ." She got up from her chair to feed the fire and throw on some herbs to sweeten the smoke. "I did not like it so much at first, but I remembered what you said—I told myself again and again that I am a Princess of Tir Gwyngelli and nothing could rob me of dignity. And I must say it is much more interesting to do these things than just sit idle all day long."

"And the magic she teaches you?"

Her face brightened, as she came back to the leafy chair. "Oh, Cousin, that part is wonderful. I had a great many spells inside my head when I came here, but most of those were horrid and I wanted to forget them. Ceinwen just wiped them out of my memory, and now I am learning all over again, healing spells and growing spells and things of that nature. I wish I could tell you what it is like, but . . . it is not like anything else, and the words simply fail me."

"Aye, well," he said, looking down at his feet. "If you are content, then I must be also." And he *was* perfectly happy here in this place—though he suspected it would all be different when he arrived at Caer Ysgithr and Gwenlliant was not there waiting for him.

In the morning, when the witch led his horse around from the stable at the back, when he was almost ready to leave, Tryffin turned back toward Gwenlliant and pulled her into his arms again.

"Come to visit me at Midsummer," she said, turning up her face to receive his kiss.

That kiss was long and lingering. He tasted her mouth, moved his hands down her back, rehearsing the shape of her bones, the feel of her skin through the cloth, so that he would be able to remember exactly what the kiss was like, many months later when they were far apart. They were both a bit breathless when it was over.

"And will you go home with me . . . if I come to you at Midsummer?" he asked.

Gwenlliant shook her head. "I think . . . not so soon as that. But perhaps next year at this same time. I have so much to learn, and I suspect that you will be busy, too."

"Yes," he said, reluctantly moving away from her, walking toward the door. "Now that Lord Cado is dead, I think that a year should be sufficient to put things in order and make all safe—so the Emperor may name Morcant's successor, and my work in Mochdreff will be done. Then I will take you to Castell Maelduin, present you to all my relatives, make you a princess in very truth, and after that . . ."

"And after that?" she said.

Tryffin paused with one foot in the stirrup, a hand on the saddle. He realized suddenly that Gwenlliant would no longer be a child untrained in her gifts. She would be a Mochdreffi wise-woman, capable of revealing or concealing her power as the occasion demanded.

"After that," he said, "we can live at Caer Cadwy, or on my lands in Gwyngelli. Or I can take you north to Rhianedd, to visit your mother and my grandfather." His face lit with a sudden smile. "The fact is, being who and what we are, we can go where we please, live where we choose, and no one will hinder us."

He swung up into the saddle and took up the reins, stole a final look at Gwenlliant, standing there in her homespun gown. It was difficult to leave her, there was no denying that, but it was a splendid future they had before them—in another year, or maybe two—and that was what he must think about now.

He gave the roan gelding a light tap with his heels and the word to go ahead, and began the journey home to Caer Ysgithr.